THE CALAMITIES OF CAMDEN CALLAHAN

FIRST
FRUIT PRESS

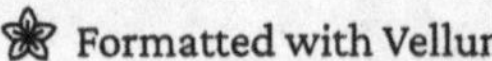

THE CALAMITIES OF CAMDEN CALLAHAN

BRITTANY TUCKER

This one is for Mom.
I miss you.

COLD! BRING A
ROUENN
ENOCH
CAMDEN'S
BEST CAMPING
DON'T GO BACK!
ALMOST GOT STABBED
PORT LEBANON
NEW HAVANA
SHAR CRUE

THE FOUR CORNERS
TOO MANY TREES
SLEET FIELD
RAVELS
ADAH'S ARCHIPELAGO
ITCHY BUGS
BRISTOL WATCH
ABNER
SNAKES. STEP CAREFULLY

TEN YEARS EARLIER

Almost there.

She huddled tighter into her shawl as she walked, clutching the boy's hand so tightly that he whimpered. The sun had just begun its ascent over the sails of the cargo ships in the harbor. Fish merchants set up their stalls, mingling with the leftover nightlife, selling vagrants their supper at breakfast time.

The boy slowed to take in the fresh snapper frying in a vendor's heavy, cast-iron skillets. His torn, stained clothes had grown so loose. The way his stomach growled in the night, huddled under their threadbare blanket, haunted her.

"Mother," he whispered, licking his cracked lips. "I want—"

"I know, baby, soon." Her voice broke, dry. How long had it been since she'd spoken? "Soon. Just a little further."

He didn't argue as she led him toward the docks. *There are so many people.* Her breath hitched. *So many faces.* She scanned each and every one. Searching for features she knew, for the figures she'd seen in her nightmares, keeping her awake for days on end.

But they were all strangers. Solemn workers, heading home to their families after a long, thankless night. Bitter restaurant owners, haggling down ingredient prices, barely able to keep their doors open. She kept her gaze fixed on the pale, grey sails fluttering in the cool breeze.

Their lifeline. Their salvation.

Almost there. Almost there. The boy ran to keep up with her long strides, but he didn't complain. Despite the exhaustion, he trusted her and only her.

The crowd grew dense closer to the docks. A long line had formed to board an anchored frigate, ready to sail East. She found an empty place to the side of the ticket booth, and they waited. The boy kicked gravel to pass the time. She held her free hand to her chest, counting every breath. Her contact would be here soon—with their boarding passes, identification, and a small amount of cash. New names. A new life. That's what she'd give them. *We're almost there.*

"Cassie?"

She startled at the sound of her name, one that she couldn't wait to leave behind. A stranger approached, and the boy scrambled to hide behind her skirts. She reached back and ran a hand through his sandy, blond hair. "Yes?"

The stranger—heavily bearded and dressed as a common sailor—nodded as he slipped her a large, faded envelope. She took it, and he disappeared back into the crowd as quickly as he'd come. She exhaled, nearly crying in relief.

A new life. They were so close.

We're going to make it. She slipped open the seal of the envelope, tipping it to spill the contents into her waiting palm. Instead of papers and bills, a single vellum letter waited for her. Her fingers shook as she flipped it open.

Nice try.

All feeling left her limbs. She pressed her back against the side of the booth. *No, no, no, no.*

"Mother?" The boy tugged her sleeve, his green eyes widening in terror.

Booted footsteps creaked on the wooden dock. She glanced up in time to see a blade sink into her gut. Once . . . twice . . . thrice. A high-pitched gasp escaped her lips. The pressure was enough to take her breath away. *We were so close.*

The new stranger—dressed in black—held her panicked gaze as he gently lowered her to the ground, leaning her back against the booth. He straightened, blood dripping from a thin dagger. In one smooth movement, he turned and squeezed the stunned boy's shoulder. "Your daddy says he misses you."

The boy swatted the man's hand away and spat. "Tell him to burn."

The stranger chuckled. "I'm sure he'd love to see *you* burn."

"Hey!" a gruff voice called across the docks. "What the blazes is going on?"

The stranger fled, blending back into the shadows.

"Did you see that, Mother?" The boy turned, smiling. *Bless him.* He thought he'd scared her attacker away. His eyes widened again, color draining from his golden skin, when he noticed the blood leaking from her abdomen. He crumpled beside her, tears staining his cheeks.

She couldn't breathe. Drowning from the inside, she took his face in her red-stained hands. "Get on that ship, Camden. Leave."

"*No.*" He laid his head on her shoulder and sobbed.

Oh, my sweet baby. She clutched him to her chest, breathing in whatever scent she could of his skin, his hair. Of the thousand nights she'd rocked him to sleep. Of all the tantrums and skinned knees.

"What's all the fussin' about?" The voice belonged to a stocky, dreadlocked sailor. By his look, and the pack of men behind him, he was a pirate—a captain. She managed a smile. *God is good.*

"Help!" The boy rushed forward and grabbed the captain's hand, dragging him down to his level with surprising strength. "Help her!"

The captain pursed his lips. Her breath grew shallower, the pain spreading deeper, as he prodded at her wounds. He sat back on his heels, wiping her blood on his trousers, and exhaled. "You don't have much life left, hun. Sorry to say. Nothing I can do."

The boy let out a gurgling sob, but the ringing in her ears drowned him out. She gripped the captain's fingers. "Are you getting on that ship, sir?"

"Naw." He shook his head. "I'm getting on my own. I was just meetin' a friend."

"Here." She dug through the pockets of her gown until she found her small purse. Shaking, she dumped the contents in the captain's open palm. A thin, diamond bracelet. A pair of ruby earrings. A few golden hair clips. All she had left of what she'd taken the night they fled. She'd planned it perfectly. It would have been enough to feed them until they reached the far side of the ocean.

"Take these." She closed his hand, holding tight when he tried to pull away. She smiled lovingly at the boy. "He's smart. Strong. Take him with you. Somewhere his father won't find him."

The captain had the decency to look saddened, still in her grip. "I don't have room."

"Take him," she managed, breathless. Every inhale was a

new knife in her heart. "Promise me. Keep him alive. Give him a life far away from here. Promise me."

What life he'd have with these men, she didn't know, but it would be better than here. Anywhere was better than here.

The boy sobbed, clawing at her skirts as one of the other pirates restrained him. The captain glanced between them, then sighed. "Fine." He stood, gesturing for his crewman to release him. "Kid, say goodbye to your momma."

"*No.*" The boy fell beside her, running his fingers through her hair, over her face. "I'm not going. I won't leave you."

She stroked his cheek before pulling the ring off her left hand and sliding it over his thumb. A lovely fire opal wreathed in golden leaves. He stared at it in confusion. She lifted his chin, both their eyes streaming tears. "Don't lose that," she whispered. "You might need it one day."

He fell against her shoulder, trembling, and she kissed him one last time. "Goodbye, Camden. Remember, I love you."

Oh, her beautiful, sensitive, angry boy who never listened. But he'd always loved her, though. From the moment they laid him on her chest, he loved her and only her. She hoped he wouldn't miss her too badly. That wherever he ended up, he would flourish. That he'd conquer every corner of the world.

She nodded to the captain, and he threw the boy over his shoulder as he kicked and screamed. The boy continued to scream even after the pirates disappeared into the crowd. She stared at the space he'd been until his voice faded into the songs of the waves, gulls, and creaking, stained hulls.

No one bothered to help as she lay there against the booth, her mouth agape as she struggled against the red sea inside her lungs. *We were so close.* She took one breath, two, three—then her heart went still.

So close.

CHAPTER I

CAMDEN

Cam had done many things and worn many names, but never had he thought he'd become an old man's bloody paper pusher.

"This can't be it." He sifted through a stack of papers littering the desk of his captain, the once glorious Edmund Resh. Cam tied back his hair with a bit of string to get it out of his face. "I distinctly remember doing that shill job last week. Where's the contract?"

"No idea." Resh glowered at him from his plush red armchair, dreadlocks loose over his shoulder, fingering the jade fishhook pendant he wore around his neck as he nursed a half-empty fifth of whisky. An unused glass sat on the floor by his feet. *How typical.*

"Five dollars." Resh's words were slow, his eyelids droopy. "That's what's left. That's what they get."

Cam tossed the papers at him. "I can read. The last *written* invoice was three months ago. After that, what? There should be double this—triple. What did you do with all the money?"

Resh rubbed his temples and grunted. "Spent it."

"On what?" *Why do I bother to ask?* Cam glanced around at Resh's finely furnished cabin. At the hand-woven rugs and crystal chandelier. Blazes, even the booze he drank cost more than Cam made in a month.

Resh honored him with eye contact. "Do you think runnin' a crew is cheap . . . or easy?"

Cam rolled his eyes and Resh straightened in his chair, scowling. "I've been burdened with the task of feeding you lot. Not to mention repairs on the ship, supplies, coin spent on the blasted healer when one of you catches something unsatisfactory. Have you ever thought of that? What I do to keep you lot alive?" Resh took a long drag of his whisky and smacked his fat lips. "Five dollars. That's what they get."

"You know what *I* think?" Cam gave him a polite smile. Resh scowled. "You're not going to be worrying about us much longer. Not when your men leave you to rot for their five bucks."

Resh ran his tongue over his yellowed teeth, eyes narrowing, unfocused. "They can try. They won't get far."

Cam clenched his jaw and held his captain's gaze. Resh hadn't always been this way. There was a time when he would have given his leg for the lowest of his crew—done anything to keep them afloat—but time and poverty had a way of changing people. Cam had no choice but to let it change him, too. "It would be better than being stuck here with you."

Resh's thick, black brows furrowed, then he spat, "Get out."

Cam snatched the bag of coins off the desk and bowed. "As you wish. If only I could promise good tidings to come and not woeful tales of mutiny."

"Get out, Barnes, *now,*" Resh growled.

Cam was already halfway out the door.

arnes was Cam's current last name. He switched it every year or so to keep the city officials on their toes. Eight assassination attempts in ten years could make any man paranoid.

Cam inhaled as he stepped onto the deck of *The Nightlady*, taking in the city of Port Lebanon's friendly stink. Gulls flew overhead, doing what they did best—cawing and defecating—as a mangy dog barked up at them from the street.

Bells chimed the new hour. Strolling folks on the docks argued over fish prices and curfew times, oblivious to anything but their own imagined troubles. Under Cam's feet, the frigate swayed with the comforting rhythm of the ocean. The smell of salt and brine filled his lungs, and he closed his eyes, trying to let the breeze carry away the angry pressure filling his chest.

It didn't work.

Instead, the merciless air left his rage there to fester.

Out across the bay, dozens of ships were docked in the harbor. Merchant vessels, private sailboats, and privateer ships waited, stuck. Even a frigate flying the Callahan flag—a leviathan rising from a golden sea, the symbol of the most powerful family in the West—was forced into submission by martial law.

They were trapped. None could leave with the city on lockdown. All because that bloody ship anchored about a mile out along the sand drifts, its sails drawn and complacent. On its mast flew a yellow and black flag, a declaration. The ship and all its passengers were infected with The Rot.

Cam wrinkled his nose at the phantom stench of death. This had been his reality for the last six months. No one could enter or leave the city from the harbor, not until Port Lebanon's government decided to set that cursed rig on fire. It only took one infected entering the city for the pandemic to begin again.

The disease had killed millions since its spread into The Four Corners. The fear of it had been instilled in Cam since he was a boy.

But he was a man now—an exceptionally bored one—and his evenings were presently spent in the Portside slums. That same pressure in his chest spread into his shoulders and gut, made all the worse as he glanced up at the tall wire fences separating the harbor and the slums from the rest of the city. *I'll get out of here. Soon enough.* He'd repeated that lie to himself so many times, he'd almost started to believe it.

Cam hopped off the ship and entered the bustle of the crowd. The setting sun shone through the wire, leaving orange squares on the cobblestone streets. He forced himself to watch the light dance across the toes of his boots as he walked. Listen to the click of his heels on the chipped red rock. Anything to keep his attention from the narrow cage that had become his life. Anything to keep him from burning this place to the ground.

At least I have more freedom than some. He never could stop himself from looking as he passed the kennels. Never could get used to the scent of pus, urine, and stale blood. Once used to house the animals waiting to be boarded, the kennels were now the city's official dumping ground for the infected. They'd be burned, too, at some point.

Grown men—squeezed into crates too small for hounds— somehow managed to sleep despite their faces being smashed against the bars, their blue, festering blisters pressed against cold metal. A woman lay curled up in the back of another cage, a babe at her breast, singing softly as she gently stroked her child's wispy hair.

Her sunken eyes met Cam's as he passed, and a familiar leaden sensation spread through his limbs. He pulled his scarf over his face, fingering the revolver on his hip. *I have my own problems. They're beyond help. I'm not. You can't save her. Just like you couldn't have saved Mother.*

Another lie he told himself.

It was late by the time Cam reached the Yellow Bunter, one of the slum's more popular taverns. Its cheaply painted doors were propped open, spilling warm light onto the slick, cold streets. Barefoot courtesans ghosted through the moon's shadows, some with leering men on their arms. Others scanned the faces around them, looking for any sign of interest—hungry wolves on the prowl.

Usually, a shapely female silhouette would be a welcome distraction, but not tonight. No, tonight, he would be the bearer of bad news—a role he'd grown used to playing.

Inside, drunken laughter and the crashing of overturned tables hit Cam's forming migraine like a sledgehammer. He shoved his way through the packed tavern, dodging a few thrown chairs, and found his crew at their usual spot in the back.

Nathan Williams, *The Nightlady's* navigator, bridged a deck of cards between his fingers. A smile spread on his dark, acne-scarred face as Cam approached. A short, black ringlet fell into his eyes as he patted the stool beside him. "Thought you weren't coming. Just started a new game of Old Maid. Wanna join?"

"I'll pass." Cam plopped into his chair. Besides Nathan, only Dean and Gerald were at the table. "Where is everybody?"

"Turned in for the night." Gerald inspected his cards as Nathan dolled them out, veins throbbing on the back of his thick, bald head. "When you didn't show up, they figured they weren't gettin' paid."

A serving girl set a dark, foaming beer on the table. Cam eyed it bitterly. Years ago, he'd almost died when his wine had been poisoned with arsenic. Some of his fingers were still numb from it. He hadn't touched alcohol since, but tonight was one of those nights he wished he could stomach it.

Nathan shot him a nervous glance every few moments as he and the others began to play.

Cam filled the awkward silence by popping his lips.

Nathan was young—younger than Cam's nineteen years—and had yet to learn there wasn't much to gain by avoiding inevitable questions. *God, I hate this job sometimes.* "Spit it out."

Dean and Gerald glanced up from their cards.

Nathan cleared his throat. "You talked to the cap?"

Cam nodded slowly.

Nathan chewed his lip. "Are we . . . ?"

"Yes."

"How much?" Dean's black eyes sparkled.

Here it comes. Cam sighed. "Five."

"Five?" Nathan's eyes lit up. "Hundred?"

Cam's stomach dropped, his mouth going dry. The serving girl set a glass of water down in front of him—she'd remembered—and he sucked it down gratefully, even though it was warm. "Five dollars . . . each."

Silence.

"*Hang it all.*" Dean pushed back his chair and knocked it into the table, sloshing beer all over the cards. Cam didn't try to stop him from storming out. His anger was justifiable. Gerald stared down at his ruined cards.

Cam watched a dark stain spread across the chest and shoulders of the queen of hearts. *He won't be able to afford another pack anytime soon.*

Nathan cupped his face in his hands. "The healers . . . my sister—"

"I know." Cam grit his teeth.

"How will I—"

"I don't know."

Nathan opened his mouth to answer, but jumped as the tavern door slammed. The room went silent. Two men stood at the bar, speaking in low voices. A chill crawled up Cam's spine at the look of the newcomers. One wore the hood of his cloak thrown back, revealing the vivid, pulsing tattoos covering his skin.

Stripes—what commoners called the Revenant.

Men claiming to have come back from the dead, able to wield all kinds of powers. When Cam was a child, his nurse-maid told him stories of Revenant, dozens of them. Undead figures from storybooks, so twisted in death that even hell couldn't swallow them. He never believed her theatrics, even then, but the Revenant were intimidating all the same.

A hiss rumbled through the room, followed by the squeak of chair legs as everyone turned their backs to them. The barkeep nervously pointed to the farthest corner of the tavern. The Stripes obliged, and angry curses and gestures followed them to their table. The Stripes seemed completely oblivious to the hatred following them as they took their seats.

They leaned their heads together, whispering, and the older one slipped a small red card from the sleeve of his robes, setting it carefully on the edge of the table.

A calling card.

Cam cursed, swallowing roughly. *You've got to be joking.*

Green for local contracts, blue for road jobs, red for over-seas work. Work currently forbidden in Port Lebanon . . . the kind that could bring in cash, lots of it.

Blazes.

Cam looked at Nathan. A young, but hardened sailor, nearly put to tears. Gerald, catatonic in his current state of poverty. There was a time when he'd seen them prosper, when all of them lived as if they owned the blasted earth they tore apart. Taken what they wanted, stolen whatever they pleased. When they'd been respected, feared, and coveted.

Now what did they have?

God bless it. Cam stood, pulling his new and only dollar coins out of his pocket, and slid them to Gerald. "Buy some more cards, mate."

Gerald glanced up at him with watery eyes, nodded, then shoved the coins into his pocket.

Cam tapped Nathan's shoulder, and he lifted his head from his hands, scowling. "What?"

"Follow me," Cam muttered. "And let me do the talking."

Nathan jumped up and fell in line behind him without hesitation. Cam headed toward the Revenant's table, Nathan at his heels. Curious eyes followed them, but none carried any judgment. Desperate times called for desperate action, and everyone of them knew it.

"Don't." Nathan tugged on Cam's coat sleeve. "We can't."

Cam jabbed his elbow into Nathan's gut. "Shut it."

"Why *me*?"

"Because you're the only one around here I can tolerate for more than fifteen minutes without wanting to shoot. Now quiet."

The air seemed thicker, vibrating, as Cam slid into the booth across from the Revenants, snatching up the red card in the process. He gave them an impish grin. "Gentlemen."

The two men exchanged glances. The younger of the two smiled back at him, his eyes an unsettling cat yellow. Matching golden tattoos twisted up his neck. "You're a captain?"

"Quartermaster." Cam straightened his patched grey coat. "Acting on behalf of his captain. This is Mr. Williams, our navigator."

Gold Stripe frowned. "We'd rather speak to your captain."

"Well, you have me." Cam popped his collar. "Would you like to speak here or somewhere more private?"

Gold Stripe studied his face for a moment, thin lips spreading into a knowing smile. "Follow me."

Checkmate.

The entire tavern watched, whispering amongst themselves, as Cam and Nathan were led into one of the tavern's bedrooms for rent. Inside, the sheets on the bed were unmade and reeked of vomit. Broken beer bottles and cigar ash crunched under their boots, scuffing the hardwood floor.

The Stripes sat beside each other on the sunken couch by the fireplace. Cam and Nathan propped themselves on the end of the bed across from them. Sweat poured down poor Nathan's chocolate skin, his eyes wide and fearful.

The older Stripe cleared his throat and threw back his hood. Green swirls tattooed the older man's sizable, wrinkled forehead, made more prominent by a receding auburn hairline.

"Before we get this show on the road." Green Stripes had a poor man's accent and a mouth full of missing teeth. He passed Cam a small, corked bottle. "Do ya' know what this is, boy?"

Cam squinted as he examined the object. It contained a shimmering pink powder, the consistency of sand. "Pearl Dust." Cam walked the bottle between his fingers. "A potent and extremely rare narcotic. What of it?"

Nathan studied the bottle curiously.

"Do you know what it's worth?" Gold Stripe asked.

"To the right buyer?" Cam tossed it back. "Quite a lot."

Gold Stripe laughed, a gentle musical sound. "That bauble you held is worth more than your last three hauls combined."

"How do you know what we've hauled?" Nathan snapped.

Cam glared at him, and Nathan's eyes turned to his hands, wringing on his lap.

Gold Stripes cocked his head. "We've been following your

work. It's difficult to find a trustworthy crew these days. I'll make this short. We need a large supply of Pearl Dust moved. We're willing to put half payment upfront."

"Half?" Cam's brow rose. *Interesting.* "And where would we be headed that requires such heavy insurance?"

"New Havana."

"New Havana?" Nathan repeated. "That island just a bit south of here? Owned by some spice merchant?"

"Formerly owned by," Gold Stripes corrected. "It was purchased several years back by a wealthy prospective client of ours. We're seeking a sound crew to make the journey."

They shared a glance, and Cam could see the glint of gold in Nathan's eyes. Heaps of cash. Mountains of it. Red cards were blood oaths—unbreakable—and it was worse than disgraceful to make a deal without Resh's approval.

But if they succeeded?

Cam could buy a ship of his own. Make Nathan his quartermaster. He'd pay his crew properly, treat them decently. Find somewhere nice for Resh to retire and live out the rest of his days in comfort. Cam owed him that much.

But most enticing of all—escaping this festering, dunghole that'd become his personal hell. An image of that woman and her baby flashed through Cam's mind, and he shook his head violently to chase the thought away.

The Revenant watched him intently.

Cam reclined on the bed, a wicked smile spreading on his face. "Deal's done." *I'm so dead.* "When do we leave?"

Gold Stripe's brow rose. "That's it? No questions?"

"Nope, that's it. When do we leave?"

"We sail in one week."

"What about the lockdown?" Nathan asked.

Green Stripes waved dismissively. "Don't you go worrying. We have contacts to handle that. Just show up when you're supposed to, do your blasted job, and no one will have any problems. Agreed?"

"Sounds fair." Cam nodded. "I look forward to doing business with you. I'm sure this will be an . . . enlightening experience for us all."

Gold Stripes smiled, wide and charming. "Oh, I promise it will be."

CHAPTER 2
CAMDEN

I am truly and whole-fully screwed. Cam's fingers hovered over the handle of Resh's door, his heart dancing against his ribs. It was past two in the morning now. Maybe he could wait to confess his sins until daybreak.

Cam inhaled, running a clammy hand through his hair. *No, I have to get this over with.*

The door swung open. Cam smiled in panic. Resh stood on the other side, blinking at him in confusion. "You need something?"

Blazes. Sweat beaded on Cam's temples. *Blazes.* Resh was still fully dressed. "Heading out?"

Resh harrumphed and nodded. "Can't sleep. Figured fresh air and a smoke would do the trick. Join me?"

"Sure," Cam exhaled. "Might as well." *He's going to kill me.*

They walked from Resh's quarters out onto the deck of *The Nightlady.* Cam shrugged deeper into his coat. The overcast skies from earlier in the day had cleared, allowing the cold to creep in. Fog rolled into the harbor, shrouding the surrounding anchored ships in mist.

Resh flipped his lighter open, puffed his cigar to life, and took a long drag. "You got that guilty look about you, kid. What'd ya do?"

Cam sucked on his teeth. He'd had always been a good liar, since he was young, but Resh had the amazing ability to see straight through him. Cam focused his attention on his feet, scraping a bit of algae off the wooden deck with the toe of his boot.

"I, uh . . ." Cam began. *Screw it.* "I made a deal for you. Red card."

For nearly a full minute, the only sound between them was the squawking of a few noisy gulls and Cam's quickened breathing.

"Hmm." Resh took another drag, not even bothering to look at him with those black, beetle eyes.

"It's a good one," Cam muttered.

"Yeah?"

"Yeah." *God, end me.* "Moving Pearl Dust to New Havana. Heard of it?"

"Yep." So slow, drawn out. "Nasty waters down that way, you know. Lots of pirates waiting to pick off ships coming out of the harbor."

"We'll make a fortune." Cam wiped his sweaty palms on his trousers. "Enough to get us back on our feet, get us out of here. They're going to pay off the city watch. We'll finally be at sea again."

More quiet thinking. The end of Resh's cigar burned a deep orange. "They?"

There it was . . . Resh's anger brewing below the surface. He'd felt it plenty of times before.

Cam pulled the contract from his pocket. "A couple of Revenant propositioning down at the Bunter. They're looking for a crew to work steady."

"Revenant, aye?" Not actually a question. Resh took another puff, then reached to grab the contract.

Cam moved faster and stuffed it back in his pocket. "Before you think of tearing this up, they've got their own signed copy. Deal's done."

Another minute passed.

Slowly, Resh turned and put his cigar out against Cam's shoulder, embers burning into the worn fabric of his coat. "Have you lost your thrice-blasted mind?" The fact that he'd said it calmly—didn't yell or scream—made it so much worse.

"It had to be done." Cam brushed ash off his lapel. "You'd have let us sink. There was nothing else to do about it." He meant to say more but decided against it when he saw the waves of emotion running over his captain's face. Fury and disappointment, but most unnerving of all . . . fear.

They just stared at each other for God knows how long before Resh stepped forward and slipped his hand around the back of Cam's head. "You've sold yourself to the devil now, you stupid boy, and there's no going back. No paying the price it'll take to please him."

"I can do this." Cam's breaths were faint and rushed. "I'll run it for you. I did what I thought was right."

Resh's expression softened. "I know you did." He patted Cam's cheek . . . too hard. "And you know I love you, Camden— like my own—but if it wasn't for the promise I made your momma, I'd throw you over the edge for the bloody sharks."

Cam's jaw stiffened as he pulled away, his mother's final gasps echoing through his mind. *Take him with you.* She'd begged his captain. *Give him a life away from here. Somewhere his father won't find him.*

Never had Resh used his mother against him, never. Not when he was thirteen and gutted an official, getting them chased out of town. Not when he'd run off with another crew, abandoning them, only to find them half a year later, sick and starving. Not in their years of training, when Cam spit blood on Resh's boots as they fought with blades for hours on end.

Never.

Cam took a step back, reflexively reaching for the handle of his revolver, running his thumb over the hidden compartment carved into the pommel. "I should put a bullet in your head for that."

Resh let out a low laugh, moonlight glinting off the jade pendant peeking out of his stained shirt. "Trust me, boy, you already have."

CHAPTER 3
CAMDEN

And here we are now—so far away from home. Cam gazed over the sea, watching his doom grow closer every passing moment.

The Revenant, the deal, his bloody soft heart—that'd all been weeks ago, and Cam had regretted every moment since.

They were deep in Southern water, and there would be no turning back. Not with the massive ship approaching on the horizon, black storm clouds engulfing it like smoke. Its crimson sails had haunted him for the last three days, and with the amount of Pearl Dust on board, Cam doubted they were coming for a friendly chat.

He'd known this would happen—Resh had cursed him for it—but Cam loaded the drugs onto their ship anyway. Any lives lost, any wounds taken from this point on, were his fault. Another failure he'd have to live with.

"Bring down the sails," Cam ordered as he tucked his spyglass into his belt.

Nathan chewed on his thumbnail. "The cap never said to—"

"I'm telling you now." Cam shot him a glare. "Get the boys loading the cannons. I'm sick of this cat-and-mouse garbage. Time to light this ninny up."

Nathan was right, of course. At his rank, Cam had full control of *The Nightlady* on most days, but when it came to battle, only the captain could give orders.

Nathan ran a hand through his curly locks. "Cam—"

"Let me worry about Resh," Cam said, more softly. Nathan looked a little green, so he patted his shoulder. "Relax, mate. What's the worst that can happen?"

"We get blown to bits." Nathan groaned. "Gutted. Hanged. Keel-hauled. Would you like me to start a list?"

Cam sniffed and rubbed his hands together excitedly. "Smells like a perfectly fine day to me. Ready the ship. Don't start until I get back."

Nathan laughed, then bowed before striding off toward the main deck.

God bless him. Cam headed toward Resh's quarters.

The Nightlady rocked and fought against the powerful waves crashing against its hull. Despite the oncoming storm, gulls circled above the masts, settling when the wind allowed them to watch the chaos below. Smart enough to know when to wait for a carrion.

When Cam tried to enter Resh's quarters, the door was locked.

Bloody ridiculous. "Open up." Cam pounded his fist on the door. There was shuffling on the other side. "I can hear you, Cap."

The shuffling stopped. "Go away, Camden."

Cam stepped back, sucked in a breath, and slammed his heel into the door just above the lock. It flung open. At the back of the room, Resh sat at his desk, writing a note. There was an open bottle of booze in front of him. Crusty vomit stained his nice rug, filling the cramped space with the stink of a sour stomach.

"I don't know if you've noticed." Cam pinched his nose and grimaced. "But we'll be having company soon. Maybe—I don't know—you should clean up a bit?"

His captain didn't even bother to curse him. Instead, he ran his fingers through his beard. Dark, purplish shadows encircled his eyes. "I've noticed."

"And?"

"And what?"

"What are you going to do about it?" Cam sat down across from him and propped his feet up on the desk. Resh glared but didn't tell him to move. Cam smiled. "We've got six barrels of Pearl Dust below deck, just ripe for the taking. Blazes, I'd probably steal it, too, if I were them."

"You can keep talking, Camden." Resh rubbed his brow. "Keep making your jokes. Go ahead and drive me silly to make yourself feel better, but that doesn't change the fact that we die today because of you. Because you were too bloody greedy to wait for a safer option. The right option."

He might as well have stabbed Cam in the heart. "There wasn't time. We would have rotted there."

"There's always time. It just wasn't convenient for you."

An ugly, ugly hurt settled itself in Cam's stomach at the tone in Resh's voice—abandonment. If Resh kicked him off the crew, he'd have no one—nothing left. He'd be alone. Cam chewed his tongue. It felt irregularly thick and dry.

"I need you to help me fix this mess, Ed. I promise, I'll protect you, but I need your help."

"Protect me? How?" Resh asked with a bitter laugh. "Death here will be more pleasant than any future the Revenant have in store for us. I can assure you that."

"What's that supposed to mean?"

"It means leave." Resh stood, knocking into the desk and spilling his drink. "I have nothing else to say to you, boy, and your promises mean nothing."

Cam wanted to curse him, to scream—to wrap his hands around Resh's throat and slam his head into the wall. Before he could, Nathan appeared in the doorway, his eyes round and wild. "The ship hit a good wind. They're upon us."

Cam rose, his eyes never leaving Resh's hard stare. "I thought you were better than this."

Resh smiled. "I could say the same for you."

Too much. The slide of anger and hurt threatened to spill over the edge.

I've killed for you. The words almost slipped from his lips. *I've faced death a thousand times for you. Why won't you fight for me?* Instead, Cam turned and followed Nathan out onto the deck. At the prow, dozens of crewmen stared out across the water, mouths forming silent prayers against the approaching leviathan.

"What are you doing?" Cam shouted. *I need to hurt someone.* "Fire a shot over her bow!"

The crew came back to life and, within seconds, had a warning shot sailing toward the oncoming vessel. The shot splashed harmlessly a dozen or so meters from its target. Cam counted his heartbeats as they waited for the returning shot, Resh's words eating at what remained of his self-control. Twisting and gnawing until it flowered into a violent rage burning just below the surface of his skin.

He needed to fight. To bleed. His blood longed for it. To release this poison in the most unpleasant ways possible.

A flash, then a deafening crack, split the coming dawn. Instead of a warning, a cannonball slammed into the side of *The Nightlady,* blowing open a splintering hole.

"Load 'em up!" Cam cried over the explosion of wooden

shrapnel, adrenaline, and hate singing through his veins. A cheer went up from the gun deck as the cannons were readied. Nathan joined Cam at the prow, his face plastered with dust and sweat.

Nathan was breathless from exhilaration. "Are we ready for this?"

"Of course, we are." Cam shot him a wry look. "Have I ever steered you wrong?"

To his surprise, Nathan leaned in and gave him a tight hug. "Don't die, Cam. You're the only friend I've got left."

Cam's throat tightened. "Don't you start this again." He hugged him back anyway. He hadn't realized how much he needed it.

An unnatural wind caught the enemy ship's sails, and it swerved just in time to scrape along *The Nightlady's* side. Across the space between the two ships, dozens of unfriendly faces jeered down at them. Ugly, toothless, wind-burnt faces. Their steel and firearms were of far better quality than anything his crew could afford.

A heavy, metal boarding plank fell from the other ship, embedding steel spikes into *The Nightlady*. Endless numbers of screaming men spewed onto the deck like water from a burst drainpipe.

Cam closed his eyes and inhaled, tasting blood and fear. *Somewhere his father won't find him.* Her words were always the last nail to the coffin of his self-control. He breathed out. Their shouts were his war cries, gunshots, the beating of his raging heart, the sweat and stink of bodies, now the scent of prey.

Somewhere his father won't find him. Cam checked to make sure the compartment on his gun was sealed tight—the only place he felt safe keeping his mother's wedding ring. She probably meant for him to sell it, but he'd rather slit his own throat.

Most nights, he wished the assassin had taken him, too. He often wondered why he hadn't.

Seconds later, the ship was overrun. Gunshots rang out. Men on both sides fell, some dead, others partially disemboweled by enemy swords. Cam dove into the action, howling, revolver and cutlass in hand. He embedded his blade between one grunt's eyes and took a shot at another. He cut a throat, then stabbed another man beneath the armpit. In a matter of moments, bodies piled around his feet like flies to fresh feces.

A sailor dove for him, bloodied sword raised, and Cam parried him before opening his guts over the deck. The poor man's eyes widened in shock before blood loss turned them glassy.

A blindingly bright light flashed from somewhere to his right. Cam turned just as a Revenant stepped onto *The Nightlady*, his clothes covered in blood and ash.

Cam's heart quickened as time slowed.

He was no longer the top predator. All the stories he'd been told . . . they didn't prepare him for the truth. The reality of what happened to a man when death was cheated.

The demon in front of him was thin, with rich, fiery hair. A ruby red tattoo ran down his forehead, over his nose, his chin. The air around him distorted as he raised his arms, and a burst of flame exploded from the aura, lighting *The Nightlady's* sails into a vortex of fire. One of the crewmen charged after him, but the Revenant torched him mid-stride, leaving the man in a crumpled, charred heap.

A second Revenant appeared, hovering above the corpse-strewn deck. Older than the first, with long black hair braided down his back, the tail of his pale overcoat streaming behind him in the wind. He shot a strong gust, sending several screeching men overboard. His sleeves blew back, exposing the silver marks twisting up his arms.

His grey eyes locked onto Cam's, despite the clashing of steel around them, and he curled his finger. Cam's stomach lurched.

"You there!" The Revenant called out to him—over the screams, the sound was like animals being butchered—and the commotion froze.

Cam straightened, inhaling sharply to catch his breath. "Aye?" *God, you sound like an idiot.*

"Where is your captain?" The Revenant lowered himself to the deck. "This bloodshed need not continue."

All eyes were on Cam. He couldn't show fear or else lose the crew's morale. He sucked in another deep breath and took a few confident strides toward the Revenant. "All this bloodshed wouldn't have happened *at all* if you had heeded my warning shot. What business, Stripe?"

The red-haired Revenant grinned. "Don't be rude. You have something we want."

"Ah, the Pearl Dust." Cam nodded as he moved closer. They were only about twenty feet apart now. The only thing that brought him any kind of comfort was that he was about six inches taller than either of them. "It saddens me to say you can't have it."

Resh burst onto the deck then, strapping on his sword belt. When he saw the Revenant men, his face drained of color.

Cam could have choked him. *God no. Just go back to your cabin, man.*

"You must be the captain, yes?" the black-haired Revenant asked, cocking his head to peer around Cam.

"Aye." Resh swallowed as he took in the mayhem. "What business?"

"As we were just telling your friend here." Black Hair nodded to Cam. "We've come for your cargo. It would be greatly appreciated if you would hand it over without any further violence."

"I already told you." Cam drew his revolver and cocked back the hammer, sights falling directly on Red Hair's stupid horse face. "You can't have it. Don't make the mistake of thinking I'll miss from this distance. So why don't you and your fairy friend get the blazes off my ship?"

Red Hair began to laugh—a terrible, haunting sound that echoed across the water, chilling Cam to his core. He closed the space between them in less than a blink, wrapping his hand around Cam's throat. A putrid stench filled Cam's nose: the smell of his own skin melting.

He struggled—tried to cry out—tried to break free, but the Revenant's grip was inhumanly strong. He couldn't move.

"I don't like you," Red Hair whispered, leaning in close, his breath stinking of cigarette smoke and old coffee. "I don't like talkers. I don't like little kids—like you—trying to wear bigger men's boots."

Despite the agony, Cam shot him a quick grin. "Then maybe you should have bought yourself smaller shoes."

Red Hair scowled and squeezed his throat tighter, a fresh burst of pain radiating from his burnt skin. It spread to his jaw, his ears. The pain reached its peak as the blood vessels began to burst in his eyes, then everything went black.

Cam woke to acrid smoke filling his lungs. He squinted past the burning in his eyes.

He—and what remained of the crew—were tied to the blackened stump of the mast, a fire kindled around them from pieces of *The Nightlady's* ruined body.

Across the deck, Nathan, Resh, and about twenty other

crewmen were being loaded onto the Revenant's ship, along with the Pearl Dust.

Cam moaned—half a laugh, half a sob. *They're going to burn us alive.*

"*Oi,*" Cam tried to cry out, but his throat was raw and ruined. Smoke choked him.

Red Hair noticed and grinned, striding across the deck overtop of the slowly building fire. His trouser legs caught, but he seemed not to notice. He pressed his nose into Cam's face. "I hoped you'd come around before we'd gone. We had specific orders to take the captain and his second alive, but we decided the navigator would do just fine. I didn't feel like listening to you talk the entire trip."

Cam didn't know whether to laugh or cry. How could he be afraid when the fire surrounding them was so breathtaking, so serene?

It's beautiful. Cam burst into hysterical laughter. *It's beautiful and I've lost my bloody mind.*

Red Hair's brows scrunched in confusion.

"I'm going to haunt you," Cam rasped. "You think you hate me now, just wait until I come back for you."

Red Hair patted Cam's cheek, blistering it as he did so.

Cam groaned.

"I look forward to it," Red Hair crooned. "Enjoy your stay in hell."

Cam spat at his feet, his saliva disappearing in a puff of steam before it could stain Red Hair's boots. "I'll do my best."

The fire really was beautiful.

Cam watched them sail away, listening to the men around him screaming for help—to God, to their mothers, and even one or two for him. The Revenants sailed away as the flames licked up his legs and split his flesh in two.

He watched until that ship was once again a speck on the stormy horizon.

The screaming grew louder.

Flames swallowed him, but there was no pain. Only the euphoric bliss of being wrapped in a warm, loving blanket.

It had been a long day. Death called—a black and sorrowful song—and Cam closed his eyes, answering gratefully. This was not how he expected to die, but it was the only way he wanted to.

Safe and embraced, with no one left to hurt him.

CHAPTER 4
ANNIE

"Be on the lookout for false teachers. They are wolves amongst sheep." Lady Duskin copied the day's lesson down on the classroom's large, slate chalkboard. "They will tear you apart. Their tell is the product of their actions. Just as an apple tree will only ever produce an apple, the fruit of evil will always be evil."

Annie suppressed a yawn, trying to stay straight in her chair despite the ache in her shoulders. The other girls scratched notes down on their slate boards. Annie never took notes. She just remembered. Though she couldn't remember the last time she had a full night's sleep.

A light brown curl escaped from Lady Duskin's loose bun as she turned, the voluminous skirt of her navy day dress swirled around her. "Can anyone give me an example of a sin in disguise?"

At the desk to Annie's right, the hand of pretty, red-headed Jenny shot up. "Fibbing to spare someone's feelings?"

"Very good." Lady Duskin smiled sweetly, showing off her perfect white teeth. Jenny beamed. "Anyone else?"

"Taking food from the kitchens without asking," Rose asked, "even if you're hungry?"

"Dressing above your station?" Jenny added in.

Lady Duskin nodded. "All wonderful examples." Her cool grey eyes locked onto Annie. "And you, dear? What do you consider a secret sin?"

Annie held her stare, unwavering, her expression a stony mask. "Murder."

Lady Duskin's smile faded. "Um, yes, murder is the most terrible of all sins, and one the Lord does not easily forgive."

"And being a hypocrite?" Annie responded flatly. "Does He forgive that?"

Lady Duskin clicked her tongue. "That's enough for today. Run along. You are all at your usual stations."

Annie remained at her desk as the other girls scooted their chairs back, stood, and placed their slate boards back in their assigned cubbies on the shelf. She took her time putting her supplies away, watching as Lady Duskin jotted down new notes on the chalkboard, preparing for the boys' class. Why she bothered separating them, she didn't know. Out of the four Duskin children, little Nathan was her only brother—and the youngest at eleven. Jenny and Rose were both sixteen, two years younger than Annie.

Brother. Annie exhaled. *Sisters.* She didn't share blood with any of them. She'd lost her true siblings a long time ago.

"Richard expects you downstairs," Lady Duskin reminded her after several tense minutes, followed by the exaggerated screech of chalk on slate.

Without a word, Annie nodded and headed for the door. *No more stalling, I guess.*

"And dear?"

Annie turned stiffly. "Yes, Mother?"

Lady Duskin's smile was no longer sweet. "Next time . . . "

She continued with her notes, shoulders visibly stiff through the fabric of her dress. "Watch your bloody mouth."

Annie curtsied, hiding her smile as she left the classroom.

Every day was the same. Mornings were meant for education. The Duskins' could afford tutors, but Lady Duskin preferred teaching class herself. Afternoons were meant for chores. Again, they could hire servants, but what responsibility would the children learn? Evenings were spent attending one of the Duskins' nightly social events. They always had guests in and out of the house.

Annie waited behind every day to be told to head below ground. Today was no different than the hundreds that had come before or the hundreds that would come after.

She walked the stone hallways toward the kitchens, her dainty, slippered feet hardly making a sound on the polished coral floors. This morning was particularly humid. She twisted her straight, white hair into a low bun, her pale skin damp with sweat. At least it was always cool in the bunker. The mansion was built over one of New Havana's numerous volcanic lava tubes, which—thankfully—seemed impervious to the island's tropical heat.

Annie had lived here with the Duskins for three years, and still hated the weather as much as she had the evening Lord Duskin purchased her from the slavers.

Too much sun. Too many colors. What she'd give to feel again the icy winds and snowfall of home.

She missed the North. She missed Rouenn—the village she'd grown up in. When her family had still been together. When Papa hunted deer, she skinned them while he prepared the fire. Mama died when she was born, so her older brothers expected her to do all the women's work alone, even though she was too young.

And she always did, diligently . . . until the day they were slaughtered. She'd been thirteen.

But that was a long time ago now. Lord Duskin had found her two years later.

Inside the kitchen, the chefs were busy preparing the day's meals. At least cooking was one thing she didn't have to do anymore. From the smell, they must be serving white fish and crab cakes for lunch. Annie scrunched her nose. She hated the bottom-feeder taste of crustacean, but it was better to eat what you're given than to starve.

No one paid her any attention as she entered the pantry. They knew better than to bother her. Behind a fat sack of flour, covered in cobwebs, was a lever. She pulled it and waited impatiently as the false back wall let out a loud creak before stuttering open. *I'll have to oil the hinges soon.*

Just another thing to add to her endless to-do list.

The customary stench of death, rotting flesh, and human waste wafted up the tunnel to greet her. The smell no longer fazed her. The staff didn't question it. Annie descended the steps carved into the lava tube's slick, grimy stone.

As she'd hoped, the air below ground was pleasantly cool. Water dripped from the ceiling, tickling her scalp as it sent goose prickles down her spine. Annie walked with confidence in the complete darkness, trusting her feet to keep the path, until a dim light became visible up ahead.

Lord Duskin spared no expense on the gaslights he'd had built into the black rock walls. She squinted, eyes adjusting to the light, and she ducked into one of the smaller side tunnels that led toward the teaching room and the patient quarters. Along with the gaslights, dozens of candles lit the low-ceilinged cavern. To the left, a second tunnel opened into a larger cavern, used to house their test subjects.

It was a prison, really. If it weren't for the lamps, they'd be living in constant darkness.

Noiselessly, she entered the teaching room, closing the door to the chamber gently behind her. Dressed in a stained, white medical coat, Lord Duskin leaned over the table in the center of the room, lost in thought. His lips twitched. "Bring me a vial, girl."

Annie took a small, corked bottle out of the cabinet and walked to the table. Elain's naked body lay stretched over top of it, in the advanced stages of The Rot.

Annie quickly looked away, burying that small aching part of herself still seeking to mourn. Elain's long, golden hair trailed off the side of the table, her once-pink cheeks emptied of color.

Not Elain. She's patient 478 now. She had been one of the Duskins' adopted daughters, just like Annie. Elain had been lovely, had been sweet. She'd sang and danced, had picked flowers for Lady Duskin from one of the gardens she'd grown herself, but that had been the extent of her talents. Lord Duskin may have kept her around—solely for her beauty—but Elain started asking questions.

Questions were dangerous.

Lord Duskin's gaunt jaw was clenched, his black eyes fixated on the bit of flesh he peeled away from Elain's thigh with his scalpel. Annie stuffed the vial beneath her armpit, slipping on a pair of gloves before offering it to him. Lord Duskin squished the mottled blue bit of skin into the vial, and Annie replaced the cork. Blood leaked over the seal.

"Note the time of death as one hour ago. No need to watch this one further. No detectable signs of change." Lord Duskin cut into the blue blister oozing on the girl's shin. "Cause of death: dehydration from excessive excrement."

Annie did as she was told, her eyes flickering to Elain's

pallid face every few moments. The Pearl Dust had worked alarmingly fast on her. She'd been exposed only four days ago. This state of deterioration—un-medicated—usually took weeks, if not months, of illness.

The Rot was not typically a quick death. The bacteria festered inside the body, transmitted by an infected touch, contaminated water, or feces, until it erupted from the skin. By that time, though, your organs were a blackened, mushy mess. There was no cure.

She knew—she'd seen the autopsies.

Every morning and evening, when Annie came to feed the patients, Elain begged her to free her. To plead to Lord Duskin to let her go. But Annie ignored her. She hated it—hated herself—but hated the thought of being the next one on that table even more.

All she knew how to do anymore was survive. Self-preservation was the only emotion she allowed herself to feel.

"Mother taught us about evil today." Annie labeled the vial and set it back in the cabinet. The Duskins made sure all their children knew how to read and write. For the first time since she'd entered, Lord Duskin looked up, his lips curving up slightly in amusement. Annie turned back to her work. She should have kept her mouth shut.

"And?" He removed his gloves carefully, so as not to touch the contaminated blood. "Did you find the subject of interest?"

Annie pretended to busy herself with some papers, stalling. It wasn't often he rewarded her with conversation. *I need to be careful.*

"She spoke that evil can often hide itself in an innocent act." Annie chewed her lip. "It made me curious . . ."

"Yes?"

It's too late, just say it. Annie straightened her back. "Are we the evil within the act, using people in this way?" *Am I a monster for helping you kill Elain?*

Lord Duskin laughed, almost cheerfully, and smoothed back his dark hair. "Is it wrong for a wolf to hunt? For a lesser creature to kill for its own survival?"

"I guess not."

He stepped closer, cupping her chin in his cold hand. "Such is the sacrifice of life, and this girl may save thousands. Millions. She began life as a transient's whelp and ended it helping to stop a future pandemic."

"Forgive me for asking, Father." Annie lowered her gaze. "My curiosity got the best of me."

Lord Duskin kissed her full on the lips. His mustache tickled her nose and cheeks. "It's not a sin to doubt," he said as he pulled away. "Only to act upon it—to allow the seeds of uncertainty to grow. Take care of this specimen in the usual manner. I have more work to do." He turned and strode from the room.

Annie stood, frozen, until she could no longer hear the click of his footsteps echoing through the cavern.

Elain's empty, dead eyes watched her.

Not the eyes of the body on the table, but from the shadow in the corner—her ghost. The shadow grew steadily darker, sadder, as Annie wrapped Elain's corpse in a cloth and rolled it onto the waiting cart.

The ghost followed her through the tunnels, but Annie paid it no mind. They'd started following her the day she'd arrived at New Havana. The cart bounced and caught on every lump in the hardened lava floor, Annie's breath heavy and ragged from the exertion.

The lava tube split, and she swung into the cavern on the left, the path hidden by stalagmites, and it expanded into a cave mouth that led out to the ocean. The ground here was soft soil, instead of rock. Annie took a shovel from the cart and began to dig.

Waves, from the sea outside, lapped at the narrow shore a few yards away. Hundreds of white crosses surrounded her, marking the graves of Lord Duskin's patients, and she'd nailed together each and every one.

How many lives had she seen taken in her eighteen years of life? How many souls had she watched pass from this world to the next?

Annie dug until her calluses split and bled, staining the shovel's wooden handle. Elain's ghost emerged from the shadows to watch as Annie struggled to lower the frail body into the hole.

Tears streaked the ghost's pale face, but Annie couldn't bring herself to cry with her.

What would it do?

Tears didn't bring the dead back to life. If that were true, her entire family would have come back to her by now.

When the hole was filled, Annie glanced back at the grave one last time before heading back into the tunnels. Elain's grey form stared down at her only lasting mark on the world, weeping.

She would never sing again, never dance.

Don't stay here. Annie turned back to the darkness, praying Elain would find the light. *Anywhere is better than here.*

CHAPTER 5

CAMDEN

Cam was suspended in the abyss, neither rising nor falling.

It was warm here—safe, even.

The fire he'd grown to love was all around him, comforting him. Whispering kind words into his ears when the pain became too much to bear.

A creaking groan echoed somewhere out in the endless void. Above him? Below him? Cam shied away from it. He didn't want to go. *I might find Mother here.*

A distant voice began to murmur. The groaning grew louder, and the world began to shake. An explosion of light flooded Cam's darkened kingdom. He squinted. *Please, don't take me away.*

"Ah, there you are," a familiar voice said. "I thought I'd never find you."

"No—" Cam choked on a mouthful of ash. Something tugged on his arm, and he tried to pull away, but he wasn't strong enough. Cam dared to open his eyes.

A hazy figure stood over him. A black terror against a pale

sky. A wave of heat rushed through his bones. He hated the terror. It was the reason everything burned.

The heat grew and grew. It wouldn't stop. The terror reached out for him, but it would never reach him. The heat loved Cam, and only him. A raging fire ignited the air, making the terror scream.

Cam was safe in his private world again. Nothing could touch him. He drifted away happily, wrapped in his guardian flame.

In the darkness, Cam swayed. Rhythmic. Slow. He counted every breath. If he opened his eyes, would hell be waiting? He'd entered the abrupt nothingness of death—the absence of time and space—but now the air smelled like unwashed bodies and stale bread. Rough fabric covered his sensitive skin.

Wool? Cam dared to open his eyes again.

He was in a plank wood cabin, lying on a cot. The constant *drum-drum* of waves echoed from below. Slightly crooked shelves lined the walls, filled with scrolls, boxes, and creepy painted dolls.

Cam sat up—wincing as a dull ache shot through his muscles—and rested against his pillows. *Is hell a stuffy, windowless room and a cheap bed?*

"Not so quickly, now, Mr. Barnes," a voice said to his left. "Your body needs to rest."

Cam twisted, too quickly, and nearly fainted from the throbbing in his skull. A man sat on an ugly green armchair on the far side of the room. Maybe in his early thirties, clean-shaven and Roman-nosed, wearing grey robes. Bandages covered his hands and part of his face.

Cam blinked, noticing the yellow tattoos on the man's neck. "Gold Stripe?" It all came rushing back. The deal. New Havana. The Revenant's hand around his throat, searing his flesh.

"*You killed them!*" Cam's scream filled the cabin as he leapt from his cot. His knees buckled out from under him, and he landed on all fours. "Nathan . . . Resh . . ." Cam's throat tightened as he choked back tears.

The Nightlady burned. The only people he gave any kind of care about were taken away. *It's all my fault.*

"I assure you, Mr. Barnes." Gold Stripe folded his gauzed hands over his lap. "I had no part in that."

"*Liar*," Cam growled. "I saw. The Revenant—"

"You were attacked by two Revenant, yes." Gold Stripes threw back his hood. "But they have no affiliation with us."

Cam tried to control his breathing, but no matter how hard he tried, he couldn't get enough air. "Explain. Now—before I beat you to death with my bare fists."

"My name is Elias Bennett," Gold Stripes chuckled. "I found you buried in the wreckage of your ship as I searched for what may have remained of the cargo I hired you to carry. You're aboard my vessel, *The Armageddon*."

"Why?" Cam grit his teeth, staring at the floor. It was a little too clean for his taste, too shiny. Unused.

"Pardon?"

Cam clenched his eyes shut. "Why didn't you leave me to die?"

"Mr. Barnes—"

"You should have let me rot."

"Mr. Barnes, please—"

"They're all dead—all of them, aren't they?"

"*Mr. Barnes!*" Elias jumped to his feet.

"What?"

"You're smoking."

Cam opened his eyes. The floor beneath his palms was indeed smoking. He jerked his hands away, leaving scorched handprints in the polished wood. Cam stared at the burn marks, stunned.

The burning, *the burning.*

"I *did* die, didn't I?" Cam murmured. *The fire that protected me . . . was that real, too?*

"And now . . ." Elias smiled wide. "You've been born into your true life. Have a look."

Elias lifted an old mirror off the wall and set it in front of him. Panic bubbled in Cam's throat, the eyes staring back in his reflection round and frightened. He still looked the same . . . sort of.

Same long, sandy-blond hair, same green-gold eyes, same skin—tanned from years in the sun. But now, sunset-orange tattoos zigzagged down his cheeks, starting from his lower eyelid, trailing down to his jaw. A second set of tattoos started at the corner of his eyes, stopping at his cheekbones.

"You'll get used to them in time." Elias grimaced.

Cam was almost surprised when a dark laugh escaped his lips. "Is this God's punishment for what I've done? For signing your bloody contract?" *For letting my mother die?*

If he hadn't gone behind Resh's back, would all of them still be safe in the slums? Drinking at the Yellow Bunter, slowly but surely, losing their minds. Or would The Rot have spread, forcing them into kennels of their own?

Elias knelt and touched Cam's shoulder. "God has given you a second chance, not His judgment. You're alive." He stood and held out his hand. Cam took it. Elias pulled him to his feet. "Come with me, Camden Barnes. There's much to explain."

Elias headed for the door, then paused. "But maybe you should dress first."

Cam peered down at himself. "Oh." He was stark naked. More orange tattoos trailed from his collarbones down his chest like lightning.

Elias chuckled. "I've brought clothes down for you. They're in the dresser. Meet me above when you're able." He left without another word.

The trembling began in Cam's fingers again, spreading through his arms and shoulders until his whole body broke into convulsing sobs. In the mirror, the demon where his reflection should be stared back at him, changed but still so familiar.

The glass shattered. It wasn't until he saw the blood dripping from his knuckles that he realized he'd struck it. *Why couldn't you have just let me die?*

For the first time in his life, Cam curled up on the floor and cried. Cried, but the heat inside burned away the tears as they left his eyes. *This is all my fault.*

He would not be allowed to mourn.

Not this time.

Cam stepped onto the main deck a short time later, a rush of hot salt air stinging his eyes. He squinted against the sunlight. Every part of him felt wrong. His feet were too light, his vision too sharp. Every emotion sent waves of heat rolling through his skin.

He wasn't sure yet if any of this was real and not just some prank being played on him before he fell into hell.

Subconsciously, he reached for his waist where his gunbelt should be and found it empty. His heart cracked. *I lost the only piece of her I had left.* Who was he without her ring? He rubbed his fingers together, then blinked at them in surprise.

They weren't numb anymore. The scars he bore on his knuckles from years of fighting had disappeared, too.

He clenched his fist.

There was one thing he knew for sure: he'd already caught Elias Bennett in a lie.

The Armageddon wasn't just a ship—it was a fully staffed, steam-powered war machine. He'd never seen anything like it. Hundreds of crewmen darted about like ants, all wearing grey uniforms, supporting their bug-like appearance.

There were footsteps behind him. Cam turned, and Elias strode towards him, the wind whipping his robes around his knees. He stepped up to Cam's side and glanced out across the clear, blue sea. He let out an exasperated sigh. "I'm not sure where to begin."

"Well . . ." Cam shielded his eyes from the sun. *Why is it so bloody bright?* "The beginning is always a good place to start. You were tailing us, weren't you? All the way from Port Lebanon?"

Elias nodded absently.

"You knew we'd be attacked?" Cam was too exhausted to be angry. "Why even hire us, then? Why let the Pearl Dust get stolen?"

"I had my suspicions." Men shouted from the bow, and Elias had to wait to speak to be heard over the noise. "I just didn't think Julian to be so bold. We took precautions, though. Had the barrels lined with fireproof material, just in case."

Where the hell do you get fireproof material? Cam shook his head. *Questions for later.* "Julian?" he asked instead.

"Julian Price." Elias' expression darkened. "The Air Brand you encountered. His companion, Frank Boyle, is a Fire Brand. Which I'm sure you're aware of . . . all too intimately." His eyes flickered to Cam's tattoos as he spoke.

Cam shifted under his stare, directing his gaze out to the

water, watching as the waves parted for *The Armageddon,* helpless against its massive girth. With his keen new eyes, he could see straight to the seabed below, spotting brightly colored fish scrambling out of the behemoth's path.

Frank Boyle . . . that was Red Hair's name. A vengeful fire burned in Cam's gut, curling, twisting. He would kill him. If he had to sacrifice the last of his soul, he would kill him.

Cam swallowed back his hate, fighting to stay on topic. "By brands, are you referring to the tattoos?"

"In a sense," Elias said. "The marks we earn at rebirth are not ones we choose, as you now know. Each brand is unique to the individual, but the colors seem to be consistent with a gifted element. Shades of blue for water, browns for earth, and so on."

"Clever." Cam shook his head. It was all too much. "Does that make me a Fire Brand, too, then?"

Elias regarded him thoughtfully. "So it seems. Ironic, isn't it? Revenant of destruction are quite rare. It takes a certain kind of person—certain personalities—to bear that much power. Frank Boyle was one of only few Fire Brands I was aware of . . . before you. Most are reborn with gentler gifts. The ability to grow plant life, bring in a breeze, manipulate the paths taken by water." Elias rolled his eyes. "Gifts the government love to manipulate."

A certain kind of person? Figures. Cam sighed. "So, I'm a freak?"

Elias laughed and rolled up the sleeves of his cloak, revealing more gold marks that wrapped around his wrists like bracelets. "You're among like company."

The Armageddon jostled slightly as it navigated through a small series of islands. A larger island sat ahead of them, encircled in its own peninsula. A village sat along the coast, not too far away.

"Were you murdered, too?" Cam asked once the ship steadied. The conversation had to keep flowing, no matter how tired he was. There were too many questions that remained unanswered. *Like where the blazes are Resh and Nathan?*

"Not exactly. I was a fisherman once," Elias said as the coast grew closer. "One day, my brother and I sailed out, despite a coming storm."

"Not very smart."

"No, it wasn't." Elias blew out a breath. "But we were poor, and no fish meant no food. Our ship sank. I woke, washed onto the beach, covered in strange marks. Not only that, but I found the lightning answered my call. Storm Brand."

"And your brother?"

"Died as well."

"A cruel *and* ironic world, isn't it?" Cam smiled wryly.

"That it is."

With a loud bellow and thick puff of steam, the ship began to slow as it approached the village. It chugged violently as it came to a stop, and Cam nearly lost his footing. He'd been a sailor since he was nine—after leaving his old life behind—but in all the years he spent at sea, he'd never been aboard a steamer.

Pirates didn't have such lavish things unless they stole them, and Resh had never been that ambitious.

"Welcome, Mr. Barnes." Elias turned away from the railing and spread his arms wide. "To Shar-Crue."

CHAPTER 6
CAMDEN

Shar-Crue, on the outside, was much the same as most of the wayward fishing villages Cam had seen in his travels.

Plank boardwalks supported by wooden stilts, made it possible to walk and build over the water. Most of the huts closer to the harbor had roofs thatched from coconut palms. Dozens of canoes were tied to the docks, waiting idly for their masters to return.

Cam followed Elias off *The Armageddon* and onto the boardwalk, salt rotted planks creaking under his feet. Oyster shells were strewn everywhere, but they weren't fresh. Locals stopped and stared as they walked by, their mouths agape.

At first Cam thought it was the sight of the steamship that startled them, but then the people started crossing their fingers in the shape of an X, hissing and cursing in their strange Southern tongue.

"*Torva Messor!*"

"*Torva Messor—*"

Cam pulled up the hood of his borrowed cloak. Elias gave him an apologetic look.

"Persecution is part of our lifestyle." He seemed unfazed by the crowd of locals that had gathered, parting for them to pass. "You will either drown in it or use it to your advantage, as my associate has done."

"Associate?" Cam dodged an egg thrown by a heavy-set woman. He shot the thrower a nasty glare, and the woman burst into tears, running back into her hut.

"The natives believe eye contact with a Revenant will bring a death curse down upon their families," Elias scolded. "That woman will probably never sleep again."

"Good," Cam laughed. "She deserves it."

"Does she?" Elias' brow rose. "If I remember correctly, you were one of the egg throwers not too long ago. Mocking and jeering without considering the humanity we still share with you. For the traumas we've had to suffer."

Cam wasn't sure what to say to that. He folded his arms over his chest, trying to quell the heat inside him, and grudgingly drudged on.

In the previous villages Cam had visited, there had always been merchants selling dried fish and fruit, waving down tourists to sell them cheap, hand-carved trinkets they swore had been blessed by some idol or another. Shar-Crue had a different feeling to it.

Wicker baskets lay empty beside vacant stalls. Palms on the roofs were brown and flaking. There was none of the excitement he'd grown to expect. Just a sad excuse for an even sadder community, one no longer interested in growth.

But why?

Elias led Cam out of the village and onto the island itself, followed by the sound of voices chanting, *"Torva Messor."*

A thousand questions buzzed on the tip of Cam's tongue,

but he knew better than to ask. He'd met men like Elias before. Clever, educated. He'd string Cam along until he was too deep in his games to back out. Only share information when he felt it gave him the most leverage.

Cam admired him for it, not that he'd admit it out loud. *He reminds me of Father.*

The path they followed led them quickly into a grove of dense banyan trees. Their tawny brown branches stretched out across the forest—like thick, inviting arms—and burrowed themselves into the ground a few meters from the trunk.

Thin green vines wove around the limbs of the banyans. Delicate, pink flowers grew from them, shaped like a tiny bell. At the center of the bell sat a shimmering pearl.

Not a pearl. Cam leaned in closer. An iridescent, crystallized drop of nectar.

Cam gently brushed the nectar. "Is this—"

"Pearl Dust?" A Revenant stepped out of the trees. "It is, and I'd appreciate it if ya didn't disrupt my product." Green swirls decorated the Revenant's forehead, framed by a receding hairline.

"Ah, Green Stripes." Cam grinned. *Of course.* "I should have guessed."

Green Stripes grinned back and extended his hand. Cam shook it. "Vernon Douglas." He bowed. "You're mighty calm for a man just come back from the eternity box."

Cam ran a hand through his hair. "Only on the outside."

"I can tell." Vernon grimaced, flexing his hand, now pink and blistered.

Cam scowled. *Oops.* "Sorry."

"Don't worry about it." Vernon waved dismissively. He wore the clothes of a common worker—a loose white shirt, stained yellow from sweat, and a pair of knee-length sailor's slops. His feet were bare, caked with a healthy amount of dirt. "Just a flesh wound, and a long way from my heart."

"Mr. Douglas and I have been working together for quite some time," Elias said as he, too, shook hands with his companion.

Vernon smiled. "Too long."

Cam turned back to the flowers, curious. Once—as a child—he'd stolen Pearl Dust out of his father's private quarters, wanting to see what all the fuss was about. In small doses, the nectar could be used as an effective painkiller, but anything more than the tip of the teaspoon would send you on a hallucinogenic, psychoactive high for hours.

He learned that lesson the hard way—waking up after an accidental binge covered in ugly burns. His father had beaten him for it.

"So, you two run drugs off this island?" Cam clarified. "How classy."

"You've got no room to talk, Barnes." Vernon rolled his eyes. "I know all about you. Poor man's pirate, is it?"

"Sticks and stones, mate, sticks and stones," Cam said with a coy smile. "But my crew runs bigger jobs now."

"*Ran,*" Vernon shot back. "Heard they all caught a nasty case of death, eh?"

Heat burned relentlessly beneath Cam's skin.

Hurt him, it purred.

He wanted to act upon it—he *could* act upon it. All he had to do was . . .

"How about we take Mr. Barnes for a tour, hmm?" Elias stepped between them.

Vernon chuckled and shook his head. "Kid thinks he's king because he can light a match on his own. I can do that with a bit of flint and a bowl of beans, if you catch my meaning." Vernon looked Cam up and down and shrugged. "But you're right, Bennett. He's perfect for the job. Come on, let's take that little tour."

Job? Cam hesitated.

A job got him into this mess. Did they really think he'd dive into another? All he wanted was to get what remained of his crew back and try to rebuild the pieces. Murdering the cowards who killed him was second on the list. Cam shoved his hands in his pockets and started after them, despite his reservations. He wasn't in much of a position to do anything but play along for now.

They led him deeper into the banyan forest, Vernon chatting all the while. They rounded a bend, and six or seven men were visible high up in the trees, tending to the pearl vines. Two were Revenant—one's brands were green, the other's brown—and they seemed to be in charge.

Cam's brows furrowed. "You hire Revenant to tend your crops?"

"Of course, I do," Vernon spat. "Mortals are as many as roaches in a cave. Takes the mitts of a skilled Flora Brand to keep the pearls flowing. Of course, with all these setbacks, I've had to resort to bribing the locals into working for me, too."

Cam felt like he'd been punched in the chest. Vernon had already started on another topic.

Mortal? Cam gripped his head against the ringing in his ears. *As in, I'm not?*

He'd died. Some force—whether God or chance—brought him back, but never once had immortality crossed his mind.

Vernon froze, glancing between the two of them. "You haven't told him?"

"There is no valid research to suggest our kind is immortal." Elias wiped his palms on the edge of his cloak. "Scientists predict our lifespan to be anywhere between six hundred and a thousand years. Politicians try to keep this knowledge from the public as much as possible to keep fear at bay. Revenants seem to age just as slowly. But don't make the mistake of thinking you can't be killed. Time won't hurt you. Bullets still can."

"Yeah, okay." Cam swallowed back a wave of nausea. "Whatever you say."

Vernon laughed. "Lucky ya died so young, mate. I've spent the last hundred years looking like a dried-up cockroach."

"Oh yes," Cam replied dryly. "I'm so fortunate."

Immortality. No, he couldn't think about it now. Better to wait until . . . well, never. His mind already felt like it was about to be torn in half.

They continued and found more men up in the banyans, combing through vines and flowers. One man—an Earth Brand, Vernon had called him—picked through the soil, stopping occasionally to scratch at the dirt. "Do you know how Pearl Dust is harvested, lad?" Vernon asked.

"I'm afraid I don't."

"Let me tell ya then." Vernon found a small flower bud, just beginning to wilt. "It takes three years for a vine to mature enough to produce pearls." Vernon blew gently on the bud, and it opened. A vibrant pink hue spread throughout the petals. "And in the best of circumstances, it takes a miracle for mortals to keep them alive."

He plucked the pearl from the center and placed it in Cam's outstretched palm. "It takes one thousand forty-six dried and ground pearls to make one cup full of dust. How many years do ya think it took to harvest the barrels you loaded onto your ship?"

Cam ogled the pearl in his hand. As far as he could tell, there were about two hundred mature banyan trees with thousands of flowers each. With six barrels, at about a hundred pounds each . . .

Cam let out a low whistle. "Years."

"We'll go with that." Vernon grinned. "So, you can imagine my bitterness toward a certain two Revenants for even risking ruining so many precious years. Seems we share a common hate."

"So, it seems," Cam replied. "But why hire us in the first place if you knew we'd be compromised?"

Vernon broke out in raucous laughter, his mouth wide enough to see all his missing teeth. "Because it was fake, boy. Those barrels were loaded with sand."

Sand. The word buzzed through Cam's mind like a bee in a hive. "I died—my men gone—for sand?"

Elias grimaced.

Vernon raised his hands. "Tough world, mate."

Cam sucked in a heavy breath, his fingertips burning hot. *Stay calm.* "I think I need to sit down."

"I've got what ya need." Vernon waved him on. "Come with me."

Vernon's hut was the least shabby Cam had seen so far. The roof was tin instead of palm, and most of the holes had been patched. The door was no more than braided strips of leather to push aside.

Vernon gestured for Cam and Elias to sit on the mess of cushions he had strewn on the dirt floor. He took a jug down from his top shelf, poured three glasses, and handed one to each of them.

Cam sniffed it and shuddered. "No, thanks."

"Ninny." Vernon knocked back his own in one swallow.

Elias set his glass aside, eyeing it warily.

"I'd like to know what you planned to do if we *weren't* attacked." Cam licked his dry lips. "If we'd made it to New Havana and delivered your client a load of beach sand?"

"We had alternate plans in place." Elias rested his elbow on his knee. "If our suspicions had proven false."

"You said in Port Lebanon you were doing business with the owner of the island?"

"We were." Vernon picked at one of his remaining teeth. "*Are*, I should say."

"Doesn't seem like you're off to a good start, mate."

"We needed proof that the Revenant employed by Richard Duskin were the same ones responsible for the attacks on the Pearl Dust shipments and suppliers in recent months." Elias slid his drink to Vernon, who chugged it down gratefully. "We have it now. You are our proof."

Cam groaned. "Glad my death was for such a noble cause. Who's Richard Duskin?"

"Here's the deal, Barnes," Vernon began. "We had a plan. Plans fall apart. Nearly every ship carrying Pearl Dust through the South has been ransacked. Terrible for business. Growers, like me, have been selling out to an anonymous buyer and won't say a word about it. Meanwhile, this Duskin fellow buys himself an island, builds a town, acting like he's some god. Makes me wonder where he's gettin' his money, catch me?"

"You think he's buying out the growers, stealing the ship-ments, and . . . what?" Cam made a face. "Reselling it?"

"That's the mystery." Elias raised his hands. "None of the Pearl Dust has gone back on the market. It simply vanished."

"And what do I prove?"

"It's a known fact that Julian Price and Frank Boyle are associates of Lord Duskin." Elias hesitated, then sighed. "Julian was one of us . . . once. A dear friend. We sent him to New Havana a year ago after rumors started swirling about the island, but he betrayed us. I never thought he could have been swayed by greed, but it seems I was wrong."

Cam chewed his thumbnail, thinking. "And Boyle?"

"Nothing." Elias shook his head. "All we know is his name and the nature of his powers. Not where he came from, or how he came into the Duskins' service. We've suspected for some time that the two of them have been responsible for the attacks on all the pearl shipments in the South, but until now, there have been no witnesses. Your rebirth has not only connected the attacks to them and Lord Duskin, but also may have given us the leverage we need."

I should have known . . . I did know.

These men wanted to use him, just like everyone else, but instead of political or social gain, this time, he was a weapon. Cam folded his arms over his chest. "I fail to see how this became my problem."

"It's your problem," Vernon growled. "Because I bet your shiny, hairless backside, your men are on that island."

Cam's mind flashed back to *The Nightlady*—to the terror on the faces of his crew when the Revenant hauled them away. What had Frank Boyle said? *We had specific orders to take the captain and his second alive.*

Cam's eyes widened. *Blazes.* "He's taking prisoners. Why?"

Elias nodded. "We aren't sure. About three months ago, we contacted Lord Duskin, suggesting a partnership on building a pearl grow on his island under the guise that we are an outside party. Share the profits. We've been in slow contact ever since and have arranged to meet in New Havana to settle on the terms of a partnership. The shipment we hired you to carry was a last-ditch effort to prove Julian's guilt."

"Why does he need a grow when he owns half the world's Pearl Dust?"

"Our spies reported back that the island doesn't have one." Elias rubbed his forehead. "It was a shot in the dark. Fortunately, greed is predictable."

"That doesn't make any sense." Cam ran his hands through his hair. It felt oily. "Resh knows as much as I do. What do you think will happen if he rats about the haul? It all comes back to you."

"That's not your worry, kid, but we need to act soon," Vernon said. "Our plan was to infiltrate the island, pretending to be some high-to-do toady, and find out what happened to the Pearl Dust. You see, most of that product stolen came from my groves. I'd like it back to mediate my losses, and we want you to do it."

"Oh, no." Cam shook his head. "I've been dragged through your mud enough. I'll get Nathan and Resh back my own way."

"We'll pay you." Elias wrung his hands on his lap.

"Yeah?" Cam scoffed. "You offered to pay me last time, too, and look where that got me. Why can't you do it?"

"In regard to business,"—Vernon took another shot—"men like me don't like doing dealings face to face. Too many risks. Duskin is expecting a man made of money, and you're just the right fit, with your pretty face, good teeth, and all. Plus, you're Revenant now, one of us."

One of us.

"We need you, Mr. Barnes." Elias was almost pleading. "You know the trade, the underground, better than I ever could. Why go alone when you can walk in plain as day with a new identity and resources? Not to mention a fat wallet."

"Do you see any bills in my pockets?" Cam patted his trouser legs. "I don't see any money."

Vernon stumbled to his feet and made his way to a chest in the corner of his hut. With a grunt, he pulled out an enormously large sack and dropped it at Cam's feet. It spilled open, littering the floor with gold, jewels, and cash clips.

Cam's jaw dropped. *Blazes.*

He owed it to Resh to rescue him. He took him in when no one else would. Gave him a hot meal, a place to sleep, taught him to fight. But even more so, there were things Resh knew about him that Cam would rather he not share with anyone else. Not to mention, Cam wanted revenge. To make Frank Boyle suffer in the worst ways possible.

But?

Cam picked up an uncut diamond—the size of a peach pit—out of the pile and examined it. *Flawless.* His eyes narrowed. "By the end . . . how much?"

"Triple what we paid your captain," Elias answered. "And interest every day you work past your contracted time."

Cam's stomach bottomed out. *Triple.* He could buy an island of his own for that price—maybe even two.

"Do we have a deal, Barnes?" Vernon asked. "You work for us, get your boys back, and do some good for once in your blasted life? Like it or not, your current career is gonna tank if we don't get these drugs back on the market. You know it. I know it. You're the only one for the job."

Something good? Hang it all. For triple, Resh would be asking *him* for forgiveness.

But as much as he hated it, Vernon was right. Pearl Dust was the most coveted drug in the underworld. He and his crew wouldn't have a life left to go back to if he didn't try to fix this.

Cam grinned as he tucked the diamond into his inner coat pocket. "I'll hate you both for this." *Or I'll hate myself.* "But I'm in."

CHAPTER 7
ANNIE

Annie woke to a cold hand clamped over her mouth. Elain's ghost straddled her, a finger over her lips, gesturing for silence. Blurry grey eyes stared down at her, the skin around Elain's lips splitting as she smiled.

Annie tried to swat her hand away, gasping, but she touched only frigid air. *Relax. She won't hurt me.*

Elain crawled off the bed like an animal, still smiling, and waved for Annie to follow.

"What do you want?" Annie mouthed then glanced up at the clock. Three in the morning. Two hours before she usually woke. Didn't matter, she never slept much anyway. This wasn't the first time she had a nighttime visitor. The ghosts came to her quite often.

Jenny and Rose were fast asleep, oblivious their lost sister had come back to visit.

Elain tapped her ear, pointing to the door. Annie held her breath and listened. *Voices.* Men's voices carried up from downstairs. Angry and shouting. Two? Three?

Elain faded away, reappearing beside the door. Giggling, she waved for Annie one more time before disappearing again.

Her hands trembled as Annie slipped from her warm blankets, tugged on her robe, and headed out after her. The voices grew louder as she crept down the hall, amplified by the pounding of her heart. Goose prickles crawled up her arms and thighs, the marble floors chilly against her bare toes.

When she reached the top of the stairwell, she lay on her stomach and shimmied to the railing, peeking over the landing to look down on the grand entry several floors below.

A chill ran across Annie's skin, and Elain appeared beside her, again pressing her finger to her lips before looking over the edge. Annie nodded and followed her gaze.

"How could this happen?" The voice was Lord Duskin's. "If you expose my work, years of research and observation will be ruined. If the authorities intervene—"

"No one knows, I swear to you." Julian Price emerged from the shadows beneath the stairway. His usually crisp, grey suit was torn and travel-stained, his pale skin sallow. It had only been a few weeks since the Revenant left. Usually, they were out at sea for months.

What could bring them back so soon?

Lord Duskin had many secrets—and not all he shared with her.

Her stomach sank back against her spine. If the law comes here . . .

They'd execute me, alongside the Duskins, if they figure out what we've done. Annie looked over to Elain, hoping for answers, but she was gone.

"*Sand!*" Lord Duskin pointed at Mr. Price, his hand quivering. "Those blasted barrels are filled with sand, and you come with promises and apologies? You said this was the best way, and I was fool enough to trust you. Someone is trying to make a mockery of us. How did you not know?"

Mr. Price raised his hands. "Listen, my lord, please—"

"I'll find out who did this, Rich." Frank Boyle leaned against the wall, looking weary and defeated in his torn green duster. "Give me an hour with the captain, I'll—"

"You'll do no such thing." Lord Duskin glared at him. "Finish unloading the new patients. Get the girl when you're done, have her check them in, then send her to me."

Mr. Boyle stiffened. "I can handle it—"

Lord Duskin wheeled on him. "The girl, *now*." He stormed from the room, swearing.

Once he was out of earshot, Mr. Boyle groaned. "When are you going to tell him the truth?"

Mr. Price shot him a glare. "I'm not . . . neither will you."

"You better start paying me more, then." Mr. Boyle sneered and rolled his shoulders. "This is getting ridiculous. There's only so many lies I can tell before he figures out what you've been doing. I mean, *so* many ransacks."

"Keep your voice down." Mr. Price pinched the bridge of his nose. "You'll get your money. Just do your job."

Mr. Boyle shook his head, chuckling. He turned and headed for the stairs. "Sure, whatever, but I better go get the *girl* before he gets pissed."

Oh no. Bile rose in Annie's throat. She scrambled back, smacking her head on the railing, clacking her teeth together. She sprinted back to her bedroom as quickly as her light feet allowed, ignoring the pain, tasting blood in her mouth.

Please, please, please. Her feet were wings, weightless as feathers. Annie burst through the bedroom door, barely stopping to close it before throwing herself into bed and pulling her blankets over her head. *Please, please, please.* She had to slow her heart, her breathing.

Thunk, thunk, thunk. Frank Boyle did not have light feet. His presence filled the room as the door creaked open. That heat followed him wherever he went, covering everything—a constant smoky scent clinging to his skin. Overtop the blankets, Mr. Boyle's fingers latched onto her bony shoulder and shook it.

"Move it, sunshine." There was a drunken slur in his voice. "Richard's waitin' for you. Got some new toys for you to play with."

He didn't wait for her to answer. He yanked her from the bed, and Annie's hip hit the floor—hard. She bit her tongue to keep from crying out. Jenny and Rose were awake now, watching with fearful eyes, but they would not speak, not move. Not unless they wanted to be punished.

Mr. Boyle dragged her halfway down the hall before Annie was able to catch her breath. "Let me walk!"

He dropped her arm, laughing, and Annie's chin bounced off the floor. Blood filled her mouth, and she spat.

Mr. Boyle rolled her onto her back, his face inches from hers—weak-chinned and pointy-nosed—breath hot and stinking of beer. She wanted to scream, fight with every inch of her soul, like she'd done all those years ago, but she forced herself to lie still. *You're here, not there. That was different.*

"So sharp." He stroked her cheek, licking his dry lips. There was a small phoenix tattoo on the underside of his left ring finger. "So icy. I bet you could cut me with that tongue of yours."

Annie collected herself, willing her features to harden. *Breathe.* "Touch me again and you'll lose your hand."

"And *you'll* be the one to take it off?"

"If I have to."

He laughed again but let her stand.

Annie closed her eyes as she followed him down the stairs,

counting each step, blocking out the fear trying to fill her. *They are like wolves and will tear you apart.* Frank Boyle was a wolf, and she would not let herself become a sheep.

Not again.

The sun had begun to rise as they led the last of the prisoners into the cavern from the sea. The Revenant kept them in a queue. Annie's head spun from lack of sleep, but she kept on. Elain's ghost hovered beside her, a constant reminder of what could happen if she fell behind.

A grubby sailor waited for her to call him up, eyes darting around wildly. Taking in the lava tunnels, the patients hiding in the backs of their filthy cells, and the blood coating Annie's wrinkled nightgown.

She waved him over, slipping on a new pair of gloves, her eyes drawn instantly to the deep, veiny bruise on his neck. "What's your name?"

"Ernest, ma'am." The stubble on his jaw poked her through the gloves as she looked over his face.

"Don't talk to her!" the man behind him shouted. "What are you thinking, man?"

"Not talkin' won't help either!" Ernest yelled over his shoulder, sending an angry murmur through the line of sailors.

"Quiet," Mr. Price snapped. The sailors fell silent in an instant.

"Ligature marks, petechiae, abrasions." Annie waved the man on and glared at Mr. Price, who leaned against the cavern wall, arms crossed. "Who gave you permission to strangle him?"

Mr. Price's grey eyes flickered to hers. "That's none of your concern."

Annie slipped off her gloves, the rubber snapping against her wrists. "No, but it's Lord Duskin's."

He pursed his lips and looked away. "We needed information."

"On what?"

"That's none of your concern," he repeated.

Fine. She wasn't going to get anything more out of him. He was especially somber today. Most likely from the fight she'd overheard. *I was fool enough to trust you,* Lord Duskin had said. What had he trusted Mr. Price with?

Mr. Price . . . but not her.

She shook her head. *Mind your own business.*

Annie finished her report as Mr. Price's crewmen chased the last of the prisoners into their cells. They wept and moaned as they were locked away. They'd never get to see the sun again or the ocean they loved so well.

They're my patients now. She'd come back later and tend to their wounds when no one knew she was out of bed. Lord Duskin wasn't the only one with secrets.

Annie startled as Mr. Price touched her elbow. "Come," he murmured. "He's waiting."

By the time they reached the teaching room, Annie had artfully set her expression back into its usual mask. Mr. Price hovered beside her.

Extra gaslamps had been lit. At the center of the room, two metal tables had been set up. Mr. Price rushed forward to help Mr. Boyle subdue the prisoner he was attempting to tie down.

More sailors.

Both prisoners wore torn slops and loose-fitting shirts, blood-stained from split lips and broken noses. The younger of the two screamed and thrashed as the Revenant bound him.

Lord Duskin watched from the side, his expression cold, and he was dressed in his medical coat.

He noticed her waiting and inclined his head to her. "Get dressed, girl."

Girl. That's what he always called her. Often, she wondered if he even knew her name at all.

She stepped over to the table. The sailor's personal belongings were strewn over it haphazardly. Knives, cans of chewing tobacco, bits of this and that—but what caught her attention was a lovely jade pendant shaped like a fishhook and strung on a black leather cord.

"Girl?" Lord Duskin's voice was sharper now, agitated.

Annie hesitated only for a moment before she grabbed the necklace and slipped it over her head along with her medical gown, tucking the pendant down the front of her bodice. She never wanted to be a thief—in fact, she hated thieves—but part of her hoped one day she'd be able to sell the trinkets she'd collected. That she'd be able to buy her way onto a vessel and escape to the mainland.

The Revenant struggled as they tied up the second captive. This one was older and portlier than the first, black, dreadlocked hair beginning to grey. He struggled, and Mr. Boyle punched the man square in the jaw, and his head snapped violently to the side.

Annie forced herself not to flinch. She'd been hit like that before, back in her days on the slave ships. It wasn't pleasant.

Lord Duskin stepped forward, hands laced behind his back, looking every bit the nobleman he was. "You may be wondering why you're here."

The captives raised their heads to listen. The mouth of the older man bled profusely.

"And I must state, I do not like to begin any relationship this way, but integrities *are* at risk, so I have no time to waste. Who hired you, and what was your destination?"

The younger man spat up a wad of congealed blood. "What's it matter? You're just going to kill us anyway."

Lord Duskin cocked his head. "No one is going to die today."

"New Havana." The older man's voice was so hoarse. "Our mark was New Havana."

"What are you doing, Resh—" the younger one began, but the man named Resh shot him a glare. The boy fell quiet.

Annie glanced at Lord Duskin. *They were coming here?*

That didn't make any sense. She knew the Pearl Dust they used had been stolen. She wasn't stupid. Lord Duskin was always squashing rumors around town about the shipwrecks, the sailors gone missing.

But why do the work of taking a ship already coming to the island?

Lord Duskin seemed to be thinking something similar. His already narrow lips pursed even tighter. "New Havana, you say?"

Resh nodded. "Two Revenant contracted us to ship the Pearl Dust. I never saw them. Don't know their names. They only ever spoke to my quartermaster. We're just middlemen, mate. I don't know what you want or who you're looking for." Calm, controlled. He'd been in this kind of situation before.

So, he must be the captain.

Mr. Boyle and Price exchanged nervous glances at the word Revenant.

Lord Duskin looked like he'd sucked on a lemon. "Are you telling me . . . that you were not aware that the cargo you carried was fraudulent?"

"Fraudulent?" The younger one shook his head, shocked. "Hang it all, of course not!"

Lord Duskin scowled, smoothing back his hair. "Then it seems this has all been a mistake. My apologies."

Liar. Annie knew him better than that.

Lord Duskin nodded to the Revenant. "Bring me the quartermaster."

The younger one burst into laughter. "How do you expect to do that? They bloody killed him. Burned him alive with most of the others."

The Revenant looked like they were going to sink to the floor as Lord Duskin's gaze fell upon them. "Leave."

They were gone in seconds.

"Get my scalpel, girl—and the vial from the other night."

Obediently, Annie stepped back to the table, the tools already laid out. Lord Duskin would use them whether they were guilty or not. There was no use fighting it. *Please, God, forgive me.*

She turned to hand the scalpel and vial to Lord Duskin, but he shook his head. "Go on, just like the others."

Resh's olive skin turned green at the sight of the knife.

Far away. I'm far away. Annie forced her mind to travel somewhere else. Somewhere where the winds were cold, and the blood of men had never stained her skin.

The captain didn't cry out, didn't struggle as she cut a short incision into the inside of his bicep. There was nowhere to go tied to that table.

Annie removed the bit of Elain's infected skin from the vial, inserting it into the wound and squeezing until the blue pus of the blister leaked into his flesh. Lord Duskin handed her a needle and thread, and she sewed his arm shut, bandaging it up after.

Dozens of times she had done this—had watched her so-called father do the same to Elain—but every time, it got harder.

After all this time, shouldn't this be easy, thoughtless?

The contaminated bodily fluids would release the The Rot into his bloodstream. Soon, it would eat through his organs until it had no other choice but to burst through his skin.

Just like it did to Elain.

Annie's fingers trembled as she set the supplies back on the table.

"W-what did you do?" the younger one screamed. All the color left his face. "What did you do? You said no one would die!"

Lord Duskin tsked. "Today. No one will die today." He turned to Annie. "Leave them here for a few hours, then find them a cell. Keep the captain separate. He'll contaminate the others. Make sure their meals are properly supplemented. With guests arriving soon, he'll be our last experiment for some time."

Annie stared at the ground, clenching her shaking hands into a fist. Obedient, submissive—everything he liked best in his children. "Yes, Father."

She came that evening to feed them, as she did twice a day, and sprinkle minute amounts Pearl Dust into their oats. They only fought the first meal. Once they caved from hunger and wolfed down their supper, the drugs would become all they wanted. The only relief they'd find was in their small personal hell.

With the way it caused The Rot to burn through them once infected, fortunately, they never suffered long.

Annie moved steadily down the corridor, dread increasing

every step she took toward the captain's cell. *It's not my fault. I didn't want to.*

He was dead—she smelled it before she saw him—hanging from the cell bars by the suspenders he'd used as a noose.

Annie stared at his body, completely blank.

"This is your fault, you know."

She withheld her wince, turning slowly toward the voice that spoke. The younger one had his head resting against the bars of the cell opposite, his dark skin stained with tears.

Annie took in his face. The pock scars on his cheeks and neck, the chapped lips. *He can't be any older than I am.* "What's your name?"

"Does it matter?"

"It does to me."

"I'm Nathan." He nodded to the captain's body. "He wanted me to tell you that you'd never have him."

Another Nathan. Annie's brow furrowed, trying to think through the numbness clouding her thoughts. "And who was he talking about?"

"Don't know. Doesn't matter now." Nathan shrugged. He looked at his friend one more time, clenching his eyes shut. "But I want you to know I cared about him like a father."

Don't think about it. You can't. Annie sucked in a breath, her body going rigid.

She was nothing. No one. No better than the ghosts. She just wanted to sleep. Before she walked away, Annie whispered. "Eat your oatmeal, Nathan. It doesn't taste as well when it's cold."

CHAPTER 8
CAMDEN

The next few weeks passed in a haze. Vernon and Elias spent their time going over preparations, ironing out every detail, while Cam sat in the corner . . . brooding.

He was a Revenant. Denying it wouldn't stop it from being true.

As much as he tried to go back to sleep, dreaming he'd wake up back on *The Nightlady*, he'd always find himself back in that godforsaken hut, the scent of pearl flowers drifting through the slat windows.

He'd learn to accept it, they said. That one day he wouldn't remember what it was to be mortal. Cam wasn't so sure. He wasn't the same anymore. Not just in his body, but *he* was different. Something was off . . . wrong. Like pieces of him no longer fit into their assigned spaces.

"We've sent word to New Havana," Elias began as he and Cam walked together down one of Shar-Crue's many dirt paths early that morning. "Lord Duskin is expecting your arrival within the month." Elias wasn't wearing his usual robes today. Instead, he wore the garb of a workman, the gold brands on his neck alarmingly bright against his pale skin.

"Wonderful." Cam yawned, not bothering to cover his mouth. "You have no idea how much I've been looking forward to sailing out to my death . . . again."

"No one is going to kill you," Elias shot back. "I have a contact, Thomas Wilkins, who will be expecting you. He works as a tavern keep on the island."

"What's your take in all this, anyway?" Cam ran a hand through his tangled hair, watching the dust they kicked up from the road. "Vernon has his business concerns, but that doesn't seem to be your niche."

Elias smiled at him pleasantly. "Have you ever heard of equality, Mr. Barnes?"

"Here and there." Cam rolled his eyes. "People are always rattling off about it."

"There are those who seek to protect Revenant life," Elias said. "I seek to aid them. All throughout the Four Corners."

"So, you're a vigilante, then?"

"Oh, God, no." Elias let out a laugh. "Nothing so outrageous as that. There was a political party founded two hundred years ago to give shelter to newly turned Revenant and protect them from mortal social agenda." Cam tripped over a rock, but Elias seemed not to notice. He just kept talking. "We are solely responsible for orchestrating the laws that now protect Revenant from such hate. We've persuaded the governors of three of the four continents to allow us full, unprejudiced citizenship. Of course, sadly, no law can protect from ridicule. Other parties have since risen to combat against Revenant acceptance. I am to stop them."

Cam exhaled. "Interesting."

"We've been abused, hated, defiled." Elias clucked his

tongue violently. "I will accomplish, acquiring for our kind, the equality we deserve. I will . . . no matter the cost."

Cam thought for a moment. It was a lot to take in. "So, you're a member of this pro-Revenant party?"

Elias smiled again, "I took over leadership of it eighty years ago. The contact you'll meet is also a dedicated member."

"What's all that have to do with New Havana? With Duskin?"

He didn't answer right away, appearing lost in thought as they passed through a dense thicket of ironwood. Cam swatted one of the low hanging branches out of his face.

"You must understand, Mr. Barnes." Darkness spread over Elias' features. "My group is dedicated to peace. Julian Price was a loyal, prosperous member for many, many years. Respected and well-loved. I didn't want to believe the rumors that he was involved in the attacks on the suppliers . . . that he'd turned on us. Like I said before, he was a good friend, but I can no longer keep turning a blind eye. He must be stopped, as much as it pains me to do so."

"Ah." Cam popped his lips. "Revenge, then."

"I prefer to say justice."

They headed north, out into the more remote parts of the island. The dirt road came to a fork, and Elias led them right, toward the ocean.

"You will be posing as a wealthy merchling from the Western cities." Elias changed the subject. "A successful upstart in the drug trade, seeking out connections and a base in the South to broaden your market. You will have to take on an assumed surname: Callahan."

"Callahan?" Cam blurted, shocked. *Blazes. Blazes. Blazes.* "No, pick another name. Any other."

Elias' brow rose. "The Callahans are the most influential family on this half of the world. Lord Duskin won't be able to resist the temptation of making contacts with one of their kin."

Blazes, blazes, blazes. Cam swallowed roughly. "Pick another."

"No."

"I won't do it."

"You signed a contract, I will remind you." Elias' expression darkened. "And Lord Duskin already expects someone wearing the name. They are a large family—lots of siblings and cousins —so you'll be able to whip up a believable backstory, I'm sure."

Cam grit his teeth so hard it was a miracle they didn't crack. "Fine."

"Well, then . . . what is your trade, Lord Callahan?" Elias said, but he still looked cross. "What are your exploits?"

"Firearms, opiates, explosives." Cam repressed his irritation and gave Elias his most charming smile. "Anything weaker men are too afraid to carry. I've recently decided to settle on my most profitable score: Pearl Dust. Expand. As for my suppliers, I'd prefer to keep their identities private until we come to know each other a bit better, Lord Duskin."

Elias exhaled, relaxing. "Very good. You'll do fine." He continued off down the path, and Cam had to jog to keep up.

"You've failed to mention the point of today's excursion," Cam called from behind.

"Soon, soon, patience."

The path opened into an expanse of waist-high reeds, then thinned out into bone-white sand, waves rolling gently onto the shore. Cam breathed in the sea air, desperate for something familiar. The ocean stretched out into a flat green-blue sheet of glass, begging to be broken. There was nothing in all the corners of the world like the waters in the South, so clear you could see your footprints in the seabed.

Someone cleared their throat, and Cam turned to see

Vernon standing a few yards away next to Elias. Vernon spit out a wad of tobacco into the sand, what remained of his teeth stained with black juice.

"Training day, lad," Vernon said with a clap.

Cam's brow rose. "Training?"

"You didn't think we'd send you off into the unknown without at least a few new skills in your pocket, did you?" Elias rolled up his sleeves, revealing the gold bands on his forearm.

"Have you gotten attached to me?" Heat burned in Cam's fingertips as his fists clenched. *He's manipulating you.* "You didn't teach any tricks to the fifty men you sent off to die last time."

Elias' face fell, and a pang of guilt settled in Cam's stomach. *That was uncalled for.* No one forced him to take the job, but he wanted someone to blame for his misery, and now, Elias was an easy target.

A loud sound crackled around Cam's ears, making his hair stand on end, and he jumped back. A bolt of electricity shot from Elias' pointer finger, striking the ground at Cam's feet, sending a painful jolt up his shins. He cursed.

"If you're gonna have a mouth that big," Vernon hollered from the sidelines, "you better learn to back it up." He waved over his head in a quick motion, and the reeds around Cam doubled in height, snaking around his arms and legs, binding him.

Just kill me. Cam grit his teeth. *I don't want to live like this.*

He may be impervious to time but not to pain. His body jerked, reacting out of a sense of self-preservation, but the reeds only grew tighter the harder he struggled. Elias shot a second bolt, hitting him square in the chest. Cam gasped, his vision growing dark, his muscles seizing.

Heat ripped from Cam's core, molten as it filled his hands

and mouth. It crawled up his neck, whispering in his ear. *Let me help you.*

How?

Burning. Just like on the mast. Smoke filled his lungs. It was going to turn him to ash.

The fire. A pulse reverberated through his skin, and Cam stood, despite the reeds. *The fire is mine, right?* If he died now, he'd never get to kill Frank Boyle.

Maybe later. Later, he could die . . . but now he had a score to settle.

Elias raised his hands, and lightning swirled and cracked around him.

What would happen if he set the fire free? *Only one way to find out.* Cam exhaled and let go, releasing the dragon clawing inside his flesh.

Everything happened in the span of a breath.

Reeds hissed, exploding within the firestorm raging around him. Vernon yelled. Elias cried out. His fire surrounded him, begging to rage for just a little longer, but Cam couldn't hold it. His head swirled, lungs empty of air, and he realized he was falling into a pit of blackness.

"Barnes?"

The darkness shook.

"Barnes!"

Cam's eyes flickered open, and Vernon stood over him, covered in soot.

"Oh, hello." Vernon chuckled. "Over-did it just a bit, did you?"

Cam sat up and groaned, his whole body aching. Most of

his clothes were gone except for a small swatch of trousers and the lower half of his left boot.

"Blazes." Cam yanked off the boot and tossed it. Blinking through his foggy head, he looked around. They were alone. "Where's Elias?"

Vernon squatted beside him and handed him a handkerchief. Cam wiped the soot off his face.

"Ran to get ya some more clothes," Vernon chuckled. "Don't need the poor villagers seeing ya in all your glory." He kicked Cam's thigh. "Get up. Time for round two."

"Round two?" Cam rubbed the sore spot where he'd been kicked. "I don't think that last mess counted as round one."

"I'd say it does." Vernon packed his lower lip with more tobacco. "You burned everything green for a quarter mile. Now I don't have anything to use against ya."

He was right, unfortunately. The beach looked like a war zone. The ground still smoked in places, and what wasn't burnt was left grey and ashy.

"Serves you right." Cam stood. "Bloody cheaters."

Vernon tapped Cam's nose. He was quite a bit shorter, so he had to crane his neck back to look Cam in the eye. "And when in your experience, pirate, have you trusted a man not to cheat in battle?"

Cam shrugged. *He has me there.* "I can hope. From what I hear, honor tends to disapprove of tricks."

"To the honorable." Vernon raised his hand in mock salute. "May they die happy in their self-righteousness as we drink over their gold."

Cam threw his head back and laughed. "Here, here."

Steady footsteps came from their left, and moments later, Elias crested the hill, carrying a sack. "I must beg your pardon, Mr. Barnes." Elias dropped the sack on the ground and began removing its contents. "I lost my temper. I should never have attacked you like that. Forgive me."

Why does he have to be so bloody likeable? "I deserved it," Cam exhaled. "I've been called an ass once or twice. Guess I should have warned you."

Elias tossed him some clothes and smiled. "I guess you should have."

Cam slipped them on. They were loose but would do the job. "Thanks."

"So where did you two leave off?" Elias asked.

"Never started." Vernon gestured to the singed reeds. "Barnes didn't leave much to work with."

"Very well." Elias nodded. "We'll begin where we should have in the first place. Have a seat, Mr. Barnes."

Cam did as he was told and sat across from the two Revenant, tucking his legs beneath him. Elias stretched his hands toward the sun, then folded them over his lap as if in prayer. "Focus. Mental clarity. All the power in the world means nothing if you cannot control it. We must channel it into an art form."

Cam fidgeted. "I always preferred chaos over art."

"Hush." Elias' voice never rose above an eerie calm. "Chaos *is* art, wielded correctly. Hold out your hand."

Cam extended his hand, palm up, and watched him expectantly.

"What do you feel?" Elias asked.

"A headache forming," Cam drawled. "And maybe some sand in my crack."

"Camden."

"Fine." Cam sighed. "I feel heat all the time. It gets stronger when I'm angry."

"Good." Elias nodded, eyes closed. "Now imagine the heat building in one place. The tip of your finger, for example."

Cam glanced over at Vernon, but the Flora Brand just smiled at him. Cam shook his head and let his eyes close. He'd felt the heat every moment since he died—had grown used to it, and was comforted by it, even. How hard could it be to condense that feeling?

Cam imagined a pin pricking the tip of his finger, a dot of red beading on his skin. Was the heat the blood or the pin? It didn't matter. He needed to concentrate. A small burst of energy escaped him, but didn't spread. Cam allowed a little more energy to flow. Sweat ran down his temple.

"Very good, Mr. Barnes," Elias whispered. "Very good."

Cam dared to look and let out a low gasp. A small flame flickered over his fingertip, dainty as a candle. A surge of euphoria rushed through him. *God, it's beautiful.* Blue at the base, fading out into a soft buttery yellow. *And it's mine.* He couldn't contain the adrenaline. The flame flickered, then exploded outwards, bathing Cam's skin in warmth. *All mine.*

Vernon shouted and shoved his face in the sand.

"*What?* What happened?" Cam jerked back to attention and tried to pull him up, but he just rolled away, cursing. Finally, Vernon turned over onto his back, rubbing the bare patches where his eyebrows had been. "You singed my brows off, you blasted ninny!"

Cam couldn't help it. After all the stress and turmoil of the last few weeks, the laughter came roaring out of him before he could stop it. Doubled over, Cam laughed until he was out of breath, eyes filled with tears. The others laughed with him.

"Well." Elias collected himself. "With some practice, I'm sure you'll do just fine."

Cam just grinned.

A couple of hours later, the three of them were headed back to Vernon's hut. Cam could focus a small flame now, but nothing larger than an apple. Apparently, he lacked self-discipline.

Like I've never heard that before. But as much as he didn't want to admit, Elias was a good, patient teacher, and he was grateful for the help.

"It will come in time," Elias said. "Perfect practice makes perfect."

"If you say so." Cam stretched. They came to the fork in the road, and Elias and Vernon started in the wrong direction. Cam jogged after them. "Now where are we going?"

"To my warehouse," Vernon called over his shoulder, "I want to show ya something." He led them to a large warehouse. It was rusted and full of holes. Vernon must not be too concerned about thieves. He dug an equally rusted key and inserted it into the matching lock on the door.

"Welcome to paradise."

Vernon opened the door and waved Cam inside. As he entered, Cam's jaw dropped. Is this what he called a warehouse?

It was a full-blown armory.

Rows and rows of swords and knives hung on the wall. Headless mannequins were dressed in all assortments of odd clothes and laden with expensive jewelry. Cases with glass tops showcased cap-and-ball revolvers, flintlock pistols, and endless rifles. A lovely musket hung from the ceiling, equipped with a bayonet.

"You fantastic sod," Cam breathed, and Vernon shot him a semi-toothless grin.

Forget his powers. This . . . this was worth dying for.

Cam lifted one of the cutlasses off the rack and rested it across his finger. Flawless balance. The gold braided hilt was weighted perfectly with the tang of the blade. A true piece of art—his favorite kind.

"It's yours, if you want it." Vernon's chest swelled in pride. "I've got more than I'll ever need."

"Where did you get all this?" Cam tested the edge of the blade on his thumb. It left a thread-thin wound.

"Where do ya think?" Vernon gestured to the walls. "Pillaging. Looting. Ships go down off the coast all the time, thanks to the rocks. That one I won off a bloke in Rouenn. Ever heard of the place?"

"Been there." Cam slid the cutlass back in its scabbard and placed it back on the rack. He picked up a long hunting knife next. It was a gorgeous damascus blade, etched with an orchid. He hooked it onto his belt. "Mountain village in the North. Lovely country. Lovely women. Cold as hell."

Vernon winked. "That's the place."

Elias opened a cabinet, turning and holding out a velum package. "I had these made for you. After today's incident, I think they'll prove useful."

Cam opened the package, careful not to tear the velum. Inside, he found a charcoal grey frock coat with a delicate black thread brocade into the fabric. Orange borders had been sewn onto the tail and lapel, matching Cam's brands. There was a matching pair of trousers with it, made of the same material. Both were tailored to his exact size.

Cam rubbed the fabric between his fingers and raised a brow. "Let me guess—fireproof?"

"Of course," Elias smiled, "my own design."

Cam slid the coat over his shoulders. It fit like a glove. Elias beamed. "A tad ostentatious." Cam shoved his hands in the pockets. "But it will do."

Elias turned and lifted something silver out of the cabinet: Cam's revolver.

A shudder ripped through Cam's body, and it took everything he had not to fall to his knees.

"I found this in the wreckage." Elias held the weapon out to him. "I had it refurbished for you."

My revolver. Cam bit the inside of his lip to keep from breaking into a sob.

Resh had given it to him for his eleventh birthday. The worn wood grip had been replaced with a pearl finish, the barrel fresh and polished, but it was his. He spun the chamber and cocked back the hammer. *Music to my ears.* Cam turned away to hide the wetness building in his eyes. The seal on the hidden compartment was still intact. He popped open the pommel's hollowed-out bottom, and his breath hitched in his lungs.

There it was.

A tiny, cloth sack fell into his palm. It had been years since he opened it, but he had to see. As he undid the strings, a glimmer of gold peeked out from between the folds of fabric. A dainty golden band, wreathed in gilded leaves, held a teardrop-cut fire opal. After all this time, the deep red jewel still sparkled.

Cam scowled. *It's almost the same color as my brands.* A queasiness filled his stomach, and he tucked the ring away safely back in its hiding place. Plastering on a fake smile, Cam slid the revolver into his waistband, beside the knife. Nothing like cold steel to bring back some sense of self.

"Thank you. Truly." He did a quick spin. "How do I look? Good enough to fool ol' Dick Duskin?"

"Good enough to fool me." Vernon stifled back a laugh. "If I didn't know any better, I'd say you came straight from some lord's sack."

They laughed. Vernon turned and headed out of the warehouse, whistling. Cam made to follow, cheerier than he'd felt in weeks, but Elias grabbed his arm. "I must ask a favor of you, Mr. Barnes."

Cam's brows furrowed. What brought on such intensity? Anxiety flowed through his grip much the same as his electricity. "I've tried to instill in you time, and time again, that destructive powers—like yours, and mine—are rare," Elias whispered. "Please . . . please, at least while you're on your mission, try to avoid using your powers as much as possible. It's a terrible thing to ask. Like asking a bird not to use its wings, but the consequences of an accident would be insurmountable. I will teach you when you get back . . . I will, but promise me."

Cam hesitated, saw the fear in Elias' eyes. "I promise."

Elias let out a heavy sigh, then smiled. "Thank you." He hurried off after Vernon, leaving Cam alone to contemplate what he'd just been asked to do.

Don't use my powers? The heat inside him flickered, as if recoiling from the thought. It was like a friend he didn't want but grew attached to anyway. What else did he have in his empty life anymore besides his fire?

The man who raised him was gone. The only friend he'd ever had was gone, too. Now he was being asked to turn away from the only thing he had left.

I'll try . . . for now. I owe him that.

It would take a great deal of honor to keep such a large promise.

Cam wasn't known for his honor.

CHAPTER 9
ANNIE

"*G*o *away!*" Annie screamed, alone in her empty bedroom. *"Go away!"*

Except she wasn't alone. She placed her head between her knees, rocking, trying to block out the ragged voice that now refused to leave her.

The captain—Resh . . . he hated her. Clawing and yanking on her limbs with misty shapeless fingers. His black, scaled lips screaming words she could only understand in bits and pieces. *Don't. Touch. Him.*

Elain's silvery entity sat in the corner, weeping crystal tears that pooled around her pale feet like shadows. *Does he haunt her, too?*

"Go away . . ." Annie moaned, covering her ears, but it didn't help. She didn't want to be a monster. She didn't.

She didn't.

She didn't.

The jade pendant dangled around her neck, and Annie clutched it tight. It wasn't her fault. It wasn't.

Was it, though?
She didn't know.

CHAPTER 10
CAMDEN

Waves thundered against the sides of *The Armageddon*, but they would never conquer it.

Cam stood at the steamship's bow, watching the shores of New Havana grow ever closer. A thick line of trees blocked the view of the island's interior from the coast. Walnut? They looked like walnut. Must be imported.

The incoming harbor seemed rather dainty for all the grandeur he'd been promised. Cam watched the crew shout back and forth with the men gathering on the docks, working together to anchor down the massive vessel. Six smaller ships were docked further down, in various states of repair.

Cam chewed his lip. *Reaped from the dead, I'm sure.*

Soon, *The Armageddon* would sail back to Shar-Crue, leaving him alone in this nest of vipers.

Late summer was in full swing, the sun overhead scorching and relentless.

Cam stretched, breaking in the shoulders of his new coat. It was too formal for his taste, but it would be nice not to have to put down the coins for a new one every time he lost his temper.

Though he supposed it didn't really matter now. If he pulled off this job, he'd be able to afford to wear a new coat every day of the week. Why the nobility insisted on wearing so many layers in the hot months was beyond him, but at least he couldn't feel the warmth in the air anymore.

The only heat he felt lay curled inside his core.

A bulky, covered coach waited for him at the end of the street leading out of the harbor, drawn by two smooth, bay thoroughbreds. It was painted an ungodly shade of yellow, adorned with the crest of a sea serpent and wrapped around a golden cross. Cam had never seen the sigil before, and he'd seen plenty in his time. *Lord Duskin must have fashioned his own. What a fop.*

A uniformed man ducked out of the coach as Cam approached, an officer's sword strapped to his hip. By the look, the piece was meant for ornament, not combat. *Good.* The fewer real fighters in his way, the better.

Sweat dripped down the man's ebony-black skin, clinging to his thick, groomed mustache. "You must be Lord Callahan?"

I never thought I'd hear that again.

"The one and only." Cam smoothed back his shorter hair. It had taken weeks for Elias to bully him into cutting it, but he'd still managed to allow him to keep the front and sides long enough that, with a little grit, he could still look like he'd spent the last week sleeping in an alley. It was probably silly of him to care, but since rebirth had buffered away all his scars, only his sun-bleached locks remained to remind him of his years at sea. "And you are?"

"Commander Carter, my lord." He bowed. "I lead Lord Duskin's house guard."

"I wasn't aware that Lord Duskin was in need of a house guard."

Commander Carter's eyes flickered up to Cam's brands,

then back to the ground. "One can never be too careful. Please, follow me. My lord will be meeting you at the city's gate."

Cam climbed into the coach, taking the seat across from the commander, the gold curtains drawn back from the rectangular windows. The road from the harbor was paved with smooth red cobblestone—much like Port Lebanon but cleaner. Ginger plants lined the road, topped with stunning red flowers wider than Cam's body.

"Your lord must have many groundskeepers and gardeners in his employ," Cam asked. It would be a pain remembering to shed his commoner's tongue. The wealthy spoke . . . pretentiously. The difficulty wasn't in the words themselves, but the way they were said. When to extend a certain tone into a drawl, when to pause for added suspense. Picking up subtle hints in conversation. The politics. *This is going to be exhausting.*

"Yes, yes." Commander Carter nodded animatedly. "About four hundred workers maintain the island on rotating shifts, twenty-four hours a day."

Cam smirked. "That sounds rather expensive. Who pays the bills?"

"Lord Duskin himself, of course," the commander replied. "He also finances the current construction happening in the town—along with the harbor, six stables, blacksmiths, three separate medical units, and much more. More estates are being built to accommodate the growing nobility wishing to call New Havana their home."

They passed a family on the road, leading a grey draft horse. Cam took in every detail. *Field workers, most likely.* They appeared lower class in birth—weak boned from poor nutrition—but even so, they were clean and well-dressed. Smiling, laughing.

Cam scratched his chin. *Interesting.* "How do the poor pay for such services?"

"Poor?" Carter's brow rose. "We have no poor here. Every man is given work—a chance to provide for their families."

"And if they refuse to work?"

"Forgive me. I don't understand."

Cam turned his attention back to the commander. "If the men stop working—demand higher wages or other such protest. Then what?"

Carter straightened his uniform, polishing the silver buttons on his coat with nervous fingers. "I assure you, my lord, you need not worry about such things."

Cam watched him, smiling slowly. "If you say so." It wasn't the first time he'd heard that in recent weeks. Elias shirked his questions all the time.

They spent the rest of the trip in silence.

As they approached the gates of the city, Cam couldn't help but be impressed by the design. A ten-foot-high wall, made from tightly stacked lava rock, stretched for miles in either direction. The gates themselves were polished brass encircled in a golden arch and adorned with the same cross and serpent.

A man waited for them at the gate. He was maybe in his early forties, with slicked black hair covered with a top hat. Along with a crisp black suit and burgundy waistcoat, his white shirt beneath was ruffled at the collar and pinned with a cross brooch.

Cam's eyes narrowed. *Ah, you must be Duskin.*

Lord Duskin stepped forward to greet them as Cam and Commander Carter exited the coach. "Welcome, my Lord Callahan, to New Havana." Lord Duskin extended his gloved hand. Cam shook it. "I am Lord Richard Duskin—but please, just Richard. I greatly look forward to doing business with a man of your breed and caliber."

Breed? Arrogant blatteroon. Cam put on his most winning

smile and bowed. "The honor is mine, Lor—I mean—Richard. I've heard much about you." *God, I'm out of practice.*

Richard gestured to the open-topped carriage, waiting just inside the city gate. "Shall we, my lord?" Richard's mouth twitched. His upper lip was covered by a groomed mustache.

Must be the current trend. Cam rubbed his upper lip. *I wish I could grow a 'stache.*

One of Richard's front teeth shone golden. "It would be an honor to present to you my crown jewel . . . New Havana."

Richard led him to the carriage drawn by a couple of chestnut sport horses. Cam had to admit, Richard had good taste. The horses were as fit and well-bred as any he'd seen on the mainland. Cam restrained a huff. *My father would like him.* A nervous tremor ran through Cam's limbs, but he ignored it.

"So . . ." He seated himself beside his host. "New Havana. Was the city already here when you acquired the island?"

"There was a small village down on the western coast," Richard replied as he straightened his collar. "Three years ago, I began the city's construction and recently contracted further expansions to accommodate the rising numbers of denizens. A few noble families—the Carters, the Appletons, and whatnot—are residing in estates on the island. I'm having more built as we speak to accommodate the growing number of families eager to fund my campaign. As for the locals . . . they were quick to see my side of things."

"I'm sure they were." Cam pursed his lips. *Quick to see the side of greed, you mean.*

The streets of New Havana were the same red cobblestone as the road without, and despite being under construction, the city seemed immaculately clean. Plumeria trees—in all shades and colors—filled the spaces between buildings. Most of the houses were set together in the usual southern fashion: yellow, orange, and red-painted stone. Lattices, filled with hydrangeas, shadowed the windows, all in all, giving the city a cheerful vibe. It made Cam's skin crawl.

The *clip-clop* of the horses' hooves echoed through the streets, causing people of all different ethnicities to pop their heads out their windows, each looking as clean and healthy as the family Cam spied on the road.

"Tell me about yourself, Lord Callahan," Richard asked. "What brought you into this line of work?"

"Would you like the honest answer?" Cam let out an exaggerated exhale. *Time to work my magic.*

Richard nodded, dark eyes glinting in amusement.

"Money," Cam shrugged, leaning back. "Moving guns and petty comforts pays the bills, but I wanted more than that, if you catch my meaning. Wealth. Respect. Opportunity."

Richard let out a breathy chuckle. "I can appreciate an entrepreneurial spirit."

The driver turned the carriage right onto a wider avenue, leading them into what looked like a market district. Instead of open-air stalls, citizens crowded around shops of every kind. Bakeries, produce, clothing boutiques, and on and on. The avenue opened into a large square filled with more shops, packed with customers. A grand fountain stood in the center of the square—a marble angel, balancing golden scales.

"And you, *Richard*?" Cam drawled. "I must admit, you don't seem the type to have an interest in the illegal drug trade. I'd expect you to be the kind to have your wife iron your undergarments."

Richard's stache twitched, but he smiled. "Would you like an honest answer?"

"Of course."

"Would you believe me if I said that I consider this small evil necessary for the greater good? I aim to be a godly man,

Lord Callahan, and whether you believe it or not, I foresee our partnership being beneficial to His work."

"Small evil or great." Cam crossed his legs. "I expect a continued amount of honesty if we are going to have any kind of partnership."

"That's fair." Richard nodded. "But let's leave negotiations until the end of our tour."

"As you wish."

They took another right out of the square, onto a slimmer road, and headed into a more residential area. The streets were slightly rounded, channeled out on the edges to provide proper drainage to the sewer drains. Cam leaned over the side of the carriage to get a better view. *What an interesting concept.* Everywhere he'd travelled, mainlanders and islanders alike just threw their sewage onto the streets, leaving it to pool there, until it was eventually scraped up by night-soil men. Along with that, streetlamps were spaced about every fifty feet apart. Beneath every five, a red water spicket.

"Are those gaslights?" Cam asked, "Must have been pricey to import, seeing as The Rot has most of the harbors shut down."

"No price is too great in terms of quality of life," Richard answered. "We in my house believe that The Rot is born from the sins and filth of the mainland. Sin spreads, and the pandemic continues. We have proven here that clean living can bring salvation from the disease, God be good."

Cam looked around. Children played in the streets, giggling and shrieking in happiness as their dogs chased after them, dashing between their knees. Blazes, even the blasted dogs looked fat and healthy—not the mangy animals that usually roamed city blocks.

Could Richard be on to something? Cam shook his head. Another thought for later.

They chatted amiably for the next hour as the carriage took them from the city deeper into the heart of the island. The cobblestone road split, snaking out in several directions into the thick, tropical jungle. Wild bananas and coconuts grew here. At least the fruit would be fresh.

The jungle thinned, opening into a wide open plain. Rising beyond, a sharp, jagged mountain seemed to jut from nowhere out of the earth. Despite the clear blue sky, mist surrounded the peak.

Richard must have seen Cam's confused expression because he chuckled. "It's a volcano," he said, and Cam shot him a nervous look. "Don't fret. It's been dormant for a century. Tomorrow, I plan to take you to the pearl groves on the northern side."

Cam cleared his throat. Something in his chest pulled toward the mountain, and he crossed his arms to keep it from escaping. "I look forward to it."

Richard just smiled.

The Duskins' estate stood mid-way up a smooth, grassy cliff, overlooking a one-hundred-and-fifty-foot drop down to the blue, blue sea. All of it was impressive. Lava rock walls and a square gate—matching the entrance into the city—surrounded the property. Their carriage halted at the gate, and a uniformed guard stepped out of a booth beside it, bowing animatedly as they passed through.

The manor itself was extraordinary, too, of course. Three stories high, each floor having its own wrap-around balcony. Though the main bulk of the mansion was white, the pillars that held it were ribboned with gold. Cam rolled his eyes. It was just another way for them to show their wealth.

Several acres of neatly trimmed lawn surrounded the mansion, complete with private gardens. The carriage circled the estate, and Richard pointed out pieces of the building's architecture, explaining some of the island's history as he did so.

Cam smiled when he was supposed to, nodded, and laughed when he should. He'd played this game a thousand times as a child, back in another life. Sit and listen to the rich folks as they show off their beautiful, worthless things.

They left the carriage and walked up the pathway onto the mansion's coral-rock front porch. Five people waited for them, standing as still and lovely as statues. How long had Duskin been planning this show?

One boy—maybe eleven—stood to the left. Three girls stood to the right. All wore matching black ensembles, except the girls wore dresses instead of trousers. At the center of them stood a stunning, smiling woman—maybe in her twenties—wearing a high-necked sapphire day gown. Its bodice was absurdly tight, and the train behind her was ruffled and draped, her curly brown hair pinned into a tall coif.

"I would like to introduce you to my wife." Richard beamed. "Lady Charlotte Duskin."

Charlotte smiled, dimples forming in her round pink cheeks. "I have heard so much about you, Lord Callahan." She curtsied. "It's an honor."

What has Elias been telling them? Cam kissed her gloved fingers. She blushed prettily.

"The honor is mine." He glanced up at the faces waiting on the porch and was met by a wall of disdain. He swallowed. *What have I gotten myself into?*

Richard followed his gaze. "These are my children. The Lord chose a different path for us in terms of family. We've adopted unfortunate children from across the Four Corners, bringing them up under a roof of morality. They help serve and take care of the household to teach them work ethics. When they're old enough, they'll be given the opportunity to prosper, just like anyone else in New Havana."

"How . . . generous of you." Cam held back a grimace. Looking at these *children,* he doubted they were picked for their misfortune. Never had he seen a more visually appealing group of people, each of them unique in one way or another. Cam stepped onto the porch, walking down the line of them, fascinated.

The boy stood nearest to him. With the deep coppery-brown skin of the far Eastern countries. His inky-black hair shone like crystal. Crude black suns had been tattooed under his eyes, giving him a wild look.

"He was found on the ship of a spice trader that had come to port a year back." Richard watched Cam intently. "I convinced the trader to give him to me in exchange for full bellies for his crew. A wonderful find."

He thinks of them as toys. Dolls. Cam's stomach rolled. He patted the boy's shoulder and couldn't help noticing the way he cringed. Cam paused. "What's your name, kid?"

The boy wouldn't look at him—not in the eye. "Nathan."

"Nathan, *my lord,*" Charlotte said sweetly. "Speak properly, darling."

Nathan flinched. "*My lord.*"

Nausea again. This time, it threatened to bend him over. Just like his own childhood. Cam patted Nathan's shoulder again, attempting to regain his composure. "Nathan is a great name." Cam knelt beside him. "And the name of my closest friend. You should be proud to share it with him."

Nathan's black eyes lit up. "I will, my lord. Thank you." The boy leaned in and whispered in his ear. "Don't go into the basement."

Cam pulled back, brows furrowing, and Nathan's gaze flickered between him and Richard, pleading.

Beside them, Charlotte went rigid. She placed her hand on Cam's shoulder, her jaw tight. "Shall we continue?"

Cam rose and continued down the line, feeling the eyes of the Duskins follow him as he glanced back at the boy. *What in the blazes?*

Charlotte dragged him forward, but Cam paused when he reached a girl in her early teens, with fiery red hair and freckles. He'd never seen hair so vivid—a true ruby red. Her irises the purest gold. Again, no eye contact. *What have these people done to you?*

His heat flickered, and the older girl beside them stiffened. She was maybe close to his age, and when he met her stare, the two palest eyes he'd ever seen stabbed through his soul—so light blue, they gave off a silver hue. To be honest, there wasn't a part of her that *wasn't* white. Her hair, her skin, her brows, even her lips, all the color of freshly fallen snow—and there wasn't a single inch of her body that didn't scream *hate, hate, hate.*

For the first time in his life, Cam was at a loss for words. He backed up a step.

"Don't let Annie alarm you," Richard chuckled. "She can be . . . intense, especially where her sister, Jenny, is concerned, but I promise she is an absolute treasure."

Annie. Cam stored the name away to process later. He met her gaze again, expecting the rage he'd seen a moment before, but instead . . . there was nothing. A cold, empty distance filled her eyes, void of all emotion.

A void he'd seen before, a long, long time ago. *Blazes.*

"I freed her from a slaver. It took a hefty sum to convince them to let her go." Richard grinned. "Her coloring is called moon-vein in the North, but it's actually a form of albinism. Not many families carry the trait any longer. Lovely, isn't she?"

"Lovely." Cam's insides crawled as the girl continued to watch him.

The third girl was far less intimidating. She was also in her early teens, with dark curls and an equally curvy figure. She introduced herself as Rose and shook his hand excitedly. Annie's dead glare never left him.

Charlotte clapped sharply, and the children snapped to attention. "Inside, inside. Lunch must be served."

She turned to Cam and cocked her head. *She really is pretty.* "You must be hungry, my lord."

"Famished, actually." Cam watched as the line of odd children filed into the mansion. Lord and Lady Duskin fell in behind them, arm in arm, looking as much in love as two parakeets forced to share a cage.

Cam shoved his hands in his pockets and followed them. What else could he do? This had been the strangest day of his life, and it was only halfway over. *Even dying hasn't topped this one.*

CHAPTER 11
CAMDEN

Cam hadn't known what to expect of the Duskins' household, but the mansion's interior was exactly that: simple in its extravagance, yet every detail was chosen with care and symbolism.

In their sitting room, the stitching in their leather furniture picked up the pinkish tones in the coral flooring. The brocade in the scarlet drapes matched the pattern of the wine glasses, carefully arranged on the low table.

"Your things have already been brought to your rooms." Charlotte looped her arm through his as she took him for a tour through the rest of the mansion. "I believe you'll find your lodgings suitable."

"I'm sure I will." Cam smiled wide. "Especially if you chose them. Your taste is exquisite."

Charlotte blushed, as if on cue—a practiced proper lady—and led him on.

Every wall in every room and on every floor held exactly eight paintings.

Cam counted. They ranged wildly in theme. Death, life,

God, angels, and the occasional basket of fruit. Some of the work he recognized belonged to the top artists from the mainland. Others could have been custom pieces.

Fortunately, Charlotte talked enough for the two of them, gifting Cam precious time to think, his mind flashing back to the faces of the Duskins' children.

The anger he felt pouring from that girl—Annie. That couldn't be a coincidence. Rage always had a cause—a trigger —and he'd like to know what triggered her. *I need to keep an eye on the kids.* If anyone knew what was going on here, it would be them. He saw enough and spied enough when he was young. They weren't stupid.

Don't go into the basement, the boy had said. The mansion didn't *have* a basement, from what he could tell—and he'd looked. Every floor and room she led him through, Cam scanned for any sign of a lower level, but nothing stuck out to him.

He and Charlotte entered the dining room half an hour later to find an expansive table set. A roasted hog was sliced onto their plates in generous portions, served over a bed of roasted vegetables and rice, drowned in decadent sauces. The three girls swooped into the room in a synchronized dance and poured them each a separate glass of ice water and fruity, red wine.

He pushed the wine aside.

Cam couldn't stop himself from studying Annie as she moved—silent as a cat, her dainty feet gliding over the smooth, stone floors. She was small—chest height to him, perhaps—and grossly thin, the bones of her hips visible through her silk dress, her pale hair braided down her back.

Their eyes met, for the briefest of moments, and he was hit by that same cold emptiness again. A black hole where life was unable to thrive. Cam's stomach lurched, and he looked away, shifting in his chair.

"You're excused, my loves," Charlotte cooed to the girls, waving slightly.

Annie curtsied with the others, with no regard to him, and left as silently as she came, hands folded behind her back.

Richard sipped at his wine before setting it down with a sharp clink. "I imagine you'll be wanting answers to your previous questions, Lord Callahan."

"Aye," Cam quirked his lips. "But I must admit your ice has made me a tad more patient. What a novelty."

Richard raised his glass. "Spared no expense."

"I must ask a question of my own before we begin." Charlotte leaned in close, brushing Cam's fingers. "If it's not too bold?"

Cam chanced a glance at Richard. Not a hint of jealousy. *Maybe the dinner isn't the only thing that is a show.* "Ask away."

"I would *love* to know how you ended up in your current . . . condition." Charlotte's grey eyes sparkled. "You must have quite the tale to tell."

"Charlotte!" Richard's wine glass froze halfway to his lips.

"It's quite all right," Cam winked. *Play the game.* "We did promise each other a certain amount of honesty." Cam leaned into Charlotte, mimicking her movements, their faces only a foot apart. "If you must know . . . I was murdered."

She gasped, her mouth a perfect O. "How horrifying! You must tell me what happened."

"I assure you." Cam straightened. "Such details are not meant for the dinner table, but I will tell you this—I have yet to avenge my death. When I do, it will be a terrible day, indeed."

Charlotte clapped excitedly. "Give us an example!"

"Of what, my lady?"

"Your powers." She smiled, lips curling up at the edges. All that sweetness was replaced with a vicious hunger. "Show me."

God help me. Cam raised his hand, inhaling deeply. *Narrow as the head of a pin. A bead of blood.* A ball of flame formed as he flexed his fingers, pulsating like his own personal sun. He exhaled, allowing the energy to spread. The light burst out into a flash of yellow and orange, then disappeared, leaving behind the faint scent of smoke.

Charlotte squealed in delight. "Marvelous! Again!"

"My dear, please." Duskin patted his wife's hand. "Lord Callahan didn't sail all this way just to entertain us."

Charlotte pouted, pushing food around on her plate.

Richard sighed. "Back to the matter at hand. How much do you know of me, my lord?"

"Not as much as I would like," Cam said through a mouthful of pork, cooked to tender perfection. "More than you might think."

Richard picked at his meal. "When I was a younger man, I wasn't as blessed as I am now." He sipped his wine. "I worked the shipyards, running for this man and that, and as you can imagine, I saw a great many things."

Cam bit a green bean in half. "I have a wild imagination."

"Quite." Richard took Charlotte's hand again. "Day in and day out, I watched men and women step off those ships. Many died two or three weeks later from the pandemic, infecting all exposed to them." He paused for more wine. "One day, I noticed a group coming off a cargo ship from the South. It had been a rough journey, but they seemed in perfect health despite. Jubilant, really."

Cam traced his finger around the condensation building on the edge of his glass. "Strange."

"Strange, indeed." Richard nodded. "The group was quarantined, of course. Within two days, the disease came upon them. Two more, and they were dead. So, I asked myself, what caused the disease to burn through them so quickly?"

"One can only guess."

"And I did," Richard continued. "I dug up every scrap of information I could find on those poor people. They were all from different regions, different colors, lifestyles, but I did find one common trait among them."

"Let me guess," Cam said. "They all had a taste for Pearl Dust?"

"Smart man." Richard winked, an unsettling gesture on his face. "After years, and years, of grueling research—I'll spare you the details—I found that the drug accelerated The Rot at an alarming rate. Weeks of exposure, condensed to hours."

Richard's eyes were feverish as he propped his elbow on the table. "Soon—in another two weeks—I will be receiving the patent back on my discovery. Lords and ladies from all over the world are coming to celebrate it. Then—imagine—sharing this knowledge with every harbor in the world. The demand for Pearl Dust will become unimaginable. Screening people for the disease before they ever set foot on land—"

"And preventing another pandemic," Cam muttered, eyes widening. *This is bigger than I thought.* "You'd be a hero."

"And you'll be rich, Lord Callahan, beyond your wildest imaginations," Richard said. "You're associates began the discussion, but I will ask you—man to man—to bring your operations here and set up a permanent grow on New Havana. You will never want again."

Cam leaned back, blowing out a long breath. *Blast.*

Whatever Elias and Vernon imagined was happening here, it was clear the situation was much more complicated than they expected. *Improvise, adapt.* "It's a tempting offer, my lord." Cam cleared his throat. "But I need some time to think and go over the numbers. See if what you want is even attainable."

"Very good." Richard downed the last of his wine. "Like I said, in two weeks, I will have my patent, and my research will become public. Dealers will be groveling for the same offer I just gave you. Think quickly."

"But why the island?" The question leapt from Cam's lips before he could stop it. "Why the fairytale experience for the people living here?"

Richard smiled. Charlotte stared down at her folded hands. "Happy citizens make happy trophies. None of this is a mask. Besides, every experiment needs control. The healthy to compare to the sick. When others see the results of my work, they'll come around quickly. And, well . . . if the public needs an example, I have plenty of clean test subjects. You asked for honesty."

Dear God. Cam swallowed, aware of how closely they watched him. "I see. If the lamb sees the knife . . ."

"If the lamb sees the knife," Richard repeated, relaxing. "I'm showing the world—as my city flourishes—what a life free of sin can bring."

Cam's stomach rolled as he looked down at his plate. He'd lost his appetite. "If you'll excuse me." He stood, nodding to each of them. "It's been a long journey. I would like some rest and would appreciate a later start tomorrow."

"Of course." Richard jingled a small bell that sat beside him on the table.

Annie appeared around the corner, looking as guilty as a dog that had stolen food from his master's plate. Cam smiled to himself. *She's been listening the entire time.*

Richard frowned. "Annie, dear, escort Lord Callahan to his quarters. Make sure he's well cared for."

Charlotte offered Cam her hand, and he kissed it. A ruby

the size of a small grape sat on her wedding finger, the band thick and gaudy. She batted her thick lashes. "Goodnight, my lord."

Annie curtsied, and he could have sworn she rolled her eyes. "If you'll follow me."

Cam stepped in line behind her, feeling eyes on his back, and she led him up the nearest staircase. His room was at the end of a well-lit hall on the third floor. Annie opened the door for him, and he stepped inside, keeping his body poised respectfully away from her.

His room was decorated much like the rest of the manor, with black oak and leather furniture. Red velvet everywhere. To his surprise, he had a washroom all to himself, including a large claw-foot tub. All his things were stacked neatly atop the chest at the end of his king-sized bed. *I wonder how many times they've been searched.*

Annie waited for him to get acquainted without saying a word, just watching him with a bored expression. Cam tried to think of something—anything—to say to her, but for once his tongue betrayed him. Instead, he fidgeted awkwardly with the corner of his sheet.

"Is there anything else you need, my lord?"

Cam looked at her—those pale eyes—wishing he could unlock all their secrets so he could get the blazes off of this island and go home. *You don't have a home anymore.*

"Umm . . . " Cam scratched his head. "Play some cards with me?"

Annie huffed and gave him a subtle, close-lipped smile. "I'm afraid that's not my vice. Sleep well."

As she turned to leave, a glint of green caught Cam's eye. A jade fishhook pendant sat against her pale throat, peeking out over the modest neckline of her black bodice.

Cam reached to grab her elbow out of instinct, but stopped himself. *It can't be.*

Annie closed the door softly.

He stood, completely still, staring at the space she'd just occupied. *How did I get here? What have I started?*

Most importantly, why did she have Resh's necklace?

He pushed the desk from the far wall, the wood screeching as he blocked off the door. He added a chair and his suitcase, too, just in case.

Cam collapsed into bed without undressing and blinked up at the dark ceiling above. He didn't want to think about Annie, about Resh, and didn't want to think about where life had brought him at all.

Good job, Camden. You've found yourself back in hell. He rolled over, exhaustion settling over him like a thick, prickly blanket. Within minutes, he was fast asleep.

CHAPTER 12
ANNIE

"When are you going to tell me what's the matter, dear?"

Annie refused to look up from the hot rags she wrapped tightly around the old woman's fingers. Today felt like a day her face might betray her. Instead, she blew out a long breath.

"Your knuckles are getting worse." Annie took another rag from the steaming bucket beside her. Water dripped over her gloved hands, back down toward her elbows. "I'm going to have to find something for the swelling."

Lowana had been a cook on a merchant vessel—happy, respected, full of life—before Mr. Price and Boyle ended that for her. Too old—she was too old to survive down here much longer. In the cold and damp. In a right world, she would be sitting beside a fire, drinking tea, and laughing as her grandchildren wrestled at her feet.

But she wasn't. She would spend her last days below ground, blanketed in her own filth.

And through all her walls, all her shields, Annie had come to care for her.

Lowana pulled her hand away back through the cell bars and closed her eyes. "It's been a long time since I've felt any pain. That's why I eat my oats." Lowana chuckled. "And that's not what I meant. Spill the beans to Mama Lowana. What's troubling you?"

Annie tossed the used rags back into the bucket, sighing. She was going to collapse if she didn't get some sleep soon. The captain hadn't let her shut her eyes in days. "It's nothing. At least, nothing you need to be bothered with."

Lowana smiled. All her teeth had rotted out. "At this point, sweetie, I'm dying for a little trouble."

Nothing good came from talking, but lately . . .

A chill ran up her arm. Elain stood behind Lowana, shaking her head, finger over her lips.

Don't worry, I won't betray you. Annie sat and crossed her legs, cupping her chin in her palm. "He brought in another one."

It wasn't just another one, but *him*. Arrogant and self-appreciating. The type who thought he could get anything he wanted by having a handsome face.

And he *was* handsome, which made it so much worse. Rose wouldn't stop talking about it. About his tall, muscled body. His square jaw. His piercing green-gold eyes and the cheeky way his lips curled when he smiled.

Rose was young. She just saw another man to ogle, another spectacle, but Annie knew what he really was . . . another monster that could burn her.

The old woman blinked at her slowly, wrapping her arms around herself. "Another what?"

Annie picked at her gloves. "Another Revenant." *You don't*

understand. "After Frank . . . Lord Duskin promised me no more."

"And you believed him?"

"I—" She did believe him. It was the only promise he'd ever made to her—the only thing she'd ever asked of her adopted father. Saying it out loud, though . . . it was foolish of her to think he'd hold to it—to think he cared that much. Especially if it meant the success of his work. "I guess I just hoped."

"What about them bothers you so, dear?" Lowana asked gently. "They're just people—a little different than you and me, but people."

"They're evil. Cursed," said a voice behind her.

Annie looked over her shoulder.

Nathan—the navigator—pressed his forehead against his cell bars. He grimaced. The Pearl Dust hadn't yet rotted his large, white teeth. "You're right to hate them."

Lowana shook her finger at him and spat, "Quiet! Enough of you, boy. We're all sick of your spouting."

A murmur of agreement rippled through the neighboring cells.

"You wouldn't say that if you'd seen what I saw." Nathan scowled, raising his voice over their mumbling. "Two creatures, blowing a ship apart like a kid's toy. Friends burnt to ash. There's no believing after that."

"We all know Boyle's a chicken gizzard." Lowana waved him off. "But the decisions of two don't govern the action of all."

"No." Nathan shook his head. "You didn't see. Folks aren't supposed to get back up after they die. Something goes wrong in the head—"

They broke into a full-blown argument, shouting back and forth across the hall. Annie covered her ears. Someone would hear. The captain's ghost laughed in the shadows of the nearest gaslight.

"I need to leave." Annie stood, breathless, and dusted off her skirts. "I'll find something for the swelling."

They didn't seem to hear her. The echo of angry voices and the captain's laughter followed her deep into the tunnels.

Annie walked faster, trying to drown out the noise with the *clap-clap* of her rushed footsteps. They didn't have much else to do, she knew, as much as she hated the noise. Still, the stress wasn't good for the old woman's arthritis.

More voices, more echoes. It sent her back to her days with the slavers. All the fighting. Torturing prisoners out of boredom. The screams of the men and women forced to share their captor's beds. Well . . . beds if they were lucky. Usually, they were chained to the cold floor. She still wore the scars on her wrists and ankles.

Annie shook it off and composed her mask. Those days were memories now and could no longer hurt her, no matter how hard they tried. The pantry's hidden door swung open, perfectly smooth. The fresh grease had done its job. Annie crept through the door and closed it behind her.

"What are you doing in here?"

The blood in Annie's veins froze, her heart slamming and sputtering in her chest. Across the kitchen, Lady Duskin stood facing the sink, tears streaking her round face, clutching a large glass of brandy.

"I—" *She's going to tell. He'll kill them. Kill me.* She wasn't supposed to be down there at this time. Annie's legs were useless, wobbling meat columns. "Please."

Lady Duskin's lips curled, and she snorted. "Relax, I don't care. You just startled me."

Breathe. Her eyes searched for something, anything, some detail to latch onto to keep her heart from bursting. They settled on the thick coat of red staining Lady Duskin's hands, smeared on her gown, and across the lip of the sink. Diluted reddish drips streaked down the white kitchen cabinets.

Annie's breath slowed. Blood was okay. She could handle blood.

Lady Duskin turned away from her, hands trembling as she sipped her brandy. "I'm glad you're here. I need the second left-wing guest room cleaned up. Be sure it's done before morning."

No more. I can't handle more. Annie forced a shaky smile, wanting to rip her hair out. "Is there anything else?"

To her surprise, Lady Duskin let out a sharp laugh. "Nathan's a liability. That's what Richard said, his reasoning. After today's outburst, he couldn't risk him with the rest of the guests arriving soon. He told me to take him to the bunker." She took another drink. "But I didn't do that. I spared him. I *saved* him." Lady Duskin shook her head violently, curls falling loose from her bun. "Fix it, and I don't want to hear another word about it."

I'm so tired. Annie's mind was too frazzled for the weight of Lady Duskin's words to even reach her. The thought of another night awake almost sent her into tears. The beginnings of delirium whispered in the corner of her mind. The captain knew it. His manic laughter found her from all the way down in the prison.

But there was nothing left to say. Nothing to do but obey.

As she left the kitchen, Lady Duskin broke down into racking sobs.

When Annie arrived, the guest room was painted red, just like Lady Duskin's hands. Little Nathan looked so small lying on that bed. His black eyes, tattooed with suns, stared up at the canopy. Blank, empty. His beautiful, shining hair fanned out onto the pillows, crusted with blood.

Annie stepped forward, touching the jagged edges of skin along his opened throat, several smaller wounds carved above and below it. *Hesitation marks.* She wiped some of the blood away. He'd been cut to the bone.

Out of all of them, Nathan was the only one Lady Duskin had formed any kind of bond with. A real bond—not the ridiculous performance she put on to keep her husband happy. He'd been sweet to Annie, too. Brought her shells he'd found on the beach once or twice, but he hadn't been good at pretending or playing house with the rest of them.

Lord Duskin had an image to maintain, and that image required the perfect, happy family. If they threatened that— stepped too close to the edge of reality—no bother. There were always more children in need of a father. The islanders didn't ask questions. Not if they wanted to keep their extravagant, new lifestyles.

A cold arm wrapped around her, and Elain—her form that same dove grey—laid her head on Annie's shoulder, her touch icy but not unpleasant.

Annie clenched her teeth and pulled away.

Not now. Now was not the time to mourn. Elain began to cry, and Annie fought back tears of her own.

"Hush, hush, now. Close your eyes, and dream," she sang as she wrapped Nathan in the ruined bed sheets, lifting the little boy into her arms. *"Hush, hush, now. You're home, now. Close your eyes, so free."*

Her father had sung the same song to her as he bled out on the floor of their hut, the bodies of her brothers lying in pieces around them. Snow fell that night, gentle, sweet. The Revenant man found her there as she tried to wrap up the stumps of her father's arms with fabric torn from her wool dress.

So small—she'd been so small—but he took her anyway.

Violated her. Sold her for a pretty price after, because of her coloring.

She'd been ruined by a branded animal dressed as a man. His face had been covered, but she'd never forget his laugh . . . or his companion's. Another golden-eyed Revenant had watched, sitting at the table her father had carved for her mother. It haunted her where the ghosts couldn't, and now she shared a house with three more monsters.

CHAPTER 13
CAMDEN

He checked the note Elias had given him for a third time.

Wilkins' Whistle—this was the place.

Cam looked up at the freshly painted sign hanging above the tavern—some jolly-looking buffoon, knocking back a pint—the establishment itself hidden away in an alley. The exterior walls were painted a whimsical sky blue, lined with flowerpots filled with daffodils.

He'd ridden out at dawn to be here before opening hours. At least Richard's horses were faster than his carriage. It took less than an hour to get into town, but another hour he spent wandering and asking for directions before he finally found this blasted place.

Even here, people averted their eyes from him. Talked to the ground when he asked them a question. Part of him could hear the chanting of Shar-Crue's villagers echoing in his ears.

Richard could promise perfection all he wanted, but he couldn't change what Cam was—unnatural.

Just the thought made his skin itch. Elias never told him

how *uncomfortable* not using his powers would be. He didn't remember it being like this on Shar-Crue. New energy in his blood clawed at his pores to escape. *Burn, burn, burn,* his power whispered, *burn, burn, burn.*

Cam twitched all over. It didn't help that he'd spent most of the night tossing and turning, trying to figure out what to do about Richard's daughter.

He fingered his revolver, calming himself. He could confront her, sure, and likely blow his cover in the process, ruining any chance of doing business with the Duskins.

I can't worry about that now. Cam shook his head. The tavern door was locked, its shudders drawn tight. There was no light between the cracks. Cam pounded his fist on the door, harder than he meant to, and chipped the paint. *Oops.*

Oh well, it was time for Tommy Wilkins to wake up.

Silence.

Cam knocked again. The wood splintered. He glanced at his balled fist. *Since when could I do that?*

This time, a thumping came from the second floor. Heavy footsteps thundered toward the door from inside, and it flung open, revealing a young man with slicked-back yellow hair. His brows rose so high they could have shot off his forehead. "Can I help you?" Each word was annunciated deliberately slow.

Cam smiled wide and moved to block the damaged door out of view. "Are you Thomas Wilkins? You must be Thomas Wilkins. May I come in?"

"Like blazes, you will." Thomas rubbed his eyes. "You woke me from a dead sleep, which is a sin, if you didn't know. What could you possibly want at this hour?" His brown eyes flickered over Cam's brands, then widened. "Ah, forgive me. You must be Mr. Barnes. Come in, come in."

Thomas ushered Cam into the tavern, taking his coat and hanging it by the door. The interior of the place was as cheery as the outside. Buttery yellow walls, painted with red, pink, and blue swirls and flowers. The stools in front of the bar were green with absurdly tall backs, like a baby's highchair.

Cam held back a snigger. "This is . . . cute."

"Thank you." Thomas squeezed behind the bar and disappeared below the counter. By the sound, he was rummaging through shelves. "I apologize for the mess. I'd have cleaned up if I'd known when to expect you."

"Have a rough night?" Cam poked a bit of broken glass with the toe of his boot. Tables were flipped on their ends. Chairs were smashed. An empty keg lay on its side in the corner.

Thomas's head poked up. "Do you have any idea how rowdy ladies get when they're drunk? Maybe. The weekends are always busy, but last night was particularly awful." He ran a hand through his thin hair and sighed. "I was too tired by closing to clean. Thought I'd do it this morning before I opened, but here you are." He continued to rummage. "Can I get you anything? Coffee? Sausage?"

"Both would be nice." Cam slid onto one of the green stools. "Elias said you could help me. Can you? Or are you just going to feed me, because I can go anywhere for that?"

"Yes, yes, don't be snippy." Thomas set two steaming mugs on the counter, scowling. "But not before breakfast."

Cam sipped his coffee as he watched Thomas work. He had a full kitchen behind the bar, complete with stone and wood stoves. Thomas slapped a couple of thick sausages on a skillet and drizzled them with olive oil in a practiced flourish.

Elias said Thomas was part of the political group fighting for Revenant rights, but he didn't have any visible brands. Was he Revenant, too, or were mortals allowed to join?

"What are you?" Cam asked, unable to contain his curiosity.

Thomas didn't look up from his sausages—still pink and spitting grease—but he did smile. "I'm just like you, kiddo. Pillar, stones, and all."

Cam frowned. "That's not what I meant."

"No, I'm not Revenant." Thomas yelped as hot grease splashed on his thumb. "Just a devout supporter. My mother died when I was young, turned Revenant, and was never treated the same after. I do what I can to help."

"Huh." Cam pursed his lips as Thomas set a hot plate in front of him. He shouldn't have been so rude. "Sorry about your mum, mate."

Thomas shrugged. "Like I said, I do what I can."

Cam stuffed a huge bite of sausage into his mouth without letting it cool. Nothing was too hot anymore, not with his fire prowling just below his skin. He sighed and closed his eyes, enjoying the mixed flavors of black pepper and garlic. Just like the meat pies some street vendors sold back in Port Lebanon.

"Righty then." Thomas pulled a map out from beneath the counter and spread it between them. "I don't have much time this morning, so best get to it."

"Oh, wow." Cam glanced over the rim of his mug. "A map, how thrilling."

"Do yourself a favor"—Thomas shot him a nasty look—"and keep your mouth shut. You'll get yourself stabbed around here with that attitude." He wiped his sweating forehead with a handkerchief and pointed to the drawing of a town on the southwest edge of the map. "Here's the city." His finger moved to the southeast end. "And here's the harbor."

"There is a lot of unsettled jungle between these two points and the estate. Lord Duskin is trying to cultivate pearl groves on the far side of the volcano, out of sight."

Cam nodded. "He told me as much . . . at least about the groves. He's taking me to see them this afternoon."

Thomas circled two points to the far left and right of the Duskins' estate. "This is where the housing is going in for the new lords and ladies under his employ. They're empty at night. We could use it as a rendezvous area later, or we can meet here."

Cam wiped his mouth on his sleeve. "I don't plan on being around long enough for any of it to matter. What I need to know is where all the missing sailors are being kept, and where he's keeping all the Pearl Dust he's been buying out. It's the only reason I'm here." *I'll find them and kill Boyle . . . somehow.*

"You should see this through . . ." Thomas' blond brows furrowed. ". . . if you plan to convince these people of your status long enough to attempt a rescue. You're going to have to take it slow, play your part right. The supporters and I have been trying to locate his stores for a year, with no luck. We were going to attempt and smuggle it out ourselves, but Mr. Bennett decided we needed outside help."

Did he decide that before or after I died? Another thought for later. "Supporters?" Cam asked.

Thomas nodded and refilled Cam's coffee. "Workers, shop owners, ship-rats out of the harbor—people enlightened to the horrors happening at sea. Like the one that ended your life, I'm told."

"And what of Price and Boyle?" Cam said quickly to change the subject. "I've yet to be reintroduced."

"You will soon, I'm sure." Thomas rolled up the map and leaned against the counter. "Frank is a hot head—excuse the pun—and he's dangerous. The kill-first-ask-questions-later type. Likes to strut around town to remind everyone how powerful he is. Julian is the one you need to watch out for, though. He's smart and must know Mr. Bennett will be coming for him."

Cam shoved another piece of sausage into his mouth, using

chewing as a chance to think. He liked the idea of having backup on the island—people on his side. Trained killers would be nice, but shopkeepers would do in a pinch. There were a lot of undeveloped areas where Richard could keep prisoners, but he'd need somewhere with access to food and medical supplies. Someplace where he could have them brought in discreetly.

Someone on this blasted rock knew something, but he didn't blame them for staying quiet. They had it all here—a safe life for their families, comforts available on every corner.

"Let me worry about the Duskins for now," Cam said. Thomas's eyes narrowed. "I want you and your friends to keep an eye on Price and Boyle. Everything they do, everywhere they go. We need to know why they're here in the first place. Why they're serving Richard. Think you can do that?"

"*Aye*," Thomas said, mocking Cam's harbor accent. "Anything else?"

"Who does Richard keep company with?" Cam mused. "I mean, besides his lovely wife."

Thomas swirled the contents of his mug, deep in thought. "No one comes to mind. Despite his showiness, he's very reclusive. As far as I know, he doesn't leave his work or home for long."

That means a lot of time around his children. Maybe they weren't just bystanders to whatever he was doing. Maybe the whole adoption and generosity act was just a way to ensure their loyalty. Young, impressionable minds were trainable.

"And what of his work?" Cam asked. "He said he's discovered how to screen for The Rot."

"I don't know," Thomas sighed. "Lots of rumors, but nothing concrete. Some say human sacrifice—yuck—but you know how people like to talk."

And I know now who I need to talk to. Cam stood and drained the last of his coffee. "Thanks for your help—but mostly your food. I'll come back soon. Find a way to send me a note if you come across anything good."

"Will do." Thomas handed Cam his coat and opened the door for him. "Be on your guard."

"Whatever you say." Cam waved him off as he headed out, and Thomas locked the tavern door behind him.

God, this is going to be a long day. He was to meet Richard in about two hours, but Cam took his time as he wandered back into the main square. Silent and empty just a short time ago, the city seemed to awaken with the rising sun. A few early birds were already out and about, arms loaded with shopping bags, some with sleepy-eyed kids at their heels.

A familiar, welcome smell found his nose. *Cinnamon rolls.* Cam's mouth watered. His mother used to make them. It only took him a matter of minutes to find the source. Steam leaked from the window of a small bakery out into the cool morning air. An old man sat in a rocking chair on the front steps, puffing on a cigarette.

His wrinkled eyes widened in fear when he noticed Cam approaching, but at least he looked at his face. *At my brands, most likely.* Cam stopped just short of the steps and nodded toward the window. "Those ready yet?"

The old man blew smoke from his nostrils, tense. "Just out of the oven, too hot for eating."

Cam dug into his wallet and dug out a few bills. "I'll take three. I'm not scared of getting burnt."

The baker just nodded and wrapped his pastries.

A short time later, Cam sat on the edge of the fountain in the square's center, sucking the last of the sugary icing off his fingers. Water sprayed from the fountain, tickling his neck. Cam sighed, enjoying the sweetness still on his tongue, feeling relaxed for the first time since he'd gotten here.

I could get used to this. He sat back, watching the square fill with people of all kinds, laughing together, genuinely embracing each other's company. For all the talk he'd heard about abductions and murder, Pearl Dust, and backwards research, these people seemed . . . happy.

He'd seen more smiles in the last ten minutes than in the last ten years. Couples with fat babies on the breast, elderly folk accompanied by caretakers. No Rot. No new scars.

What kind of sacrifices did it take to make this happen? At what cost?

A swift white movement in the corner of his eye caught Cam's attention. Richard's daughter disappeared into the growing crowd, carrying a pale pink parasol, heading into the heart of the market.

Annie. Cam was on his feet in an instant, a smile spreading on his face.

What a coincidence, a tempting opportunity. He should play it smart, keep his distance. He couldn't afford to blow his cover after only one day.

Annie ducked into one of the smaller shops a few blocks down from the bakery. A bell jingled as she stepped through the door.

Blazes with it.

He didn't have to push and shove—the crowd parted for him. Parted for the excited heat that surrounded him like a shield. He ignored the nervous looks and whispers—didn't care—as he jogged across the square.

Richard would have to wait. If he played his cards right, this day was about to get much more interesting.

CHAPTER 14
ANNIE

"Do you have anything for inflammation?" Annie leaned against the pharmacy's cedar countertop to steady herself. She hated the way her words slurred lately, like some drunken invalid. *Just a few more hours.*

"Hmm, let's see here." The young apothecary gentleman dug through his cabinets, clacking glass bottles together noisily. Annie pinched the bridge of her nose, breathing slowly.

Too loud. The sound scraped at her teeth.

At least the inside of the pharmacy was warm. The heavy scent of frankincense covered her like a blanket, mixed with orange peel and rosemary. It was easy to imagine each scent soaking into the wood walls like a sponge, releasing whatever smell best suited its visitors. It didn't help her drowsiness one bit.

"I have white willow bark." The apothecary set a couple of slender bottles on the counter. Annie jumped, forcing her eyes open, fighting the weight of her eyelids. "I have ground chili powder, too."

Annie's head swam. *Just a few more hours.* "I'll take the chili powder. Do you have any turmeric?"

The man dug around a bit more, then set a knobby brown root on the counter. "Anything else?"

"No, thank you, that will be all." Annie reached into her satchel. Empty. *I forgot to grab some more money.* She chewed her lip, trying to swallow the lump building in her throat. She'd have to put it on store credit. Risk Lord Duskin seeing the bill before she could get it paid. He'd only caught her once, but she'd convinced him the herbs were to treat an embarrassing rash. She wouldn't be able to get away with it again.

The apothecary wrapped the herbs in a small paper bag and pushed it across the counter with a smile. "It's on the house, ma'am, please take it."

"Oh." Annie blinked up at him. "Thank you." She didn't know what else to say, so she grabbed the package and shoved it in her bag before rushing out the door, the bell jingling behind her.

In the few stops she'd made, the market had filled considerably. Annie popped open her parasol, grateful for the small bubble of space it gave her between people's shoulders and elbows. Lord Duskin made her carry it so her skin wouldn't darken beneath the tropical sun. Hauling it around didn't really bother her. She burned like a lobster anyway.

She flinched as the heavy-set woman beside her called to a friend across the square. She grit her teeth against the howling of dogs and children behind her.

Too loud. Her skull was going to split open. Too many smells. Fresh bread and meat, fish and spices, rich perfumes and sweating workmen's bodies. Sucking in a breath, she focused on placing one foot in front of the other, one in front of the other.

The carriage waited not far off. Just a little way left to go.

Despite the heat of the bodies pressed around her, a chill crawled up her arms. *Not here, not now.* She resisted the urge to look over her shoulder. He'd never followed her this far from the mansion.

His shadow grew darker and more humanoid as he wove through the crowd. Unseen by everyone but her. There were times when his form was a lighter color—more like Elain's— and those days, he left her be. Now it was black and dripping like ink.

Not now, not now. Annie walked as quickly as her wobbly knees allowed, ducking into an alley at the edge of the market. She slid behind a stack of crates, holding her breath as she pressed her back against the alley wall.

Of course, the captain followed, his figure solidifying, empty eyes searching—always searching. When they didn't find her, he vanished into a cloud of black mist. Annie exhaled, rubbing her eyes with the heels of her palms.

He wouldn't go far. It was like he could smell her. No matter where she went, he was there. In the corner, laughing. Breathing on her neck. Stroking her hair with blackened fingers. Worst of all, when he hung himself over her bed by his suspenders, his thick, bloated tongue lolling from his open mouth.

It was the necklace. It had to be. She fingered the jade fish-hook. *I should just throw it in the ocean.* It was the only reason she could think that he would torment her this way, but destroying it . . .

As much as she hated him now, she couldn't bear to disrespect his memory that way. Not after what she'd done to him.

Across the alley, a church spire pierced the sky over the market buildings, casting shadows over the orange and yellow bricks. *I'll be safe there.* Class would be starting soon, and Lady

Duskin would have her meals cut back again if she missed another. *Just for a minute. Just a quick rest.*

Maybe she could leave the necklace there. Let God decide what to do with it.

Annie stood, straightening her dress, and made a beeline for the chapel.

The captain was on her in an instant, hovering just behind her elbow, groaning, clawing at her.

Just don't look. Don't look.

She did.

His upper lip pulled back, revealing rotting gums and silver teeth. She didn't allow herself to shudder as she looked away.

Why him? What was different?

Since she came to New Havana, the ghosts had been coming to her. She often wondered if they were ghosts at all. Usually, they were grey shapes, bustling here and there, as if on some sort of mission. Sometimes they were black and hateful. They'd never frightened her, never wanted to hurt her . . . until now.

Leave him, he screamed at her in the dark. *Leave him.*

The chapel was a forgotten oasis in a lifeless desert. A sanctuary.

Warmth spread through her chilled fingers as she pushed open the freshly painted, white double doors. Simple, clean. Everything she needed right now. He didn't follow her inside.

Despite not having service today, the pew had already been swept spotless. The stained-glass windows were wiped clean, and white wax candles sat ready in golden sconces in between the windows, ready to chase the darkness away.

Slowly, Annie walked up the carpeted aisle toward the altar, every step lightening some of the weight on her shoulders.

Evil couldn't enter here. She would be safe. Safe from the

nightmares, safe from the phantoms. A few minutes of peace where she could pretend nothing existed outside these walls. No death. No rotting corpses waiting to be buried.

After lighting the candles, Annie knelt in front of the altar and looked down at her hands. They were shaking. No matter how hard she scrubbed, she could still feel little Nathan's blood beneath her nails. Tears dripped onto her knuckles. She blinked, then wiped her cheeks. They were wet. When was the last time she cried? Months, years?

Annie lay her head on the steps, savoring the feeling of her damp cheeks. It was good to know she was still human, could still feel after all she'd seen and done. Her eyelids fought to close. Maybe she could sleep, just for a minute. Just a rest, then she'd go to class—

Footsteps jerked her awake.

"Did I interrupt something?"

It took her a moment to place the voice—low and scratchy. Lord Callahan stepped inside the chapel, closing the doors behind him, a lazy grin spreading on his face. Heat rolled from his muscular body, filling the hall, covering every inch of her skin.

"I *would* say I'll come back later, but you look like you're about to do something you'll regret. Probably for the best if I stayed."

How dare he.

The words put her on edge, worse than the invasion of her privacy, worse than the fear of being cornered in an empty room by a stranger. Not *just* a stranger, but one of the same monsters that had taken away everything she loved. The only things she'd ever loved.

You know you've thought about it. Annie shook her head violently, chasing the thought away. *Not here. Not now.* "What are you doing here?"

Lord Callahan's brow rose, the deep orange brands marring his tanned face blazing bright. "Me? I'm here for the same reason you are, I imagine. For some peace." He looked around, almost bored. "What are *you* doing?"

Trying to get away from terrible creatures like you.

"I . . ." Annie chewed at her stubby nails, tasting blood. What could she say to him? Beast or not, he was still Lord Duskin's guest and prospective client. He could still ruin her. "I—praying."

Lord Callahan's smile widened as he moved from the door, stalking closer. Predatory, alien. The heat coming from him dried her throat and nose. His green-gold eyes fell on the pouch at her side. "What did you find at the pharmacy? Anything good?"

He's been following me. For how long?

Annie collected herself and stood. "Herbs." *Best not be caught in a lie.* "Nothing that would be of any importance to you."

He moved another row closer, outstretching his hand. "May I see?"

It didn't matter if Lord Duskin called her daughter. She'd learned obedience was the safest option with these types. The arrogant and entitled. Annie handed Lord Callahan her bag. Resisting only ever brought pain.

Lord Callahan gave the contents a quick once-over before tossing them back. "Chili, turmeric. You're too young for joint problems."

Annie's brows furrowed. "I don't have joint problems." *Stupid, stupid.* Her legs wobbled, and she sat back down on the steps, looking up at him. Surprisingly, his expression was filled with concern.

No, that doesn't make any sense. She rubbed her forehead,

trying to fight off the exhaustion just a little longer. "How did you know what they were for?"

Again, he smiled. He had nice white teeth. "You learn a lot of things when you've been the places I have." He cocked his head. "Like how to tell when a woman is hiding something."

Laughing. The captain peeked through the chapel window, laughing—his mouth an open gaping hole.

"I'm not hiding anything." Annie's eyes never left the captain's horrid face. He wouldn't stop laughing.

Lord Callahan's eyes narrowed, and he shot a quick look over his shoulder when he noticed her staring past him. When he turned back, he was smiling again.

He smiled too much.

"See, I also learned to tell when a woman lies." He walked closer. Annie considered backing away, but she didn't have the energy. Didn't care.

Lord Callahan knelt in front of her and reached out. She didn't pull away as he tugged on the black cord around her throat, lifting the jade pendant up from the front of her dress.

He let it fall against her chest as his eyes met hers, lips curling up at the edges.

Annie held his stare.

"This." He tapped the fishhook gently. "I know for a fact it doesn't belong to you." His expression darkened. "Where did you get it?"

Reflexively, Annie gripped the necklace. "There's a lot of jewelry in the world."

"But only one like this," Lord Callahan said. "I stole it for a dear friend of mine when I was a kid. If you turn it over—" He opened her hand and flipped the pendant, revealing the initials *ER*—Edmund Resh.

"Ah." He batted his lashes. "Just as I thought."

Annie shoved him, scrambling back until her back pressed against the altar, her head swimming. "You're a criminal."

Lord Callahan scoffed. "Criminals can't have friends?"

Yes, but monsters can't. "You're here to serve Lord Duskin," she said. "What I wear is no business of yours."

He began to laugh, low at first, but it grew louder until Annie could feel it vibrating in her bones. "Serve? Let me let you in on a secret, Kitten. I don't give two blazes about your lord, and I don't *serve.*"

"Then why are you here?" Annie snapped. *I can't talk to him this way.* Whatever her feelings, he was still Lord Duskin's guest. If they found out she'd been disrespectful . . .

Lord Callahan inched even closer. There was nowhere for her to go. He leaned in, and she turned her face away, his warm breath tickling her ear.

"About six weeks ago," he whispered, almost a purr. "That dear friend I mentioned went missing. He was heading this way, you know. Headed this way and never came back. I've been through hell looking for him. When your lord offered such a convenient opportunity to snoop around, how could I pass it up? The worst I could find was nothing, but then I found you"—He tapped her nose—"my client's pretty daughter, wearing my friend's personal property. Strange, don't you think, how things work out?"

Breathing heavily, Annie faced him. His brands pulsed like a heartbeat, alive. If only she had a knife, she could carve them out and keep them as a trophy. "So strange." She forced herself to look him in the eyes. "What do you want from me?" *What can I do to make you go away?*

"Tell me where he is."

"Who?"

"Don't play with me," he growled.

"I don't know what you're talking about," Annie said. "And if I did, what makes you think I'd betray them. Just like that?"

"Because you *hate* them." He was every temptation. Her demise made flesh. "Don't deny it. I knew it the first moment I saw you. I've been there myself. You'd be amazed how liberating betrayal can feel."

Annie blinked at him slowly. *Do I hate them?* "You're insane."

Lord Callahan leapt to his feet inhumanly fast, and his demeanor snapped from a dark anger to a boy-like excitement in the span of a breath. "I'll tell you what," he said, his eyes bright. "How about a deal? I like you. Work with me, and I won't tell your lord that I'll be declining his offer on the account of his daughter being a lying thief."

A heavy numbness spread through Annie's limbs up into her chest, neck, and lips. *He'll put me on the table. Just like Elain.* "You wouldn't." She placed her hand over her throat. "You wouldn't dare."

"You can't fathom the things I'd do, the things I've done," he whispered back.

He really was insane. *Why, Lord?* Hadn't she given enough —done enough? She dealt with enough insanity of her own. She didn't need anyone else's. *Save me.*

The captain's face pressed against the chapel window, howling in laughter. He never stopped. If anything was going to break her, the noise would be it. Groaning, screaming, laughing, and crying. All day, all night. When she ate, when she worked. It never stopped.

Madness broke through the numbness. *"Go away!"* She snatched a candle off the altar, throwing it as hard as she could at the window. Lord Callahan ducked just as it flew over his head. The candle hit the window, breaking in half, the glass barely quivering. She held her breath, hoping and praying. *Go away.*

Still, the Captain laughed.

Annie sank back to the ground, head in her hands, and burst into tears.

"If you're trying to scare me off with crazy," Lord Callahan chuckled, running a hand through the sandy hair that danced around his eyes. She met his gaze, still gasping, and he clicked his tongue. "It won't work . . . I'm into that."

He stepped over and picked up the two halves of the broken candle, holding the pieces together in his hand. He held the candle out to her, and for some reason, she took it. It was whole again, the center still warm where the wax melted back together.

"Three days." He knelt in front of her again, grinning, and handed her his pocket square. "Deal with me, or deal with the Duskins—make your choice. I'm happy to wait, but I will say working with me has its benefits."

"*With* you?" She clenched the hanky in her fist. "Not *for* you?"

He shrugged. "I prefer equal partnerships."

Annie leaned her head back. Spinning, everything was spinning. "If you're going to kill me, just do it. I don't care."

"That's no fun." Lord Callahan stood and spun on his heel, waving flippantly as he did so. "Three days, Kitten, let me know. You know where to find me."

The double doors swung closed behind him with a low thud. The chapel fell into the same stunned silence she had.

The captain was gone.

For the first time in days, she was alone.

Annie curled her arms around her legs, pressing her forehead into her knees. Too much. She didn't want to think, didn't want to feel, and was glad for the numbness creeping back into her skin. It spread through her body, threatening to choke her, but this time she didn't care. Especially now that it was finally quiet. Her eyes closed.

When they opened again, there was no light coming through the windows, and the candles had burnt down to dripping stubs. Elain had cuddled up beside her, breathing in soft rasps. How long they sat like that, she didn't know. They were safe . . . warm from the heat Lord Callahan had left behind, trapped within the chapel walls. If she stayed, would everything outside wither away? Forget she ever existed?

Of course not.

But she knew what she had to do. The only thing she could do.

Annie and Elain left the chapel together, hand in hand.

Annie knocked on the door of the pharmacy. It was well after dark, and it took several minutes of relentless hammering for a light to flicker on inside.

The same young apothecary opened the door, sleepy-eyed and wearing rumpled night clothes. "I'm sorry, we're clo—" He froze when he realized who she was.

Annie folded her hands behind her back, her mind clear for the first time in days. "I'm sorry to bother you." She rocked on the balls of her feet. "But do you carry anything that contains hemlock?"

The boy's eyes widened, his shoulders stiffening. "Yes . . . but it's poisonous, ma'am."

Annie smiled, wide and sweet. "I know."

CHAPTER 15
CAMDEN

"The pearls are dead." Cam popped his lips.

They'd ridden to the foothills north of the mansion . . . late.

Cam had made a good show of blaming his tardiness on too much wine and sound sleep. If Richard had been angry about the delay, he'd done a good job of keeping it to himself.

In fact, he'd been quite animated as he narrated the entire six-mile ride to the groves. Lavish habitat, full of thriving wildlife. Crumbling stone buildings, left behind by the island's previous ancient inhabitants. Cam found the wild tobacco, growing tall in the fields, to be of most interest. Richard could make a fine penny on them alone.

Now they stood amidst a small patch of jungle, still damp from the mist rolling down the side of the volcano. Amongst the concentrated reds and yellows of the local flora, dozens of walnut trees had been planted, their wiry branches stretching desperately upward toward the sun. Ruddy brown vines wove lazily around the young, thin trunks. Pearl vines. Dead pearl vines.

Richard dabbed his sweating forehead with his handkerchief, scowling. The afternoon had grown warm, along with his temper.

"We've been working tirelessly to keep them alive." He pointed out the plethora of gardeners darting this way and that—raking, digging, doing anything they could to look busy. "But with no success."

"You're using the wrong trees for one," Cam drawled, scratching his head. "They're supposed to leech off banyan."

Richard's brow furrowed as he sucked on his front teeth. Sunlight shone off the polished, gold hunting medals pinned to his cherry-red riding coat. All show—he'd probably never done any of his own shooting in his life. "Mr. Price has assured me that walnut is the key and that we just need more time, more experience."

"Well, Mr. Price is *wrong*."

Richard peered at Cam from the corner of his eye, biting his thumb. "Why banyan?"

"No idea." Cam shrugged. "If it works, it works. Am I right?"

"It doesn't make any sense," Richard said. "Mr. Price said—"

"*Wrong*." Cam coughed, patting his chest. "Excuse me."

"And how are you so sure?"

"I've seen it," Cam said. "Look, take my advice or don't. I came here with the promise of revenue, but keep this up, and we aren't going to be able to afford the tissue to wipe our bums."

Richard shot him an enraged look, lips pursing. *Maybe I shouldn't push him.* After a tense moment, he sighed before turning and calling to one of the gardeners. "Tear these blasted things up," he growled. "Then go to the harbor and have an order put in for banyan."

The gardener bowed, forcing a smile, before striding off to bark orders at the other workers.

Richard turned toward the horses, his jaw tight. "Shall we? I have other appointments."

Cam nodded, smiling. *He's furious.* They hopped back on their mounts and started back toward the main road, riding side by side. What a loathsome afternoon, but at least the morning had been interesting.

Annie . . . he'd taken a gamble with her, one that might prove disastrous. One word to her adopted father, and *poof*—mission over. If it had been anyone—*anyone*—besides her, he might have chalked it up to a coincidence—that Richard had given his child a gift, the wearer oblivious to its origin, but not her. He didn't doubt for one moment that she saw and heard everything that happened in that house.

Not only that, but she . . . intrigued him. The cold hatred, her manic behavior in the church—he'd seen it all before. In those last weeks before her death, his mother had acted so similarly. Talking to herself, curling into her desperation and anxiety deeper and deeper until she was merely a husk, void of happiness and light.

That white-haired snowflower wasn't far from that fate, and something or someone had made her that way. To be frank, it chaffed him. *It probably was Frank.*

Somewhere his father won't find him. Cam shook the memory away and brought his attention back to Lord Duskin, still bitter and red-faced.

Fine, let the man stew in his silence. At least it gave Cam more time to think and collect himself.

A red and blue parrot crashed noisily through the branches overhead, squawking. It landed just long enough to eye him, bobbing its head. *Take me with you, friend.* Cam watched it glumly as it soared away.

What would it be like to fly? To soar across the sleek, flat plains, pushing his wings to the limit, wind whipping through his feathers. Free, wild, uncontainable—able to do and go wherever he liked.

Julian could fly.

Julian Price. He'd told Richard to plant walnut trees, but he'd known better. If Elias had sent him—if he'd seen Shar-Crue—he'd have known. But for some reason, he'd lied. It didn't make sense. Julian had ransacked half the ocean to hoard away the world's Pearl Dust. You would think he'd *want* a grove on the island.

"Forgive me for my shortness earlier," Richard said suddenly, and Cam jumped. "So much work, so much time has gone into that grow . . ."

"Don't apologize." Cam waved him off. "I'd have a knot in my knickers, too."

"I just don't understand." Richard shook his head, sweat beading on his temples. "Julian was so sure."

Cam's eyes flickered to the strain in Richard's neck, to the bulging vein in his forehead. He was still angry, still doubting. *This is my chance.* "How'd you and Price come to work together, anyway?"

Richard's horse started to veer from the path, grabbing for a patch of grass, and he dug his heels in the animal's side to straighten him. "It's a long story."

"We have time."

"I guess we do." He grunted, then sighed. "Well, one ordinary day, Mr. Price knocked on my door, claiming to have heard stories of an island city—free of disease—and came to see if the rumors were true."

Cam bit his tongue. *Wanting to find out what the hell you were doing with all that Pearl Dust, more like. Elias sent him.*

"I showed him New Havana," Richard continued.

"Explained to him my dream of a world without The Rot, and he believed in it. Believed in me. He offered to invest and has been working to better the community ever since, as well as acting as my advisor. That's the quick version, at least."

Advisor. Liar. Traitor. Julian had racked up a whole list of titles.

He needed to keep him talking. "And Mr. Boyle?" Cam asked. "Did he come with him?"

"No, no," Richard said, distracted as he tried to rein in his horse again. "He's been here since the beginning. I did my best to help him during his early days of Revenancy. Mr. Price has been a mentor to him."

"So, he died here?" *Very interesting.*

"I never said that." Richard shot him a quick glare.

"You implied it." Cam smiled knowingly. "How does a man die on an island with no violence?"

"There are many ways to die, Lord Callahan," Richard said. "And the island hasn't always been as serene as it is now."

Cam huffed a laugh. "If you say so."

He'd have to get this news back to Wilkins, see what he could dig up about Boyle's origins. *I wonder what Annie might know about this.*

The dirt path through the jungle opened back onto the cobblestone road, as clean and pristine as if it'd just been swept. It probably had.

Bored, Cam allowed himself to take in the scenery. Surrounding the volcano, barren, lumpy, brownish ground stretched for miles. Remnants of the last eruption, he'd been told. It all just looked like gritty, wet coffee grounds to him. The lava rock used to build the city's walls must have come from these fields.

Richard said the volcano was dormant, but did any magma

still burn deep down in its center? Could it one day come back to life?

As if it had a mind of its own, his heat called out to the mountain, stretching, commanding. *Obey me. I am you.*

Cam shuddered as he forced his power down deep, deep, deep inside him. He was glad the mountain didn't answer.

Richard must have noticed the direction of his gaze. "Entrancing, isn't it? Are you enjoying the island so far?"

"Immensely so," Cam answered. "But I'm curious—I haven't seen any lakes or streams. How are you supplying the city with water?"

"Underground aquifer, if you can believe it." Richard's dark eyes lit up. "We stumbled across it during a dig. I hired engineers from the mainland to rig a plumbing system to pump water throughout the island. Very sophisticated. Very expensive."

"Very," Cam replied. "Makes me wonder why I'd never heard of New Havana until so recently. Especially with such revolutionary discoveries being made."

"Privacy has been essential to protect the integrity of my work. If the public had gotten wind of my operation before the completion of my patent, Pearl Dust would have been bought at historical rates by others wanting to replicate my work in cheaper, faster ways. New Havana is proof of what it takes to free a society of disease. Once my patent is secure, I will open the island to the public."

"So, that's the reason for buying out all the growers and suppliers?" Cam asked. "To leave nothing for the competition?"

Richard's head snapped around so fast that only a miracle kept it from flying off his shoulders. "Buy out—what in the world are you speaking of?"

Huh. Cam's smile faded. *He doesn't know.*

"Nothing." Cam slapped on another fake grin and let out an even faker laugh. "Just rambling. Where do you get your current supplies from, anyway?"

Richard blinked at him, his mouth slowly turning into a frown. "It can be difficult, with how complicated it is to grow the substance, but I scraped by. Buying from this seller and that. Nowadays, I just give Mr. Price the order, and he takes care of it. A stress off my shoulders. Gives me more time to spend on my research. You can imagine my pleasure at your associates' offer. I was surprised to receive it."

You don't say. Everything—Price, Boyle, the Duskins—it was getting sloppier by the minute. The power inside him crawled through his ribs, angry, making his heart start and stammer. He was starting to feel he hadn't met a single person who had told him the truth since he'd come back to life.

Richard peered down at the shiny, gold pocket watch he'd dug from his coat pocket and tsked. "As much as I'd like to continue this conversation, we'd better hurry." He looked up and chuckled, snapping the watch closed. "Charlotte would never forgive me if I returned you late for her luncheon."

Luncheons . . . noble life's deepest level of hell.

Hours of sampling tiny gourmet dishes, incapable of filling the stomach, and all the tasteless gossip. Not that sailors were tasteful, but at least they were honest. Not to mention all the outrageous clothing in endless, hideous layers. He'd rather run buck naked through the streets than put on another cufflink.

Cam stared into the ornate mirror of his private washroom, having excused himself to bathe and change before lunch was served. Truthfully, he'd just needed a moment to himself. A chance to relax and unwind before he continued through another minefield of torment.

He straightened the rich, brown angora vest he wore over his white dress shirt topped with a slimly cut, plaid three-button suit. He combed back his shorter hair, the tropical sun picking up the bits of gold in his strands.

If he forced himself to stare at his reflection long enough, would he begin to like what he saw? Would he become the high-class, well-bred man looking back at him—the man his father had wanted him to be when he was young?

No.

Cam let out a shaky exhale.

He looked utterly, bloody ridiculous. His brands saw to that. So did the outlaw seed that had grown and spread through his soul. He could pretend, but he could never be part of this world again . . . not really. That world had never really wanted him.

No one had really wanted him.

Just a little longer.

Unfortunately, all his plans relied on Annie coming back to him with a yes. For her to agree to betray the man that fed her, dressed her, and put a roof over her head—sociopathic or not. And he knew from personal experience that it wouldn't be an easy decision, even if she despised him.

More than once, Cam wanted to put a bullet through Resh's skull growing up, but decided otherwise because he felt he owed him. Because Resh had saved his life—given him a life—and had given his mother the mercy she deserved. It was why he was here now, pretending to be something and someone he wasn't.

Resh and Nathan were here somewhere, possibly suffering.

After another quick glance in the mirror, Cam headed down to the first floor and toward the dining room, where the Duskins' younger daughters were cleaning. *Guess they weren't exaggerating when they said they didn't have any servants.*

But they did have cooks. Men and women wearing matching black aprons dodged and weaved around him, carrying heaping platters of food and drink. Cam's stomach growled. The smell was heavenly and ripe with the promise of roasted meats.

Cam scanned the room, eyes narrowing. *Where's Richard's son . . . Nathan?*

"Lord Callahan!" Charlotte called and rushed toward him, her waist impossibly slim in her snug lavender gown. Her dark hair tumbled down her shoulders in a sea of coiled ringlets, her cheeks and lips painted bright pink.

Richard wasn't far behind her, having cleaned up and changed into a somber, black suit—plain compared to his usual attire. Who was he meeting with whom he would feel comfortable showing up so casually?

"You look ravishing, my lady." Cam kissed Charlotte's outstretched hand. "Your husband is the envy of every man here."

"That I am." Richard grinned and kissed her cheek, smudging his chin with pink, then gestured to the party behind them. "Pardon my rudeness once again, my lord. I won't be able to stay." He bowed slightly, sunlight glinting on his oiled black hair. "Charlotte will introduce you to my partners. I hope you don't mind."

"Not at all." Cam's brows furrowed. "I'd hate to make you late for your . . . appointments."

Richard looked like he was about to say something, but Charlotte swooped in and looped her arm through Cam's. "Come with me. I want to introduce you to my dear friends."

Cam gave Richard a quick farewell nod as Charlotte

dragged him deeper into the dining room, strong despite her soft appearance.

"I'm so glad you're here." She lessened her death grip on his elbow. "Finally, someone who shares my taste for trouble. I smile a lot, but all these repeating teatime conversations can grow so very dull."

Cam laughed, taken aback. "You didn't strike me as one who enjoys trouble."

"And how did I strike you?" Charlotte grinned wickedly. "As an angelic housewife that spends her time baking sweets for the sheer pleasure of it, reading romances in my armchair?"

"Well, yes, actually."

Charlotte leaned in closer. "It seems you haven't read me well at all, my lord."

"If reading you is on today's agenda," Cam shot back, equally wicked, "then I'm looking forward to every word and page." *God, that was lame.*

Charlotte laughed anyway, her round cheeks blushing prettily. She proceeded to lead him to a small outdoor parlor adjacent to the dining room. The soft whites, greens, and buttery yellows of the décor were a striking contrast to the dark, saturated colors of the mansion's interior. A delicate glass table sat at the center, surrounded by several women. Seated among them were Julian Price and Frank Boyle, lions prowling around the hills of grazing sheep.

Frank bloody Boyle.

Time slowed as Cam's eyes gobbled up every hideous ounce of him, all the details exactly as he remembered. The pointy ferret chin, tomato-red brand striped down the center of his face, thin lips set with that same sneer.

Kill him. Something shifted in the way the heat bubbled in Cam's core—shifted into something deeper, primal. *Kill him.* A sweet, seductive purr, begging to be set free. *Kill him.*

It crawled under his skin, moving with a mind of its own. Smoke seeped from Cam's clenched fist, and he inhaled slowly.

No, not yet. As tempting a thought as it was. His heat growled back at him. *Soon, soon.*

Frank's eyes rose from where they had been set on the breasts of the woman across from him and drifted to Cam's smoking hands. His eyes narrowed as he next studied Cam's face.

No recognition—none—only bored suspicion.

Elias assured him they wouldn't recognize him. That the blood-soaked sailor they'd murdered was a far cry from the high-standing Revenant he was now.

Cam wasn't convinced . . . and a small part of him hoped they'd remember. Remember what they did. Remember the good men they'd killed. So he could just slaughter them and get all this over with. Cam's heat purred again, but this time he just tried to shrug it away.

Julian noticed him and Charlotte then, and Cam could almost feel his internal groan. He pushed himself up, scraping his chair legs against the parlor floor. "Julian Price, my lord," he introduced himself, extending his hand. Cam shook it. Julian's palms were dry and callused. "So good to finally meet you."

Was he so . . . stiff back on *The Nightlady*?

"A pleasure." Cam avoided Julian's eyes. They hadn't had close contact back on the ship, but Julian had more of an awareness about him than Frank. That might end up being a problem.

Charlotte cleared her throat. "Other than a wonderful business partner, Mr. Price has become a close friend." She gestured to Frank. "As has Mr. Boyle."

Kill him.

No.

Frank smiled broadly—an attempt at charm, no doubt—and tipped his cap. "Good to have another fire lover around. Maybe we can do a little compare and contrast later, eh?"

Cam's entire body twitched. *Enjoy your stay in hell.* Lying, useless piece of sewage.

Kill him.

Reflexively, Cam's hand slipped to where his revolver waited in his waistband, carrying his mother's last heirloom.

Frank jolted from his chair as he caught the movement, hand moving toward his own pistol. Julian was on his feet as well, arm extended, as if he meant to block the attack.

Smiling, Cam slipped a pack of cigarettes from his inner coat pocket. "Sure—need a light?" Cam didn't smoke, but Vernon had insisted he keep them as cover if he started smoking out of the nose or needed a fun party trick.

Frank's body relaxed, but it didn't reach his eyes. "Yeah, okay." He took a cigarette and lit it on his thumb. After a long drag, he blew a series of tight smoke rings.

Julian slowly returned to his seat, watching them cautiously.

"Oh my!" The beautiful, heavy-set blonde beside him squealed. "I'll never get tired of that. Who needs a lighter when we have you two around?"

"Lord Callahan," Charlotte said. "This is Lady Helena Appleton. She and her family moved to the island, as investors, about a year ago."

Cam gave Helena a bow, and she smiled back with dimpled cheeks.

"And this is Lady Amelia Carter." Charlotte touched the second woman's shoulder. "Her family has been with us from the start."

Amelia's smile was tight-lipped, her skin a deep ebony, and her eyes a lovely caramel brown.

"Carter?" Cam asked. "As in the wife of Commander Carter? Stern look, nice mustache?"

"That's him," Amelia said with a groan. "He's also a good, honorable man. We are thankful to be here, living among the Duskins' generosity. My people are not so accepted in the Western countries, where I'm from." Her knowing eyes brushed over Cam's brands. "I'm sure you understand how unpleasant discrimination can be."

"I do now," Cam replied. "It's a shame. Your people don't deserve such heartless treatment."

"Neither do yours."

"Thank you."

Charlotte cleared her throat. "Now that we're all acquainted, it's high time we eat."

The pretty, red-headed girl in the corner jumped to life as her mother spoke. Cam hadn't noticed her until now. What was her name again . . . . Jenny? She skittered from the room in response to Charlotte's pointed stare. Frank's gaze followed her as well—a little too closely.

After pulling Charlotte's chair out for her, Cam took a seat beside her, tucking the long tails of his suitcoat beneath him. "Will your husbands not be joining us?"

Julian watched every move, his hands wringing.

Jenny returned a moment later, carrying a platter filled with glasses of sparkling, white wine. Cam sipped his water.

Helena rolled her eyes. "They're off hunting, of course. Always hunting or working, you know how it goes."

"What is there to hunt?" Cam asked. "I didn't see any game animals on our excursion to the lava fields this morning."

"Who knows," Helena said with a shrug, "But you've joined us just in time, Lord Callahan. Mr. Price was just telling us a fascinating story."

"I can tell it another time." Julian shifted uncomfortably.

"I'm sure you don't want to hear it over again from the beginning."

"We don't mind." Amelia sipped her wine. "Please, go on."

"Yes, *please*." Cam rested his chin in his palm. "Go on."

Dull. So, so dull. Julian picked at his cuticles. It was hard to believe this man was the same creature that helped turn *The Nightlady* into a pile of sticks.

That Julian had been powerful, confident, and dangerous. But now, he just seemed weary.

Like he was sick of life and everyone in it.

"If you insist," Julian sighed. "I was just telling these young ladies of a mission Mr. Boyle and I carried out a couple of weeks ago, well overseas."

"Oh?" Cam said. *You mean when you burned down my livelihood?* "Do tell."

Either Julian didn't notice Cam's mocking tone or didn't care. He just nodded and continued. "We've been working to secure trade relations in the South to help in the distribution of the Pearl Dust—once you and Lord Duskin reach an agreement, of course. Under the protection of Lord Duskin's new procedures, there will never be fear of another pandemic again."

"Southerners are a superstitious lot." Cam rapped his fingers on the table. "I'm surprised they'd agree to meet with you."

"I don't understand," Julian said with furrowed brows.

Frank's eyes peeled away from the Jenny girl long enough to shoot Cam a suspicious glare.

"With all the attacks on Pearl Dust shipments in recent months." Cam sighed dramatically. "Some might say the gig is cursed."

Frank snorted, spewing crumbs over his hideous maroon

blazer. It clashed horribly with his hair. "You're an idiot. Coincidences don't mean curses. Pirates . . . all it is."

Julian's skin paled.

Amelia's jaw dropped. "Mr. Boyle!"

"It's quite all right, I've been called worse." Cam patted Amelia's arm as his lips curled into a half smile. *Go ahead, give me another reason to kill you.* He fixed his gaze on Frank, who just stared back defiantly. "The way I hear it, ships are turning up empty. Crew gone. Probably dead. Must be ghosts or an inside job."

"Nonsense," Frank spat. "Ships are raided all the time."

"What makes you think they're dead?" Charlotte raised a brow. "The government hasn't released an official report. Nor have the papers, for that matter."

"Just a feeling." Cam met Julian's eye for just a little too long. *Where are you keeping them?* "Dead men are much easier to care for than living ones."

"There is a good chance they're still alive," Julian said. "Disappearances are still common in the East, for example, where human trafficking is a common practice."

"We're not in the East."

"Again, it was just an example."

"Ah," Cam said. "I guess you would know, voice of experience and all."

Frank and Julian exchanged tense glances.

"Truly awful." Helena nibbled on a tart and shook her head. "All those poor souls."

It was stupid—truly stupid—but part of Cam wanted them to know, wanted them to see their ruin coming. As he watched them and this whole charade, some little part of the plan clicked into place. He would save what remained of his crew, he'd get the stolen drugs back, but God knew he'd pull every brick of this tainted building down in the process.

Leave them with nothing left to live on but ash.

Just then, the kitchen staff swooped in, arms loaded with steaming portions of roasted chicken and fresh garden vegetables, drizzled with oil and vinegar. Jenny fell in behind them, helping to distribute plates. Frank's gaze promptly returned to her backside. The girl took a seat beside her mother.

Charlotte clapped her hands together happily. "Excellent! Let's dig in!"

Cam packed his mouth full of chicken, chatting animatedly with the women, while Julian and Frank picked at their food, sulking.

This was turning out to be a pleasant afternoon, all in all.

CHAPTER 16
ANNIE

Annie's knuckles showed white as she gripped the edge of the kitchen sink. Lady Duskin's hands had been here such a short time ago, dripping little Nathan's blood down the pristine white cabinets. Scrub marks still showed through the fresh coat of paint.

Outside the window, lightning bugs danced in what remained of the summer dawn.

Maybe she should wear the petal-pink satin day dress they'd given her for her last birthday. A gift of obligation—what a mother and father are supposed to do for their eldest daughter.

Daughter. Slave. Pawn. She wasn't sure what she was. Annie's hand slid to the satchel at her side, fingering the small vial within through the fabric. A humid breeze trickled in from the opened windows, tickling her hair over her damp forehead. Nervous sweat.

She'd imagined one day it would come to this, but not now . . . not so soon. Concentrated, ground hemlock mixed with wood alcohol, for potency, should do the trick.

Hopefully, she bought enough. It hadn't been cheap. If not, a knife to the heart would have to suffice.

Maybe she should wear the white dress. It would let the blood stand out nicely.

A hysterical giggle escaped Annie's lips. *When did I become so dramatic?* She stroked the jade pendant around her neck. For some reason, she couldn't bring herself to put it away. Not yet. Maybe the captain would be there to watch when it happened and keep her company.

It was nice to know she may not be alone when she died.

A loud crash and short scream, followed by scuffling, drew Annie's attention out the window and across the lawn. Her breath caught as her body stiffened, ready to run.

More muffled screaming.

Annie closed her eyes, exhaling. She should stay inside, mind her own business, but what did it matter anymore? She wouldn't be here much longer.

From the kitchen, Annie crept out to the front porch. The sun was just beginning to paint the sky in swirls of pinks and oranges, threatening to be smothered out by the dark clouds approaching on the horizon. Moisture clung to her like a second skin, promising another tempid day.

Annie leaned against the porch's gold-trimmed banister, stilling herself to hear above the chattering of morning birds and the crash of the ocean, far, far below. After several minutes, there was nothing more than that—white noise. *This is dangerous.*

She let out a low but piercing whistle.

More silence. She was about to head back inside when she was met by the sound of indistinct muttering to her right. *The woodshed?* More than one voice, one lower-pitched than the other.

They can't hurt me. Annie stalked across the manicured

lawn, too numb to care who saw her, the damp grass sharp against her blistered heels. The walk back from town last night had been a long one. The carriage hadn't waited for her.

Every step she took closer to the shed, the air grew hotter and drier, like all the moisture had been sucked from the sky with a sponge. Annie swallowed, trying to wet her throat, but desert heat dried out her eyes and nostrils. The shed was not too far, visible now in the pre-dawn gloom.

Laughter—a horrid, piercing laughter pulsed in her ears—threatening to burst her eardrums, and the shed door slammed open like it had been kicked.

Out stepped Frank Boyle—slicking back his rumpled red hair, and tucking it under his ruddy, brown cap. A thrill of adrenaline ran through Annie's blood and muscles. *Monster.* Flight instinct told her to run, to duck out of sight before Frank noticed her, but she didn't have time. Didn't have the energy.

Just take it. Annie straightened and didn't stop moving. Frank's gaze found her, and he grinned. She fought back a grimace, and his smile grew wicked.

"Look who it is." Frank dug a flask out of his coat pocket and took a swig. She could smell the liquor from here. "Richie was pretty pissed when you didn't show up last night. Where were ya'?"

Annie's thoughts flashed back to the cold, calm way Mr. Price spoke to his inferiors, then mimicked it. *Deep breath.* She wiped the emotion off her face. "That's none of your concern."

"Icy, icy." Frank made a mock hissing sound, then laughed. "You won't be so stuffy when you find the surprise we left you." He jerked his chin back toward the shed and chuckled. "And when you see the mess I left in there." More of that awful laughter. He blew her a kiss and waggled his fingers. "Good day, Annie-wannie. Always a pleasure."

Annie remained rigid as Frank pushed past her, scalding

even through his jacket. *Don't look at him. Don't react.* She kept her eyes locked on the shed, listening as he headed back into the mansion, still laughing.

Annie walked, trying to keep her mind off her pounding heart.

For being the same kind of monster, Mr. Boyle and Lord Callahan seemed so different. Frank was an itchy, burning spider-bite, where Lord Callahan . . . he was blazing fire on a frigid night. A charming, smooth-tongued tempter come to destroy her.

Three days. That's all she'd been given. He was the reason her life had to end so soon. She'd planned on waiting until Lord Duskin had grown tired of her. Annie's fists clenched. Years or days, it didn't make a difference. Death was death, and it was coming for them all. She might as well get it over with.

Up ahead, a small whimpering sound escaped the shed.

Breathe. She shook the stiffness from her limbs. It was too late to turn back.

Whimpering turned to sobs. Her hand hesitated over the handle. *It doesn't matter, it doesn't matter.* Too bad trouble always seemed to find her. *You have three days, Kitten.*

Annie's stomach reeled as she pushed open the door.

Small amounts of daylight wormed its way through the cracks in the shed's paneling, illuminating the cobwebs hanging from the corners of the doorway. In the back, partially hidden behind some well-used garden equipment, Jenny was slumped against a cord of firewood.

Burned.

Every part of her was left blistered and singed, the worst of it concentrated around her shoulders and inner thighs, exposed by the holes burnt through her white, satin night-gown. A burned handprint lay over her chin and part of her lower lip.

I hate him. I hate him. Annie kept her expression blank. "Morning, Jenny."

God bless her, Jenny pushed a strand of ruby hair from her eyes and managed a smile. "M-morning, Annie—" She gasped, choking back a sob. "I . . . I really hurt."

Annie chewed her lip. "Did he . . . ?"

"No," Jenny exhaled. "Almost. Your whistle stopped him." Attempting to stand, Jenny stumbled and fell back against the wood. Her mouth opened and closed, a fish gulping for air, as her hand flew to her throat, eyes round and wild.

She's going into shock. Annie grabbed an old wool sheet from the corner and wrapped it tightly around Jenny's shoulders before kneeling in front of her, holding the girl's ankles. "It's over," she whispered. *I sound so cold.* "Block it out. Nothing happened. It was all just a nightmare. Your bed sheets caught on fire. That's all."

Between gasps, Jenny looked stunned. "M-my bed sheets?"

Annie squeezed her ankles tighter, holding Jenny's stare. "Yes, your bed sheets. You know what happens to children who tell lies."

Jenny's gold eyes grew wider.

"Especially when the person being lied about is an even better liar than the child." Annie released her grip. "Then if that person goes and tells their own lies . . . the child might get punished. Killed, even."

Nodding slightly, Jenny inhaled, slowing her breathing. "I fell asleep with a candle beside my bed."

Annie forced a smile. "How unfortunate."

"W-what should I do now?"

Annie looked her over quickly. The wounds on her thighs were worse than she initially thought. "Can you stand?"

Jenny tested a little of her weight on her legs, then winced. "No, not yet. It hurts too much."

I hate him. "Come on, then." Annie reached for her. "We need to get you cleaned up."

"No." Jenny pulled away and wrapped her arms around her knees. "I don't want to leave yet. Can't we wait?"

"The cooks will be starting breakfast soon. We can't wait," Annie said. There was nothing in the shed she could use to move her. "I'll have to carry you."

After a pause, Jenny nodded, wrapping the sheet tighter around herself as Annie hauled her up into her arms. Trying to hold back a scream, Jenny hissed behind clenched teeth as Annie's grip pressed against her wounds.

Annie's shoulders and back strained against the familiar weight of a body, something she was forced to move often. *At least this one is living.* Thankfully, Jenny was as slender as she was.

Slowly, Annie pushed the shed door open with her hip and peeked out. The sun had risen higher in that short time, but the coast was clear. "Whatever you do," Annie whispered as they started across the lawn, "don't scream."

Jenny whimpered, tearing up, and she bit down on the collar of her nightie.

Just a bit further. A lie, but one she often told herself. Her thighs and arms burned with every step as she hauled Jenny back to the kitchens.

As she headed toward the pantry, Jenny started to squirm. "Not down there," she said in a rushed breath. "Not in there."

"Hush." Annie shifted Jenny's weight, then kicked the pantry open. "I can't clean your wounds without supplies, and my supplies are downstairs."

Downstairs . . . such a nice way to describe the hell that grew down in those tunnels. The disease, terror, and hopelessness.

"Please." Jenny began to tear up again. "Please, *no.*"

"Quiet." Annie kicked the lever over, and the pantry's back panel swung open. Without a second's hesitation, she hauled Jenny deep into the darkness.

Jenny's warm body twitched in her strained arms, reacting to the droplets of chilly water falling from the lava rock ceiling. *Too warm.* Sweat rolled down Annie's forehead and sides from the excursion. She had to find a way to cool Jenny's skin, and quickly, before the pain got worse.

Shadows moved in the darkness—behind her, beside her, they slithered across the ceiling. Not Elain. Not the captain. Just a few of the many angry souls stuck down in these tunnels, confused as to why their lives were taken so suddenly and violently.

The shadows grew closer as Jenny's breath grew shallower. Despite her throbbing muscles, Annie lengthened her stride, wetness pooling in her slippers as her blisters burst open. *Just a bit further.*

The bright orbs of the light broke through the still blackness as they approached the gaslights, further down the tunnel. Jenny sighed in relief.

Once in the teaching room, Annie set her down on the cold metal table in the center, the same one where Elain's body had lain. Did Jenny know her sister had died here? She and Elain hadn't been related, but they were as close as two people could be in their circumstances.

More movement in the corner. Annie glanced over her shoulder. Elain peered out from the shadows, her stringy blonde hair partially covering her gray, sunken face, weeping.

I'll do everything I can to save her. Annie only hoped Elain could hear her thoughts. *I promise.*

Over the years on the island, Annie had accumulated a large collection of herbs, tinctures, and medicines—it had become a bit of a hobby. Lord Duskin had been kind enough to let her keep her treasures in the cupboards lining the teaching room's back wall.

As she opened the first cabinet, her eyes fell on the little black box in the corner—dusty and partially hidden beneath half-used rolls of gauze. Her cache of stolen things she hoped to sell one day. Again, her fingers found the pendant around her neck. *I'm not ready.* Maybe she will put it in there one day, but not yet.

She grabbed the gauze and shoved it under her arm.

Jenny let out a loud whimper. When Annie looked, she was wiping her eyes with the corner of her singed dress.

"Stop crying," Annie said, too sharply. "Don't."

"The table is just cold, is all." Jenny sniffled, frowning. "It hurts."

"I know." Annie continued to rummage through the cabinets. After finding the jars she was looking for, she grabbed a mortar and pestle and unloaded her supplies on the table.

Without giving her a chance to protest, Annie lifted Jenny and sat her down inside the room's wide, steel surgical sink—the size of a small bathtub. Annie reached for the faucet, but Jenny stopped her. "No—"

"We need to run the worst of the burns under cold water." Annie jerked her arm away. "Sit still."

"Please." Jenny was on the verge of another panic attack. "It will hur—"

"It's going to hurt no matter what," Annie snapped. "Hold still, come on."

It's not that she wanted to be heartless. But if she faltered —showed emotion for even a moment—she might break. No weakness . . . not when the images of little Nathan's opened throat were so near in her mind. Jenny had to become another patient, at least for the time being, so she wouldn't crack.

Again, Annie reached for the faucet handle. This time,

Jenny scrunched her eyes shut, clamping her hand over her mouth to hold back a scream as a stream of cool water poured over her ruined skin. She opened her mouth to shriek, but no noise came from her throat. After a tense moment, filled with full-body tremors, Jenny's shoulders finally began to relax.

Annie breathed out, willing her pulse to slow. "It will help."

Rocking in the stream of water, Jenny nodded as she took long, slow breaths.

After turning back to the table, Annie began sorting through the jars she'd taken from the cupboard. She placed strips of soaked aloe leaves and cubed beeswax in the mortar, then added a few spoonfuls of bran. *I hate him. I hate all of them.*

Lord Duskin, Charlotte, Julian—all the lords and ladies that stayed in the estates, using the children and staff like soulless toys. All her pain—all the battered walls of her being—went into grinding that poultice. But not her tears.

She wouldn't cry again. Not for them.

What makes you think I'd betray them, just like that?

Because you hate them.

"You can stop now." Annie slammed her pestle down on the table, flicking green goo all over the metal surface. She sighed and wiped it up with her sleeve. "Come here, please. When you're ready."

Behind her, the faucet shut off, followed by the wet patter of Jenny's approaching feet. Slowly, she crawled onto the table, her cheeks and eyes tomato red from crying.

"Here." Annie held out her hand, and Jenny rested her elbow in it, barely flinching as Annie began spreading the poultice over her burns. "Put this on three times a day, and keep the wounds clean the best you can," Annie said. "It's going to scar. That can't be helped, and don't pop the blisters. The fluid in them keeps bacteria out."

Jenny clenched her teeth as Annie moved up to the hand-print on her face. "How do you know all this?"

"Necessity." Annie grabbed her scalpel and cut back a bit of dead flesh before Jenny could protest. "And lots of experience."

Jenny managed a smile. "It's too bad we're here, isn't it?"

Annie looked up from the burn on Jenny's chin. "What do you mean?"

"If things had been different, I meant," Jenny answered shakily. "I would have liked to make quilts. For the elderly, you know?"

Despite herself, Annie burst into laughter. "Quilts?"

"Uh-huh." Jenny's eyes lit up. "Lots of quilts. I would own a shop. And you . . . you would have been such a wonderful nurse. You're always helping people." She let out a sigh. "Elain loved you for it."

Annie tried not to let the tremble in her fingers show. *She loved me?* Sweet Elain, with her flowers and her pretty songs. She never knew. Annie bit down on the inside of her cheek. She wouldn't cry.

"But we *are* here." Annie handed the poultice to Jenny so she could finish the last of her wounds between her legs. "It's better not to entertain useless thoughts."

Jenny winced as she prodded at her thigh. "But what if we weren't?"

If we weren't, you would still be playing in your mother's garden, innocent and untouched. I would probably be at the bottom of the sea.

"Stop it." Annie snapped, then forced her voice to soften. "There are matches in the upper left cabinet. When you're done there, set your bed on fire. Go to Lady Duskin after and tell her what happened. She won't take you to the medical wing, so people don't get suspicious. Don't forget to use the medicine."

Jenny's eyes widened. "And what about you?"

"I have to start my chores." Annie turned and headed for the door. "I'll see you in time for class."

"Annie?"

When she looked back, Jenny gave her a strange look. "Yes?"

"It's Saturday. There is no class today."

"Oh." *How could I have forgotten?* Annie blinked. "Silly me. I'll see you later, then. Remember, three times a day."

*I*t would have been better if he'd killed her.

Annie measured small amounts of Pearl Dust, gently mixing it into the bucket of warm oats she'd prepared for the patients, as she did twice a day. Lord Duskin stored the drugs in a separate chamber, across the hall from the teaching room. Along with insulating the room itself, the Pearl Dust was kept in rows and rows of lined barrels to keep the moisture out. Not only did the insulation keep the room dry, but it left it insufferably hot. Her skin itched, her lungs scratchy from trace amounts of pearl residue floating around her head.

Annie sat back on her stool, back aching, and rubbed her eyes. No one would believe all that damage was caused by a candle, but maybe not calling out Mr. Boyle would buy Jenny some time. Maybe Lord Duskin would see her for her loyalty instead of being damaged goods.

Even then, she only had so long. Jenny was a marr on his flawless world now. It would take time, but when he finally looked up from his specimens and samples, he'd notice. Once all the guests and distractions were gone. When it was only them again, he'd get rid of her. Just like Elain.

A shudder ran through Annie's limbs as a chill pooled

around her ankles. She breathed in slowly, lowering her chin just enough to look at her feet. They were hidden beneath a layer of mist.

Not again. She wasn't in the mood.

The captain stood in the doorway, but this time, his body was a pale grey instead of black. His face blurred instead of rotten, more like Elain.

I don't have time for this. Annie's lips pressed into a thin line. "What do you want?"

A swirl of silver mist formed into a cigar, which he pressed to his lips, curling his finger for her to follow.

If she hadn't been heading out anyway, she wouldn't have bothered to acknowledge him. Bucket of oats in hand, Annie brushed past him, heading back into the tunnels. If he wanted to follow, he could follow, but she had work to do.

Follow he did.

His whispers followed her from one gaslight to the next. His fingers brushed against her in the spaces of darkness between the lights. Annie kept her chin high, her gate steady. *He will not frighten me. Not today.*

He waited for her at the entrance to the dungeons, puffing on his cigar. Inside, the patients were moaning and crying for her, banging their bowls against their cell bars. Hungry, but more than anything, desperate for their next fix.

The captain sauntered ever slowly down the hall, hands behind his back, stopping only when he stood outside Lowana's cell. His blurred eyes met hers before he faded away. They looked almost . . . remorseful. Sad.

No. Warm oats splattered the stone floor as the bucket fell from her fingers.

She couldn't feel her legs. The lump forming in her throat threatened to strangle her.

You won't be so stuffy when you find the surprise we left you.

Lord Duskin wouldn't do that to her, he wouldn't—not after all they've been through.

Annie willed her feet to carry her forward, treading every step. Mr. Boyle was lying to her, trying to antagonize her. There was no way they could have known.

But, of course, they did.

"Hello, sweetie." Lowana glanced up as Annie peered into her cell. "It's not as bad as it looks."

Of course, it was much, much worse.

A bandage covered Lowana's bicep. Annie didn't have to ask to know what was beneath it. *He said no more experiments until the guests left. He promised.*

Behind her, a male voice said, "I'm sorry."

Annie turned.

Nathan's bruised face stared back at her from across the hall. "That piece of trash, Boyle, asked which of us you liked best. I—" He rubbed his battered jaw. More than one of his knuckles were bleeding. "Don't get me wrong, I hate you, girl, but I did like *her*. I'm sorry."

"Don't worry, hon." Lowana smiled her toothless smile. "With all the phlegm in my lungs, it was going to happen one way or another. I'm too old for this gristle, anyway. Good riddance."

So much death. Annie remembered the vial of hemlock and slipped it from her satchel.

I'm done. Let it end. I don't want to do this anymore.

Lowana was right—at her age, she wouldn't last more than a couple of days. The vial's cork popped off easily with the scrap of her thumbnail. Annie pressed the vial to her lips, her skin tingling where the mixture touched.

If only things had been different.

Deal with me, or deal with the Duskins—your choice.

Choices. For the first time in her life, she had one. Neither of her options were ideal, nor promised safety, but it was her decision to make—hers.

Hers.

Mine.

"Here." Annie reached between the bars and placed the vial in Lowana's open hand. "You need this more than I do."

Lowana's eyes never left hers as she tipped the contents of the vial down her throat, strong and unafraid. The old woman smacked her lips. "Do me a favor, honey."

"Anything."

"Make him suffer."

CHAPTER 17
CAMDEN

Mr. Bennett,

It seems that our mutual friend is unaware of any of the recent events happening at sea—or refuses to believe it. Your former associate seems to have an agenda of his own. What that is yet, I have yet to discover. Regarding the product in question—

Hang it all.

Cam slammed his pen down, splattering ink over his black oak desk. At least it wouldn't stain. He crumpled the paper, tossing it over his shoulder. More material for the tower of failed letters piling up on his bedroom floor.

Cam pinched the bridge of his nose and exhaled. Where did he start? What could he say? As terrible as he was at writing with such subtlety, he wasn't sure how much he really trusted Thomas with what he had learned.

Cam took the diamond from his coat pocket—the one he'd swiped from Vernon's hut—and rolled it between his fingers. He'd already sent a note to Thomas. They planned to meet on Sunday. Cam wished it were sooner, but he had too many meetings planned with Richard to sneak away before then. Discussions of future profit margins, packaging, and scheduling product shipments. It was exhausting just to think about. Especially when he was making it all up as he went.

Cam rested his head in his hands, watching the ice shift in his glass of water, condensation dripping down the side. Such a luxury—ice and chilled glasses.

I should be drinking coffee. Something to clear his head. He'd already taken in more information than he had the energy to process, but one thing was for sure: he had to learn more about Julian Price. To figure out what reason he'd have to steal away so much Pearl Dust if Richard hadn't ordered it.

It has to be for the money.

He must be stashing away the drugs he'd stolen, just to try to sell it back to Lord Duskin once his patent went public and was desperate for product. It was an easy story to believe, an easier one to spin, but . . .

Something just doesn't seem right. With a groan, Cam let his head fall and hit the table. It didn't hurt enough.

A soft knock came from the door, barely audible.

Blazes. Cam looked up. *Could it be? It must be.*

The knocking came again. Cam jumped to his feet, tucking his button-down back into his trousers, and crossed the room in two strides. *Please, please, please.* He yanked open the door, his heart pounding in his throat.

His initial reaction at seeing Annie standing in the doorway was one of intense relief, but that feeling quickly fell into one of shock.

She looked like a corpse. Along with being covered head to

toe in fresh mud and her nails caked black, her expression was dead. Vacant. Not really looking past him, but through him, to some distant place no one could reach her.

"Um." Cam shifted awkwardly. "Want to come in?"

Annie walked into his room without a word and sat gently on the foot of his bed. She just stared at the floor as Cam returned to his desk.

"Can I get you a drink?" Cam asked. "Wine? Maybe a fifth of whisky?"

"No," she said. Flat. Lifeless.

"Okay . . ." Cam rapped his fingers. "What have you been doing, may I ask?"

"Digging."

"I can see that."

Finally, she looked at him. "Then why'd you ask?"

"Oh, I don't know." Cam shrugged, crossing his legs. "Just trying to make small talk. Have you thought about my offer?"

Annie nodded, chewing on her dirty thumbnail.

"And?"

Slowly, her silver eyes met his. "I will work for you . . ." She hesitated. "B-but I have conditions."

Praise God. He needed to go to church more. Cam leaned on his elbow. "Let's hear it."

The dim light shining from the lamp on the bedside table illuminated the purple shadows beneath her eyes, the hollowness of her high cheekbones. *She hasn't been sleeping.*

"I want a new identity and citizenship on the mainland—out west," she said in a rush. "Also, a position in one of their local hospitals. I want the patients freed, and my sister, Jenny, comes with us when we leave."

Well . . . that's not what I expected. Cam exhaled, raising his brow. "Anything else?"

"Frank Boyle dies."

Cam burst into laughter. *Girl after my own heart.* "I will gladly kill that meathead for you." He shifted in his chair. "But it won't be easy to falsify records well enough to fool the West's harbor customs, let alone their medical community."

"You'll figure it out if you want my help," Annie muttered. "Or I'll go to the Duskins and let them deal with you."

"Ooh, an ultimatum." Cam bridged his fingers. "I like your style. Sounds like a deal."

"Y-you'll do it?" She seemed surprised. The first emotion he'd seen from her.

"If—"

Her face fell.

Cam raised his finger. "I'll get you to the mainland. Get you a job if that's what you want—but I need one thing from you."

There it was again . . . that deep-seated hate. Annie gave him the same look she'd given him when they'd first met. She picked at a loose thread on his bed sheet, waiting for him to continue.

She thinks I want to use her body. "Get your head out of the gutter." Cam gave her a cheeky smile, but bile rose in his throat. "All I want is your unfaltering loyalty."

She watched him warily. "Loyalty?"

"All of it," Cam said slowly. "No hidden motives, no secrets. You be honest and upfront with me, and I'll do the same for you. This doesn't have to be unpleasant, yes?"

"If you say so," Annie said after a few quiet moments. "But what assurance do I have that you won't just take what you want and leave me here with the rest of them?"

Cam paused, thinking, then his eyes fell to the black leather cord around her neck. "That necklace."

Annie reached for her throat.

"There's your assurance. That's solid, pure jade. Easily

worth a few hundred bucks—or more if you find the right fence. If I screw this up, you can keep that as collateral."

Annie fingered the pendant, brows pinched, then she sighed. "Okay."

"Excellent." Cam stood and extended his hand. "Deal's done, then. Welcome to the seedy underbelly of the world."

Hesitantly, Annie reached out and shook it. Her palm was cold and gritty with dirt. "Deal's done."

"Very good." Cam grabbed some of his paper and scribbled out a quick note. "My associate and I are having a meeting soon. Here's the time and the address. Don't be late."

Annie briefly scanned the note before tucking it into her bodice. *Good, she can read.* Just like that, her mask returned. "Is there anything else I can do for you, my lord?"

Cam opened the bedroom door for her. "Yes, actually. Don't ever call me that again. Just Camden is fine. Or Cam if you prefer."

Annie paused in the doorway, craning her neck back to look at him. *God, she's beautiful.* "You're not really a lord, are you? You don't really own pearl groves?"

Cam shrugged. "Yes and no. Not everything I've told your precious Lord Duskin is a lie." Something struck him then. Something that had been bugging him. "I haven't seen that Nathan kid running around with the others. Is he sick?"

"Don't ask about him." Annie shot him a look that was nothing short of vicious. "Ever again."

Cam swallowed. "As you wish."

She turned to leave, then paused. "You were right before. I do hate them."

"Oh, I know," Cam crooned as he closed the door. Blank papers littered his desk, begging for him to get to work. Cam sat, picking up a fresh paper. *At least I have something interesting to write about now.*

CHAPTER 18
ANNIE

This is dangerous. Annie bundled herself deeper into her coat, keeping up a quick stride. The sun's rays were just beginning to fade away the night's stars, but she still imagined them watching her. Judging.

It's a good thing the Duskins were such late-nighters. It gave her the whole morning to get real work done. Besides, if they woke and found her missing, they would just assume she was at church. Regularly, they allowed her to attend one of the chapels in town—one that followed the less ceremonial Northern customs—and didn't complain too much that she didn't come to their private sermons.

But it's too late to turn back now. Annie exhaled as she made her way toward the far-east corner of the market square. A narrow alley waited in the shadows, but no ghosts waited within it. Not today. It was Sunday, and even the worst of spirits respected the Lord's special day.

If it wasn't for the address she'd been given, she would have never noticed the alley in the first place.

I shouldn't be here. She pushed onward, allowing the gloom

166

to swallow her. Annie clenched her fist, her nails biting into her palm. *Yes . . . I should be.* She'd made her bed. Now she must lie in it—even if it means lying in the dirt with him.

She turned a sharp corner and paused. Several yards deeper into the alley, Lord Callahan sat on a bench outside a colorfully painted establishment. He checked a small silver watch, his expression serious. The orange brands beneath his eyes glowed brightly, then faded in quick succession. He stood, running a hand through his uncombed hair, then shoved his watch back in his pocket.

He doesn't think I'm going to show up. Annie held her ground, fighting the urge to run. She disliked him—he was so horrifically vain and self-imposing. Acting like he owned the world and everything in it. She hated what he was even more. But the thing that bothered her most of all was that she wasn't afraid of him. Not like she was of the others.

Lord Callahan—Camden—was strange to her. With his blunt words, it would be easy to believe all that rubbish about honesty and loyalty. Part of her even wanted to believe it, but the sailor Nathan was right. Human beings weren't meant to come back from the dead. From her experience, Revenant were liars, murderers, and monsters. Frank Boyle, and the beast that killed her family, were all three.

Don't let your guard down. Inhaling, Annie stepped out into the alley. "Good morning."

Cam whipped around, his green eyes intensely scanning her face, before his full lips broke into a smile. "Good morning, Kitten. You're looking as lovely as ever."

Don't give him any ammunition. Annie kept quiet.

He wore simple clothing today—a brown pea-coat and matching trousers—a startling change from his usual extravagant attire. It looked . . . good on him.

He cocked his head in that predatory way, looking her up

and down, then smiled. "Are you ready? It's too early. I need some coffee."

Annie just nodded, then followed him to the building's door, glancing up at the sign overhead. Wilkins' Whistle. The caricature on the sign was drinking. It took everything she had not to roll her eyes. Of course, he'd want to meet at a tavern.

Gently, Cam knocked on the tavern door. There was a lumpy white spot in the center that looked like it had recently been patched. Cam kept eying it.

On the other side, there seemed to be a lot of commotion and shouting. The smell of booze seeped from the available space between the hinges. She would expect this type of behavior at night, but at this time of the morning? They should all be passed out by now.

After a minute or two, and several loud crashes later, the battered door swung open. A slender gentleman stood in the doorway, his light blond hair gelled into an artful swirl over his forehead. A dried, pink orchid was pinned to the lapel of his gingham suit. "Ah, Mr. Barnes." He dabbed sweat from his temples. "Good to see you."

"And you, Thomas." Cam nodded.

Barnes?

The man named Thomas' lips pinched as his gaze fell onto her. Annie forced herself to stare back, cold and unflinching.

"I assume," Thomas drawled, looking back to Cam, "that you have some cute explanation for why you brought *her* here?"

How does he know me? She knew for a fact she'd never seen him. She would have remembered.

"I don't do explanations," Cam said. "Or apologies, for that matter. Are you going to let us in?"

"Of course," Thomas ducked out of the way, ushering them inside.

Annie took one step inside and froze. The air within the tavern was too sticky and thick to breathe, the inside just as colorful as the out. Dozens of women were packed into the cramped space, seated around circular, corkboard tables. They laughed, shrieked, and shuffled cards as huge plates of steaming entrees were passed around.

"Are they. . ." Annie blinked. "Gambling?"

Thomas chuckled. "What else is there to do on the weekends, hmm?"

"Gambling is illegal," she said. A burst of snorting laughter erupted from the table next to her.

"So is the betrayal of familial trust, but here we are." Cam winked. He turned to Thomas. "Got any coffee? I'm desperate, mate."

"Trot upstairs, and I'll have some brought up," Thomas shouted to be heard over the raucous. "I have to finish a few things down here first, if you don't mind."

"Not at all." Cam offered Annie his arm. "Shall we?"

Annie crossed her arms and ignored him. He followed her up the staircase, the heat rolling off him making her sweat. Hot but a comfortable warmth. Not the scalding aura Frank produced.

No, Cam's was more like the well-loved hearth inside the cottage she and her family shared when she was young. Familiar, safe. Annie chomped at her lip, hard enough to draw blood, bringing herself back to reality. *It's part of his façade. Keep your guard up.*

The loft above the tavern was surprisingly demure. White walls and a lush blue carpet that matched the patchwork curtains over the window. A small bed sat tucked in the corner. Four armchairs sat around a short, narrow table in the center. Mr. Wilkins must have visitors often.

Cam plopped into the nearest chair, propping his heavily

worn boots on the table. Anne removed her coat, folding it over her lap, and took the seat furthest from him.

A young boy thumped into the loft, carrying a tray with a large thermos, three mugs, and a plate of glazed pastries. Annie had seen the boy in town before. His mother was a florist. He set down the tray, bowed, then rushed from the room without a word.

"Oh, yes, *please*." Cam poured hot, black coffee into two of the mugs, dumping half the dish of sugar into one, then looked up. "Do you like sugar in yours?"

"No, thank you," Annie said instinctually. "I can't."

"Really? Why?" Cam's brow rose, and he gave her a knowing look. "Who's stopping you?"

Lord Duskin never allowed them to have any kind of sweet or stimulant. He didn't like fat, hyper children. Annie picked at the hole she put in her lip. The coffee really did smell good.

"Maybe . . ." she began. *He doesn't own you anymore.* "Just a teaspoon, please."

Cam grinned, measuring a perfect, level spoonful, and carefully stirred it into the steaming liquid before handing her the mug.

The warmed glass felt wonderful beneath her stiff fingers, still sore from digging Lowana's grave. Annie's chest spasmed, and she tried to ignore the fresh, open wound the old woman had left on her heart. *I must be cursed.* Anyone she'd ever gotten attached to was either dead or would be soon.

To distract herself, she took a sip of her coffee, and a rich, powerful taste exploded over her tongue. Bitter, yet sweet. Harsh, yet velvety smooth. "Oh," she gasped, putting her hand over her mouth. Drinking this almost felt indecent.

"Sweet blood of life." Cam drained his mug, then poured another. He looked at her, and his expression softened. "Your dress is very interesting, by the way. It's so dark. Bold colors seem to be the fashion nowadays. It's all I see anymore."

Annie glanced down at her charcoal grey shift. Plain. Boring. "Sorry to disappoint you."

"No, not at all." Cam looked away as he swirled the contents of his mug. "It's peaceful."

"If you say so."

His brands flickered, and he smiled. He had a nice smile.

Heavy footsteps pounded up the staircase, and Thomas entered the loft. "Pardon the wait," he said, looking slightly more disheveled. "I had to keep those devilish creatures out of my scotch."

"Who's the kid?" Cam asked, the softness he'd shown a moment ago replaced with his usual cocky demeanor.

"Oh, I pay him to help out from time to time." Thomas waved dismissively. "Gives him some spending money, while also keeping him out of his mother's hair."

Annie set her mug back on the tray. "His mother is a nice woman."

Thomas smiled, showing gapped teeth. "That she is." He took the empty seat beside her, gesturing between her and Cam. "So, are you going to tell me how this happened?"

"Miss Annie can tell you all about it later, if she wants," Cam replied. "But for now, we have work to do." He shoved a pastry in his mouth. It smelled like an apple tart. "Shall we fill in our new teammate on what we know so far?"

Thomas shifted. *He doesn't trust me.* "I'm sure your new friend is more informed than we are, but sure." He grimaced at her. "Don't be impressed, it's not much." He proceeded to tell her about his ties to the radical groups in the West, fighting for Revenant rights. About the missing sailors and the attacks at sea. Annie had heard all the politics before—who hadn't?—but had never suspected they were involved, or even cared, about what happened on New Havana.

As Thomas carried on, Cam downed the rest of the pastries, barely paying attention.

"Have you considered that Lord Duskin is telling the truth?" Annie interjected when Thomas finally paused for a breath. "That Mr. Price really does believe in his work, and his abandonment of this Mr. Bennett is just a civil matter?"

"It's not like that," Thomas said. "What I mean is once you've seen the atrocities mankind inflicts upon those they deem less than themselves." He shook his head. "It's not something you walk away from. If you can turn your back on that, murder innocent people . . . you deserve the fate in store for Mr. Price once Mr. Bennett gets a hold of him."

"Maybe," Cam said through a mouthful. "We would better understand if we knew what Richard actually does with all the Pearl Dust he's been helping himself to."

"He—" Annie bit her lip. *This feels so wrong.* "Lord Duskin, I mean. He uses the sailors to continue his research. Studying how The Rot affects the body to increase the efficiency of the Pearl solutions and speed up the time of death. There are dozens of lava tubes inside the cliff the mansion is built over. That's where the patients and the drugs are being kept."

"God bless." Thomas signed the shape of a cross over his chest.

Smoke stung Annie's nose as the arms of Cam's chair began to smolder. He just watched her, his eyes growing dark. *Don't look away, don't.* Annie forced herself to stare back—hold her features in place. She wouldn't let him intimidate her.

Finally, Cam spoke. "Edmund Resh. Nathan Williams. Have you heard those names before?"

Annie's stomach crumbled. *No . . . not the captain . . . it can't be.*

She clutched the jade pendant. *My pendant.* "I know Nathan," she said slowly. Cam's stare was a crushing weight. "I don't know an Edmund Resh."

"That necklace belonged to him."

"I took it from a pile of valuables taken from the dead," she said, palms sweaty. "I didn't know who they belonged to. I swear. There have been hundreds in the past few years."

"How do you know the prisoners?" Thomas asked. "Patients, as you called them?"

"I help him with his experiments," Annie answered. Saying it aloud . . . admitting what she'd done . . . she shuddered. "I feed them, supplement them, and document their process or lack thereof."

"Excellent, excellent." Thomas leaned forward, rubbing his hands together. "So, you have access to the lava tubes and Lord Duskin's full confidence?"

Annie nodded to him, but her eyes never left Cam. His brands pulsed so intensely and quickly she thought they might crack. Staring at the floor, he didn't seem to notice the way his arms and shoulders twitched.

He noticed her watching then, and smoke curled from his clenched fists. "Bring me Nathan. You can get him out."

Don't be afraid. Don't show weakness. "No." The words left a numbness on her lips. "They all go, or none of them go. That was the deal."

Something happened then, not physically, but she felt like he maybe really did crack. His whole body convulsed, and he smashed his eyes shut. She may have imagined it, but for a moment, she thought she felt the atmosphere around her ripple. *What is he?*

"Mr. Barnes?" Thomas cleared his throat. "Mr. Barnes, when do you want to get started?"

Just like that, Cam snapped back to attention like nothing

happened. "We can't do anything without a way off the island. We need a ship. I'll handle that. Do you think you can ready food and supplies to travel?"

"Yes." Thomas' brow furrowed. "But what about—"

"Miss Annie will dig up what Julian's been doing with the stolen drugs."

"How?" Annie shot back. "I've never done this kind of thing before. Where do I start?"

"Use your imagination." Cam shot her a cocky half smile. "Where does he spend his time? Who does he hang out with? We have a week and a half before Richard's patent goes public and he realizes I'm a sham. We need to be out of here before then."

A week and a half? She couldn't fathom being somewhere else, starting anew, let alone in so short a time. Annie inhaled, then chugged down the rest of her coffee. She was going to need the energy.

"Speaking of certain Revenants." Thomas slipped a note from his inner coat pocket. "I did as you asked and had my friends keep an eye on Mr. Price and Boyle." Quickly, he read the note, letting out a long breath. "Boyle is what you'd expect—bars, shopping for clothing he shouldn't be able to afford. Not to mention hawking and drinking with the Appletons."

"Good." Cam nodded. "What else?"

"Well, then things get interesting." Thomas wiggled his brows up and down. "It seems Mr. Price spends a considerable amount of time with New Havana's own Lady Charlotte Duskin."

"Hmm," Cam said, amused. "An affair, maybe?"

"No." Annie's eyes widened. "He wouldn't risk it. Lord Duskin would kill him if he found out."

"You'd be amazed what a man would risk for a round backside." Thomas rolled his eyes. "The meetings do always seem to be held in private off mansion grounds."

"No," Annie repeated. *They can't be. They wouldn't.* "I don't believe it."

"Then find the truth," Cam said. "Prove us wrong. If they are just meeting, we need to know what they're discussing. In case we're missing something. "

Annie grit her teeth and nodded, anger swelling in her chest. They didn't live with them, serve them, understand. Even if Lady Duskin did have an affair, Mr. Price wasn't her type. He was too quiet and brooding.

Outside, the sound of horses' hooves on stone streets resonated through the window. The town was beginning to come to life. Annie glanced at the clock. Six-thirty. The Duskins would be waking in a couple of hours.

"Good work, Thomas," Cam said. "We'll plan to meet in another three days. Search the grounds." He looked at her. "Miss Annie, come to me as soon as you find anything. Give me some leverage."

She couldn't stop herself. "What about you?"

"Me?" Cam leaned back in his chair, feigning offense. "I'll continue to be the fantastic, exuberant Lord Callahan. Keeping the attention on me, giving you two the time you need to fight the real battles. Sound good? Sounds good. Now let's get to work. Time's a wasting."

The two men grinned and shook hands like old friends. Annie forced herself to put on a small, fake smile. *What have I gotten myself into?*

After goodbyes were said and done, Annie found herself side by side with Cam, astride their borrowed horses, riding the path through the jungle back toward the mansion. *He's still upset.* The darkness in Cam's eyes hadn't lessened since she'd told him of Nathan and the captain.

Speaking of which? Annie glanced over her shoulder. Behind the broad fern leaves, he wasn't there, watching her from the shadows. Not from the tree branches. Nowhere at all. Even on Sundays, he still harassed her close to the manor. What had changed?

Annie blinked at Cam, his expression focused and drawn. *Is the captain afraid of him, too?*

Cam noticed her watching. "Is something wrong?"

She looked away. "It's nothing."

He shrugged deeper into his coat. "So . . . what do you think?"

"Of what?"

"All this." He made a show of gesturing around. "Of what we're doing. Of this place."

"My opinions don't matter," Annie replied flatly. "Only that the job gets done so we can move on."

"Don't be so self-depreciating." Cam huffed. "I find you enthralling. Slave turned adopted daughter turned evil minion to a mad scientist. It's fascinating."

Annie ignored the compliment. At least, she thought it was meant to be a compliment. "You make him sound like a horrid man."

"And he isn't?"

"In my opinion, you are," Annie said. A cranefly flew into her horse's mane, and she leaned forward to pluck it out. "What Lord Duskin wants is good, life-changing. It's just . . ." *I can't be a killer anymore.* "I have to do this. For them. For Jenny."

When he didn't answer, Annie looked over and was surprised to find Cam smiling. "I haven't always been this way, you know," he said. "I had a mother, a future planned out for me. Even when that was gone, I still had friends I called family."

They came around a bend. A wagon rumbled toward them, heading back to town. A boy and a girl, twins by the look, sat in the back with their mother, hands linked, singing a nursery rhyme.

The same one she and her brothers used to sing, playing together as their father baked shepherd's pie for supper. Annie sucked in a breath. "What happened to them?"

Cam's smile disappeared. "They were taken from me."

"Dead?"

"Most of them."

The path split into a Y ahead, and where the wagon kept straight, to the left, Annie caught a glimpse of a grey coat and inky-black hair. *Julian.* He was on foot, returning the wagon driver's friendly wave. She couldn't see his face. "Speak of the devil . . ." Annie murmured.

". . . and the devil shall appear." Cam's lips twisted into a cruel grin, his brands lighting up like a candle. Again, she felt that ripple of energy wash over her. "Where does that road lead?"

"To the estates still being built on the hill," Annie whispered, "not more than two miles from here."

Cam grinned and swung off his horse, tossing her the reins. "I think you have some work to do, Kitten."

"What?" Annie said. *Oh no.* Her mare nickered nervously as Cam's horse jigged alongside her.

"I'm going to make an excursion. One that will leave Julian's private quarters empty for at least an hour or two." Cam stood up straight, cracked his neck, and threw back his shoulders. Just like that, he was Lord Callahan again. No more softness. No more vulnerability.

She just stared at him, blinking numbly.

Cam winked. "Ride fast." He took off at a leisurely stroll

after Mr. Price, his hands in his pockets, not a care in the world. He didn't even glance back in her direction.

Annie hesitated before pushing the horses into a run, questioning whether she should leave two of the most dangerous creatures on the island alone together. *At this rate, there might not be an island left for me to run from.*

CHAPTER 19
CAMDEN

What are you doing here, Price? What do you want?

Cam was determined to find out.

He peered around an azalea bush, watching as Julian rose in the air and levitated over the gates leading into the partially built estates. An extraordinarily useful gift. There was only one way in, the rest of the property was already enclosed in lava rock.

The road led to an ugly, cleared patch of jungle. Large amounts of earth had been pushed to the edge of the clearing, littered with rock and bramble. The foundations and bones of a large manor stood at the western edge. Foundations for at least three more structures had been dug, as well.

Seeing as there were only the Carters and the Appletons so far, the Duskins must be hoping for more investors soon.

Once Julian was a safe distance ahead, Cam approached the gate. Whether it was luck or a higher power, he couldn't believe the opportunity that had fallen into his lap. Not only did he have the chance to spy, but he'd be able to give Annie the time to dig up the dirt she needed. He imagined she'd had a lot of disappointments in her life, and he had no intention of being the next one.

The gates were solid iron bars, chained and sealed with a heavy padlock. Cam reached into his boot, digging for the lock pick he always kept hidden in his sock. After several minutes of fiddling, the pick snapped. *Blazes.*

Cam stepped back, inspecting the surrounding area. The lava walls were too high to climb, the rocks mortared too tightly to get a good foothold. He didn't feel like tearing his nice, new pants, anyway.

He rubbed his neck, eyeing the lock. *I wonder.* Hesitantly, Cam reached out and gripped the chains, pinching his eyes shut. *Come on. Bead of blood, bead of blood, head of a pin.*

Nothing.

"Hang it all." Cam threw down the chains and groaned. Elias had taught him plenty of parlor tricks to impress the nobles, but anything more than that and he was useless. He knew the heat—constantly felt it simmering beneath his skin, but it seemed to have a mind of its own. Came when it wanted, waned when it wished. He didn't know how to use it.

But his anger . . . that was the center of it all. One day, maybe, he'd learn to control it, but for now, he needed to provoke it.

Okay, who's pissed me off lately? Images of Frank's stupid face filled his mind. That sneer, the way he stared at the Jenny girl. Cam's temper rose, but the creature inside him happily ignored it.

Come on. He forced himself to think of Resh. Was he burnt alive before ever making it to New Havana? Or did he rot away in some Godforsaken hole in the ground, a tortured lab rat?

Annie knew—knew and did nothing to stop it. Now Nathan wouldn't be long for it.

The creature stirred.

But how could she? Could he blame her for trying to survive? For trying to keep the people she cared about alive just a little bit longer? *Take him somewhere his father won't find him.* His mother had tried to do the same for him. Tried and failed.

And how had he honored her? By becoming a murderer, thief, and a fraud. He'd even gotten killed for it. Lost the life she'd died to protect. The least he could do to make it up to her was to do right by Nathan, Resh, and Annie—to get *them* somewhere safe. Somewhere *their* demons couldn't find them.

His fingers bit into his palms, and Cam opened his eyes. Molten metal dripped down his coat sleeves, singeing the fabric. When he uncurled his hands, the chains fell to the ground with a heavy thud. Cam inhaled slowly, steadying his trembling body. *Thank you.* He didn't want to think anymore, didn't want to remember.

Cam slid through the gate. Julian was long out of sight.

The noble's manor, when completed, wouldn't be near the size of the Duskins', but still enormous compared to what the common folk could afford. Two stories, with the standard wrap-around porch on the lower level. The exterior was still raw, exposed wood, and the windows and doorframes were unfinished and empty.

Cam hopped inside the open window, landing in a light crouch onto a scuffed baseboard floor, littered with tools and empty beer bottles. Julian must be lurking in here somewhere. Besides, around back, there was nowhere else to go. Large slabs of rock lath were stacked in the corner, waiting to be hung and plastered.

As he stood, a surge of new energy hummed through Cam's limbs, fueling his muscles, clearing his senses. As if he was waking up for the first time since the day he'd stepped onto the deck of *The Armageddon.*

Cam flexed his fingers, and they filled with a fresh wave of heat. It leached up his throat and caressed his cheek, a sensual purr. *Promises be damned,* Cam's lips curled, *this feels good.*

The room adjacent to his was empty as well. The beginnings of a dining room. The door opposite and across from him was cracked open.

Voices. Julian was in there. Cam slid along the wall, careful not to crunch any of the broken glass strewn around his feet. He peered through the gap in the door.

Apparently, when you speak of the devil's mistress, she comes too.

Julian paced the room, and Charlotte was with him—arms crossed, and expression twisted with frustration. By the half boots and breeches she wore, she must have ridden here herself instead of taking a coach. A bold and unladylike move. Cam's father had never allowed his mother to wear pants. Even as a boy, Cam found all the upper-class societal constructs to be complete bull.

Women looked fantastic in pants.

"We need more time, Char." Julian's coat tails flowed behind him like a storm cloud as he continued to pace.

"*You* need more time," Charlotte corrected. "I've done everything you've asked. If all this goes to blazes, it's not my fault."

"Just until the patent clears," Julian muttered, "then there is nothing he can do. Not if he wants to keep the government out of it."

"Then you'd better find me something new to use," Charlotte said with a huff. "I can only keep feeding him the same sob stories for so long. I'm worried he might be getting suspicious already."

Julian sat on a bucket of plaster, rubbing his face in his hands. Charlotte leaned forward and rubbed his shoulder.

Hmm, Cam narrowed his eyes, pressing deeper against the wall to listen. *Maybe Annie was wrong about the affair. They're closer than they let on.*

"Why are we doing this, Jules?" Charlotte's voice softened. "So much work. All the cloak and dagger. What if he does get his way? How can he hurt us any more than he already has?"

"You think I'm doing this for myself?" Julian snapped, stirring up a gust of wind strong enough to stagger Charlotte backwards, throwing her chocolate curls over her shoulder.

"Sorry." Julian winced. "But you know what would happen. So many lives." He shook his head. "Blast it, I just need more time. Every time I get close, he jumps five steps ahead. He has the money, the resources . . ."

Charlotte bit her lip. "What about Callahan?"

"What about him?"

"He could help. He's young, set in his ways, but you won Frank over."

"I didn't win over Frank." Julian snorted. "The cash clip I handed him did. Not Callahan. It won't work on him. He's involved somehow. I know it."

"You don't know that. He's been here less than a week. I've spent time with him, and you haven't. We need the muscle. You said it yourself. He's powerful."

"Not Callahan," Julian said, stern. "I know what my brother likes, and Camden Callahan is exactly it. Flashy, reckless. A dangerous distraction."

Brother? Cam pinched his brow, crouching, trying to piece together everything he'd just heard. If Richard really was Julian's brother, that would explain his sudden abandonment of Elias, but not the missing drugs. Why would he invest in his brother's cause, while also trying to sabotage it? Plus, why hadn't anyone mentioned they're related? Richard's story about Julian's arrival on the island made it sound like he was a stranger.

And if he had some moral stick about Richard's experiments, why would he *want* the procedural patent to clear? He could just blow the whistles to the officials now and let them tear it down.

Julian and Charlotte left through the back entrance, arm in arm, still entranced in conversation. Cam stood to follow, scowling. He was missing something. The pieces didn't add up. Hopefully Annie found something in Julian's room or—

A firm grip on his shoulder stopped him. Cam wheeled. Frank stood behind him, grinning.

Blazes, he's sneaky.

"Hello, handsome," Frank sneered, then slammed his fist into Cam's jaw.

By the time Cam's head stopped spinning, he found himself flat on his back in the dirt outside the estate house. Frank had sent him sailing through the wall, and now the Fire Brand was standing over him, smirking.

"You know." Frank cracked his knuckles. "I always suspected you were a pile of garbage. Don't you know it's rude to eavesdrop?"

Cam propped himself on an elbow and rubbed his jaw. He was going to have a bruise later. "It's also rude to assault an innocent person. Eavesdropping? I've done no such thing."

"Sure, sure." Frank's brands brightened, his clenched fists smoking. "How stupid do you think I am?"

Cam shrugged. "Pretty darned stupid."

Frank lunged, inhumanly fast, his fist now wreathed in

flame as it hurtled toward Cam's face. Time slowed as another wave of energy rushed through Cam's body.

The creature inside him growled. *Move.*

Cam twisted, and Frank punched a shallow crater into the bare ground. Cam rammed his heel into Frank's gut, sending him flying back through the destroyed wall, burying him in rubble.

Breathing heavily, Cam scrambled to his feet. The heat filled every part of him, his blood was painted with it. He looked down at his hands. They were illuminated from the inside, the fire snaking up his veins. This strength . . .

Has this been here the whole time? Of course, it had. The connection had snapped into place when he burned on that mast—he'd just been too scared to touch it.

Trust me, the voice whispered. *Trust me.*

The building groaned, and Frank burst from the rubble, his hair stained white with plaster. "I'm so glad you did that." He brushed dust off his shoulders. "So glad. Because now I have an excuse to kill you."

All the pain. That he'd caused him, that he'd caused those girls. *Frank Boyle dies.* Annie's words rang through his mind.

Not yet, Kitten. Cam grinned. *Not yet, but I guess I can allow myself the pleasure of hurting him.* He owed Resh that much.

"Bring it, princess." Cam straightened. Julian could wait. It had been too long since he had a good fight. "Let's see what you got."

Frank responded by hurling a fireball at him, then another, laughing.

They exploded as Cam dodged, spraying the air with soil and roots.

"Why ya' running, Callahan?" Frank threw another blast. "Can't back up that fat mouth of yours?"

Technically no. The fireball glanced off Cam's arm, and an acrid chemical smell hit him as his coat sleeve burned. Frank's shirt was half-burned as well, smoldering the plaster with it, revealing his pale, freckled chest. Wood and scrap from the house surrounded him. An orange glow from the cinders glinted off the steel hilt sticking out of the top of his boot— a dagger.

Bingo. He had to get his guard down long enough to swipe that knife. He'd brawled with thug types like Boyle before. You just had to get them mad enough to make mistakes.

"You know, Frankie." Cam paused mid-stride and stretched. "You didn't have to strip to win me over. With some flowers and a moonlit stroll, I would have been all yours."

Frank smoothed his collar. "I've never been subtle."

"I believe that," Cam spat. "Especially by the way you look at the Jenny girl. Can't find any willing partners your age?"

The air around Frank fluctuated, a mirage in a desert. His eyes darkened. "It's not wrong to take what I want from lowly, mortal trash." He raised his hands above his head. "That tart should be honored to be coveted by an immortal."

Here's my chance. Frank lunged at the same time Cam dove, snatching the knife from Frank's boot as he slid behind him. He kicked the back of Frank's knee before he could react, throwing him forward, where Cam had the knife waiting.

"You know." Cam allowed the blade to bite into Frank's throat. "It's dung holes like you that give men a bad name. Why people hate Revenants."

Frank's body went strangely limp. "They hate us because we're better." The mirage around him thickened, making it difficult to see. "Because they're our playthings."

"The world belongs to them, not us."

"Not for long." Frank arched his back, and the mirage ignited. The force of it threw Cam into one of the porch's support beams, crushing it. Fire rained down onto the roof of the estate and the mounds of cleared foliage. After all the time spent beneath the hot sun, they lit up in seconds.

Uh oh. Cam got to his feet, wincing at the pain shooting through his ribs. The fire spread into the surrounding trees. Frank looked out over the jungle, laughing wildly, waving his arms like he thought that would help the flames spread faster.

"What are you doing?" Julian ran from around the back corner of the estate house, black braid whipping behind him. He pointed at Cam. "What are you doing here? How did this happen?"

"Ask your friend." Cam spat blood. "He started it."

"Good God, are you a child?" Julian cried, furious. He turned to Frank. "Put it out. What are you doing? Put it out!" The roar of the growing inferno drowned him out.

Frank continued to laugh. That horrible, piercing laugh.

Kill him. Cam covered his ears, clenching his eyes shut. *Do it now.*

I can't, he pleaded. *Not yet.*

If he killed Boyle now, Richard would cancel the deal. He'd never get Nathan and Resh back, Annie would be stuck here, and he'd lose all the money Elias had promised him. *Not to mention any chance of learning to use this power.*

He didn't realize he'd picked up a rock until the weight of it left his hand and he lobbed it across the clearing. Julian cursed as the stone hit Frank's temple with a loud thud, and he fell face-first into the dirt, still and lifeless.

The roof of the estate caved in, releasing an updraft of hot ash. Julian swung his arms in a downward motion, creating a gust that sent the ash straight back into the ground. "Do something, Callahan, before it destroys half the island!" He screamed as he used his wind against the fire, all the while protecting Frank's useless body.

I can't stop it. The realization hit Cam square in the gut. *I don't know how.*

Flames licked up the tree trunks like they'd been painted with tar, curling the leaves into black soot. Wild, unchecked. The master of its own will. How could he stop something like that?

I can, the gentlest of whispers brushed his ear.

Cam exhaled. A sense of calmness filled him. *Will you show me how?*

Trust me.

Okay.

The creature locked inside him crept from his pores, gagging him as it spilled from his throat. The force of it flattened the surrounding trees, blowing apart the house. Julian braced, creating a shield around him and Frank as wood and debris flew past them.

My fire.

The energy ignited like Frank's had, but this time it stretched and shifted until it took on a vaguely humanoid shape. It glanced back at him and smiled. Cam watched as the fire around them paused, waiting. Waiting for what?

Command me.

He felt the draw then, a tether from him to the inferno. Cam pulled, and the fire redirected toward him. No longer a bead of blood, but a monster on the end of a leash.

In his mind, Cam kept pulling. The fire sucked away from the trees, from the house. Changing, until the full force of it combined into a massive tornado of heat and rage.

"Get rid of it!" He could faintly hear Julian shouting. "Stop it!"

Cam exhaled. *Here goes nothing.* He raised his arms—just like Julian had—and swung them downwards. His monster mimicked the movement. The jungle groaned as the tornado lurched forward, spiraling toward the earth at an incredible speed. When it made contact, the earth shook, violently exploding mud and water into the air like a bomb had been set off below ground. Earth rained down on them.

Cam took a shaky breath, fighting to keep his body upright as exhaustion overwhelmed him. Julian stepped beside him, wet hair plastered across his face and grey eyes wide. Water continued to shoot out from a hole in the ground.

"I think . . ." Cam let out a breathy chuckle. "I think I broke the plumbing."

To his surprise, Julian burst into laughter, his hands on his knees.

Cam glanced around the clearing. All that was left of the house was stone and coal. "Where's Boyle?"

"I got him away in time, but you singed his arm," Julian said. "And you nearly caved his head in."

Cam's jaw clenched. "He deserved it."

Julian grabbed what remained of Cam's collar and spun him until they were face-to-face. Cam didn't have the energy to fight back. He found himself staring at Julian's hawk nose.

"Don't try to lie." He squeezed tighter. "If you repeat anything you *may* have heard, I will not hesitate to kill you."

"Bold talk coming from the man fooling around with his employer's wife." Cam smiled wide. "Or should I say his brother's?"

Confusion flashed across Julian's features, then for a moment what seemed like relief. He released his grip, taking a step back.

Cam straightened his ruined coat. He should have worn the one Elias had given him. "You have no leverage to threaten me with, mate."

"No?" Julian scowled. "You think I didn't recognize you from the start, boy? Out for vengeance, are you?"

Cam's stomach dropped.

"Listen, Callahan—if that's your name." Julian's eyes were red-rimmed and bloodshot. "I don't care. I'm too busy to be concerned with trash like you. Stay out of my way, and I'll stay out of yours. Cross me, and I'll ruin you."

He should be enraged, but all Cam felt was numbness. "You ... you helped him kill me."

"I did," Julian leaned in. "Don't make me do it again."

CHAPTER 20
ANNIE

Of course, it's locked.

Annie jiggled the handle of Mr. Price's door again, just to be sure.

By the time she'd gotten back to the mansion—sweating and smelling of horse—the cooks were busy prepping the morning meal. Her sisters had already begun their chores. It had been easy for her to just grab a stack of clean sheets and head upstairs. No one seemed to notice her entering or asked where she'd been.

Normally, she'd have been assigned the master key to change the lord and ladies' sheets, but it was Rose's turn today. She'd have stolen it, if she'd had the time, but she'd learned long ago to improvise.

Annie glanced up and down the hall. Empty. The others would be preparing the tables for breakfast, feeding the animals, and cleaning the classrooms. If she did this right, she would have a good fifteen minutes before anyone had any need to come to the third floor.

Please, Camden, give me some time.

She set down the sheets, reaching into her low bun and pulling out the pins, letting her hair fall down her back. She stretched the pins open and slipped them into the lock, closing her eyes and working it by feel.

After a tense minute, the lock popped, and Annie smirked. *Camden Callahan isn't the only one with tricks.* She let herself inside and locked the door behind her.

Now that she had a moment to breathe, she realized she'd never been in Mr. Price's room. He'd always requested to do his own cleaning. It was messier than she would have expected. The bed unmade, books strewn across his tall, mahogany desk and stacked in unruly piles on the floor. The candles he'd burned the night before had dripped onto some newspapers and dried into thick, white lumps.

Annie picked through some of the papers on the desk, finding nothing of interest. A metal filing cabinet sat beside it. One of the drawers lay partially open. The inside was overflowing with documents. Organized by alphabetical order, date, and topics that seemed most important to him.

Come on, come on. Annie flipped through the files, fingers slick with nervous sweat.

She had to admit she was curious about this Elias Bennett. Even in Rouenn, back home, there were always arguments about how much Revenant should be allowed to own, operate, and reproduce. If they even *could* reproduce. It wasn't a new topic. You'd think she would have heard of Mr. Bennett in her travels if he were so important.

As she sifted through the stack of papers, Annie picked up a small slip that looked like it might be a receipt. She chewed her lip, squinting, as she tried to decipher the worn ink. What had been purchased, she didn't know, but Lord Duskin had signed it, and there were a lot of zeros in the number.

A photo clipping slipped from the pile. Annie lifted it to

take a closer look, the browning paper brittle between her fingers. It was a black and white photograph of a well-dressed gentleman shaking hands with a Revenant man. The men smiled up at her, familiar though the picture was dated several years before she was even born. The Revenant looked a little like Mr. Price. Something in her stomach turned as she studied the man. She'd seen him before—somewhere. Her mind blocked it out.

She turned her attention to the second man. There was no denying his good looks. The slicked back light hair and wide jaw, his smile bright and energetic.

Maybe Camden will recognize one of them. Gently, she folded the clipping and tucked it into her bodice.

The last paper in the folder was a letter written on thick velum, folded where it had once been sealed with red wax. Annie opened it, scanning the words over quickly. The top third of the letter was too worn to make out. Mr. Price must have read it so many times he'd rubbed out the ink. It was dated ten years ago.

"—have turned out better than we could have ever hoped. The Pearl Dust will prove it. I know it. Rebirth is not a random act of nature, like so many believe.

There are signs. Clues.

Symptoms that are detectable even in infancy. We are born into our first life wearing pieces of what we truly are. A woman who can grow her garden more beautifully than any of her neighbors may be called a green thumb . . . but is it just a stroke of luck, or something more?

But why, you may ask, does not every man with special talents come back as we are? These are questions yet unanswered, but do not fear, continue your good work. Always remember . . . death is the catalyst for life—"

"What are you doing?"

Annie shoved the letter up her sleeve and slammed the drawer shut. Rose stood in the doorway, mouth agape, long brown hair curled into a coif, just like Lady Duskin's.

Annie's heart thundered against her ribs. "None of your business."

"Father told me to come find you." Rose's eyes darted in every direction, taking in the scene. "You shouldn't be in here. You're going to get in trouble."

I forgot teatime. She and Lord Duskin always had tea on Sundays to discuss plans and experiments for the patients. *I can't believe I forgot.* Annie's knees trembled as she stood. Too much coffee in her bloodstream. She wiped her sweaty palms on the skirts of her dress. "I'll be down in a moment. M-Mr. Price asked me to get something for him."

"Mr. Price is out right now." Rose glanced over Annie's loose hair, the folder spread out on the carpet, and pulled a small, black key from her pocket. The master key.

She knows I broke in. He has the only other key. Annie swallowed nervously, and the two girls stared at each other in complete silence.

Rose took two slow steps backward before bolting back down the hallway.

"*No!*" Annie stumbled as she ran out of the room, her ankle twisting. Rose was already down to the first landing. Annie's throat tightened as the panic set in. *It's over.*

She'd wanted to save them. After Lowana, she'd been determined to do something more than cower. All she'd ever done was let others trample over her. She'd *let* them do it to stay alive. *But I'm done with just living.* If Rose made it downstairs, she wouldn't be alive much longer. Cam would probably die, too.

A bright, grey light blasted through the hall. As the light touched her, Rose froze on the second flight of the stairs, eyes filled with terror. The bedroom doors on both floors slammed shut, and a loud click echoed as all the locks bolted shut.

"*What's happening?*" Rose mouthed to her.

Annie shook her head and pressed her finger over her lips.

Pale mist began to pour from the walls around Rose. She cried out as it dripped over her shoulder, pooling around her feet. An arm and hand formed out of the mist and latched onto Rose's leg, continuing to grow until it became a full-bodied figure.

She screamed, and the figure clapped a translucent hand over her mouth, its other wrapped around her throat. As the figure's features solidified, looking at her over its shoulder, rage rampaged through Annie's blood instead of fear.

The captain.

He grinned at her with blurry features and nodded toward Rose. He'd stopped her, she realized.

Now he was asking what she'd like done with her.

Part of Annie wished she *were afraid*—that she could continue to be the girl who always followed orders. The girl who lay her head down at night, hoping by some miracle she'd die and wake in heaven, instead of continuing on in this hell.

But as she watched the terror flickering in Rose's eyes, she knew she couldn't be that girl anymore. She'd died slowly. . . piece by piece, along with the bodies she'd buried.

Electric energy buzzed through Annie's core.

The captain inclined his head to her again, blurry eyes widening, almost as if he felt it, too.

Rose's body went limp.

Annie stood, ignoring the throbbing in her ankle. "Let her go." She was surprised at the commanding tone her voice had taken. "Now."

The captain's cracked lips curled back from his teeth.

"Now," Annie growled back, and the captain smiled at her.

Why is he helping me? It was still the captain, but not the same one who tormented her day and night. What had changed?

He released whatever hold he had on Rose, and she fell hard, hitting the stairs with a loud thud. She sucked in a choking gasp and sobbed, curling around herself.

Annie blinked, and the captain's face was a mere breath from hers. Gently, he stroked her cheek with a light, icy touch. *"Tell him he's sorry."* The captain's voice was a sickly drawl. *"Tell him he loved him like a son."*

"Who?" Annie whispered, but she already knew. He was talking about *him* all along.

He placed his crumbling hands over her eyes, and when the darkness lifted, he was gone. The hallway and stairwell free of mist and light. Like he'd never been there at all.

Rose's eyes fluttered open, her tawny cheeks pale, and Annie knelt beside her. "Speak a word of what you saw today, and I'll make sure you find yourself below with the rest of them. Understood?"

Rose clutched her throat, nodding frantically.

"Good." Annie stood, smiling, and continued down the staircase. When she reached the bottom, she slowed, stepping into the grand entrance with precise footsteps.

Something felt . . . off.

Is it the captain, still? The entryway and the living area were well-lit. No signs of his shadows lurked in the corners.

The air.

Annie inhaled. That's what it was. It seemed to be . . . buzzing. Like right before a lightning storm. It set her on edge.

"What is that?" Rose had followed her down the staircase, her voice hoarse.

Annie watched her for a moment, trying to sense if the girl meant to run. "I don't know."

Rose's eyes rose to the window, looking out over the

valley between the grounds and the jungle. She moved closer, fingers brushing the sill, and her jaw dropped. "Annie, look."

She felt it before she saw it. Annie's limbs trembled as she moved to the window. When she looked outside, her heart nearly stopped.

The northeast edge of the island was on fire. Black smoke billowed into the air, smothering out the beautiful blue skies. Somewhere far below—maybe in the city—an alarm began to sound.

Camden. If only she could have stopped him from following Mr. Price. She should have known he'd ruin everything. An orange glow reflected in Rose's eyes, her hand moving up to cover her mouth.

The ground shook. Dust broke free from the stone ceiling as Annie gripped the windowsill. Rose screamed, then outside the trees . . . bent.

An invisible wave rippled over the jungle, flattening the plant life. The fire sputtered, only to be sucked into a cyclone of flames that hovered over the earth, waiting to destroy.

Annie watched the grass bend as the wave crashed over the estate grounds. Then it hit the manor. More screams echoed through the halls as a rush of energy leaked through every crack and open space, reverberating through Annie's bones, her blood.

Rose crumbled to the floor, but Annie found herself grinning. *No . . . that is Camden.*

She'd felt that energy before, leaking from him at Thomas' tavern.

The cyclone lunged for ground, disappearing below the tree line. A second earthquake shook the manor before everything went quiet. The only evidence of the event was the black smoke still lingering on the horizon.

Annie sucked in a deep breath, a second one. Rose got to her knees, body shaking, then repeated. "What was that?"

Annie exhaled, her mind clear for the first time in years. "The reason you will stay quiet."

She didn't wait to hear Rose's response before she was out the door and heading to the stables.

CHAPTER 21
ANNIE

Annie had never ridden so hard in her life. Side-saddle, her horse's sweat soaked into her grey day dress, her hair whipping behind her like a moon-white flag. The horse's hooves thundered over the cobbled road, eating the distance between her and New Havana with its wide, surging strides.

Was it too much to hope that Frank Boyle was dead? That Camden had burned him into a blackened stump and left him to blow away in the wind? No, that would be too quick. For Jenny, for Lowana . . . he should suffer.

She knew where they'd be. If any of them were alive after that event, they'd be at the hospital wing on the west side of the city. Annie pushed her horse harder, and it happily obliged. Lord Duskin's sport horses rarely got to run the way they craved.

The beast was drenched when she reached the hospital wing. The actual building was yet to be finished, but Lord Duskin had an elaborate tent constructed, with several wings as a temporary medical center. She could hear the chaos before she saw it. When the enormous white tents came into view, there were people everywhere. Not only nurses—dressed in their slim, crimson gowns—but citizens craning to get a view of whatever lay inside the tents.

Annie didn't have to guess. She could feel them. The Revenant.

She swung off her horse before it had fully come to a stop and passed the reins to a waiting attendant. Lord Duskin may be angry with her for showing up, but she had to know, had to see. Was the monster she'd sworn to work alongside more powerful than the monsters that haunted her?

If Camden was dead, then she needed to reevaluate her future—quickly. She refused to wind up on Lord Duskin's table.

None of the nurses even looked up from their work when she entered the hospital wing, shoving the tent flaps out of her way. Annie spent a considerable amount of time here. Between collecting supplies for the patients, she'd come and linger in her free time. Watching the nurses work . . . watching them heal—whether it be a broken limb or an upset stomach—it made her feel not so dead. That there was life still in the world, even if she couldn't be part of it.

After a time, the nurses began leaving an extra chair in the exam room for her. She'd never been able to tell them how much it meant to her. If she did, Lord Duskin might find out and take it away.

"*Destroyed?*" Lord Duskin's voice shattered the usual calmness of the wing. "Do you have any idea how much gold you've just thrown into the mud?"

Found you. Annie leaned against the tarp separating her from the next room, sweat clinging to her brow. Lord Duskin never raised his voice in public where his citizens might see. This must be worse than she thought.

"I wouldn't say thrown," Cam's voice drawled. "More like incinerated."

He's alive. Annie exhaled in relief. *But for how long?*

Lord Duskin inhaled sharply, and she could imagine just the way he was pinching the bridge of his nose right now. "I have every mind to ship you off this island, Lord Callahan. Don't press me."

"As stated." She jumped as Mr. Price spoke, his tone soft and calming. "As much as I hate to admit it, the fault wasn't with Lord Callahan. He may have been skulking where he didn't belong, but it was Mr. Boyle who set the blaze."

Annie's eyes narrowed. *Why is Mr. Price defending Cam?* He and Mr. Boyle had always been thick as thieves. Now he was blaming him for whatever happened at the estates.

"And I'm to believe that Mr. Boyle's attack was completely unprovoked?" said Lord Duskin.

"Of course, it was provoked." She could imagine the cocky sneer on Cam's lips. "But it's not my fault that Frankie's an idiot."

Annie couldn't stop the amused huff that escaped her.

"Gentlemen." The curtains pulled back, and Mr. Price smiled at her. "It seems we have a visitor."

Panic sent Annie's heart lurching into her throat, but she molded her expression into her usual icy stare. She'd survived worse than this. She would survive again. It took every ounce of her will to force her gaze to settle *only* on Lord Duskin, to read him. He looked surprised. She used it to her advantage.

She gave him a slight, yet yielding, bow of the head. "Father, I saw the . . . explosion from the manor." Annie let her eyes flash to Cam's. He winked. "I came to see if you needed any help."

Lord Duskin sighed as he stepped toward her, leaning in to kiss her brow. As he did, she allowed herself to survey the room, and she held back a grin at the sight of Frank Boyle lying on a cot. Unconscious, his head wrapped in a blood-soaked bandage. His clothes were scorched and filthy.

She forced herself to meet Lord Duskin's eyes as he held her face in his hands. "You are *too* thoughtful, darling." She didn't miss the warning in it. He turned and glanced over at Cam and Mr. Price, finally letting his gaze settle on Mr. Boyle, wounded on the cot. He paced a few steps, chewing on the edge of his thumb. "Annie, dear, by their account, Mr. Price and Boyle found Lord Callahan surveying the new estate grounds without permission. They confronted him, and Mr. Boyle attacked Lord Callahan, leading to the *explosion* you witnessed. How do you suggest they should be punished?"

The room went silent, all eyes falling on her. She was more surprised Lord Duskin had said her name. She looked between the four men, letting her gaze linger on each. Mr. Price was as filthy as Mr. Boyle and Cam, but the way he watched her was intense, his brows furrowed tightly—the liar. She didn't know why, but he'd chosen to keep information from Lord Duskin.

Cam leaned against the tent's supporting beam, arms crossed, as smug as ever. *No.* Something was different. He seemed calmer, less fidgety, his brands not as chaotic as they'd been this morning.

I've gotten too bold. Annie folded her hands behind her back. "Was Lord Callahan *told* not to visit the estates?"

More silence.

Lord Duskin exhaled. "No, he was not."

Annie continued. "Was Mr. Boyle directed to watch his temper?"

It had been just a guess, but it was easy to imagine the conversation had happened. Lord Duskin smiled. "Yes . . . yes, he was."

"Then punish the rules that were broken, not the ones

unsaid," Annie whispered. Why was Mr. Price working so hard to catch her eye? She glared at him, allowing his silver eyes to try to convey whatever message he held. Her brows furrowed. "And if Mr. Price tried to stop it, how could he be at fault?"

Lord Duskin clapped, splaying his hands toward her. "See how well my wife has taught her? The sense of justice that's been instilled in my children?"

Annie kept her expression blank.

Lord Duskin ran his hand down her back, pausing at the base of her spine. She knew better than to shudder. "I agree with my daughter. Annie, please, escort Lord Callahan back to the manor. Mr. Price, we have more to discuss."

She gave him another nod, and as she turned to exit the tent, her eyes snagged on the mangled wound on Mr. Boyle's left ankle. *Burns.* Oozing blisters showed through the blackened hem of his trousers, red and inflamed. She allowed herself a glance at Cam, to where she'd seen the scorched sleeve of his coat. His skin was smooth and tanned as ever.

"No need to stare. I'm coming with you." Cam bowed to the other men. "Gentlemen." He offered her his elbow, giving her a challenging look. "Miss Annie?"

Reluctantly, she took his arm and allowed him to lead her from the tent, feeling the others' eyes boring into her.

Cam leaned in and whispered, "Don't look back. They're watching us."

Annie scowled. "I'm aware."

Cam let out a fake laugh as if she'd said something oh-so-humorous. "And why are they so suspicious of you, Kitten?" He glanced over his shoulder. "Richard looks like he's seen a ghost."

If you only knew. "Because I'm letting you touch me."

"Hmm," was all he said as they continued out of the tent. He didn't let go once they were out of view. Instead, he held her close. He leaned in again, the oven warmth of his breath caressing her neck. "And why, pray tell, would you touch me if you knew it'd draw attention?"

Annie's eyes flashed to his, giving herself a moment to appreciate the orange glow circling his pupils. She looked away. "Because Mr. Price covered for you. I'm curious why. I'd rather we kept him on his toes, if at all possible."

Cam grinned at her, letting out a breathy chuckle. "I noticed that as well. I have my suspicions. Would you like to hear them?"

"If I must." Annie chewed the inside of her cheek. Up ahead, she could see her horse tied to a post under a separate tent, a bucket of fresh water within reach. Several attendants bustled about, caring for the other horses waiting for the return of their riders. She continued. "Just not here."

"Obviously," Cam snorted.

She glared at him.

He just smiled.

When they approached the stable tent, a thought struck her. "You don't have a horse." She'd led it back to the manor with her on the way to search Mr. Price's room.

"That I don't," Cam replied.

Annie thanked the attendant as he re-tacked her horse and passed her the reins. It nuzzled her cheek, its breath sweet from alfalfa. She turned to Cam and smiled. It hurt her cheeks. She wasn't used to smiling so much. "I'll guess you'll have to call for a carriage or make the trek back on foot."

His eyes lit up. "Or we can ride double? You can drive."

She crooned as she adjusted her stirrups. "Not on your life."

"We have lots to talk about. We can chat on the way?"

"Enjoy your walk." Annie mounted her horse, tucking her

dress tightly against her knees. "The mangos are divine this time of year if you get hungry."

She wasn't sure which was more satisfying—the absolute, wicked delight on his face or knowing he had at least six miles to hike in the tropical heat.

Annie urged her horse into a canter. The captain and his shadows were nowhere in sight.

She was afraid to hope the rest of the evening would go so well.

CHAPTER 22
CAMDEN

The sun was burning brightly overhead by the time Cam returned to the Duskins' estate. With a bow, a guard—adorned in gold and white—opened the manor's heavy double doors. The man kept his eyes trained to the ground, sweat dripping off his chin. Cam gave a curt nod as he strode inside.

He'd barely set foot into the grand entry when a shrill wail assaulted his ears. Charlotte Duskin hurried down the staircase, arms stretched toward him—dressed now in an embroidered, pink day gown, instead of riding leathers.

Cam couldn't help rolling his eyes when she fell into his arms. *The conniving snake.* Little did she know he'd seen her only hours earlier, conspiring with Julian Price . . . against her own husband. He hadn't been sure what to make of the conversation he'd overheard. He hadn't had the time to process it. Not after the earful he'd gotten from Richard.

Tears streamed down Charlotte's round cheeks. "Lord Callahan, I'm so relieved you're unharmed." A big sniffle. "When I saw the jungle burning, I feared the worst."

206

"There, there." Cam patted her shoulder. She smelled like roses. "I'm not dead. Or at least, not dead again."

Charlotte looked up at him with watery eyes. "And the others? Mr. Price and Boyle?"

"Julian is fine. Frank is mostly fine."

She sniffled again and wiped at her tears. "That's good to hear."

Over her shoulder, Cam watched Annie step into the entry, the Jenny girl on her tail. Annie had changed out of her dirty grey dress into a black one. Her eyes trailed from him to Charlotte's weepy outburst, and she rolled her eyes, too. He held back a laugh as Charlotte pressed her head into his chest.

Then he noticed Jenny Duskin's face.

A scorched handprint blistered the skin over her mouth and chin. She wore a high-necked bodice, barely concealing the burns on her neck.

That piece of retched trash. Cam's heat flared so fast and hot that Charlotte jumped away, letting out a gasp.

Jenny's eyes dropped to the floor when she realized he was staring. The question escaped his lips, though he already knew the answer. "What happened to you?"

Jenny glanced quickly between Annie and Charlotte, then swallowed. "I fell asleep reading. My candle set my sheets on fire."

I'm going to kill him. Cam smiled bitterly. "Is that so?"

Jenny nodded, head low.

"Jenny, dear, run along, would you?" Charlotte scowled, any hint of her former tears vanishing. "Annie, make sure your siblings finish sweeping up after the earthquake, then have some tea brought out." She turned to Cam. "You're too late for lunch, but shall I expect you at dinner?"

Cam took her hand, kissing her knuckles, but let his gaze

roam back to Jenny once more. *Frank is going to die in the worst way possible.* "I wouldn't miss it."

Charlotte nodded, dabbing her eyes with a handkerchief as she headed towards the sitting room. Once she was out of sight, Annie let out a weak sigh, hands folded behind her back.

They stood in silence, just watching one another. Cam cleared his throat. "I hope your day was . . . productive."

Not a flicker of emotion passed over her features. "It was. More so than yours, it seems."

Cam gave her a crooked smile. "I'm glad to hear it."

Annie's nose crinkled. "I imagine you'll be wanting a bath before dinner. I'll bring fresh towels to your room."

Ouch. Cam made a point to brush against her as he passed, leaning in. "Kitten."

"Camden."

He let out a breathy laugh as he headed up the staircase.

Annie was right—he was drenched in sweat and wanted nothing more than a long soak in his personal claw-foot tub.

Gently, Cam closed his bedroom door behind him, clicking the lock into place. He was done with these people. Done with this place. He missed the sea and salt air, the wind in his hair, and the daily routine of caring for *The Nightlady.*

Stripping down to his undergarments, Cam flopped into the cushioned armchair by the window, then leaned back and let out a long breath.

He'd acted like an idiot. Picking a fight with Frank was stupid and could have ruined everything he'd set out to do. What if Richard had decided to fire him right then and there?

He leaned forward, rubbing his face in his hands. *I'm feeling sorry for myself.*

There *had* been successes to the day. Annie had smiled—actually smiled at him. He knew he shouldn't care, but seeing it was like watching an iceberg crack. Breathtaking and terrifying all at the same time.

Cam flexed his hand, his heat coiling sweetly in his veins. *The second great part of the day.* He'd broken his promise to Elias and used his power, but if he hadn't, Frank would have gladly murdered him—again.

Frank. His heat writhed up his neck, stroking his jaw. *The slack-jawed prick.* He knew what caused the burns on Jenny Duskin's face. It hadn't been a blasted candle.

Annie had been right about Julian, though . . . he'd covered for him. Most likely out of fear that Cam would repeat what he'd heard at the estates, but maybe he could use this to his advantage. Blackmail Julian into staying out of the way.

Cam pinched the bridge of his nose, a headache forming. *I just want Resh and Nathan back. Is that too much to ask?* He didn't want all this drama and scheming. It's why he'd resented his inherited title in the first place.

I know Nathan. I don't know an Edmund Resh. If she was telling the truth, he couldn't blow this. Not if there was a chance of getting Nathan out of here alive. *Would she lie about Resh?* He couldn't see any reason she would, which meant either his captain was dead, or he'd escaped between his capture and New Havana.

Either way, Cam wouldn't be able to rest until he knew for sure. Not only about the fate of his mentor but also of the knowledge that came with him.

There was a soft knock at his door. He glanced at his clock. Quarter past three.

When he swung open the door, Annie's eyes widened at

the sight of him in nothing but his underwear, fluffy towels in her arms. "Should I return when you're decent?"

Cam stood and opened the door wider. He didn't miss the pink flush on her cheeks. "Do you have long?"

"I have thirty minutes until I'm expected for dinner prep." Annie cleared her throat, keeping her eyes on the wall behind him as she lowered her tone. "I thought we might discuss the day's findings."

"I would like nothing more." Cam stepped into his private bathroom as Annie closed the door behind them. She lingered outside the room as Cam turned on the faucet over his tub, letting the gushing water run over his fingers. "I can't believe Richard has plumbing."

Annie leaned against the doorframe, dropping the towels on the rack. Letting her eyes fall everywhere but him. "Lord Duskin has a lot of things he shouldn't."

"Like you?"

Annie shot him a quick glare. "That's not what I meant."

"It should be." Cam dumped some fragrant soaps into the tub as it filled. "Your talents are far wasted here."

"You know nothing of my *talents*." Annie paused and sniffed, still looking away. "I didn't take you as a lavender man."

"Oh?" Camden slipped off his undergarments and climbed into the tub, wincing at the frigid water. "What do you take me as?"

Annie's cheeks were bright red, locked on the opposite wall. "I'm not answering that."

"Amuse me?"

"You know you could have asked to have the water warmed?"

Cam leaned back his head and exhaled, releasing the heat building in his muscles. The water boiled with a hiss, steam fogging the bathroom mirrors. He sank deeper into the tub, letting the bubbles cover his chest and neck, only his knees exposed. "It's alright. I can do it myself."

They remained silent for a moment before Annie finally whispered, "You're not actually a lord, are you?"

Cam scooped some bubbles in his hand. "Yes and no."

"What are you?"

"At the moment?"

Annie rolled her eyes again. "Before you came to New Havana."

"Ah." Cam sighed. "Just a pirate, I'm afraid."

Annie crossed her arms. "That explains a lot."

"Explains what?"

She gestured to him in the tub. "All this. Your horrid manners."

Cam laughed. "I had terrible manners before I became a pirate, trust me." He let out another burst of heat, bringing the bath back to a boil. "Julian Price knows, by the way. That I'm a fraud. Which makes it all the more curious that he's covering. But enough of me. What did you learn about our friend?"

Annie stepped closer to the tub, pulling a few slips of paper from her bodice. "He has ties to the groups fighting for Revenants. Or at least interest in them." She held the papers toward him. Drying his hands, Cam read them over them as she continued. "I'm not sure what to make of the rest."

Cam glanced over the receipts she gathered. "Richard mentioned that Julian takes care of his Pearl Dust orders. I imagine he just signs the check and lets Julian do the rest."

Annie scowled, picking at the sleeve of her dress.

Cam's brow rose. "What?"

She chewed her lip. "I don't think Mr. Price has been paying for the Pearl Dust brought to the island."

It's still hard for her to betray him. "No?"

Annie shook her head. "Whenever they bring in new stores, my job is to assess and catalog all the sailors they bring in with them—the new patients." She sighed. "I take care of those men and women. None of them are here willingly. Lord Duskin knows that much, at least."

"Hmm." Cam thought for a moment. "Which means Julian is probably pocketing the money for the drugs."

She looked stressed. "Perhaps."

"I wonder why."

"I wouldn't know."

Cam turned his attention to the next document: a worn letter. He read over it six times just to make sure he understood it right. He looked up to Annie and found her watching his face anxiously. He held up the letter. "Did you read this?"

She nodded.

"And?"

Annie swallowed, running her fingers through her long, pale hair. "Whoever wrote that thinks Revenancy can be predicted? Lord Duskin has me wait a short time before disposing of deceased patients, but I always assumed it was out of caution. He always says we don't need a new Revenant crawling out of their grave. Maybe there's more to it than that?"

"Do you think Richard is trying to make Revenants?" Cam asked.

Annie's silver-blue eyes widened. "No, no. Of that, I'm sure."

"Interesting." Cam licked his lips. He turned over to the next document—an old photograph—and his heart nearly stopped.

Elias Bennett . . . standing beside a much younger version of his father, Alexander Callahan. God, when was the last time he'd seen his father's face? Ten years? *This must have been taken before I was born.*

Annie watched him intently. "You know them." Not a question.

Cam nodded. How much did he trust her? *When have I ever trusted anyone?* "This . . ." He pointed to Elias' face in the photograph. "Is the man who sent me here." He ran his finger over his father. "This is Alexander Callahan."

Annie's brows scrunched together. "The Governor of the West?"

Cam nodded. "And my father."

Annie actually looked surprised. "So, you *are* a lord?"

"Am I?" Cam exhaled, passing her back the documents. "I gave up that title a long time ago."

"Yet you're here, wearing it."

"For Resh and Nathan." *How did it come to this?* "To get them back."

Annie sat on the edge of the tub. She let her fingers trail through the bubbles. "That's a lot of dedication . . . coming from a self-proclaimed pirate."

"They're all I've got. But that's why I need to get out of here as soon as possible. Before my father catches word I'm here."

Annie looked him in the eye, and she seemed sad . . . very, very sad. She whispered, "What's next?"

"I'll find a ship." Cam sank deeper into the tub. "I need you to find a safe way to get Jenny and the patients out of the manor. Once you have what you need, signal me, and we'll find a way to meet with Thomas Wilkins."

Annie nodded, drying her hands on her apron as she stood. "I need to leave."

Cam nodded back. "See you at dinner."

Before she left the bathroom, Annie paused, hesitating. "Camden?"

His name on her lips had his heat surging toward the surface. "Yes, Kitten?"

She chewed her thumbnail. "Do you want Nathan to know you're here?"

Cam breathed, holding all the broken pieces of himself together. "Not yet. I . . . I don't want him to get his hopes up."

"Fair enough." With that, she was gone.

That was unexpected. He shouldn't have told her who he was. Mistakes like that could get him killed.

Cam sat in his tub until the water went cold.

CHAPTER 23
ANNIE

She knew the summons would come.

Not only had Annie missed teatime this morning, but she'd missed a shift in the bunker a few days before. Honestly, she was surprised she hadn't been punished already.

It took everything she had to make it through dinner. To keep her eyes anywhere and everywhere *but* Camden Callahan.

He'd stripped and climbed in that bathtub—right there in front of her—and for the first time in her life, she felt something other than repulsion at the sight of another's skin.

She'd *wanted* to look. At the hard, muscled lines of his limbs and abdomen, at the sea-earned golden sheen on his skin.

Annie wanted to hate him for making her feel that way, but she still found herself watching him as she served Lord and Lady Duskin their meal. Of course, he'd spent the evening charming the other lords and ladies, smiling and laughing like he'd been born to entertain.

But she supposed he was. Cam was heir to the West.

She wondered how many knew the truth of that fact.

But he's a pirate now. That thought played through her mind all throughout the night. *Why?* Annie wondered about it while she served the Duskins' guests their second, third, and fourth glasses of wine. Cam never drank, only sipped on water or tea. When the others grew sloppy, he'd remained sharp and alert.

People became pirates for a reason—whether they'd killed someone or someone wanted *them* dead, and even then, they were never sober ones.

Cam sent her wicked smiles now and then, a reminder that he was dangerous—a spider gathering flies to feed upon—and now she was tangled in his web.

Worst of all, the thought thrilled her.

While dessert was set on the table, a rather smug-faced Rose had slipped a note into her apron. Lord Duskin wanted to see her in his rooms once they retired. Only once had Lord Duskin summoned her to his rooms, not long after she'd arrived on the slaver's ship. She'd tried to run—to where, she didn't know—and he'd brought her to his chambers after.

The things he did to her then were too unspeakable to allow herself to remember. Now that she was being summoned again, she doubted she'd survive until dawn this time.

No . . . I'm not going to die. She'd come too far for it all to fall apart now. Whatever she had to say—whatever she had to do —she'd do it. Just to stay alive a little bit longer.

Lord and Lady Duskin's chamber sat at the very back of the manor on the third floor, their balcony overlooking the cliff behind and the sea below. Annie passed it every day and pretended she didn't see it. Lord Duskin didn't even allow them in to clean. He made Lady Duskin do it.

Exhaustion crept into her limbs as Annie strode towards

their rooms. Each step felt as if she had millstones tied to her ankles.

Annie exhaled, knocking gently on the Duskins' bedroom door, counting each heartbeat as muffled footsteps sounded on the other side. A low chuckle tickled her neck, followed by shadowed fingers—the captain.

The door swung open, revealing Lady Duskin leaning against the frame, a bottle of wine in hand. Her grey eyes were unfocused as she looked Annie up and down, a sneer spreading over her lips. "Annie, dear. What a *pleasant* surprise."

"Mother." Annie curtsied stiffly. "Father summoned me?"

"Of course he did." Lady Duskin moved aside. "Come in."

Annie hadn't stepped inside this room in years, and yet nothing had changed. Unlike Mr. Price's chambers, the Duskins' room was immaculately tidy. The books on the shelves were alphabetized and color-coded. Each wall had two paintings, each of the same size. Even the coral thread in their sea-foam green bed linens matched the coral webbing in the wallpaper.

The captain crept along the walls until his shadow settled amongst the curtains, his ebony, sunken eyes filled with venom.

That is not the same captain who helped me in the hall. He'd been a lighter shade of grey, his presence free of that greasy coating of hate. Annie blinked. *Are there two? How?*

Annie turned to Lady Duskin, hands folded behind her back. "Where is he?"

"Oh, he'll be here." Lady Duskin took a long drink from her bottle. "Soon enough." Her hair was undone, letting her brown curls spill down to her waist. She sat on the edge of the bed, grinning, and patted the space on the mattress beside her.

Annie kept her face expressionless as she sat. *They can't hurt you worse than death.*

Lady Duskin pressed her cheek against Annie's hair, her breath stinking of wine, and wrapped her arm around her waist. "You've always been his favorite, haven't you?"

Annie stiffened under her touch, her mind flashing to Cam. "I'm afraid I don't know what you mean."

Lady Duskin pinched her side hard. "Don't lie. There was a point I thought I might win him over, but then you showed up."

Oh. Annie kept her breathing even, refusing to flinch away from her touch.

Lady Duskin took another swig of wine, softly stroking the place she'd pinched. "If I'd been able to give him a child of his own, it might have been different, but here we are."

"Here we are," Annie repeated.

"Is that your plan?" Lady Duskin's grip tightened until her nails dug into Annie's skin. She pressed a kiss to her temple. "To take him from me? To become the new Lady Duskin? And if that doesn't work, you'll crawl and worm your way into Lord Callahan's bed?" She laughed sharply. "I can't blame you for having a plan B. I wish I'd had one."

Something cold and sharp pressed into her side. A blade. Annie kept her breathing slow, even. *I've survived this before. I can survive it again.* If she denied her claims, Lady Duskin would call her a liar. If she admitted to working with Cam, she'd sink the knife into her ribs.

You're no longer a sheep. Annie inhaled. *Sympathize with her. Play into her fears.*

"Forgive me, Mother. The only bed a desire is mine." She let herself sink into Lady Duskin's touch. "Sometimes I'm so tired, I cry in the night, knowing that I have to rise in the morning. Have you ever felt that way? Like you can't go on?"

Lady Duskin swigged her wine. "Every blasted day."

Annie's voice softened. "How do you deal with it? The weight?"

The stroking on her side continued, the knife catching the seams of Annie's gown. Lady Duskin kissed her hair. "When I can't sleep, I imagine myself shoving this blade into his throat. Sometimes it's your throat. Sometimes I'm sinking it into the temples of all those whimpering court ninnies and watching their blood pool on the floor."

Annie let a moment pass. "Does it help?"

"No," Lady Duskin whispered. "Not at all." She set the wine on the floor, then pulled a small, corked vial from her bodice. Pearl Dust.

"Where did you get that?" Annie asked, her throat dry. "Lord Duskin and I—"

"—Have the only keys to the stores, I know." Lady Duskin uncorked the vial and dipped the tip of her pinky into the pink dust. She brushed the dust onto her tongue, and the muscles in her body instantly clenched. She let out a low groan. "How convenient for the two of you. But don't worry, dear." She patted Annie's shoulder, the dagger just grazing her cheek. "I have my own sources."

"Charlotte." Lord Duskin's words were low and harsh. He stood in the doorway, his eyes fixed on the blade in Lady Duskin's hands. "Charlotte," he repeated. "Leave us."

Lady Duskin bristled, moving so the blade now pointed at her husband. "You cannot cast me out of my own bedroom, Richard. I won't have it."

Lord Duskin's eyes darkened as he stepped slowly toward the bed. He held out his hand. "Leave us."

A pure, world-ending rage rippled over Lady Duskin's features, and she stood unsteadily, raising her blade. In the curtains, the captain laughed. For a heartbeat, Annie actually believed she might stab him, but instead, Lady Duskin set the knife into her husband's waiting palm, shooting Annie a hateful glare before storming from the room.

Lord Duskin let out a rough sigh, rubbing his forehead.

Annie stayed silent as he sat down on the bed beside her, resting his elbows on his thighs. His oiled hair and mustache gleamed in the low candlelight, and when his gaze locked onto hers, she couldn't help the tremor that ran down her spine. "My wife is a jealous woman."

Annie held his stare. "She loves you."

"Do you?" His hand whipped out and grabbed her chin. "Do you love me, girl?"

No fear. Fear will kill you. She didn't look away. "You know I do, Father."

He squeezed painfully tighter. "You've neglected me this week. I must ask, is your love waning?"

"Of course not."

"I've heard whispers. Some of the children say you visit Lord Callahan in the night. I've seen the way he looks at you."

Annie's heart thundered in her chest, but she didn't let it show. *Half-truths.* "He's requested me . . . more than once."

"And?"

Even though it curdled her stomach, she forced herself to stroke his cheek. "I respectfully declined."

Lord Duskin smiled. "I knew you would."

"I admit I haven't been myself lately. It won't happen again."

"No, it won't." He took a fistful of her hair at the base of her neck. "You know how I feel about disloyalty. It gladdens my heart that I can trust you." When he released her, Annie closed her eyes, forcing her breathing to slow. Lord Duskin stood. "I decided to throw our family a ball this coming Sunday to celebrate the finalization of my patent. I have invitations written to be delivered to the influential townsfolk and business owners. Can I expect to have your full support during this endeavor?"

"You know you do," Annie whispered, standing as well. A thought struck her. "And to prove it, let me deliver the invitations for you. In person."

Lord Duskin's brow rose. "I have couriers."

"It would mean more coming from me." She forced some sweetness on her tongue. "From your own daughter. The guests would think it such an honor."

"Hmm." Lord Duskin leaned in. "It *would* send a nice message." Every ounce of pleasantness dropped from his expression. "Do not disappoint me."

Annie allowed herself to smile, her heart pounding against her ribs. "Have I ever?"

Lord Duskin returned her grin. "We shall see."

CHAPTER 24

CAMDEN

I'm tired of riding. Cam brushed a bit of dust off the fireproof coat Elias had given him. Surely, he smelt of horse. Not only had he had to scale his bedroom balcony to sneak out of the manor, but he'd also had to trade his pocket watch to ensure the stableboy on duty kept silent.

Two months ago, he wouldn't have given a rat's behind what he looked or smelled like. He'd spent too much time with these upper classers lately. If he kept this up, he'd be requesting cucumber finger sandwiches before long.

Cam parked his horse at a station just outside the shipping yard, nodding to the attendant. The moon rose just over a thicket of walnut trees as he trekked down the road to the harbor, casting a pale glow over the red brick beneath his boots. Flowerbeds lined the road, overflowing with bright lilies in bloom—some in reds, yellows, pinks and oranges. Others were striped, and some were layered with multiple colors. Just another showcase of Richard's attention to detail.

His father's mansion had been perfectly detailed, too. From the outside, no one would have suspected or believed that the inner workings of the Callahan home were a living hell.

He'd been beaten for picking a lily once.

Cam shoved his hands in his pockets, careful not to touch the flowers, as that now familiar fire raked inside his chest.

It wanted out . . . again.

It had settled for a short while after his incident with Frank Boyle, but it soon returned with full force. He wasn't sure what to make of it—of his power's seemingly independent wants and greed—but for now, he had a mission to distract him. One that would allow him to put on an old, yet familiar, mask— that of Camden Barnes.

Pirates worked during the day, but they came alive at night.

As Cam moved closer, the horizon filled with a sea of masts and sails. A loving salt breeze filled his lungs, whipping his hair over his eyes.

God, he missed the ocean.

He needed it, craved it. Parts of his soul felt empty without it.

Even with midnight approaching, the harbor was bustling. Sailors unloaded supplies from the docks, while others hauled supplies into the harbor, already haggling prices with waiting vendors.

This . . . this is who he'd become. Who Resh had made him, and who he was afraid he'd have to let go every day Resh spent missing, leaving all his secrets in limbo.

Somewhere his father won't find him.

Only he and Resh knew the truth: Alexander Callahan put out a hit on his own wife and son.

He'd been successful in killing Cam's mother, but she'd ensured that Cam had gotten free. In his sleepless nights, Cam wondered why her assassin didn't finish him in that street. If he'd meant to let him starve as an urchin before taking him out for good.

Either way, if somehow Resh let slip what he knew, Cam's father would find him again—and he didn't think he would survive this time.

No one wanted a governor that sought to murder his family, but they *could* sympathize with a husband whose wife allegedly ran away for another man and wound up getting her and her son killed. One slip of the truth from Cam, and Alexander's entire regime could collapse. He was a liability, and Cam had spent the last ten years making sure his father never heard his name again.

Cam wouldn't leave until he had Resh back or knew for certain that he was dead. He couldn't risk it.

Oh, Resh. Cam shook his head, sighing. He knew Annie was lying to him to a degree, but *why* was the bigger question? There were times when he looked at her and she seemed . . . haunted. Scarred. A little bit like himself. Maybe that's why he always found his thoughts wandering back to her.

A shiver of fresh heat made his fingers clench. Cam slammed his eyes shut. *Just go away.*

He had a job to do. He needed to concentrate.

A towering, wooden arch stood at the entrance of the harbor, its latticework beautifully ensnared in the grips of wild, pink clematis. As he passed through the arch, Cam allowed his posture to relax, shaking out his hair until it fell around his eyes. He tucked his hands in his pockets, making sure the revolver hanging on his gun belt was visible as he strode lazily toward the piers.

He'd never seen anything like the Duskins' harbor. It wasn't large or particularly impressive in grandeur, but it was so . . . clean.

Cam paused, taking in the layout. There were seventeen

separate wharfs for the ships to moor, each with its own transit shed. Not a detail was missed, not an expense spared.

I hate it. Cam sniffed. Watersides were meant to be grimy. Filled with barnacles and fat rats crawling over your boots, with scumbags on the corner trying to slip their sticky fingers in your pockets. Where every corner and every shadow was just another place for someone to shove a rusty knife into your gut.

Cam took his time walking the dockside. Merchants of all shapes and sizes shot him wary looks as they passed, and he returned their stares with bitter glares of his own. *It's my blasted brands.* There was no reason to try to hide who he was anymore. Not when he now wore targets on his flesh. Despite the flowery façade, there were killers here, too. They were just better paid in New Havana.

Cam fingered his revolver, finding comfort in the cool steel and the warmth of his mother's jewel inside. People parted as he headed deeper into the docks, whispering, their eyes scouring the burning marks on his face and chest, visible where he'd left his shirt unbuttoned.

Well-dressed sailors sat in covered booths between each pier—Duskins' hires. In the farthest booth, a younger sailor—with rich, red-brown skin and curly, black hair—sat propped against his desk, his head lolling onto his chest as he snored.

Cam leaned against the booth, crossed his feet, and cleared his throat. "Morning, Sunshine."

"*Blazes.*" The boy jerked awake, his eyes bloodshot. What little color he had drained away when he caught sight of Cam's brands. "Ex-excuse me, my lord. I must have nodded off."

"You don't say." Cam tapped his left breast pocket. "I'm looking for someone to carry a package off the island. Got any suggestions?"

The boy's thin brow rose. "Besides normal post?"

Cam rolled his eyes. "*Yes.* Besides normal post."

The boy let out a low whistle, running a hand through his hair. "Check the Havana Inn. They don't allow booze inside, but you can usually find a few blokes drinking out back."

Cam slipped a silver coin from his coat sleeve and slid it across the desk. "Thank you."

The Havana Inn was easy enough to find. It sat like an eyesore—decorated with bright green and yellow plaster—on the far side of the harbor, well away from the stink of the tide.

Warm light spilled out into the streets from the open door and windows, a pleasant fiddle solo chasing away the tension of the cut-throat market stalls. For a moment, it reminded Cam of his time spent in Port Lebanon, stuck inside the Yellow Bunter night after night. Playing card games until he went cross-eyed, laughing with Nathan, watching his crew drink themselves into a stupor.

He glanced in the window, his heart sinking as he made his way around back. Smiling, well-dressed men and women sat around circular tables, drinking ale out of wooden mugs. He missed when life was simple. When all he had to worry over was where his next meal would come from.

Had it ever been simple, though? Cam's brows furrowed as he stepped into the alley behind the inn. *Was it simple, or was I lying to myself?*

He didn't want to know the answer.

Foul water splashed over his boots as he walked, seeping into the fine leather. A few yards down, hushed voices trickled out from the shadows. As his eyes adjusted to the darkness, six men became visible, huddled together. Some sat on empty beer barrels, others leaned against the backside of the inn, puffing on cigars.

They turned at the sounds of Cam's approaching footsteps, their expressions set into hardened scowls, and they reached for their weapons.

Ah, my people. Cam grinned, tapping the pocket on his chest. "Gentlemen."

A short, stocky bloke—with a wiry, chest-length beard—kicked off the wall and returned the gesture as his cigar lit up his dead, brown eyes. "Aye? Who sent you?"

Cam's hands went back in his pockets. "The kid in the farthest booth."

"Figures." The man spat. "He's gotten greedy if he thought to send a Stripe."

"Times are tough," Cam replied. "I took a deal with a Stripe myself not too long ago."

"Ha." The man took another puff, blowing smoke from his nose. "Is that how you got to be"—He gestured to Cam's brands— "in your current predicament?"

Cam flexed away the heat building in his fingers and smiled. "You could say that."

"Mmm." The man nodded to his companions, snuffing out his cigar on the heel of his boot. He offered his hand. "I go by Pulley. You?"

Cam shook it and winked. "You're better off not knowing my name."

Pulley chuckled. "Fair enough. Come with me, then."

He was careful not to touch Cam as he passed him in the alley, heading back towards the docks.

He stinks of gunpowder. Cam couldn't help staring at the moon's reflection off the man's shiny, bald scalp. They approached the very last moored ship—a decent-sized frigate with deep, green sails. Pulley pointed to the bench on the side of the dock. "Stay here, if ya don't mind."

Cam sat, giving him an impish grin, before that blasted bald head jogged up the gangplank and onto the ship. He must know the captain well if he'd dare board without permission.

As the minutes passed, Cam stood, allowing himself to take in the outer details of the ship.

It was a sleek, mean creature. By the look of the pine planks coated in pitch, it was Western. Even though they rotted faster, he'd always loved the look of a pine hull. He loved the smell even more. He counted it out to be around one hundred and seventy feet long, with two gun decks. Plenty large enough for what he needed, then some. Maybe he could find some men looking for work back at the inn to fill in for his crew.

Maybe it's time for Nathan to move up to Quartermaster.

Pulley stepped back onto the gangplank, followed by a second man with a scarred-up chin and a wide-brimmed hat. The newcomer froze when he caught sight of Cam, then a growling laugh escaped him. "Hang me out to dry! If it isn't Camden Barnes. Heard around town you were dead." He paused, taking in Cam's brands. "Guess the seagulls were right."

Pulley's beady dark eyes flashed to Cam curiously.

"Clyde Duffington." Cam strode toward the man and grinned. "Some say I'm alive, but I really must be in hell if you're a captain now. I haven't seen you since that gig in Rouenn." Cam ran a finger over his own smooth chin. "What happened to your face, mate?"

Clyde laughed, waving him forward. "Now that's a tale for another time. Come, come!"

Cam followed him obediently up the gangplank, closely monitored by Pulley. The glint of metal flashed off the sailor's belt—a dented spyglass.

Cam's eyes narrowed. *Interesting.*

Now that he was boarded, he got a better view of the ship. Its deck needed polishing, but it was well-maintained besides. The console sat atop the captain's quarters, the helm over-looking the deck, as was the usual fashion. Sailors working the rigging stared at them as they passed, whispering to each other. Out of a younger boy, he distinctly heard the word *Torva Messor.*

Cam snapped his teeth at him, and the poor kid nearly fainted.

"You quit that," Pulley whispered from behind him.

Cam smiled but didn't look back. "I've done nothing but what he deserves."

"He's been a powder monkey since eight and he's still alive," Pulley shot back gruffly. "What he deserves is a little respect, don't ya think?"

This time, Cam *did* look back. Even behind the massive beard, Pulley's expression was stern. No fear.

Cam just gave him a crooked smile. *I think I like him.*

"Here we are." Clyde ushered them into his quarters, shutting and locking the heavy oak door behind him. Cam let out a low whistle. The room was horrifically gaudy but lush. Bright velvet tapestries lined the walls, while heavy bear rugs covered the floor. A crystal chandelier swayed over what he presumed to be Clyde's desk—an oversized, flat-topped chest with claw-foot legs.

It looks like my tub at the manor. Cam snorted. "You've done well for yourself, it seems."

Clyde puffed his chest as he sat. "I've done what I can."

Pulley sidestepped behind Clyde as Cam picked through the novels lining the shelves. Children's stories, mostly. Cam peered over his shoulder at the captain, smiling as he snapped a book shut. "From boat lackey to captain in two short years. Explain to me how that happened."

Clyde leaned back in his cushioned desk chair, scowling. "I made friends with the right people."

"*Killed* the right people, you mean."

Clyde's scowl deepened. "That, too." He watched Cam pick through his trinkets, his cheeks reddening with irritation. Now he propped his feet on the desk. "Why are you here, Barnes?"

"I thought your mate would have told you." Cam set a particularly lovely silver chalice back in its glass cabinet along with the other fineries. "I need something delivered."

"I know what you *told* him, but why are you *really* here?" Clyde picked at the feather on his hat. Pulley's gaze darted between Cam and the captain as he continued. "The Camden Barnes I knew was a two-faced, lying barracuda."

Cam splayed his finger over his chest. "Clyde, you wound me. And here I thought we were friends."

Clyde shook a finger at him. "See, mate, you're still lying. We were never friends."

Cam let his fire light his eyes, amusement falling from his features.

Clyde leapt out of his chair as Cam swung onto the desk, inhumanly fast, and sat cross-legged. Both men pulled their pistols on him, but Cam just smiled and smiled. "You see, now I am telling the truth." He pressed his palms onto the desktop, letting his handprints burn into the wood. "I do need something delivered. Something very precious to me."

Clyde collected himself, slowly lowering his pistol.

Pulley kept it raised.

"See?" Clyde chuckled nervously. "Another fib, Barnes. You've never cared for anything."

"Things change." Cam slid from the desk and onto Clyde's chair. Pulley kept his gun trained on his forehead. "Twenty-five to thirty people will need emergency evacuation from the island when I give the signal. Since I don't know the exact time this will happen, I need the ship stocked, staffed, and ready to sail twenty-four hours a day." Cam turned his attention to Pulley. "Do you think you can manage that?"

Pulley's wiry brows rose. "Why you asking me?"

"Because that's what you want, isn't it? A new position?" Cam nodded to the spyglass on Pulley's belt. "Cheap steel, or it wouldn't have dented. If you'd earned it on promotion, I doubt your captain would have been so petty."

Clyde was furious now. "How dare—"

Cam raised a finger. Clyde went silent. "By the sulfur stains and smell coming off your clothes, you're a gunner, yes? A gunner who would like nothing more than to be a navigator?"

The two men exchanged glances. Pulley lowered his weapon and nodded.

Cam gestured to the bookshelves. "Bedtime stories and lullabies. If your crew was educated enough to read, Clyde, they'd laugh you into the sea. It's all a show. Along with that chalice—fake gems—there's no way your crew would ever know, unless they were learned enough on precious stones." Cam's smile widened. "Plus, *Pulley*, with the way you defended that boy, you must care for him like a son. Maybe he is your son. It would be a shame if such a selfish, deceiving captain left him a powder monkey forever. Promotions are expensive."

Snarling, Clyde grabbed Cam's wrist to pull him from the chair, but hissed when Cam's skin burned him. He cursed at the welts bubbling on his palm. "What the *blazes* do you think you're doing, Barnes?"

"Not Barnes." Cam pulled out the uncut diamond he'd swiped on Shar-Crue out of his pocket and tossed it to Pulley. The man's eyes nearly bugged out of his skull. "Camden Barnes is dead. It's Callahan, now. I'm taking your ship, Clyde."

Clyde's face turned a brilliant shade of red in his fury. He cocked the hammer of his pistol and aimed between Cam's eyes. "Over my dead body, you piece of Stripe trash. I—"

A gunshot went off, spraying the innards of Clyde's skull all over the desk.

Smoke billowed from the barrel of Pulley's gun, his breath coming in heavy gasps.

Cam burst out in hysterical laughter, then clapped a hand over his mouth, clearing his throat. "Sorry, so sorry. Forgive me. You know, knocking him out would have worked just fine?"

Pulley's gaze finally met Cam's, filled with confusion and a sprinkle of hope. "The arrogant pheasant had it coming." He pocketed the diamond. "You'll be the captain now, eh?"

Cam picked a bit of brains off his coat. "It seems so."

"You'll make me your navigator?"

"Can you have this ship ready to sail at the drop of a hat?"

"Aye, sir."

"Then welcome aboard, Navigator Pulley." Cam bowed at the waist. "Please inform the crew of the staff changes. Make that boy your personal assistant. We'll have ladies coming aboard. I want every inch of this ship polished until it shines as brightly as your beaming, beautiful head. Understood?" He kicked the toe of Clyde's boot, grimacing, then tossed Pulley a gold coin. "And if you could find someone to clean up this mess, that would be great."

Pulley bowed. "Anything else, captain?"

Cam paused as he turned for the door, thoughtful. "I don't know how I forgot to ask. What's the name of this rig?"

Pulley's lips tugged up at the corners. "*The Apology*, sir."

"Dear Lord." Cam shook his head. "We'll have to change that, now, won't we?"

The purple and pink halo of sunrise was just breaching the treetops by the time Cam returned to his room. Thank the Lord the Duskins were late sleepers.

He climbed back the way he'd come, through the glass balcony doors. Cam pulled off his coat, tossing it on the sofa by the window. A speck of white caught the corner of his eye. *What the—*

A folded white note sat on his coffee table. Cam ran a hand through his hair and exhaled. *I shouldn't have expected my room to be safe. But safe from whom, though?*

Stupid question. Of course, it was her.

Slowly, Cam peeled the note open, careful not to tear it—or set it on fire. He scanned over the dainty script:

Dawn. Bakery.

Hmm. Cam slid the note into his pants pocket and grabbed his coat. *I guess I'm not sleeping tonight, after all.*

And he didn't mind. He'd stay awake a thousand nights as long as she was there.

CHAPTER 25
ANNIE

"Yes." Annie forced a sickly, sweet smile on her face. The grocer's wife accepted the thick, wax-sealed envelope, skeptical. "6 p.m. on Sunday. The details are inside. It would be an honor to have you."

The young woman curtsied. *She seems nervous.* "Thank you. It's an honor to be invited. Formal dress?"

"Formal dress," Annie confirmed. They stared at each other for a moment. Annie shifted her gaze to the ground. "Have a nice morning."

"Same to you," the woman muttered quickly before shutting her cherry-red door.

This is truly awful. Annie tucked deeper into her cinched, lilac day coat, the morning mist clinging to her neck and hair. She turned back onto the main street. There were several hours until the sun was dangerous to her skin, but she hid behind her parasol all the same.

I hate this coat. I hate this color. Not only did it wash her out, but she felt ridiculous. Color was meant for ladies—for those who brought joy—not for someone like her. Lord Duskin had bought it for her months ago, though, and she'd never worn it. Hopefully, it would keep her on his good side for a little longer.

The sun was just rising as she made it back to the market square. The merchants threw open their doors, welcoming the day's first customers. Annie scanned the growing crowd for fiery brands.

Nothing.

She brushed the bag at her side. One invitation left—she'd timed it perfectly. If Cam got her note, he'd meet her at the bakery and could walk with her to her final stop, which happened to be on her way back to the manor. If he didn't show up . . . well, she could make the excuse of wanting to buy sweets for her sibling, then head back like nothing ever happened.

Her stomach growled as she wandered toward the bakery. She wanted to run—to see if Cam was there waiting for her— but she had an image to maintain . . . and self-control to keep.

For most of her life—since her family's death—other people were dangerous. They either hurt you for pleasure or they hurt you for gain. It frightened her that she didn't know yet what Cam's motives were. It frightened her more that she sometimes forgot to care.

Annie jumped when the bakery owner swung open his shop window, blanketing her in the heavy, rich scent of freshly buttered bread. An elderly, whiskered man blinked at her. She blinked back, fighting the urge to duck behind her parasol.

He cleared his throat. Hers tightened. He set a steaming platter of cinnamon rolls in the window. "Is there anything I can get you, my lady?"

He recognizes me. Annie opened her mouth to answer, but her tongue stuck to the roof of her mouth. "I—um . . ."

"We'll take four of those," a drawling, amused voice said behind her. *Camden.* She turned, her heart hammering, and he was smiling at her as he offered a few bills to the baker. "I'll take a box if you have one."

The baker glanced between her and Cam, his expression pinched, but he nodded. "Right away, my lord." He headed back into the shop, probably in search of packaging.

Cam let out a low chuckle, stepping forward until his elbow brushed against hers. His brands were bright again, pulsing. "I hate when they call me that."

"Liar." Annie tucked a loose strand of white hair back into her tight braid, collecting herself. "From what I've seen, you enjoy the attention."

"Do I?" Cam's green eyes flickered with mischief. "So, you've been watching me?"

Annie looked away, fighting the warmth building in her cheeks. "Shouldn't I be? I'm trusting you with my life, after all."

Cam shrugged.

The baker returned moments later, carrying a wrapped package of pastries. Cam took the box and thanked him, turning to Annie. Shadows purpled the underside of his eyes. "So, where to? I'm at your whims and mercy."

Something in that statement made her stomach clench. She exhaled, straightening her coat. Cam's gaze roamed over her clothing, a frown forming on his lips.

It was her turn to scowl. "What? You don't like it?"

"I'm just curious. Why purple?"

"It's lilac," she huffed. "And that's none of your business."

"Lilac," he snorted. "I've just never seen you in anything but grey or black. Did Dick Duskin make you wear that?"

Annie's chest tightened, but she couldn't stop from laughing. "Don't let him hear you call him that." She noticed what *he* wore, then. His usual grey frock coat, his shirt unbuttoned halfway, revealing his tanned, sculpted chest and brands beneath. A dark stain on his coat hem and sleeves caught her eye—blood.

He followed her gaze, expression darkening. "We should walk, shouldn't we?"

She straightened, raising her parasol. "This way."

He offered her his arm, and reluctantly, she took it, leading him towards the edge of the market square. Even beneath layers of clothing, his touch was warm. Cam popped open the box of rolls and started munching on one with his free hand, the sugary glaze coating his fingers. He noticed her watching and offered her a bite.

Annie shook her head, looking away.

"No?" he asked, "But they're *so* good."

The crowds were growing fuller. Annie could feel the eyes watching them, probably searching for something—anything—to report back to Lord Duskin. She kept her voice low. "Will you please pull up your hood?"

Cam snorted, causing people to glance in their direction. "Embarrassed to be seen with me, Kitten?"

"At the moment?" Annie pursed her lips.

Cam grinned and licked the icing off his lips.

God, save me. "Lord Duskin already suspects us. He questioned me about you last night."

Cam's smile faded. "And?"

It was Annie's turn to half-smile. "I told him you've been persistent in your pursuits, but not to worry, because I do not return the sentiment."

Cam let out a barking laugh, causing Annie to duck deeper behind her parasol and hiss. "Keep your voice down."

Cam shook his head, still chuckling. "Reciprocated attractions or not, you have to admit, this works to our advantage."

Reciprocated attractions? She didn't allow herself to stop and consider what *that* meant. Her brows furrowed. "How so?"

Cam again offered her a cinnamon roll. When she declined, he began munching on it himself. "It means we have an excuse if we're seen together. You can continue to insist my *pursuits* are unwanted, and we can go about our business."

I hadn't thought of that. Even if someone did see them and report it to Lord Duskin, she could make the excuse that she was just being polite to protect Cam and Lord Duskin's relationship. Annie's shoulders relaxed a little. "And what of Mr. Price?"

Cam spoke with his mouth full. "What about him?"

She frowned, dusting away the crumbs he spewed on her sleeve. "He suspects."

"Oh, right." Cam swallowed. "I never got to talk to you about him."

Her brow rose. "Yes?"

Cam waited until the crowd thinned before he continued. "When I followed him to the estates, I overheard a very interesting conversation between him and one Charlotte Duskin."

No . . . I don't believe it. She couldn't imagine a situation on Earth that would put those two in a relationship together. They were just too . . . different. *But I've been wrong before.* "Interesting how?"

Cam's eyes scanned the oblivious, busy faces around them as he said, "I can't be certain yet, but it sounded as if they are conspiring together against Julian's brother—Richard."

Annie stumbled, heart jumping into her throat. "*Brother?*"

Cam shrugged. "That's what it sounded like."

"You're wrong. How could she cheat with her husband's brother?"

"It happens all the time."

"There's no way."

"Is there no way," Cam drawled, "or are you choosing not to see it?"

Annie didn't know how to answer that. Desperate to change the subject, her eyes wandered again to the blood staining his sleeve. "Who did you kill?"

Cam swallowed, sucking the last of the icing off his thumb. "I didn't kill anyone."

"Sure you didn't," she whispered. "Your coat and dark circles say otherwise."

"Why does everyone always assume I'm lying?" He dropped his chin, watching the crowd. "Someone died, but *I* didn't kill him."

"Did you help?"

"Less than you might think," He exhaled, and they walked in silence for a moment, the only sound being the clicking of her heeled boots on the cobblestone street. "I found us a ship."

"Did you?" As they moved toward the edge of the market, Annie led him into an alley to the right, toward the northern residences. "Was it worth the cost of a life?"

Cam slowed, his lessened pace tugging at her elbow. "The *cost*?"

Annie wheeled on him, that blasted strand of hair falling loose, irritation building in her throat. "Was someone's *life* worth a boat?"

He looked taken aback. "*Ship*. And some would say it was."

They just stared at each other, a dozen emotions passing over his features. Annie's fists clenched. *Remember who you are. Remember why you're doing this.* Even still, she said—too honestly, "I hate killing."

Cam had the decency not to smile. "Coming from one in the *business* of death."

Annie's eyes fluttered closed for just a moment. *I can't judge him.*

If only she could be home again. To smell the snow on the wind, to watch the frost form on the windows. "Where I'm from, life is cherished. It doesn't belong to us, and it isn't ours to take—unless someone is trying to take yours or your family's away from you. Then it is forfeit." *And I am an abomination.*

Cam's eyes . . . they looked so far away. "If only we all came from your country."

Annie turned and moved to the end of the alley, knocking on the last door to the left. An older man answered the door, and she gave him all the same words and courtesies she'd given the others. He never looked at her, though. He watched, wide-eyed, to where Cam stood a few yards back, his gaze fixed on the ground as flames licked around fists and throat.

As soon as she finished speaking, he closed the door in Annie's face. Inhaling, she strode back down the alley to rejoin Cam.

As she approached, his eyes lifted to hers slowly, and they were no longer that vibrant shade of green, but aglow with living fire.

She paused as he exhaled, and a rush of something that wasn't quite fear flooded her. A wave of energy surged from him, spreading into the street, and the walls surrounding them shook.

She kept her face expressionless, wearing her mask.

He stared at his glowing palm. "Why did you ask me here?"

He's going to kill you. He wouldn't do that. He's a monster. He's killed. So have you. Annie blinked, then swallowed, gesturing to the house at the end of the street. "Weren't you listening? Richard is throwing a ball on Sunday to celebrate the finalization of his patent. It might be the only chance we have to get the patients out. It must be this Sunday."

Cam let out a low laugh, tucking his hands in his pockets. "That's the first time I've heard you call him Richard."

Her throat went dry. "Seems there are many firsts today."

"Indeed."

"You'll get in touch with Mr. Wilkins, then?"

"Naturally."

She nodded. "I'll wait for your word." As she made to move past him in the alley, he caught her arm. Not forcefully. The touch was almost like a question.

Annie paused, turning to him. When she took in his face, she'd never seen anyone look so torn and distraught. So close to the point of crumbling. *I've never seen anyone look so much like me.*

His eyes were green again when he said, "What about when it is your family?"

"Pardon?" She breathed. "I don't understand."

He chewed his lip so hard it began to bleed. "What about when the person who wants you dead *is* part of your family?"

Her heart hurt as she swallowed. "Well, I guess they've forfeited the right to be your family, haven't they?"

He nodded, watching her intently. He ran his tongue over his bloody lip. "Then what?"

Don't look, don't look. She looked at his lips. "Then you find a new family. For as long as they're beneficial to you."

"That sounds like a miserable existence."

"It's the only one we have."

He laughed softly, the heat of his breath tickling her face and neck. His eyes met hers. "Does it have to be?"

She didn't know.

CHAPTER 26
CAMDEN

After his excursion with Annie, Cam went back to his room and slept the entire day. More than once, there were soft knocks on his door, rousing him from his dreams, but he ignored them and drifted off again.

Edmund Resh stood on the bow of the point, overlooking the rolling sea. He often took his watch there, cigar smoke clouding his head, counting the stars as they appeared on the horizon.

Cam looked down at his younger body, unscarred and brandless. He felt so empty without the heat crawling under his skin. Elias and Vernon had been right—he had forgotten what it felt like to be human.

"You called for me?" Little Cam asked.

Resh turned, blowing smoke from his nostrils. "Come here, boy."

He didn't sound angry. Little Cam swallowed and moved to his captain's side, the failing light gleaming off the older man's golden buttons. Without looking his way, Resh handed him a small, wrapped package. "Here," he grunted. "For your birthday."

It was his birthday?

Little Cam had forgotten. Excitement flooded him as he greedily tore open the package. Inside sat a polished, six-chamber revolver. Wide-eyed, he ran his fingers over the smooth handle until his nail caught on a thin ridge on the underside of the pommel. He looked up at Resh, questioning.

His captain smiled. "Pull it."

Little Cam did, revealing a tight compartment hollowed out inside the pommel. A tiny, wrapped lump was stuffed inside. He dug it out and removed the object, unwrapping it. His breath caught as a blazing orange jewel shone in the sunset, so bright it almost looked ablaze. Was this his mother's—

"It's your momma's ring." Resh took a puff of his cigar. "I thought about selling it half a hundred times, but it didn't feel right. It's yours. Do with it what you will."

Little Cam struggled to hold back the tears lining his eyes. "Thank you. For all of it."

Resh just nodded.

Little Cam gently stowed the ring back inside its compartment before sliding the revolver into his belt, pride swelling in his chest.

"You know." Resh took another puff. "Your momma made me promise I'd keep you alive. To keep you safe."

"I know." Cam rolled his eyes. Resh had told him this story one hundred times. "And to keep me somewhere my father won't find me."

Resh's black eyes scoured his face. "Have you ever wondered why your papa might want you dead?"

"No," Cam lied. Of course, he did, but that would require remembering. Seeing in his mind as his mother's blood leaked over the pavement as her red-stained hands gripped his.

"Fair enough," Resh grunted, turning his attention back to the stars.

Little Cam watched the waves rise and fall, the sea air filling his lungs and clearing away all fear. "I couldn't keep my mother safe, but I promise, I will protect you."

To his surprise, Resh barked out a laugh. "Don't be ridiculous."

"I'm not." Little Cam puffed up, moving in front of Resh. His captain wasn't the only one who'd come with a gift. Little Cam pulled a necklace out of his pocket—a lovely jade fishhook on a leather cord. He lowered it into Resh's waiting palm. "For good luck. I'll protect you. I'll protect The Nightlady *. . . and its crew. I promise."*

Resh tied the cord around his neck, then began to laugh, his face twisting until it was a pool of black hatred. A smile cut through the darkness. "We'll see about that, you stupid boy. We'll see."

Cam jolted awake, dripping in sweat, as his breath came in heavy rasps. That had been so long ago. Did Resh know, even then, that he'd fail him? *The Nightlady* had burned, and its crew were dust or worse, and he had no idea whether Resh was alive or dead.

He was somewhere on this island, and Annie knew—Annie knew, and he couldn't bring himself to force it out of her. Resh would call him weak.

His father would call him weak.

A tendril of fire stroked his cheek, attempting to soothe him.

The lock on the door clicked. Annie stepped into his room, holding up a key for him to see—the master key. She quickly scanned over his half-naked body, at the sheen of sweat coating his skin. Dare he say, the faintest blush again colored her snow-white cheeks. "Dinner is in half an hour."

"Thank you." Cam pulled back the sheets. "I imagine I've been summoned?"

"You have." Annie looked anywhere and everywhere but him. "And wear something nice. All the lords and ladies have been invited. Lord Duskin expects your formal answer on the Pearl Dust arrangement."

"Great." Cam rubbed his sticky face. "Anything else?"

"No," Annie said flatly.

"No?"

"No."

"Fine." Cam stretched. "See you at dinner then?"

Annie nodded, hesitated, then closed the door behind her.

Cam tugged at his necktie as he headed into the dining room. Over a dozen people waited inside, the sound of their chatter like a beehive. Half the town had arrived to hear him declare his allegiance to the Duskins. Now the manor would be full of even more eavesdroppers.

Cam's breaths were shallow. The noise, the colors, the smells—all of it was too much right now. He'd rather drown himself in the sea than sit at the long table in front of him, overflowing with over-spiced meats, heavy cheeses, and dark red wines.

The tightness in his chest choked out what breath remained in him. Why did the flowers in the vases have to match the sofa pillows? Why did they have to wear so many layers when it was hot enough outside to fry an egg on the cobblestone? His heat flickered up his neck again, curling around his ear. *Let me go.*

I can't.

Why?

I don't trust you.

Trust me.

No. Cam rubbed his temples. People were going to notice. People were going to—

"Camden?" Annie's soft voice whispered by his elbow.

Cam's knees nearly buckled. Something cool brushed his

fingers, and he opened his eyes. Annie held out a glass of ice water, the condensation hissing against his skin. Again, she didn't meet his gaze, instead observing the growing crowd of guests. "For you."

"Thank you." Cam truly meant it. He downed the glass in one gulp, then proceeded to chew on the ice cubes. "I hate parties."

"As do I." She smoothed her gown, a lovely, layered silk masterpiece in ebony black.

"You look stunning." Cam sucked on another ice cube as he scanned for Richard. "I'm surprised Charlotte let you in here."

Annie finally looked at him, her expression flat. "Are you alright?"

He crunched another cube. "No."

"Nightmares?"

"How'd you guess?"

To his surprise, Annie patted his elbow. "I have them, too." A flicker of fear passed over her features as Richard emerged from the sea of bodies, striding toward them. "Enjoy your evening," she whispered before ghosting away.

"Lord Duskin." Cam bowed. "I apologize for my late arrival. I've been struggling to sleep of late."

"You're not alone." Richard smiled, his golden tooth gleaming. He wrapped his arm around Cam's shoulder, steering him toward the others. Cam didn't miss the tension in his touch or the way he glanced back to wear Annie stood, waiting in the corner. Richard's tone deepened. "I've heard rumors that you've made advances toward my daughter."

Careful now. He had to play this right. Cam let a few breaths pass before he answered. "Am I to deny her beauty?"

"I'm glad you're honoring our agreement to honesty." Richard led him toward the window, the setting sun reflecting off his oiled, black hair. "I may not have reacted well to a lie."

"Oh?" Cam leaned against the windowsill, his heat burning all the way into his tongue. "And what have my truths earned me?"

Richard's dark eyes cut to his. "Have you made a choice?"

Cam exhaled. "I will announce before everyone this evening that I will be building a pearl grove on New Havana under your authority."

"Good." Richard smiled again. "Good. I'm glad to hear it. And my daughter informed you of the ball this weekend?"

"She did."

"And?"

Cam raised his empty glass of ice. "Large achievements deserve even larger celebrations."

Richard took a step closer, his lips purple from wine. "At the ball, I'd like you to wear my daughter on your arm."

Cam choked. "Excuse me?"

"The Callahans are the most powerful family in the West," Richard murmured, his expression hard. "Once my patent finalizes, word of my alliances will spread far and wide."

"And you want to solidify the name of your house." Cam's stomach rolled. "And having one of your children seen being courted by a member of my household would do just that, wouldn't it?"

Richard smirked. "At least you're not stupid."

"No, but I am a fool." It was Cam's turn to smile, wide and wild. "A fool and a dreamer, it seems."

Richard gave him a quizzical look.

Charlotte's high voice called over the buzzing crowd. "Dinner is served! Please, friends, take a seat."

Excited tenors, along with scraping chair legs, filled the next fifteen minutes. The Duskins' daughters swooped in and out, serving wine, water, and whisky. Jenny was present this evening, a veil hiding her scarred face. Cam searched the table until he found Frank Boyle sitting at the opposite end, as far from him as physically possible.

Frank smiled at him when he caught Cam's gaze, raising his glass. Julian Price sat beside his cohort, pushing around the food on his plate.

As the lords and ladies sat, Cam remained standing, never taking his eyes off Frank's horsey face.

Commander Carter and his wife, Amelia, paid particularly close attention to him.

Annie swooped in and refilled Cam's water glass. He made a point of letting his eyes follow her back to her station.

"Ladies and gentlemen." Cam tapped his glass with his fork. *I'm screwed.* "I have an announcement to make."

CHAPTER 27
ANNIE

Adam Harris. Forty-three-year-old male. Advanced stages of The Rot. Time of death. Annie glanced at the clock. It had been fifteen minutes since she'd found the sailor dead in his cell and brought him to the table in the teaching room. He'd still been warm. *8:53pm. Exact cause of death to be determined.*

Exhaling, Annie set her notes on the end of the table. Of course, today of all days would be when another passed. He'd been the last one they'd infected—right before the captain—once the guests had started arriving.

She was exhausted—being around Cam always exhausted her—but it looked like she'd be having another sleepless night. This late in the evening, Lord Duskin would order her to take care of the autopsy on her own. She didn't bother reporting it to him.

Annie pinned her hair into a bun before sliding on her gloves. The man's body lay naked on the cold metal, his dark skin not yet taking on the greyish hue of death. His eyes had clouded over, though. She examined them quickly before

249

pushing his lids closed. Normal—no broken vessels or yellow tones.

What about when the person who wants you dead is part of your family?

She tried to shake away Cam's words. *Does the Governor of the West want his own son dead? Why?* Cam was a lot to deal with, but was it enough for his own father to try to murder him? *Do I want to know the answer to that?*

Annie turned to gather supplies—several, differently sized scalpels, unmarked vials, clean linens, and tweezers. Lord Duskin liked to know exactly *what* inside the body quit working once The Rot took over. She'd done this dozens of times, and the causes were usually dehydration or failed kidneys. She expected to find much of the same tonight.

Soft footsteps echoed in the tunnels behind her as she made the first incision into the man's chest.

Her back stiffened. *Mr. Price.* It was only moments later before she was met by the familiar, icy smell of the wind—a scent that always followed him. She pretended not to notice as he leaned against the doorway, instead continuing to open her patient from breast to pubic bone, avoiding the navel.

Mr. Price cleared his throat.

Annie made a point to pretend to jump and glanced over her shoulder. He stood with his arms crossed and was dressed in a thick, cream-colored coat, his inky-black hair braided to his waist. Mr. Price's cool, grey eyes scanned her face before shifting to the man on the table. His expression tightened, but he remained quiet.

Annie turned back to her practiced cutting. "Is there something you need, my lord?"

His fingers rapped against his elbow.

She opened the dead man's body, blood coating her up to the wrists. Inside, his organs were mottled with blue spots.

Common for this stage of The Rot. Mr. Price just watched her.

I'm too tired for this. "If you have something to say, Mr. Price, say it quickly." Her words came out sharply. "I have a lot of work to do."

The strumming stopped. He exhaled irritably. "You've been spending a considerable amount of time with Camden Callahan." Not a question.

Not him, too. Annie set down her scalpel, turning to Mr. Price as she wiped her bloodied hands on her apron. "If you've come to lecture me, please know that I've already had this same discussion with Lord Duskin. It doesn't need to be repeated."

Surprisingly, Mr. Price smiled. "And that conversation went . . . well?"

"Would I be standing here if it hadn't?"

Mr. Price snorted, stepping toward the table. He glanced over the man's innards, his face, nose crinkling. "Nasty business."

"The Rot is ugly. Most diseases are."

"Not The Rot." Mr. Price took a scalpel and pushed back the man's lips, revealing browned teeth. "Pearl Dust. Even without feeling the . . . effects . . . men go mad for it."

He wasn't wrong. Over the years, Annie had seen what the substance had done to the minds of her patients. *And now Lady Duskin is using.* She picked up her tools and got back to work, moving organs until the kidneys came into view. "What's your point?"

"Look at you." Mr. Price let out a low laugh, causing Annie to stiffen. "Just over a week and he has you speaking so boldly."

Just as she thought, the kidneys were in advanced stages of failure. Annie gritted her teeth. "I don't know who you mean."

"You're a liar," Mr. Price whispered.

"So are you."

"For good reason." Mr. Price's eyes darkened. "Men don't kill men to stop a disease. They do it for money . . . for power."

That made Annie pause. *What is he getting at?* "Lord Duskin has already admitted to desiring the profits that will come from his discovery. You're not speaking anything new."

Mr. Price slammed his hand on the table, causing her tools to scatter onto the stone floor. "*Blazes.* I'm not talking about Richard!"

Annie didn't dare speak or move a muscle. Not when a sharp, cold rush of air swirled through the room, slamming the door shut. Mr. Price rubbed his face, taking deep breaths. "My apologies."

Oh, she wanted so badly to ask who he'd meant, but Annie knew better. Instead, she turned and picked up her fallen scalpel. "You question me, yet you yourself have shown inclination toward Lord Callahan."

Mr. Price scowled, his wind calming with his temper, as he watched her remove the man's innards. "I have my reasons."

Intestines quelched as Annie set them on a tray. "As do I."

Mr. Price seemed to hesitate before saying, "But do they align?"

Annie forced her breathing to slow, setting down her tools before facing him. Her words came out slowly and low enough that not even the ghosts could hear. "What do you want me to say?"

Mr. Price searched her face. She made sure he saw nothing there. He swallowed. "I want you to tell me who you serve."

Annie allowed herself to hold his gaze, something she rarely did . . . with anyone. *I refuse to be a sheep. Not anymore.* "I serve no one."

Mr. Price's smile was wide and dangerous. "That's what I

hoped you'd say." As he strode from the room, the captain's silver ghost followed him out. She hadn't realized he'd been watching.

Annie sat on a barrel of Pearl Dust, wincing as she rolled her shoulders. She checked the clock—an hour and a half. Her fastest autopsy yet. As expected, the patient's kidneys had failed. A common result of The Rot.

Her mind had drifted to thoughts of bed and warm blankets as she stitched the cooling corpse closed. A good night's sleep. That's what she needed, what she looked forward to—until the irritated shouts from the hungry patients in their cells began to echo through the tunnels.

I forgot to feed them. She never used to make mistakes like this.

Annie's entire body ached as she leaned back against the cool rock wall. The patient's daily rations were kept in a separate chamber, attached to the teaching room, along with the Pearl Dust stores. Dark, dry, and well out of the heat of the sun. Her fingers were swollen, making her fresh gloves tight against her stiff knuckles. She hadn't even bothered to light the gaslamp when she entered the small room carved into the lava rock. She could traverse every inch of these tunnels with her eyes closed, and she didn't need to see to make porridge.

Just a little longer. A little longer. Annie slipped off the Pearl Dust barrel and gathered her buckets. Part of Mr. Boyle's job was to come down after dinner and boil water, which he kept in metal drums. She scooped several scoops of oats into her buckets, then topped them off with hot water. As they steeped, she turned back to the Pearl Dust barrel. Each bucket would be supplemented with a specific amount of the pale, pink powder, causing the sailors infected with The Rot to deteriorate rapidly and the uninfected to become too addicted to try to escape.

Despite the lack of light, her eyes were blurry. Even when she had the opportunity to sleep recently, it was a struggle. She just lay awake, staring across the room at Jenny's scarred face. Annie lay there as the tension and hate built in her blood until she had no choice but to get up and return to work, or else she might try to murder Frank Boyle on her own.

Annie tugged at the lid to the Pearl Dust barrel, expecting it to spring free as usual, but it didn't budge. She pulled again. Stuck.

Annie cursed, rubbing her eyes. *Why now?* She shouldn't have sat on it.

From deeper in the tunnels, the patients were shouting again. If she didn't keep them quiet, Lord Duskin would punish her for it.

Despite her fatigue, Annie braced herself, taking hold of the lid with both hands, preparing to pull with all her might, when a shadow moved in the corner—visible even in the darkness.

Annie froze, backing away as she slowed her breathing. Elain became visible from the shadows, her grey, blurred features riddled with anxiety. After not seeing Elain's ghost in days, she'd hoped she'd passed on.

I'm sorry you're still here. Straightening, Annie whispered, "What is it? What's wrong?"

Elain crouched against the unopened barrel, her blackened mouth breaking into a tight smile as she waved Annie closer.

Slowly, Annie approached, crouching down beside her. In life and in death, Elain had never done anything to harm her, had never given her a reason to fear.

Once they were at eye level, Elain muttered in a voice as dry as chalk. *"Follow me."*

Elain snapped open the Pearl Dust barrel, then clapped it

down so fast that a spray of pink powder filled the air. Annie clapped a hand over her mouth, scrambling away, but it was too late.

Her throat and nose *burned*—blanketed in a flowery scent, so rich, she gagged.

Soft footsteps grew closer, and Annie opened her eyes, barely aware of the electric current flooding her blood, singing life into her bones as a figure knelt beside her.

Elain—she was whole and . . . beautiful.

Not grey, not monstrous, but shining and radiant. Elain smiled, her lips flushed pink instead of black and rotten. Gently, she took Annie's hand and stood, her loose curls spilling over her shoulders. Her simple, white gown trailed behind her as she walked to the wall, running her fingers over the dark stones. Where she touched, a silver, glittery void opened. Again, she gestured to Annie, still smiling. "*Follow me.*"

Annie clutched her throat, shaking her head as tears spilled down her cheeks. Everything burned. "No," Annie gasped. She reached over and scooped a small amount of Pearl Dust into her waiting porridge buckets, sobbing. When she looked back, Elain still waited.

"No," Annie repeated, her chest heaving against the stimulant raging in her veins. "*No*. I don't know why you're here, but I can't be part of it! Jenny needs me." Elain's face fell as Annie sucked in a shuddering breath. "*You* needed me, but I didn't save you. I can save Jenny. I'm not going anywhere." Annie grabbed the porridge and sprinted from the room, down into the tunnels.

Even in the blackness, her ravaged senses picked up noises and shapes and colors she'd never known existed. She slowed, squeezing her eyes shut and traversing the tunnel by feel. *You'll survive this. You will. Just a little bit longer.*

The light of the gaslamps blinded her as she entered the

patient's cavern, the normally dull yellow gleam of the flames now swirling in pinks, blues, and purples. She tried to ignore the men's and women's jeers and begging as she slopped porridge into their outstretched bowls. *It's so loud.* She let out a sob as the pressure in her ears rose to near bursting.

She crumpled as she filled the last bowl, porridge slopping down her skirts. Before her face hit the black stone floor, a firm hand gripped her shoulder. "Annie?"

She looked up, scanning the room for whoever called her. *That wasn't Elain's voice. Who—*

"Annie?" The grip tightened, the voice an octave higher in alarm. "Woman, look at me!"

Spinning, everything was spinning. Annie managed to turn toward the voice, only to see a dark, pockmarked face staring at her from between his cell bars—Nathan. *Cam's friend.* "Hang it all, what happened to you?" He shook her. It felt so slow. "Look at me!"

Annie found his eyes—his round, frightened, chocolate-brown eyes—and smiled, the words spilling out of her without her permission. "Camden is here."

Shock. Pure shock flickered over Nathan's gaunt face, his grip tightening to a point she knew she'd bruise. She didn't care.

He whispered. "That's impossible. He's dead."

Her smile widened to a grin, edged with madness. "Not anymore."

Nathan paled. She may have explained if a flash of white didn't catch her eye—Elain. She strode without a sound to the end of the cavern, curling her finger for Annie to follow.

Why, she didn't know, but Annie rose.

"Wait!" Nathan tried to yank her down, but he wasn't strong enough to hold her—not when he was half-starved. Not with the Pearl Dust ravaging her.

"Annie!" He called after her as she did as Elain bid. In the rational part of her mind, she knew the curiosity and boldness replacing her fear was an effect of the drug that she should resist . . .

She didn't want to.

As she grew closer, ignoring Nathan's desperate shouts, Elain ran her fingers over the wall again. A glittering rip formed in the stone as if cut into fabric as tall as a doorway. Elain tapped her ear, then gestured to the void.

Annie leaned in, cocking her head to listen. There were . . . voices . . . on the other side. A familiar one stood out. Raspy, low, over-confident, and . . . angry?

She looked to Elain, startled. "Camden?"

Elain nodded, and, with a smile, stepped through the tear in the stone. She was gone.

Annie stared at the velvety, silver light dancing in the ghostly doorway. Again, Cam's voice met her ears, filled with rage. Elain was taking her to him.

I am not a sheep. She fingered the jade pendant around her neck. *I'm alive.*

Her blood sang as she stepped through the doorway, rejoicing as the glittering mist sealed closed behind her.

She was not afraid.

CHAPTER 28

CAMDEN

I'm going to have to throw more cash at the stable boy. With all these nightly trips, it was only so long before he blabbed to someone.

Despite his sore backside, Cam had grown fond of his usual mount—a bay stallion, called Datura. He planted a kiss on the thoroughbred's muzzle before passing him off to the barn hand in the city center's stable. *Maybe I'll pack him on my new ship when we leave, too.*

The scent of plumerias hung heavily on the humid night air as Cam headed deeper into New Havana. It wasn't past midnight, yet all the shops and restaurants were closed tight. Lights out. Curtains drawn. Cam pulled his cap down lower over his eyes, fighting a chill despite the warmth of the evening.

There was much to like on New Havana, sure—the cleanliness, the accessibility, the cinnamon rolls—but he missed the *life* of the outside world. He missed the laughing and the singing, the fist fights and bruises. Most of all he missed Resh and Nathan. He never expected how attached he'd gotten to them, nor would he admit it to their faces if he ever saw them again.

Despite the empty streets, Cam kept to the shadows—a gift of the moon—as he moved through the market square, lost in thought. He had promised Resh all those years ago that he'd protect him. Had promised him again on *The Nightlady* before it had been burned to powder. He'd promised Annie that he'd get her off this island. Blazes, he'd just stood before an entire table of lords and ladies and stated that he'd be planting a Pearl Grove on New Havana.

So many bargains, so many lies. His father would find him if this kept up. It was a miracle he hadn't shown up on the island already and put a bullet in his head.

Speaking of Daddy. He'd kept that picture Annie found in his pocket—the one of his father and Elias. He could only force his mind to blot it out for so long before he'd have to face the truth —Elias was, or at one time had been, in contact with Alexander Callahan. Meaning either Elias had known from the start who he was, or it had merely been a coincidence that their paths had crossed.

Cam didn't believe in coincidences.

Heat curled in his chest, spreading into his arms and fingers, begging to break loose. The fight to keep it in caused goose prickles to coat his skin. *I didn't sign up for this. I don't want it.* But when had he ever had a choice in anything?

Besides his mother, when had there been anyone that he could fully trust?

Cam dipped into a side alley to his left. A few paces, and an expensive gaslamp, revealed the *Wilkin's Whistle* sign up ahead.

A bald, bearded fellow leaned against the doorway, puffing on a cigar. *God, his head is shiny.* The man's eyes lit up when he noticed Cam approaching, and he gave a short bow. "Captain."

"Pulley, just the man I wanted to see." Cam grinned at his new navigator. Pulley wore a lovely, new golden spyglass on his belt. "How's my ship?"

"Spick and span, captain," Pulley answered. "Clean enough for a queen."

"That's what I like to hear." Cam knocked on the tavern door. "Because we'll be hosting one."

Pulley's wiry brow rose. "Really?"

"Well, not *really*." Cam shrugged, shoving his hands in his vest pockets. "But she's dangerous enough to be."

Pulley smiled wide enough to reveal a few missing molars. The tavern door swung open. Thomas Wilkins stood on the other side, his blond hair gelled back. He sniffed. "Gentlemen."

Pulley snorted. "Is this the queen?"

Cam jabbed Pulley in the ribs.

Thomas' eyes narrowed. "Splendid. Another wild, flea-ridden, ship rat."

"Now, don't go insultin' me." Pulley brushed past into the tavern. "My fleas are tamer than most."

Thomas looked like he was about to retort, but Cam cut him off once he got inside. "Any letters?"

"Not yet." Thomas waved him off. Sweat beaded on his temple, his expression tight. "But I'm sure you'll be hearing from our associates soon."

"Fine." Cam exhaled, allowing his shoulders to relax. It had been a hit to his pride writing to Elias, asking him to have his warship ready in case things went south during their evacuation effort. Despite Thomas' insistence, Cam sent the letters himself. He didn't need anyone doubting him or the success of their mission.

Truthfully, though, Cam was terrified. He wasn't ready to die a second time.

Inhaling, Cam nodded between Thomas and Pulley. "Pulley, this is Thomas Wilkins, my contact. Thomas, meet my new navigator."

Thomas' lips curled into a fake smile, and Pulley gave him a little bow as well. "Charmed."

Pulley pulled out one of the high-backed stools, giving it a skeptical once-over before plopping down against the bar. "You promised food, Captain?"

"That I did." Cam winked at Thomas, who then rolled his eyes before pulling out a skillet to start on some sausages. Cam leaned against the bar, resting his chin in his palms. "Did you send word to Annie Duskin?"

Thomas nodded, grease spitting in his pan as he poured them each a mug of ale. "I did."

"And?" Cam pushed the drink aside.

Thomas shot him an irritated look. "Obviously, she's not here."

Cam's heart sank. He'd arranged for Thomas to give her the time of this meeting hours ago. Nor did anything seem off during dinner. She just flitted around the room, keeping all the guests happy, as usual. *She will come. She will come.*

Will she? How well do you really know her? He shook the thought away.

"You invited a *Duskin* here?" Pulley drained his ale in one swallow. "Aren't those the hornswogglers we're supposed to be husslin?"

Thomas scoffed. "You're a smart one, aren't you?"

"Says the nance with nails cleaner than my bunghole."

"That's not an insult, you buffoon."

"You're cranky today, Tommy." Cam shot back. Instead of retorting, Thomas just gave him a nervous look.

Cam's smile fell. *Something's off.* Instinct had him rising from his chair, fingers reaching for his gun.

It was so, so faint—that creak on the stairs—but Cam's

ears were sharper now. Heat burned through him, licking up his chest and setting his brands ablaze. He cocked back the hammer on his revolver as he wheeled toward the stairwell, only to find Julian Price's pistol aimed between his eyes.

Julian's long, black braid shone in the dim light as he chuckled, "I'm sorry, was I not invited?"

"Tom, you lying, traitorous pile." He never took his eyes off Julian, a smile spreading on the Revenant's face. Cam nodded to Thomas behind the bar. "Pulley, kill him."

Pulley drew his gun.

Thomas held out his hands. "Wait! Camden, just listen! This is not what you think it is."

"Yes, *Camden*," Julian tsked. A sharp breeze blew through the tavern, dropping the blinds. "Listen for once. Or is that outside your repertoire?"

Cam groaned and rolled his eyes. "What? Are you going to tell me that he's on our side now?"

After a brief silence, Thomas winced and nodded.

Silence.

I'm done. "Bull." Cam fixed his gaze between Julian's eyes and pulled the trigger.

A shield of wind snapped around Julian, slowing the bullet long enough for him to duck to the side. The silver brands on his wrists flared, and he sent a second gust of air straight into Cam's chest, slamming him against the wall and sending framed pictures shattering to the hardwood floor.

Thomas shouted as another gunshot sounded. Pulley. That wind shield snapped in place around Julian again, and he lunged forward. He pressed a thin-bladed dagger to Cam's throat just as Cam shoved his revolver under Julian's chin. They grinned at each other.

"You really are all show, aren't you?" Julian chuckled. "With all your talk, I hoped you'd at least know how to put up a decent fight."

Cam's smile widened as he leaned into the dagger, ignoring the sting of the blade sinking into his skin, the warm blood trickling down his neck. "Try me."

Julian shook his head. "You didn't even attempt to use your powers."

"Maybe I didn't want to burn down Tommy's tavern."

"You wouldn't if you had a shred of self-control."

"And you're going to teach me?"

"I could." Julian lightened the pressure on his dagger. "But I'd have to shove a sock down your throat."

"*Julian Price.*" Cam cackled, voice lowering. "Don't threaten me with a good time."

"*Stop it.*" A faint voice floated down the stairwell. "Both of you, just stop."

Cam sucked in a sharp breath as Annie came into view. Her hair had fallen loose around her shoulders, her black dress stained and torn at the knees. Her blue eyes darted wildly between him and Julian before settling on the knife at Cam's throat.

Thomas peeked over the bar, his voice shrill. "How did you get in here? The windows are locked!"

"Oh." Annie blinked back up the stairs, fingering the jade fishhook around her neck. "I don't know." Unsteady, she stepped forward until she was at Julian's shoulder, reaching out to gently slide the dagger out of his hand. Surprisingly, he let her take it.

Julian cleared his throat. "We were having a discussion."

Annie ignored him, her gaze fixed on Cam as she brushed

away the blood on his neck with her thumb. A chill ran through him at her touch. "It's already clotting."

Cam took her trembling hand and pressed his lips to her open palm. *She let me kiss her.* "I wasn't worried about it. But you, on the other hand . . ." He looked her up and down. "Did you get into a fight with a badger?"

"There are no badgers on this island," Annie said flatly before turning to Julian, handing him back his dagger. "Is this what you hoped to find? Are you happy?"

Julian stepped back and sheathed his blade. "Depends on what our *Lord* Callahan has to say."

Pulley set a stool back on its legs and sat back at the bar. Thomas poured them each a drink and set out a bowl of walnuts.

"I have nothing to say to you." Cam kept his gun drawn, stepping away from the wall as he straightened his cap. "In fact, we had planned to have a private meeting, which you rudely interrupted. I'd appreciate it if you'd just kindly throw yourself off a cliff and die."

"Oh, I know." Julian dug a slip of paper out of his pocket. The note Cam had sent for Annie. *Blazes.* "But I thought I'd stop in and see what all the fuss was about."

Cam shot Thomas a nasty glare, and he sank out of sight.

"Mr. Price has been keeping secrets," Annie whispered, purple shadows showing beneath her eyes. "Even from Lord Duskin."

"Oh?" Cam twirled his revolver around his finger before holstering it. "Did he forget to mention to your papa that he was the one who set my entire bloody *livelihood* on fire?"

"I didn't set you on fire," Julian smirked. "Frank did that."

"Mr. Boyle murdered you?" Annie asked Cam, surprised. "You didn't tell me."

"Would it have changed anything?" Cam replied. "You already wanted him dead."

Julian gave Annie an appraising look. "Ah, it seems our intentions do align then."

"So, you want to kill Frank, too?" Cam chuckled and shivered as he brushed against Annie's elbow. "Get in line. Kitten, here, gets the first shot."

Julian crossed his arms, his sleeves rolling back to reveal his silver brands. "I can agree to those terms."

"Are we having a genuine conversation?" Cam splayed his finger over his chest. "I think I'm tearing up."

"Mr. Wilkins," Annie whispered, her eyes far away. "Will you please bring some tea upstairs? There's a lot to discuss."

"Right away, ma'am." Thomas ducked out of sight into the kitchen. Slowly, unsteadily, Annie turned and headed back up the stairs. Cam and Julian exchanged glances, the latter giving Cam a slight bow before heading up as well. Cam scowled. *Fine, I can play along.*

He didn't like this, but for Annie, he'd restrain himself. He could wait a few more minutes before pulling the trigger again.

For her . . .

A tremble ran through him, remembering the feel of her cool palm against his lips.

He found that there were many things he would do for her.

CHAPTER 29

ANNIE

The colors, the blurs of motion. One moment she was in the patient's quarters, stepping through mist and void, then she stood in the upper room of Mr. Wilkin's tavern.

Voices. Angry voices. *His* voice. Coming from down the stairs.

Annie's feet moved without her consent, taking her to him. The stairs creaked as she made her way down. Mr. Price was there, holding a blade to Cam's neck. It didn't seem to bother him. Those vibrant green eyes found hers in a heartbeat. Wild, feral, always on the edge of madness.

He'd leaned into the knife, crimson blood dripping onto his neck as he smiled. She understood that feeling, the numbness. What did it matter if the blade sank deeper? She'd be free of her burdens, her cares, and fears.

The world swayed as she wiped the blood from his neck. His skin so warm. His gaze never far from hers. He knew. He *saw her*.

More voices, words spoken. Her body moved, then she snapped awake.

She was upstairs, sitting on Thomas' brocade pink sofa. Cam sat beside her, his heat filling every cold edge of her soul. Mr. Price sat in the armchair across from her. The moonlight crawled through the window behind her and clung to his ebony hair, the shimmer like a sea of tiny diamonds weaving through the locks.

Cam began to speak, and she grappled to the sound—anything to bring her back to reality. His revolver sat on his lap, casually aimed at Mr. Price. "Talk," he growled, his voice like broken glass coated in ash. "Give me a reason not to put a bullet in your head."

Mr. Price leaned back into his chair and smiled, feigning calm, but she could feel his uneasiness. "Mr. Wilkins has been working for me for quite some time."

Cam cocked the hammer, lips curving into an equally cruel half smile. "Continue."

Mr. Price raised his hands. "We are working to take down a common enemy. *Your* enemy," he emphasized, "though it seems you may not know it yet."

A flicker of recognition hit her. "You're not speaking about Lord Duskin, are you?"

Cam shot her a surprised look before returning his focus to Mr. Price.

"Richard Duskin is a dangerous man, don't mistake me," Mr. Price explained, "but he's only a pawn to something much larger."

"Of course, he is," Cam spat. "That's the world, isn't it? Everyone climbing to overpower the bloke in the seat beside him. It makes sense, with his coming patent, that he'd have angry competitors." Cam gave Mr. Price a knowing look.

"Especially with the amount of Pearl Dust disappearing off the market."

Mr. Price's expression hardened. "You have no idea the scope of what you've done, boy."

Cam leaned forward, predatory. "I've done nothing but what you've made me do. *You destroyed me.*"

"You destroyed yourself," Mr. Price snapped back. "You could have moved on. Started a new life. Stayed the blazes away. Yet here you are. Throwing stones into a war you know nothing about. One that I'd almost won."

So much pain. Annie flinched as a jolting ache shot from her temple into her neck and back. So much pain. They'd all suffered, in one way or another. *Does the pain ever stop?*

Cam sucked in a few deep breaths, and the fiery glow burning just below his skin dimmed. Annie glanced at Mr. Price. She'd seen him and Mr. Boyle use their powers countless times, but they never seemed to . . . expand . . . the way Cam did. Like the fire was barely contained in the prison of his body.

"I'm going to assume," Cam began, resting his long leg over his opposite knee, "that Thomas has shared our plans with you."

Mr. Price nodded. "He has."

"And?"

"It's bold, I'll give you that," Mr. Price said. "Freeing the prisoners during the patent ball may work, even if Frank interferes." He exhaled, leaning back in his chair. "But you'll never escape my brother."

"Brother?" The words left Annie in a gasp.

Cam snorted. "I don't plan to leave enough of the harbor intact for Richard to follow us."

Annie jumped when Mr. Price let out a booming laugh. She'd only heard him raise his voice once or twice. "I'm not talking about Richard Duskin, you fool. I'm talking about your *master*, Elias Bennett."

A thousand emotions passed over Cam's face as he lowered his face into his hands. The energy in the room shuddered. "*Elias* is your brother?" He exhaled, breath burning the coffee table. "You're the one who drowned with him."

"Yes." Annie stared at Mr. Price, keeping her expression blank, as he continued. "Thomas has kept me posted on your letters. Your only saving grace is that you haven't informed Elias of your plan to act at the ball." Mr. Price sat forward, his eyes narrowing. "I've been working tirelessly for months to keep the Pearl Dust out of his hands. After I stopped reporting back to him, I knew it was only a matter of time before he sent a spy in to look for me and the Pearl stores. I just never imagined he'd send the son of Alexander Callahan."

"Those files I found in your room . . ." Annie breathed.

Mr. Price grinned. "I figured it was you who went through my things."

She ignored him. "That letter . . . It said that Pearl Dust was the key. That death is the catalyst for life." *Dear Lord, what am I part of?* "He wants to use the Pearl Dust to try to predict Revenancy?"

Mr. Price nodded darkly. "Imagine what governments could do with *that* kind of power?"

Cam exhaled, gripping his sandy hair, and sent another ripple of energy over them.

"But what of Lord Duskin?" Annie's head swam. "Why did you come here at all? Murder all those sailors?" *Why did Lowana have to die?* "They had families. Lives."

"Because even more lives would be lost if I did nothing." Mr. Price's voice dropped into a hiss. "Who do you think originally funded Richard's experiments? When Richard realized what Pearl Dust could do against The Rot, Elias took interest.

269

When Frank Boyle showed signs of Revenency before he died, Elias tried to buy out Richard's work. At that point, Richard had made enough from other investors that he didn't need my brother anymore and separated from him, but it wasn't enough. Pearl Dust is expensive, and he had to start buying from local drug lords."

Annie would never forget that night. Mr. Boyle had been a patient, like all the others. They'd infected him. After she'd given him his dosed porridge, he'd smoked from his nose and mouth for days—screaming—until he'd finally passed. Lord Duskin had woken her that next morning to show her what Mr. Boyle had become . . . a Fire Brand. Mr. Boyle had hated her ever since.

Mr. Price's silver brands gleamed. "If Richard gets this patent, the government will legally allow him to buy Pearl Dust to use in the ports. Elias has already won over Vernon Douglas. Once he sent me to treat with Richard, I knew it was my chance to do whatever possible to keep as much Pearl Dust out of his possession as possible. Even if it meant taking it by force. I needed to stall the patent to have more time to flush out the growers. To get as much Pearl Dust out of the underground as possible, and away from Elias."

Cam looked up, his eyes distraught, an orange glow shining behind that green. "I—I told him everything."

There was a long pause.

Cam shuddered, clutching his head again. "I didn't trust Thomas. I sent a letter myself to Elias, asking for his aid. I told him everything. About what we plan to do with the Pearl Dust. The prisoners. Everything."

Annie gripped the arm of the sofa. *No, no, no, no.*

Mr. Price closed his eyes, muttering to himself, before saying, "Then you've doomed us all."

Cam reached into his pocket, pulling out a small photograph. The edges began to burn against his fingers, and he dropped it to the floor. *The photo of Elias and Camden's father.*

Mr. Price picked up the photo, glancing over it before tucking it into his coat.

"How was my father involved?" Cam asked. "Is he *still* involved?"

Mr. Price's lips thinned. "That I don't know. Elias kept secrets, even from me."

"I heard you and Charlotte speaking about him," Cam said. "In the estates. You wanted me to overhear, didn't you? You were trying to warn me."

Again, Mr. Price nodded. "Charlotte is our sister by blood."

She didn't know why she did it—maybe it was the Pearl Dust still in her system—but Annie reached out and looped her pinkie finger through Cam's. The painful burn of his skin instantly cooled at her touch.

She didn't allow herself to look at him, but his finger tightened around hers. Annie sucked in a breath. "So, he's coming for us. The ball is in two days. Now what?"

"We do nothing," Mr. Price answered. "We continue with the plan. If my brother shows, we'll deal with him then."

"*We'll* deal with him then?" Cam let out a rough laugh. "Since when did it become *we*?"

"Since you made it *we*," Mr. Price growled. "And now I have to clean up your mess. Commander Carter is with us. He and his wife have been suspicious of Lord Duskin from the start. I'll have him ready with his guard during the ball to back us up if things go south."

The room grew sweltering. Cam looked like he was about to fight back, but then Thomas peeked into the room, carrying a tray. "Tea?"

"Yes, please," Annie said quickly.

Cam's hateful gaze never left Thomas as he set the platter

of tea and cookies on the low table between them. He cowered under Cam's glare. "I'm sorry, Cam—"

"Save it," Cam snapped as he picked at a cookie, crumbling it between his fingers. "What's done is done."

Thomas nearly fled back down the stairs.

Mr. Price stood, smoothing his cloak. "We have two days to prepare. Don't worry about Frank Boyle. He may be a heathen, but I pay him well enough to keep him out of the way."

Cam scoffed. "We'll see about that."

Mr. Price stepped toward Annie, reaching to grab her arm. "C'mon, girl. We need to get back."

Cam was on his feet in an instant, his revolver pressed to Mr. Price's chest. "Touch her and you lose your blasted hand."

Annie's heart lurched into her throat, the room spinning as she straightened. Colors and motion flashed across her vision, and she pressed a hand to her throat to keep from vomiting. She clenched her eyes shut as a pounding ache filled her skull.

Mr. Price didn't back an inch. "She needs to return to the manor."

"She needs to sleep. I'll bring her back before dawn." Cam stepped in until he and Mr. Price were nose to nose. He glanced at Annie for a moment, his expression softening. "Unless she would rather go with you, of course."

I just want to lie down. She leaned her head back into the cushions. "I—I'll stay here."

Mr. Price's voice sharpened. "But—"

"I'll be fine," she snapped back, fighting back a wave of nausea. "Go."

"You heard the lady." Cam jerked his head toward the door. "Go."

Mr. Price grunted. Annie listened to him storm back down the stairs. She opened her eyes. Cam stood by the staircase, his hand on his revolver, until the tavern door downstairs opened and closed.

As Mr. Price's footsteps faded out of the alley, Cam's shoulders finally relaxed. He turned to face her, and despite the tension haunting his features, he smiled. "Do you regularly go on Pearl trips?"

She blinked at him. "What?"

He laughed a low, rumbling sound, and sat on the floor beside the sofa, letting out a soft moan as he leaned his head back. "*Please.* I've spent half my life in the company of pirates and drug addicts. You can't fool me."

Annie let out a long breath. *What have I done?* "It was an accident."

"Sure, sure."

"I'm not lying." She wanted to sound stern, but pain in her head sent bile into her throat, and she retched.

"Here, lie down." Cam helped her stretch out across the sofa, the movement making her dry heave. "I'll be right back."

She closed her eyes, trying to stay present, as he jogged down the stairs. Below, Cam's voice mingled with Thomas and Pulley's until he returned moments later with a pillow and a blanket. Gently, he lifted her head to place the pillow beneath it and tucked the blanket over her, still warm from being in his arms.

"Thank you," she managed to get out, opening her eyes as he returned to his spot on the floor, stretching his long legs out in front of him. He took out his revolver and started twirling it absently.

She could have fallen asleep to the sound of the smooth metal against his callused skin, but not yet. Not when she still had questions. Not when the Pearl Dust still held her fear at bay. "I'm sorry."

Cam paused, turning his head just enough that she could

make out the hard line of his jaw in the dim light, the tightness in his full lips. "For what?"

"For all of it," she muttered. "For everything that just happened."

"It's not your fault."

"It feels like it."

"That's ridiculous."

"I'm still sorry."

Cam leaned his head back against the cushions as he resumed his gun twirling. "I should have known better. I had my suspicions about Elias Bennett, but I didn't act on them."

She chewed on that thought. "Why not?"

Another pause. "I guess I didn't want to be right."

She could understand that.

"How did you get in here earlier?" Cam asked. "Tom is still dumbfounded."

Should I tell him? Did she even believe it herself? Seeing Elain so beautiful again . . . what she'd told Nathan. It felt like years ago instead of hours. "I—" she hesitated. "You wouldn't believe me if I told you."

In the moonlight, a phantom smile spread over his face. "You'd be surprised."

"I think a ghost took me through a portal."

"Ah." Cam shook his head. "Those blasted ghosts."

He thinks I'm crazy. "Nathan knows you're here." She changed the subject. "I told him."

Cam stiffened, a rush of fresh heat pouring off his skin. "And?"

What do I say? After all the lies, what *could* she say? Annie fingered the jade pendant around her neck. "He said that's impossible."

Cam ran his palm up and down the barrel of his revolver. "Nathan's always hated Revenant."

"I know the feeling."

"Do you?" Cam shifted so he faced her, their mouths so close. So, so close. He grinned, causing her stomach to clench. "Do you hate me? Is that why you stayed here instead of letting the heroic Julian Price fly you back to the manor?"

She held his stare, her chest rising to meet his challenge. "Don't get snappy with me. My family was murdered by Revenant. I'm allowed to be angry."

"I'm sorry." He recoiled, turning away. "My mother was murdered, too."

Oh. More pieces clicked into place. "By your father?"

He nodded.

"And he wants you dead, too?"

Another nod.

"I'm sorry," she said back. He opened his mouth to speak, but she interrupted. "I'm sorry for your mother."

He lowered his eyes, again just green, and leaned back, thoughtful. "I'm sorry about your family. There—we've said all our apologies." He paused. "It never goes away, does it?"

It was so hard to keep her eyes open. "Hmm?"

"The hole in your heart," he whispered. "I wonder . . . will we ever stop missing them?"

"I don't think so." Annie's throat tightened. "I think we'll just get used to carrying around the emptiness in place of where they used to be. At least, I hope so."

He was silent for so long she'd started to drift off again.

"Kitten?"

When she opened her eyes, she found his lined with silver. "Yes, Camden?"

He looked at her, then away quickly, swallowing. "Are you afraid?"

She let her eyes flutter closed once more. "Yes."

"I am, too."

There was another long pause. The blackness behind her lids spun, the pearls loosening her lips again. "Camden?"

"Yes, Kitten?"

She swallowed. "Do you ever feel broken?"

He didn't laugh, only let out a long sigh. "Yes. All the time."

"Me, too," Annie admitted. "If you're lying and leave here without me, Richard will kill me." A tear ran down her cheek into the couch cushion. "And I don't even care about that, really. But he'll kill Jenny, too. I couldn't bear that."

Cam's voice was thick. "Why?"

"Because she still sees the world as beautiful," Annie breathed. "And . . . and it makes me jealous. I want to see beautiful things again. To feel again."

"I won't leave here without you," Cam whispered. "I promise."

Annie let out a low laugh. "You say that, but people lie. They always lie. Then they leave."

She opened her eyes as Cam shifted again, the moonlight coming through the window illuminating the fire behind his eyes. "I don't want to lie." His breath was warm against her skin. "I don't want to be lied to. I want one person on this blasted earth that I can trust and will remember that I wasn't just a throwaway. That I tried." Cam held out his pinkie finger. The one she'd looped hers through earlier. "Remember me and I'll remember you?"

A bewildered smile spread across her face. "Like friends?"

"If that's what you want." Cam's smile matched hers. "Whatever you want. Always."

She reached out and laced her pinkie through his, and for the first time in her lifetime, she *wanted* to. "I promise. Friends . . . and whatever else I want. Always."

Cam's mouth widened into a feral grin. Inhuman, as the brands on his face blazed in the dimming light. Shades of oranges, yellows, and reds. Beautiful. A display of power and veracity.

My friend.

Yes . . . maybe she could have that.

Cam held their conjoined hands against his cheek. "Remember that."

Annie fell asleep with her finger still entwined with his.

She woke in her own bed as soon as the soft summer sun crept through her window.

CHAPTER 30
CAMDEN

He'd ruined everything . . . again.

Only the Jenny girl had woken as he gently laid Annie in her bed. She watched with wide eyes as he tucked the thin blankets over Annie's delicate shoulders. He pressed his finger to his lips.

The purple bruises the Pearl Dust left behind were already shadowing Annie's eyes. He'd been afraid when he left her there. Afraid he'd never see her again. Afraid he'd never wake from this nightmare.

Do you ever feel broken? She'd asked. Maybe he was broken. Maybe he had been for a long time. Maybe that's why everyone had left him.

After returning to his room, Cam washed and dressed, not bothering to warm the water. The icy cold was a reminder that he was still alive. For now, at least. For another moment longer. The sun was coming up. He was running out of time.

Cam stared at his reflection in the mirror as he combed back his hair. When his hands began to shake, he paused, bracing himself against the vanity as he tried to breathe.

Breathe.

Breathe.

Who am I?

He didn't know anymore.

His father's words from so long ago clawed into his mind, never letting go. *Failure. Weak. Fragile.* Blood leaked from his knuckles as his fist shattered the mirror.

Cam climbed into bed, not bothering to bandage the wounds.

CHAPTER 31
ANNIE

"What do you think?" Rose's whiny voice grated on her like a splinter beneath her fingernail.

Annie glanced up, taking in the striking, blue, cinched waist gown the tailor had basically sewn onto Rose's body. It hugged her curvy figure flawlessly. The neckline was modest but still attractive.

With the ball a day away, they needed to get the final touches made on their evening wear. Mr. Boyle stood outside the tailor shop, picking at his nails with his dagger, their ever-lingering bodyguard. A cruel joke from their loving father.

In the window to the far left, the captain's ghost lingered in the shadows. His ugly, pustulant face pressed against the glass, screaming at her. Cursing her. He followed her through her morning chores, clawing at her face and hair. He was becoming more tangible now, able to leave red marks on her skin.

Nathan wouldn't look at her this morning, refusing to move from the corner of his cell for her to try and explain. She would have expected him to be full of questions, but perhaps he was in shock. Either way, she was thankful for it. Talking made her pounding headache so much worse.

Annie forced herself to focus on the gown and on the way the cool tones contrasted against Rose's olive skin. "It's beautiful," she said honestly. "Especially if you wear your hair up to show the bodice."

Rose grinned at her. "Maybe we can stop by the jewelers and see if they have any earrings that will match well?"

Annie nodded with a close-lipped smile. Rose squealed and went back to chattering with the tailor, an elderly man with a crooked back. His store was small and stuffy but packed with luxurious fabrics from every corner of the world. Lord Duskin saw to that.

Jenny sat beside Annie on the bench along the back wall. Her glazed-over stare never trailed far from where Mr. Boyle lingered—her personal monster. She fidgeted with the veil covering the burn mark across her face. Annie took Jenny's hand in hers, squeezing it tightly.

Jenny blinked, returning from whatever horrors were playing inside her mind, and smiled.

Annie's gown lay safely packaged in the parcel at her feet. A truly stunning thing. She'd chosen it herself, despite Lady Duskin's complaints. For the first time in her life, Annie refused to budge. The gown would be her last revenge. Especially when she wore it on the arm of Camden Callahan, heir to the West.

Whether she lived or died tomorrow, she'd go out with the little shred of self she'd managed to find this last week.

A friend. I have a friend.

Annie's stomach clenched. Only time would tell if his intentions were true or not, but she liked the idea of what they had—a comfortable truce. Whether he meant what he said or it was all just another brilliant scheme, for now . . . for now, she would hold onto the feeling of her finger coiled with his. At the pain in his eyes when she asked if he hurt.

For now . . . she'd hold onto that.

"Annie." Jenny's voice was barely a whisper, almost inaudible over Rose's chatter. "What happened last night?"

Annie didn't even allow herself the indulgence of blinking. "I don't know what you mean."

Tears lined Jenny's round, gold eyes. "*What's* happening? I saw him bring you back. Who is he, really?"

Rose stepped off the platform, thanking their tailor loudly. Jenny swallowed, her gaze falling to her lap. Annie paid for the adjustments to their gowns, and they headed back out into the market. Mr. Boyle followed closely behind them, puffing on his cigarettes, his eyes never far from Jenny.

"Gold or silver?" Rose prattled, "I know gold goes better with my skin, but silver against the sapphire brocade would be *stunning*. Don't you think, sisters?"

Annie and Jenny just nodded their agreement, smiling prettily as New Havana's citizens bowed and waved their greetings. Mr. Boyle slowed to chat up a pair of women passing by.

Annie took her chance. She grabbed Jenny by the shoulder and twirled her until her back was pressed to Annie's chest. "Let me fix your hair, sister. Can't have you looking a mess." Annie leaned in, adjusting the pins in Jenny's coif, her lips barely brushing her ear. "We're leaving tomorrow, during the ball."

Jenny stiffened, her breath hitching. "H-how?"

"All better. You look stunning." Annie said too loudly as she turned Jenny to face her. She pressed a kiss to Jenny's cheek. "Don't ask questions. Go to the bunker when Father starts his speech. Bring only what you can hide in your gown."

Jenny looped her arms through Annie's, smiling prettily as

they continued after Rose. "Thank you, sister. I don't know what I'd do without you."

Annie squeezed her arm, resting her head on Jenny's shoulder. She inhaled the rose petal scent lingering on her skin, Jenny's favorite oil. *Lord in Heaven.* Annie let her eyes flutter closed for just a moment. *If no one else, let her live. Let her live.*

Mr. Boyle's heat crawled up her back as he approached, suffocating. Beside her, a tremor ran over Jenny's body as he placed a hand on her opposite shoulder, digging into the thin fabric of her sleeve. "And here I thought this would be a boring walk." He winked, nodding to the girls behind them, chuckling as he whispered to Jenny, "I might have a date for the ball now, since Richard says I can't take you."

Annie's eyes flashed to the dagger at his hip. She could cut him in ways to ensure he'd never speak again.

Mr. Boyle patted Jenny's cheek before jogging ahead, and she let out a low whimper.

Annie tightened her grip on her sister.

Maybe she'd cut him in ways so he'd never breathe again, either. She smiled to herself at the thought. *Soon enough.*

She was tired.

Not only from the lack of sleep the night before, but from the whole charade. From the parties, the luncheons, all the fake smiles. From pretending that as soon as all the extra guests coming for the patent ball left that she and Jenny wouldn't be flayed alive.

Her heart had leapt when Cam joined them and the other guests for dinner, but he ignored her completely. Even though he sat across the table from her, he didn't try to catch her eye like he usually did. No cheeky smiles. No brushes of his hand against her sleeve.

Nothing. He just stared at the table, his cheek resting against his opposite fist as he pushed food around his plate. The shadows beneath his eyes were as purple as hers.

Annie's gaze caught on the fresh cuts on his knuckles, making her stomach drop.

He's going to back out. Her head spun, and she caught herself on the arm of her chair. For the first time, Cam looked at her, his expression dull but concerned. Annie stood, setting her napkin on her plate, and smiled at him, then at Lord Duskin. "Forgive me, Father, but I'm not feeling well. May I be excused?"

Lord Duskin's brow flickered with annoyance, but he nodded. "You may."

Beside him, Lady Duskin shot her a scathing glare. Despite not having a hair out of place, she looked like she hadn't been sleeping either. Annie stepped out of the room without another look in Cam's direction.

The nausea had returned in full force by the time she climbed the stairs. After a quick bath, she sat on the vanity in the room she shared with her sisters. She ran a brush through her hair, yanking through the snags on the way down without wincing. Her damp strands soaked into her nightgown, making splotchy stains on the pale pink linen.

It would be another hour or so before the girls came to bed and before she'd have to go give the patients their evening meals. Annie ran the brush through her hair again. She didn't want to think about tomorrow. She didn't want to think about anything at all.

The captain's ghost was a constant reminder of what she'd done. The only reason Cam was here was for Edmund Resh, and he was dead. She killed him when she sewed that flesh into his arm. And when Cam found out . . .

He may very well leave her to rot with the others . . . and she'd deserve it.

There was a click on the doorknob.

Annie froze mid-stroke, eyes wide, breath catching in her chest.

Mr. Boyle.

One, then two more clicks, and the doorknob jiggled. Annie did the only logical thing she could think of—lift her vanity seat to use as a weapon.

Her heart pounded in her ears as the door slowly creaked open, a heavy warmth leaking into the room. She closed her eyes, inhaling. One light step, then two.

Now. Annie cried out as she swung the vanity chair with all her might. The intruder dodged to the left, catching the leg of the chair and yanking it out of her grip.

"Blazes, woman." The shocked green eyes blinking at her weren't Mr. Boyle's.

"Camden." Annie slid to the floor, her breath coming in shaky gasps. "I thought you were Frank. Why are you breaking into my room?"

"I didn't want to wake you up if you were sleeping." He slid inside and shut the door soundlessly behind him.

"Good Lord." Annie set the chair back in front of the vanity and sat, willing her heartbeat to slow, and resumed her brushing. "That doesn't make it sound any better, you know?"

He winced. "You're right." He looked handsome in his navy-blue suit and grey vest, his hands tucked into his pockets. She'd forced herself not to notice earlier. He might have even tried to slick back his hair, but it had already fallen back in his eyes.

Focus. You're no better than Rose. Annie fixed her attention back to her reflection, and her eyes widened. *God save me. I'm in a slip.* That thought made her pause. She never would have cared before what she was wearing. Not after what had been done, and all the parts of her that'd been exposed.

It didn't matter—even if she knew the answer—he'd been avoiding her. He hadn't earned any sympathy. She didn't bother to cover the annoyance coating her tone. "What are you doing here?"

Cam had the audacity to look hurt. "I thought we were friends now. Friends visit."

She gave him a pointed look, and he sighed, scraping his shoe against the polished wood floor. "Sorry about earlier. I was having a moment."

"I'm aware." Another stroke through her hair. "Can I ask about what?"

"I was feeling sorry for myself. I needed to think. I'm done now."

"Good." Annie shifted to face him. He looked like a kicked puppy. "There may be time for moping later, but if you can't stay focused *now*, we'll die tomorrow."

"I know. That's why I'm here." Cam unbuttoned his coat, revealing a gun belt strapped to his waist. He undid the buckle in one swift motion and gestured for her to stand. "I won't be able to concentrate if I'm fretting about you getting murdered by these lunatics."

Annie furrowed her brows and remained seated.

Cam raised a brow, curling his finger. "Come here."

Annie kept her expression vacant. "Don't tell me what to do."

Cam let out an amused huff. "Please come here?"

Annie set down her brush and stood.

Cam sank to one knee and wrapped the belt around her waist, tightening it until it sat comfortably, but didn't shift. "I had to punch quite a few more holes in the leather." He fussed with the buckle before pulling his pearl-finished revolver out of the holster. He motioned to show that the gun was unloaded.

Annie's stomach clenched as he wrapped her hand around the pommel, moving her thumb to rest over the hammer. "You only pull this back if you want someone dead." Cam made her go through the motions of cocking and dry-firing it several times before he seemed satisfied, his expression more serious than she'd ever seen it. "This is a .45 caliber. One hit and they're not getting back up again."

"I learned how to shoot." Despite her attempts to sound confident, her voice broke on the last word. "My real father taught me."

Cam just gave her one of his crooked grins. "I'm glad." He took the revolver from her, brushing his palm down the barrel like a lover. "This is *very* precious to me. Please, don't lose it."

He handed it back to her, and Annie carefully slid it back into the holster. "Why are you giving it to me, then?"

Cam searched her face hungrily before reaching back into his coat. This time, he held up a lengthy dagger and unsheathed it, its damascus blade stamped with an orchid. He tested the edge on his thumb. It left a trail of blood behind. "If you can't get to your gun, use this. Slip it down your boot, strap it to your thigh, I don't care. Just somewhere you can get to it quickly in close quarters."

I really do *know how to use a knife.* Annie smiled slightly as she rolled the smooth, bone handle in her hand. She'd never seen anything quite like it. She clutched it against her chest, and a bit of mischief glinted in his eyes. "What about you?"

Cam smiled, and his brands pulsed. When he lifted his hand, it was encased in flame. He cocked his head, watching the fire, before blowing it out like a candle. "I have other ways of defending myself now." He gave her a quick bow before turning for the door.

"Wait."

He stopped, glancing at her over his shoulder.

"I don't want to believe you," Annie admitted. "About what you said last night."

"But you do?" Cam smirked.

"I don't know." Annie moved to her bed and sank down on the mattress. "It doesn't matter if I do or don't. What matters is that Jenny gets off the island. You said you wouldn't leave here without me, but instead, can you promise . . ." She chewed her lip. "That even if it means leaving me behind, you'll get her away. Somewhere safe?"

Cam's eyes hardened into steel. "No."

"No?" Bile rose in her throat again, making her hands tremble. "Why not?"

"Because I'm selfish." He leaned against the doorframe and crossed his arms. "Is that what you want me to say?"

"I want you to say you'll save her."

"I will, if I can." Cam exhaled. "But not at your expense, Kitten. Sorry."

I have to do it. She had to tell him about Resh. *I did it. He's dead. You don't have to be here. I'm a monster. Don't die for me.*

"I—" The words caught in her throat, strangling her. Cam's brows knitted together in confusion. Annie held her neck. "Th-thank you for the weapons. Truly."

Cam just smiled that charming, over-confident smile of his. "Anytime."

CHAPTER 32
CAMDEN

The day had come.

All the details were ironed out, all the pawns in place. Now Cam just had to sit with the anxious chasm splitting his chest in two. The guests from New Havana began flocking in shortly after lunch. He hadn't had a chance to talk to Annie, not while she was busy with preparations and her own part of the plans. The mansion was alive with activity. Cooks and their attendants darted back and forth between the kitchen and the dining room, which had been opened into the outer patio to create an enormous ballroom.

The evening had begun.

Cam felt naked without his revolver at his hip as he stepped into the party. The Duskins had not spared any expense tonight. The gaslamps on the wall had been dimmed to give the brilliance of the fairy lights strung across the walls and ceiling full attention, giving the room an ethereal glow. The tables ran in rows along the walls and on the patio outside, overloaded with top-dollar booze and cuisine.

Commander Carter caught his eye and nodded. Cam

returned the gesture. At least most of the guards would be on their side. Or at least confused enough when dung hit the fan to give them a chance to escape.

Cam swallowed against the dryness in his throat. *It's just like the night Mother and I ran away.* They, too, had left during one of his father's events while he was busy with important attendees. He could replay every moment of that night. The way his mother's mouse-brown waves fell over her shoulder, shining against the jewels in her dress. How badly his stomach had hurt from overeating at the dessert table. But more than anything, he remembered the silence.

There were no alarms, no screaming. Only a night spent without speaking, under some blanket in an alley.

She'd sold that dress to feed them. Had done a lot worse to keep them safe.

Dinner went without a hitch. He watched in revulsion as the diners guzzled their drinks, laughing and swooning over each other. Only twice did he see Annie amidst the ramble, still in her servant's attire. At some point, Richard expected Cam to dance with her in front of everyone. A show of the alliance between their houses. As much as he hated having his strings pulled, dancing with Annie was the only part of this night he was looking forward to.

The clock ticked, causing Cam's chest to hitch.

There were so many guests. Smug, vile defilers of life who only cared for themselves and their own pleasures.

Isn't that what you've become? He twitched to shake the thought away. His fire—that euphoric, endless temptation—kissed his spine, whispering in his mind. *You could kill them all, you know?*

I can't.

Why not? Do now what you couldn't do before.

Because she hates death. I'd be just like them.

For Annie, he'd refrain. He'd do better.

For as long as he could.

As you wish.

"Now don't you look handsome." Cam turned toward the high, sweet voice. Charlotte Duskin strode toward him from across the ballroom, all swaying hips and bouncing curls. Her violet, ruffled evening gown's plunging neckline and impossibly tight waist accentuated her every lovely curve. She smiled broadly, taking in his crimson swallow-tail jacket and black waistcoat, his chest bare underneath to expose his brands.

"Scrumptious, actually," she said, pinching his bicep. "I'm surprised they let you in here."

Cam chuckled, taking a step back. "Don't let Richard hear you say that."

"Oh, don't be naïve." She looped her arm through his, leading him deeper into the party. "My husband has long since stopped caring where my eyes roam."

"I doubt that." A sea of eyes followed them across the ballroom, towards the bar. Cam scanned the faces for Annie. She was nowhere to be found. "Where is our host, anyway?"

"Practicing his speech in the mirror." Charlotte patted the stool beside her, her cheeks pink from alcohol. It seemed her tongue had loosened as well. Near the end of the bar, Julian had Frank laughing into his cups. Both wore absurd outfits to show off the marks on their skin.

Richard had insisted. The creepy tool.

Julian caught Cam's eye and nodded. Cam winked in response, flicking him off. Julian shook his head.

Charlotte didn't seem to notice as she got two iced glasses of whisky. She tried to hand one to Cam, but he waved it off. "No, thanks."

She crossed her legs, her eyes giving him a once-over. "You know, it's hard to trust a man who doesn't drink."

Cam leaned against the bar, searching, and failing to find any snow-white hair in the crowd around him. *Where is she?* "I like to keep a clear head."

Charlotte sipped her whisky and pouted. "That's no fun."

"For whom?"

"For me," she laughed. "And the throngs of other women at your disposal."

God, it really is no different. He pursed his lips. "I'm not interested."

"Oh, I know." Charlotte leaned in, tugging at his jacket sleeve. "You've only had eyes for one since you got here, haven't you?"

Cam didn't bother answering. His *interest* in Annie at this point was part of their distraction. There was no point in denying it.

Charlotte scooted her stool closer, leaning in until he could feel her breath against his neck. "Annie dear is a sweet little thing on the outside. My husband has indulged in her more than once, to my dismay."

Cam's heat exploded in his core, fighting to break free and burn Charlotte alive. He inhaled as she stroked his cheek. It took everything he had not to burn her to ashes.

"Inside, though, she's as hateful as the rest of us," Charlotte whispered. "She'd stab you in the heart for a ride off this island without a second's thought. Don't forget that. You're just a means to another end."

He turned his head until he and Charlotte's lips were inches apart, her eyes glazed and wild. Cam breathed. "I'd gladly let her shove a knife through every one of our blasted hearts if it means freeing her from people like you."

Charlotte pulled back, shocked.

Cam took her hand and kissed her knuckles before stepping away from the bar.

"Do you even know what I've done and what I've risked?" Charlotte followed, grabbing his elbow. "Julian has kept me informed of everything. I know who you are."

"Of course he has." Cam shot the Revenant a glare. "Your *brother* likes to dip his fingers in many pots, doesn't he?"

The color in Charlotte's cheeks deepened. "He's done what he's had to do to keep us alive."

Cam cocked his head. "If that's the case, how did you end up married to Richard?"

Charlotte paused as a wave of anger passed over her features. "That was Elias. He and Julian share the same mother but different fathers. I was born to their mother's daughter, but they call me sister anyway. Elias is . . ." She hesitated. "Good at getting what he wants. Including getting close to Richard."

Dear God. Cam's eyes widened. "You both were spies?"

Charlotte nodded, scanning for any who might be eavesdropping. "Don't be so quick to judge me, especially when I'll be doing my own part to keep Richard and his party distracted tonight." Something over his shoulder caught her eye. "Looks like your date is here."

Before Cam could turn, Charlotte grabbed his collar, pulling him down to kiss the corner of his mouth. Cam pulled away, and Charlotte's smile turned into a grin. "Goodnight, Camden."

Blast. Cam wiped his lips on his sleeve. Annie, Jenny, and Rose stepped off the staircase just as he turned. Jenny and Rose themselves looked stunning, but Annie—

Her expression was flat, bored, and maybe a little bit angry as she ghosted across the ballroom toward him. Her pale hair was swept back so it fell in cascading waves down her back, fully showcasing her ruffled crimson gown, so deep red that it was almost black. It was long-sleeved, the collar high, and buttoning under her chin, only to spread into an open neckline that stopped just above her breasts.

She barely made eye contact as she held her hand out for him. He took it, leading her deeper into the ballroom, his heart pounding in his throat. The guests seemed to take their entrance as an invitation to begin the dance. Other couples fell in after them, and the musicians started a more rhythmic melody.

"Are you armed?" Cam whispered to her pleasantly. Eyes followed them from every corner of the room.

Annie smirked. "Yes. Your gun belt fits perfectly under my skirt layers."

"And the knife?"

Her smile widened. "In my bodice."

Cam laughed. "And here I thought you couldn't become any more appealing."

Straight as an arrow, Annie laid her gloved hand on his shoulder, the fingers of her opposite entwining with his. Her ice-blue eyes flickered to Charlotte, who'd joined Julian and Frank at the far end of the room. "Enjoying your time with Lady Duskin?"

Cam gently placed his hand on her gaunt waist and gave her fingers a squeeze. "Jealous?"

Annie's lips curled up at the corners. "You're assuming a lot."

"You wound me." Cam chuckled, then lowered his voice. "Do you want the honest truth?"

Curiosity flashed over her features as they swayed with the music.

Cam leaned in, like he meant to brush his lips against her jaw. "I think Charlotte's jealous of *you*, Kitten."

"She's a fool, then," Annie said darkly. "Sometimes I think you may be one as well."

"I've been called worse." Cam twirled her. Annie moved so gracefully. Not a hair or seam out of line. When he drew her back, a faint flush of pink colored her cheeks. "Charlotte says she's on our side."

"Did she?" Annie's brows pinched.

"You don't believe her?"

"I have an incredibly small list of people I trust, and Lady Duskin isn't on it."

"What about me?" Cam asked more seriously than he meant to. "Am I on your list?"

She didn't answer. Instead, her eyes widened as someone approached. Cam glanced over his shoulder. Frank Boyle sauntered toward them, his eyes glazed, and his gait unsteady.

Cam's grip on Annie's waist tightened. "Screw off, Frankie. We're talking."

Frank let out a rolling laugh, spreading his fingers over his chest. "I just wanted a turn with the lady. She looks pretty, doesn't she?"

"All the more reason for you to go shove your head in the toilet," Cam snapped back. "I'm surprised Richard let you loose in here, anyway. Isn't there a doghouse outside with your name on it?"

Annie just watched Cam quizzically.

"I only want to dance." Frank's smile was venomous. "No need to get huffy."

"Don't worry, Camden." Annie patted his shoulder. "It seems you've quite exhausted me. I'm going to find something to drink. Come with me?"

Cam smiled as he took her arm. Annie led him toward the buffet tables, seemingly oblivious to the wave of vicious heat rolling off Frank. Annie flashed him a look, her lips pursed. "And you call *me* jealous. You shouldn't antagonize him."

"Why not?" Cam purred, leaning in. "It's *so* much fun."

"You're going to get yourself killed," she chided. "Again."

"And *again*, you wound me." Cam poured them each a glass of water. "But what's life without a little risk?"

"Safe." Annie sipped her water, frowning. "That's what it is."

"Hmm." Cam watched as Charlotte and Julian moved toward the podium that had been set up along the far-right wall. *Richard must be ready for his speech.* The guests still danced. Swirling, laughing, trading partners.

The fire just below his skin made Cam twitch. Annie shot him another nervous look. He sipped his drink. "I guess I've just forgotten what *safe* feels like."

Annie snorted, shaking her head, but raised her glass. "Cheers to that."

Cam laughed—truly laughed—and they clinked glasses. The crowd began to cheer. When Cam looked up, Richard Duskin walked on the podium, dressed in an atrocious red, three-piece suit with a shiny black top hat.

He raised his hands, and the cheers quieted. Cam and Annie stayed back. Out of the corner of his eye, he noticed Jenny shuffling toward the kitchen. Julian stood at the edge of the stage, where he'd keep Frank out of the way, just as planned.

Richard Duskin reached out to help Charlotte onto the podium. She wrapped her arm around his waist—all smiles and poise. Richard stretched his own arms wide, addressing the crowd. "Ladies and gentlemen, it's been a long time coming, but the finalization of my patent has finally been sealed." The crowd again went up in cheers. Richard mouthed a few thank-yous before continuing. "Pearl Dust, under my direct supervision, will now be shipped to every port in the Four Corners, to fight against the plague that is The Rot."

Richard gestured to Cam across the room.

Cam gave a deep bow, and the cheering started again.

"With Lord Camden Callahan under my employment, the end of The Rot is at hand. Let us celebrate the end of a pandemic, and the beginning of a new era."

The crowd exploded into applause.

Annie looped her pinkie finger through his. "Now. Let's go."

Cam wrapped his arm around her shoulder, chuckling against her neck, just as they'd planned. Two lovers slipping away for a quiet moment. Annie smiled back, and even though, in his heart, he knew it was fake, it still took his breath away.

She led him out of the ballroom, through the grand entrance, and into the kitchen. Jenny stood near the pantry, tears streaming down her face as two unwashed cooks badgered her. They were probably wondering why she was waiting there in the first place.

They turned when Cam and Annie entered, and a growl rumbled from Annie's throat that he didn't know she was capable of. "Get out."

They glanced at her in shock, gazes then shifting to take in Cam beside her. He shoved his hands in his pockets, grinning, as he let his fire lick up his neck and chest and snake across the tiled floor. "You heard the lady."

They fled like frightened pigs, and Cam made sure his flames followed them out. Annie grabbed Jenny's hand as she yanked open the pantry, kicking a lever in the corner. The back wall swung out—a hidden door—and the strong breeze, filled with the stench of feces and decay, rushed up to greet them, blowing the women's hair back over their shoulders.

Cam scrunched his nose. "That's . . . pleasant."

Annie shot him a seething glare before diving through the doorway, Jenny at her heels. Cam closed the pantry door behind them before following, night-blinded as he shifted from the brightly lit kitchen to a dark, narrow tunnel. Annie seemed to have no trouble traversing the blackness. Water dripped from the ceiling, steaming as it ran down Cam's collar. Despite barely being a whisper, his voice sounded too loud as he commented, "What is this place?"

"Lava tubes," Annie breathed, "formed by the volcano across the grounds when it last erupted. Natural chambers have been carved into the rock that Lord Duskin uses to conceal his experiments."

"Clever." Cam ducked out of the way of a stalactite. "How very mad scientist of him."

Annie chuckled, but the rest of the trek was spent in silence except for Jenny's occasional whimpers.

How far down does this go? It felt like they'd been walking for an hour. In the darkness. In the wet. Is this where Resh and Nathan had spent their last few months? Far from the light and the sea? What would even be left of them after so long in the dark?

Cam crashed into Annie's back when she came to a sudden stop. She held her hand to his chest to steady him. It sounded like she turned a door handle. Her whisper was sharp against the cool rock surrounding them. "Whatever you see down here . . . whatever you hear . . . now isn't the time for revenge. Later. We get in, we get out."

"You think I'm that impulsive?" Cam replied, too harshly. He'd never admit to his heart beating in his throat. "I can handle it."

A sliver of light blinded him as she pushed the door open. "I hope so."

Gaslamps lit the open hall before them, sending a fresh wave of filth and decay. Jenny covered her nose with her sleeve. Annie just continued forward, expressionless, the light's dull, orange glow making her hair look aflame.

"How are we going to get out?" Jenny breathed.

Annie squeezed her hand. "Camden has a ship. His men have a small boat ready to move the patients out of the receiving chamber."

Jenny peered over her shoulder at Cam. "Won't the guests see us?"

He gave her a reassuring smile. "Not if Julian does his job."

She didn't look comforted. "And if he doesn't?"

"Then I'll blow them all off the bloody map."

To his surprise, she smiled a little before turning her focus back on their path.

The lava tube opened wider until it branched in several directions. Annie led them through the center tunnel. At the end was a heavy wooden door. She pushed it open and headed to the back of the chamber.

Cam took one step inside and froze. *Dear God, save us all.* An enormous metal autopsy table sat in the center, with channels along the side, leading to a blood-stained drain on the stone floor. Scalpels, saws, and embalming tools lined the walls—along with vials and bottles dated and timed from years back until now.

Bile rose in Cam's throat, and he let his gaze fall on Annie, who pulled a heavy duffel bag out of one of the cabinets. When her eyes met his, a flicker of guilt ran through them. She tossed the bag over her shoulder. "My supplies."

What has Richard done to you? Cam forced himself to swallow past his dry throat and took her bag. "Let me. Where next?"

Annie nodded her thanks and then led him and Jenny into the adjoining chamber. Once his eyes adjusted, at least twelve fifty-gallon drums lined the back wall. He felt his jaw drop. "Is this all—"

"Pearl Dust," Annie breathed. "Your men will have to get it from here to the boats. It's not going to be easy."

Julian wasn't kidding. How much Pearl Dust could there even be left on the market? Cam rubbed his face. "We'll take as much as we can. A few barrels aren't worth our lives. Where are the patients?"

Annie ducked her head and guided them back to the main chasm. This time, she led them to the left. As they walked, Annie lit the gaslamps embedded in the rock. A thrill ran up Cam's spine as voices began to float down the tunnel.

"What's she doing here so early?"

"Shut up. I was sleeping."

"Who cares if we get to eat?"

Cam knew that last voice. *Nathan.* He surged forward, but Annie caught his arm. "Don't. You'll rile them up. Just stay with me."

What don't you want me to see? Cam just pursed his lips and nodded. This was her realm, not his. He wouldn't push it.

As Annie switched on the final lamp, the lights spread out throughout the long hallway, revealing dozens of stone cells on each side. Cam's heat snaked around his ear and pressed against his temple. Thin, filthy arms reached from the cells, flailing, screaming. Begging for food, for their nightly fix.

Annie turned to him, pressing her finger over her lips, her eyes frozen into haunted granite. "They don't know you. We will unlock the cells and blindfold them. The less we tell them, the better. Let them fear you for now, and we'll guide them out to the boats. Understand?"

Cam's stomach curled into knots. "I'm at your disposal."

Annie raised her chin and pulled a key ring out from under the layers of her gown, then gestured for her duffel bag. Cam handed it to her, and she pulled out an enormous coil of rope.

One by one, Annie went down the line. The patients didn't

even fight—some only wept—as she opened their cells and bound their wrists and eyes, connecting them all together in a line. Jenny followed the instructions without question, her marred face frightened but determined.

Annie made it to the last cell. Her mouth moved as she whispered to the occupant, her brows furrowing in frustration. Her eyes flickered to his, then, thoughtful. Cam's heart stopped and started in his chest. *Nathan.*

Cam made himself take a step forward, his limbs trembling. The bound patients must have felt his heat because they shuddered as he passed.

But what would Nathan think of him now? *How can he ever forgive me for what I've become?*

As he reached to grip the bars, his fingers glowed with the fire inside them, illuminating the cell. Wide, brown eyes met his, but instead of the lively, exuberant friend he knew, a gaunt, terrified face stared back at him. His dark curls had grown into dreadlocks, and his acne-scarred skin was coated in filth. But it was Nathan.

It was Nathan, and he was alive. Cam hadn't failed him—not yet.

Cam leaned against the cell door and grinned, crinkling his nose. "And here I thought you couldn't smell any worse, mate."

A thousand emotions poured over Nathan's features as he scanned Cam's face. Shock, rage, relief, fear. He looked Cam up and down, still curled on the straw mattress in the back of his cell, then he finally gave him a faint smile. "And you look ridiculous. What in the blazes are you wearing?"

Cam smoothed down his vest and coat, his brands absurdly bright in the dim light. "Whatever it took to get you out of here."

Nathan snorted. "That's stupid."

"You're stupid."

"I see you haven't changed."

"I've changed plenty." Cam picked some lint off his coat. "But only that I'm better looking than you are now."

"You wish." Nathan's voice cracked from lack of use. His smile fell as his gaze fixed on Annie. His bloated tongue ran over his cracked lips. "You know she murdered Resh, right?"

ANNIE

No, no, no.

She'd had it planned out.

They'd get the patients on the ship, they'd sail away, and when they were far from the island, she'd tell him the truth. Then he could judge her—once it was too late to turn back.

But Nathan uttered the words, and Annie watched the fire light up Cam's eyes as they widened. When he turned toward her, he didn't look angry. Only hurt.

Which made it so, so much worse.

What do I say? What could she say? She didn't owe him—or anyone—an apology for what she had to do to survive. She wouldn't crumble now, not when she'd come so far. As much as she hated herself for it, she let her voice turn cold. "We don't have time for this."

Cam's gaze hardened, his flames crawling up his neck.

She held his gaze. *I'm a monster.* "Later. I'll tell you everything, but now, we're running out of time." She hesitated. "Please."

Cam looked down at his feet, to Nathan, to everything and everywhere but her, then nodded. "Fine." A ripple of energy poured from him as he reached out, using his finger to melt the hinges off Nathan's cell. The door fell free, and he threw it to the floor with a loud clang. He reached for his friend. "Are you coming? You don't have to like this, but don't die here, mate."

Shaky, oh so shaky, Nathan climbed to his feet. "I'm with you."

Cam strode toward the front of the line of patients, Nathan following, and mimicked Mr. Boyle's voice. "Keep it quiet, and stay in line, or I'll personally burn off each and every one of your digits. *Move*."

A fearful murmur moved through the patients, but they followed as Nathan tugged them forward, falling in sync immediately with Cam's plans. No wonder they'd been so close. Even now, after all that had happened, Nathan trusted him.

But Camden won't ever trust you again. Not after what you've done. Annie blotted out the thoughts filling her, focusing on keeping the patients moving steadily and quietly. Jenny stayed quiet as they stumbled through the tunnels.

A salt breeze brushed her skin as they entered the hollow of rock that led out to the sea. The navigator—Pulley—waited for them with two small boats and three other crewmen. His eyes widened as he took in Cam and the line of sickly sailors behind him. "Captain?"

Annie watched Cam take in the dark chamber—the opening in the rock, leading straight to the open ocean. The rickety, narrow dock, where she'd checked in hundreds of patients over the years. Then he scanned over to the left side of the chasm, to the field of white crosses in the soft, black earth.

His fists clenched. He inclined his head to her. "You buried them all?"

"Yes," Annie breathed. What else was there to say?

Cam shuddered, and he rolled his neck.

Nathan watched him warily, taking a step toward the boat, before clearing his throat.

Cam's eyes snapped open, and despite the fire in them, he smiled. "Pulley, this is Nathan. Nathan, this is my new navigator, Pulley."

Nathan crossed his arms, scowling. "You already got a new navigator?"

Cam gave him one of his crooked grins. "I needed someone to replace you, now that you'll be my quartermaster."

Nathan blinked, shocked. "You mean it?"

"Why would I come all this way if I didn't, idiot?" Cam shot back.

Nathan chewed his lip, glancing between Pulley and the boat. Pulley tipped his hat to Nathan in respect, who choked up. "We have a lot to talk about—like the fact you're a blasted Stripe—but for now, captain, what do I need to do?"

Cam's shoulders visibly sagged in relief. "I have a ship waiting offshore. Get these survivors on the ship first, then the Pearl Dust." He briefly filled Nathan and Pulley in on the location of the Pearl stores. If they heard any movement from the manor or in the tunnels, they were to leave immediately. Pulley gave him a respectful nod, then got to work.

Cam caught Nathan's elbow, turning him to where Jenny stood beside Annie. Nathan's eyes widened at the sight of her, and despite her scars, his dark cheeks went bright red. "This is Jenny Duskin. Make sure she gets on the ship safely, or go hang yourself. Got me?"

Annie startled at the harshness of his words until Nathan laughed. "God, don't go quoting Resh already." Nathan offered Jenny his elbow, and she took it, blushing prettily. "Of course, Captain, I'll protect her with my life."

One by one, they loaded the patients onto the boats. Jenny first, followed by the older prisoners. Nathan, Pulley, and the other crew members sailed them to the ship, then returned with the empty boats for another group.

I've misjudged him. Nathan's limbs shook, his body close to collapsing from exhaustion from the weeks in the dark, but still, he kept on and on. Before long, only one more load of patients waited to be hauled away, trembling and blindfolded.

Cam had barely looked at her the entire evening. That fire always crawling under his skin flared whenever she grew too close, creeping up into his eyes.

Annie's insides hurt. Every part of her. Hurt from hating herself, from hating the Duskins, from hating Cam for making her care. She kept her cold mask in place, not once allowing it to slip. *Block it out.* It didn't matter what he thought. What anyone thought. All that mattered was that she got Jenny away from here.

Nathan and Pulley disappeared out of the entrance of the cave, towards the ship. Only six more patients remained.

Cam smoothed back his hair, his jaw clenched. "Get on the last boat. Julian and I will meet up with you in the morning." He made to move back into the tunnels, back to the manor. Back where she didn't know if she'd ever see him again.

No, don't go. She knew the plan. She'd help get the patients settled while Cam's crew smuggled the rest of the Pearl Dust. Cam and Julian would hang around the manor just in case anyone caught word of a ship hovering offshore. But he couldn't leave . . . not like this. It took everything she had to keep her voice steady. *I'm so tired.* "Wait."

Cam paused, wavering, but his expression was so, so cold. Fire burned in his veins, crawling up his neck and jaw.

Annie swallowed. *I'm sorry. It wasn't my fault. Or was it? I don't know.* "I—" *You are no longer a lamb.* She made herself hold his eye. "I did what I had to do."

He searched her face, his gaze softening. "Haven't we all, Kitten?"

Hands in his pockets, he jogged into the tunnels, leaving her there to wait all those cold, silent minutes until the boat returned. They loaded the last of the patients. Overhead, high up the cliffs, fireworks shot off over the manor.

At least the Duskins were having a pleasant evening.

Nathan and Pulley loaded the last barrel onto the boat. Pulley glanced down at the wobbly vessel before whispering a quick word to Nathan.

Nathan turned to her. "Looks like there's no more room. I'll stay and wait for Pulley to come back for me."

"No, I'll stay." Annie crossed her arms and faced the tunnels. "If anyone comes down here, they'll expect to see me, not you. Go."

Thankfully, Nathan didn't fight. Instead, he gave her a deep bow as Pulley pushed the heavily laden boat away from the dock, the brisk current quickly pulling them out to sea.

They're gone. Annie collapsed, curling her arms around her shins. *Jenny is free.* If nothing else, Jenny was on that ship, leaving. Somewhere Richard couldn't cut her open, pull her apart, and study her insides.

Annie's mind spun, and she rested her head on her knees. *Just a little longer.* She could do it. Just a couple more hours. Then she would be somewhere Richard couldn't find her, either. Even if it meant Cam hated her. She'd find a way to tell him she was sorry. She'd make him understand, somehow.

"Beautiful, isn't it?"

Annie nearly fainted as a cool, female voice approached from behind her. Whisky in hand, the dim light glittered off the jewels in Lady Duskin's gown as she moved down the dock. "It's such a lovely evening for a stroll."

Annie reached for the revolver under the layers of her dress, but Lady Duskin let out a low laugh. "Don't worry, Annie, dear. I'm not going to kill you."

Annie just breathed, still in reach of the gun.

"Don't look at me like that." Lady Duskin stepped past her and tugged on Annie's hair. "Is it so hard to believe someone might hate him more than you? That maybe I just want to help?"

Annie didn't respond. Lady Duskin took another drink as she closed her eyes, smiling, as she seemed to absorb the murky, ocean breeze. She let out a dramatic sigh. "Or maybe I've learned something that you haven't, dear."

A slow chill crept up Annie's spine. Out of the corner of her eye, Elain screamed from the cells. Mouthing for her to run, to fight.

Annie just smiled. *Oh, Elain.* There was nowhere to go. She couldn't hide anymore. "What don't I know?"

Lady Duskin moved until she knelt in front of Annie. She brushed a strand of moon-white hair behind her ear and kissed her cheek. "That I don't need a man to get what I want. Not anymore."

"And what do you want?" Annie whispered.

"Endless life," Lady Duskin breathed, a hint of madness in her eyes. "And the power to bring nations to their knees."

Footsteps approached them. Annie shifted, and Frank Boyle stood behind her, grinning ear to ear.

"How about that dance?"

CHAPTER 34
CAMDEN

Resh was dead.

No, he was *murdered*.

Cam peeked out the hidden pantry door, slipping into the kitchen when he found it empty. He slicked back his damp hair, smoothed his coat, and slapped on a fake smile before heading back into the party.

He'd suspected—all along—that Resh hadn't made it. He'd known it in his soul. But hearing it out loud . . . and that *she'd* done it . . .

It was just another one of Cam's failed promises. Everyone he cared about either ended up dead or suffered because of his mistakes.

Cam's heart sank. *I shouldn't have left her down there alone.* He didn't know what he felt—for her, for this new life, for any of it. If only he could freeze time and scream into the nothingness chewing up his insides until either the darkness faded, or he burnt himself to dust.

"Is it done?" Julian stepped out of the shadows and fell in line beside him. Cam nodded and headed toward the outside patio. Julian followed, pretending to make small talk as they walked.

The humid air clung to his skin, making him itch. Fireflies lit up the lawn, a light show all their own. Cam leaned against the doorway. Richard still hovered over by the podium, well into his cups, surrounded by fawning guests.

Cam's eyes narrowed as he scanned the room. "Where's Frank?"

"Passed out in his rooms already." Julian picked at his nails and leaned against the opposite wall. "I think he took a couple ladies with him. I don't care what he does as long as he's out of the way."

Cam snorted. "I'm surprised he could even make it that far." *Keep talking.* He didn't want to think. "How did you two start working together, anyway?"

A cheer went out as Richard popped open a bottle of champagne, spraying the guests.

Julian let out a long breath and relaxed when he realized they weren't under attack. "As you may have already sniffed out, Frank was reborn here after dying as one of Lord Duskin's patients."

"And he still agreed to work for Richard?"

"Men will do unspeakable things for gold."

Isn't that the truth? "Then what?"

Julian's silver eyes scanned Cam's face. "After I came to the island at Elias' request, I paid Frank to work for me instead. A double agent. He's a low-life and an insufferable fool, but he's been useful."

Cam thought for a moment, crossing his arms. Julian had gone through an enormous amount of effort to stop Elias, but the man Cam knew on Shar-Crue—the man that pulled him from *The Nightlady's* ashes—had seemed so . . .

Charming? Cam sucked on his teeth. *Fatherly. Supportive.*

Caring. Patient. Everything you needed and wanted? He conned me. Simple as that.

Julian must have sensed his train of thought. "I didn't want to go fishing."

Cam's head snapped up. "What?"

Julian gave him a thin-lipped smile. "The day we died. I wanted to stay home and visit our mother, but Elias got his way. He always gets his way."

"You're defying him now," Cam replied. "You're fighting."

"I'm running." Julian shook his head, his black braid flipping over his shoulder. "He's still getting his way. It's just taking longer than he'd like."

"I know someone like that." Cam picked at a loose thread on his sleeve. "My mother only stalled her death. She couldn't stop it."

"Evil men will always rule the world." Julian watched Richard solemnly. "That's just the way of it."

Am I an evil man? He'd done evil things. Horrid things . . . but he *wanted* good, didn't he? He wanted Annie to have a new life. He wanted Nathan safe. He wanted to stop Richard from murdering any more innocent people. *But you're a coward, aren't you?*

Cam glanced down at his soil-stained boots. *I couldn't save her.* He knew that . . . deep down, he knew it. He couldn't have saved his mother. He'd been a child. His family should have protected *him*, but such was life.

Life wasn't fair.

How long could he hold on to the bitterness? To the fact that she should have been here, instead of him growing up alone.

Cam's eyes stung, but he shook it away, reaching for his revolver. His hip was empty.

Another cheer went up, and Julian peeled off the wall. "Let's go."

Cam followed him across the ballroom and out into the grand entry. The guards watching the entrance gave them a curt nod—no questions—as they passed. *Commander Carter's men.* A carriage waited for them outside. Julian held the door open for him, and Cam climbed inside.

"Thomas Wilkins knows that we, Miss Annie, and your men will be rendezvousing at the tavern." Julian watched the manor fade away, out the window, as their carriage passed into the jungle. "From there, he'll head with us to the harbor, and we'll set out to sea."

"Good." Cam decided not to mention that he planned to burn the harbor to ash. "Let's just pray those girls wore out Frank, and he doesn't become a problem later."

Julian didn't respond.

They spent the rest of the trip in a tense silence.

The carriage dropped them off outside the *Wilkin's Whistle,* and Julian handed the driver a fat, cash clip, whispering a few words before sending him off.

Cam bounced from heel to heel.

He needed to see Annie. To apologize for leaving her there to deal with the rest of the patients. Plans or no, he should have stayed until he'd watched her get on that boat. Until he knew she was safe.

Julian shrugged deeper into his coat and knocked on the tavern door.

Cam swallowed, tucking his hands in his coat pockets to hide his trembling. *She's fine. Everything is fine. She's fine.* The door swung open a moment later, revealing Thomas' anxious face. He scanned them over quickly, searching for injuries, then ushered them inside. "Thank God, you made it."

Pulley and Nathan sat at the bar, sipping ale. They stood when Cam and Julian entered.

Lord, Nathan looked exhausted, his yellowed shirt stained with sweat. They'd planned to all meet here so Thomas wouldn't have to make the trek to the harbor unprotected. Better together than apart, Julian had said.

But Annie wasn't there.

No, no. Cam scanned the bar, then sprinted up the staircase. The upstairs was empty, too. *She's fine. She has to be fine.* A panicked surge ran from his spine down into his knees. He wheeled on the others, the blood pounding in his ears. "Where is she?"

The color drained from Julian's skin as he did his own survey of the tavern. Nathan and Pulley exchanged glances. Nathan stuttered. "W-we thought she went with you. When we came back to the chamber, she was gone."

God, no. He couldn't breathe. Cam braced against the bar. He couldn't breathe.

For the first time since his death, he felt cold.

CHAPTER 35
ANNIE

Drip. Drip. Drip.

Every bead of frigid water that fell from the ceiling landed directly between her eyes.

Drip.

Annie jerked as another drop struck her, rolling down her cheek to pool at her neck. She'd just started to doze off. It didn't matter whether her eyes were opened or closed, the darkness permeated everything.

Annie tried to stretch, then grunted as the muscles in her calves spasmed as she strained against her binds. She exhaled and slumped against the table. Cam's gun belt and knife lay on the stool beside her, just out of reach. *It must be morning by now.*

Frank Boyle had strapped her to the autopsy table in the teaching room at Lady Duskin's orders. He'd bound her ankles, wrists, and neck too tightly for her to even turn her head.

They'd beaten her. She'd expected that.

She also hadn't been surprised when Frank let his hands roam to places where they didn't belong.

Annie flexed her fingers, the coolness of the stone chamber stiffening her bruised joints. It seemed fitting that she'd die here. Maybe it was even justice—for all she'd done, for all those who'd suffered at her hands.

Richard's hands, she repeated to herself, over and over.

The truth was, though, that no one made her pick up those blades. She could have chosen to die a long time ago—innocently, with a clean conscience—but instead she'd followed orders. Helped him tear people's lives apart.

A wetness ran down her cheeks that hadn't come from the ceiling. *I only hope that Jenny is safe. I hope Camden understands.*

Camden. A tightness lurched from her gut into her chest. In the darkness, she saw his arrogant, mischievous face smiling back at her. She saw the quick, cunning in his gaze and the haunted fear that lay beneath.

That would be her biggest regret. That she never got to tell him what she saw.

When she looked at him, she'd seen a chance for a new life. Not only in a new country, but maybe a sense of peace. That maybe there was someone on this planet who'd see all the violent, angry scars on her soul and not run away.

The tightness climbed into her throat, threatening to strangle her.

She'd never know now—*he'd* never know—and that was probably for the best.

The door to the teaching room creaked open, which was deafening after the silence of the night. A faint glow from the gaslamps in the hall leaked into the chamber. Then the main light in the room flipped on.

Annie squeezed her eyes shut, trying to turn her head away from the blinding bulbs overhead, but her binds held her. She didn't have to ask who had entered. She could smell Lord

Duskin's thick, expensive cologne. The sterile scent of his gloves and freshly laundered medical coat.

He ran his finger down the hollow of her neck, the rubber slick against her damp skin. She tried to squint past the lumpy, black spots floating in her vision. Lord Duskin's gold tooth caught the light as he smiled. "Hello, girl."

She steeled her expression into her cold mask. Her dry, bloated tongue stuck to the roof of her mouth. "Hello, Father."

"I hoped it wouldn't come to this." His gaze trailed from her face, down her neck, lower. "Charlotte warned me of your treachery, but I didn't want to believe her."

I knew better. She wished she'd pushed Cam harder not to trust Lady Duskin. "I'm not the only one who betrayed you. Be careful of the snake in your bed."

"True." Lord Duskin straightened, folding his hands behind his back. "But I'm quite aware of Charlotte's endeavors. In fact, I supported them."

Annie's eyes widened. "You knew?"

"Of course, I knew, you stupid girl," Lord Duskin snapped, pacing alongside the table. "I suspected others would want to steal the fruits of my research. When I started receiving requests to build a Pearl Grove on the island, and Mr. Price pushed me to decline the invitation to meet, I began to doubt his loyalty." Lord Duskin paused, licking his lips. "Then our Lord Callahan showed up, and I knew . . . I was being attacked on all sides, hunted. I am a man in the water, circled by sharks. Do you know what that feels like?"

Annie tried to gather enough moisture in her mouth to swallow. "If you hadn't spilled so much blood, the sharks wouldn't have come in the first place. Your greed killed us."

"No, *you* killed us." Lord Duskin leaned in, the light behind him casting shadows over her. "If you hadn't been swayed by gold and a famous name—"

For the first time, Annie laughed at him. A true, dark, rumbling laugh that echoed over the stone walls. Lord Duskin stood, shocked, when she said, "You think that's why I did it? For money?"

Lord Duskin just watched her, searching her face for clues to the truth.

Annie licked her cracked lips. "You murdered her. She loved you—both of you—and you cut her open like an animal."

He looked so confused for a moment . . . then Lord Duskin threw back his head in exasperated laughter. "Is this about Elain? *Elain?*"

Annie bristled at the way he said her name.

As if summoned, Elain's grey, spectral form manifested in the corner and cocked her head, listening. Annie smiled at her. Lord Duskin glanced over his shoulder to see what she was staring at.

He can't see her. "Elain," Annie whispered. "Jenny. Nathan. Lowanna. I loved them. They haunt me. Day and night, they haunt me, and you killed them."

Lord Duskin's expression grew flat. "Then you're weaker than I thought. I expected more from you."

"Maybe that was your mistake." Annie didn't bother to fight against her binds. "You expected too much. From all of us."

"Hmm." Lord Duskin stepped over and opened the coolers, picking through the vials inside. "You know, I *let* this happen."

Annie's insides dropped into her spine. "Let what happen?"

"You think I didn't know what you and Camden were doing?" He inspected one vial, then set it on the counter. He moved onto the scalpels. "You don't think I know you've loaded everything I've worked for on his little ship? I let him." He smiled at her, selecting his blade of choice. "Just to prove to the world—when I blow him and all those traitors to hell—

that the Duskin name isn't to be trifled with. Camden Callahan will die. So will Jenny. So will Julian Price."

Annie swallowed as he stepped up to the table, leaning over to brush a kiss to her lips. "And so will you," he breathed. "But you . . . you'll be the only one I regret. We could have accomplished so much together."

His mustache tickled her skin as he pulled away. She allowed herself to take in the lines of his face, the cruelty in his black eyes. "I regret," Annie barely whispered. Lord Duskin leaned in to listen. "I regret that I won't get to see him turn your entire kingdom into ash. Your name will be nothing but embers. Forgotten. Dust in the wind. Gone."

Lord Duskin stepped back, giving her a hard look before picking up his scalpel. In his opposite hand, he held up the vial he'd taken from the cooler. The label read: *Adam Harris*. The infected sample she'd taken from her last autopsy. He grinned. "If that's so, you'll rot alongside me, girl."

Annie braced herself, staring up at the ceiling. "Do it."

She would not weep. She deserved this. She only wished she'd gotten to tell Cam that he'd made her feel alive again.

Lord Duskin leaned in again, kissing her one last time. "I really do wish it could have been different."

From the mist, Elain held her hand and wept as Lord Duskin cut into Annie's arm, sewing the rotten flesh into her own.

She wouldn't cry.

CHAPTER 36

CAMDEN

Cam ripped the tavern door off its hinges and stormed back into the alley, the flames on his heels burning into the tavern's wooden floors.

He didn't hear the others shouting for him—not with the fire roaring in his ears, clouding his vision. They would burn: Charlotte, Richard, Frank . . . he'd leave nothing left of them to bury.

This is my fault. A tremor ran through his body. He gripped his temples. The streetlights were too bright, the air too humid. *I did this. I failed her. Just like Resh, just like Mother.*

Just like Mother.

"Camden—" A voice breached through the hysteria. A firm pressure gripped his bicep and turned him. Julian's eyes were hard. Stoic. A warrior. "Camden? Do you hear me? Get it together."

A cool breeze chilled Cam's skin. It came from Julian. Cam gulped the air down greedily, letting it calm the heat coursing through his lungs and veins. He pressed his forehead against the alley wall, letting the rock ground him. He sucked in another breath. "They'll *kill* her."

"Yes," Julian said bluntly. "But not yet. Richard will use her to bait you out."

"Well, it's working." Cam pressed his back against the wall, steadying himself. "I'm going back. Right now. With or without you, but I'd like to point out how much she sacrificed to save *your* hide, Price."

He'd expected Julian to refuse, but instead he nodded solemnly. "Frank will be waiting for us, plus any guards that have decided Richard's gold is worth more than mine."

"I don't care." Cam turned.

Nathan, Thomas, and Pulley watched them from the now-dismantled doorway. Cam smiled at them. "Thomas, do you have any weapons?"

The tavern owner's eyes widened. "Some."

Cam's fire traveled up his veins, setting his eyes and brands aflame. "We'll need everything you've got."

Two hours later, Cam and Julian stood outside the gates of the manor. They were sealed up tight, chained, and padlocked. There were no guards in the booth or anywhere to be seen on the grounds.

Cam adjusted the saber hanging on his belt and frowned. The revolver he'd borrowed wasn't as good as his, but it would do. At least he'd remembered to change into his fireproof suit. "Is it bingo night? Where did everybody go?"

Julian blew out a long breath, fingering his own pistol. "Many of Commander Carter's men will be heading to your ship, along with him and his wife. If any guards remain,

Richard will draw them back inside the manor for protection. If I know him, he'll have an elaborate trap waiting."

"Well . . ." Cam shot Julian a mischievous look. "Let's not keep him waiting." His fire clawed at his skin, a predator begging to be set free. He focused on the gate, imagining it twisting into oblivion. The heat erupted from his pores. The pressure exploded into a violent wave and blew the metal gate off its hinges. The flames that followed turned the rock walls molten. They dripped down and hardened over the guard booths.

Julian let out a short laugh, his arms crossed. "Very subtle. They'll have heard that."

"Good." Cam strode up the road toward the manor. Julian followed, pistol at the ready.

The acres of open land around them went silent. No birds sang to welcome the sun just rising on the horizon. No crickets chirped to greet them. Just to the north, the volcano loomed overhead. Cam's heat called out to it again, and this time, a hungry vibration answered, rumbling from deep inside the earth. Cam shuddered.

"Look." Julian bumped his elbow and then pointed to a window on the third floor. A reflection flashed across the glass, then disappeared behind the curtains. A spyglass. "They're watching."

Cam had seen enough of the grounds on his nightly escapades. He knew exactly where to go. "Too bad for them we're not going through the front door." He jogged off the path, toward the eastern courtyard. Julian followed him to the other side, the lush gardens leading them straight to the cliffs overlooking the sea.

He peered over the edge and smiled. "I had Pulley tie an extra boat onshore, just in case. We'll row in the backway through the caverns."

Julian furrowed his dark brows. "How do you expect to get down the cliffside? Even if you could climb it, that would take hours."

"Can't you fly us down?" Cam shot him a coy look. "I mean, time *is* of the essence, here."

Julian just blinked at him. "I—you—" He paused. "I've never flown *with* someone before."

Cam peered over the edge again. "There's a first time for everything. I won't wiggle much, I promise."

"Dear God." Julian let out an exasperated breath, cheeks flushing bright red, then cringed as he offered to lift Cam in his arms. "I really do hate you."

"Oh, I know." Cam wrapped his arms around Julian's neck and grinned. "But now we're even. I forgive you."

Julian grumbled. "Fine, but if we die, it's your fault."

"I'll accept those terms."

Gripping Cam against his chest, Julian only hesitated once before leaping off the edge of the cliff. Cam's stomach crawled into his throat, the rush of the wind making his eyes water. Julian's silver brands flared, and he grunted. Their descent slowed until they were floating over the water. Teeth gritting with effort, Julian dumped Cam on his backside when they were a foot above the beach. Cam let out a barking laugh despite landing on a sharp rock.

Julian landed beside him, sweat dripping down his temple. "If you ever suggest doing that again, I'll kill you."

"You enjoyed that." Cam stood and dusted the sand off his pants. "I know I did."

Julian just shook his head as he retrieved the boat from where it was tied to a fallen tree. Once in the water, Julian gestured for Cam to take the oars. "You're turn to do some work around here."

"As you wish." Cam bowed before climbing in. He knew the

only reason Julian was tolerating his harassment was to keep him distracted—so he wouldn't explode and do something rash. He appreciated it.

The sea was quiet. The waves still. As they approached the lava tubes, Cam looked up from the oars, scanning the surrounding ocean, and his gaze snagged on a massive shape lingering beneath the cliffs. All the air left his lungs. *Son of a—*

Julian must have seen the horror on his face because he turned. The color drained from his skin when he saw the warship anchored in the cave's massive alcove.

The Armageddon. It lingered, completely out of sight from the air or the shore, under the overhanging rock. It could have been there for weeks, and they'd have never known unless they were directly upon it. It would have been completely hidden in the dark. No wonder they hadn't noticed it last night.

"Well, my brother is here." Julian swallowed, his coat tails whipping in the rising wind.

No, no, no, no. Cam's heat rose into his throat, threatening to choke him.

He'd told Elias everything. Where they planned to store the Pearl Dust, where they planned to dock offshore. He'd done this. He'd brought him right to them.

Stay calm. It doesn't matter. For Annie, he'd face Elias. He'd die again. He wouldn't fail her. He wouldn't let history repeat itself. Cam shook his head and shot Julian a glare. "This changes nothing. We get Annie, then we get out. We'll deal with Elias later. Agreed?"

Julian just gave him a sad smile and nodded. "You're not the only one tired of running."

Cam's muscles strained against the weight of the water as he rowed them into the cavern, into the darkness. Into whatever Elias and Richard had waiting for them.

CHAPTER 37
ANNIE

She could feel it.

The Rot ate through her body like it had been waiting to do so for years. Hungry, rapid, hateful. After being exposed to so much Pearl Dust, she absorbed the disease like a sponge.

Hours passed. Sweat dripped down her face and neck. The chills crawling through her limbs were just the beginning of a fever. The infection would spread into her organs soon. Then it would burst through her skin. If she made it that long.

Annie closed her eyes, humming, enjoying the coolness of Elain's fingers holding hers. A dull ache had already started to spread through her abdomen. Most likely her kidneys. Her legs had long since gone numb.

But she could handle the pain. It gave her something to focus on to pass the time.

Something clattered in the hall.

Elain's head snapped up, and the corners of her eyes cracked as they narrowed. Annie's mind spun as she stilled, listening. Soft footsteps crept outside the door in the tunnel. They weren't Frank's or Lord Duskin's.

No. They were too surefooted.

Annie's heart leapt into her throat. *It can't be. He wouldn't.*

Slowly, Elain backed into the shadows, the corners of her blackened lips curling into a small smile.

Picks scraped inside the lock. The lights filtering in from the hall illuminated the barrel of the lean revolver as it breached the opened doorway first, followed by a wave of familiar heat. *Like a bonfire on a cold night.*

His skin and brands glowed bright enough for her to make out his face. His lips curved. "Kitten."

Her words barely made it past her swollen, scratchy throat. "Camden."

"I had a feeling I would find you here. Richard is nothing if not predictable."

Run. Before they find you. Her voice cracked. "You need to leave."

"That's what everyone keeps telling me." Cam shaded her eyes as he flipped on the light. This time, she was ready for it. He scanned over her body, searching for injuries. When his gaze settled on the uncovered wound on the inside of her arm, his face turned an odd shade of green.

He leaned against the table, the air in the room pulsating. "He didn't—"

"You need to leave," Annie repeated. The lights burned her eyes, making her already pounding head throb. "Richard—he knew all along. He planned this . . . from the beginning."

"I figured that bit out," Cam growled. He burned through her restraints as easily as he had the cage bars. "Hold on, this is going to hurt."

Annie bit through her lip, holding in a groan, as Cam slowly bent her knees and elbows, allowing the blood to return and setting her limbs on fire. She tried to sit up, but Cam pressed down on her shoulder. "Not yet. Stretch first. I'd be lying if I said I hadn't been tied up before."

"You can't take me onto the ship, Camden." Oh, the words tasted like poison as they slipped through her lips, brushing off his teasing. He helped her into a sitting position, and she nearly fainted as the fever made her head spin. She caught herself on his shoulder. The devastation on his face alone was enough to make her mask crumble. She choked. "I'm infected."

As she straightened, he put an arm on either side of her, bracing against the table, breathing heavily as he stared at her wound. His sandy hair windswept and wild, brushing just below his cheekbones. It looked so soft. "We'll make him fix you . . . then I'll snap every bone in his body."

He's beautiful. Annie didn't bother stopping herself as she ran her fingers through his locks, trying to imprint the sensation in her memory. She *did* stop herself from touching his face. Sadly, she shook her head. "It doesn't work like that. What's done is done."

Cam watched her from under his lashes, his voice thick. "Do you think you can walk?"

Annie let her hand fall onto her lap. *I wish he hadn't come.* "I'm staying here, Camden."

"Humor me, please."

Exhaling, she slid down until her bare feet landed on the stone floor. Pain like lightning shot from her hips into her ankles, making her legs buckle. He caught her against his chest.

Annie hissed through clenched teeth. *The Rot's spread into my nerves.* "There's your answer. Happy?"

"We'll make it work." Cam grabbed his gun belt and knife off the table and buckled them onto her waist over her ruined dress. He shoved his revolver into her hand, and in one fluid motion, he swept her up into his arms, turned, then kicked open the door. "I'll walk, you shoot."

She didn't have the energy to fight. Elain followed them into the hall, with the captain—his form smokey and grey—right alongside her.

"You'll spread The Rot to the others," she breathed, his warmth burning through her chills.

The gaslamps had burnt low. He shrugged, keeping his eyes on the ground as he carefully navigated the darkened tunnels. "I guess I will."

"Lord Duskin and Frank will kill you."

"They can try."

"Camden—"

"Stop arguing with me, Annie," Cam snapped, his eyes flaring golden. "I don't care. I made a promise. If you're going to die, it won't be here. Got it? We're leaving. You and me."

Annie exhaled slowly, letting her head fall against his chest, listening to his thundering heart. *So tired.* "I-I'm sorry for not telling you about Resh."

Cam's grip around her tightened. "I'm sorry I didn't protect you."

Annie smiled to herself. "Are we even now?"

Cam kissed the top of her head, and a chill ran down her spine that had nothing to do with the fever. "Seems like it. Now, let's go get shot at. What do you say?"

Annie let her eyes flutter closed.

Maybe she'd still die here. Maybe he'd die with her, but she wouldn't die alone. *You and me.* They'd go together.

As friends . . . and whatever else they were.

Running footsteps rushed up the tunnel toward them. Cam tensed, and Annie raised her gun, but Mr. Price appeared from the shadows. His eyes widened at the sight of her—at the wound on her arm. "He did it?"

Annie lowered the revolver. "Yes."

Mr. Price pursed his lips, glancing at Cam. "And I imagine you've warned him of the dangers of bringing you on board?"

"Of course she did—and I ignored her instructions against medical advice." Cam pushed past him. "It's time to go."

Mr. Price blocked his path. "The warship dropped a dinghy with ten men. They're sitting just outside the cave entrance. We're blocked in."

"Hang it all." Cam rocked from heel to heel before turning back towards the tunnels. He chewed his lip then swore under his breath. "I guess we *are* going out the front door."

"So, it seems." Mr. Price shot Annie a small smile, cocking his pistol. "Are you ready?"

She just waved Cam's revolver in the air, and he chuckled.

Cam turned and jogged back up the tunnels toward the manor entrance. Mr. Price moved in front of him, gun at the ready. Condensation dripped from the ceiling, turning into steam around Cam, making the air even more humid. The dampness mixed with the sweat already soaking through Annie's dress, and the chills began again, making her teeth clack.

Cam just held her tighter.

When they reached the pantry door, leading into the kitchen, Mr. Price pressed his ear against the panel, listening. He slowly opened the door with his toe, entering pistol first. He surveyed the room, then waved them forward.

When Cam entered the kitchen, he gave Mr. Price an appraising look. "Were you military?"

"I was—before Elias got me killed." Mr. Price gently closed the pantry. "After that, they wouldn't have me. I became a mercenary."

"You just keep surprising me, Julian." Cam's smile turned serious. "Kitten, stay alert. The best you can."

Annie just nodded against him, struggling to stay awake. He was so *warm*.

And the manor seemed so . . . empty.

There was none of the usual chatter of Lady Duskin and her guests coming from the dining room. The cooks were long gone. Not even the birds were singing. *That means a predator is nearby.* Annie remembered her father's voice from so many years ago. *Prey knows when to be silent.*

Annie's heart stammered as they entered the grand entry. "Lord Duskin sent the guests home."

"How courteous of him," Cam said bitterly.

The front entrance was right there within reach. Her heart wasn't the only one racing. She could still feel Cam's heart beating against her, thundering beneath his ribs.

He won't let us out. There was no way. Lord Duskin always had a plan. *He wouldn't let us leave.*

"Annie?"

Cam froze. Mr. Price wheeled, raising his pistol to aim at Rose, standing partially up the staircase. Terror painted her features, her hands trembling where she clutched them against her chest. Her eyes were fixed on Mr. Price's gun. "The door's blocked. This way."

Shaking, Rose stepped past them and headed into the dining room. Cam and Mr. Price exchanged looks. Annie tried to sit up straighter. "She'd never betray the Duskins."

"But I might be able to get through to Charlotte," Mr. Price said. "It's our best shot."

Cam adjusted his hold on Annie and then whispered in her ear, "You remember what I showed you?" Annie cocked back the hammer on his revolver, and he smiled. "Perfect. Remember, aim for the head." She watched as Cam threw back his shoulders and plastered on a wide, charming smile. Just like that, he was Lord Callahan again—heir to the West—and without a second's hesitation, he strode into the dining room after Rose, Mr. Price at his heels.

Annie swallowed, her arms aching from the weight of the revolver. *The Rot's spreading into my muscles now.* She'd be completely useless before long.

Shadows filled the dining room. The curtains had been lowered. Elain and the captain moved along the walls, hiding in the dark places behind the furniture—watching, waiting.

A slick, oily presence filled the space, and the *other one* appeared.

I was right. There are two. The hateful captain—his features vile, black, and blistered—seated himself near the head of the table, grinning at her with rotted teeth. *He knows I'm dying.*

Cam's breath hitched, causing her to pull back to reality.

Seated in Lord Duskin's usual place at the table, a lean, dark-haired Revenant sipped on a glass of red wine, a stack of papers in front of him. He wore a coat similar to Mr. Price's, golden brands swirling up his exposed neck.

Frank Boyle stood behind him, puffing on a cigar.

"Camden, Julian." The new Revenant gestured for them to sit. "We have a lot to discuss."

Beside them, Mr. Price stood rigid, never taking his aim off his brother.

"Elias. Franky." Cam sneered. "I think I'll stay standing, if you don't mind."

"Sit," a female voice purred.

Cam stiffened as a gun barrel pressed against the back of his head. Annie lifted herself to look over his shoulder, vision spinning.

Lady Duskin cocked back the hammer of her tiny revolver and smiled at her. "Hello again, Annie, dear."

CHAPTER 38
CAMDEN

"Charlotte." Cam didn't let his smile falter. "Glad you've decided to join us."

"Are you?" Charlotte trailed her fingers down his arm as she circled around them. Her brown curls loose over a tight-fitting blouse, tucked into a pair of men's breeches. Her grey eyes dilated and wild. "Because you know I've missed you."

"You've been using again," Annie said to Charlotte. Her voice barely rose past her rasping breaths. "The Pearl Dust."

That explains why Charlotte always seems so erratic. From his observed experience, Pearl addictions were a nightmare to control. Charlotte backed toward Elias, never lowering her small pistol.

"Char," Julian pleaded, braced. "You don't need to do this. Come with us. I'll take care of you."

"I don't *need* anyone to take care of me," she snapped, leaning against the table before glaring at Elias. "I *need* what I was promised."

Elias patted her arm, revealing the golden brands on his own. "Soon enough."

"What did he promise you?" Julian's voice remained steady. "Char?"

Annie stirred against Cam's chest and breathed, "Revenancy. The Pearl Dust is the key."

Dear, God. Cam's mind flashed back to the letter Annie found in Julian's desk. *But Pearl Dust can't cause—*

"You can't promise that." Julian nearly shouted at his siblings. "Elias, you fool. How many more people will you slaughter before you realize the truth? You can't create Revenants."

"No." Richard stepped into the dining room, running a lingering eye over his wife. Rose stood at his elbow, watching Charlotte warily. "But there may be a way to predict them." He glared at Julian. "I didn't want it to go this way, but you left me no choice." He glanced to Annie then, lips curling back to reveal his golden tooth. "How's the arm, girl?"

Cam's fire erupted faster than he could stop it. It burned through his veins until it burst out and slammed into Richard in a coiled inferno.

Richard screamed as the blast sent him flying into the window on the far side of the room, raining glass and rubble over him. He groaned and rose to his knees. The entire left side of his body was charred and blistered.

Annie gripped Cam's arm. "Don't." Her eyes were clouded. The veins in her neck tinged blue from The Rot. "There's been too much death already. We don't need anymore."

"Not yet, there hasn't." Elias inclined his chin to Charlotte, and she beamed. "Take care of them."

Frank let out a low chuckle. He'd been oddly silent, lingering behind Elias.

Julian raised his pistol as Charlotte stood, training his aim on her as she lifted her weapon, but he hesitated. She pulled the trigger, and a gunshot sounded as a bullet left the chamber —and blew straight through Richard Duskin's skull.

Rose screamed as Richard's body slumped, blood spreading into a crimson pool across the dark, wooden floor.

Annie stared with wide, distant eyes, her mouth slightly parted.

"*What did you do?*" Rose shrieked, rushing Charlotte. "*What have you done—*"

Another gunshot rang out, and Rose slid down the wall, an open hole in her forehead.

Charlotte broke out into a deep, rumbling laugh, continuing until it rose to near hysteria. She yanked off her wedding ring and tossed it onto Richard's corpse. "You have no idea how long I've been waiting to do that."

"Blazes." Cam held Annie tightly. "Well, I didn't expect that coming."

"Anyway." Elias ignored him, brushing a bit of blood off his sleeve. "Now that's taken care of, where was I? Oh yes, predicting Revenancy." He smiled at Julian. "You've done a wonderful job of emptying the market's Pearl Dust. I'll have more than what I need now to screen the ports. All loaded conveniently on that little ship of yours, floating just offshore."

Hang it all. That's why he'd waited to strike. He'd wanted them to get the Pearl Dust out of the caverns for him.

"This was never about The Rot, was it?" Annie wiggled out of Cam's grasp before bracing against him, barely standing. Her breath rattled. "Did Lord Duskin keep track of the Pearl Dust's progress in the patients for you?"

"No, dear." Elias lifted the papers from the table. Even from here, Cam recognized Annie's neat handwriting. "You did— and what wonderful notes you've taken." He gestured to Frank. "Mr. Boyle, here, may have been the only one to turn, but your documentation of the drug has provided me with enough information that I'll be able to know within hours whether a subject's not a candidate for Revenancy."

"That doesn't make any sense." Annie's legs buckled, and Cam wrapped his arm around her. "For that to work, you'd have to document the Pearl Dust's effects on a Revenant . . . before turning. While they're still alive the first time. Without those indicators, any observations of mine are useless."

"I'm aware." Elias grinned and finally stood. He reached into his robe and pulled out a worn, folded letter. He opened it, warmly scanning over whatever was scrawled inside. "Ten years ago, I received an incredible report from a certain governor that his young son had played with his Pearl Dust samples. In his delirium, the boy burnt down half his father's study. The governor watched as the flames seemed to form from the boy's body, like they would from a Revenant." His eyes rose and locked onto Cam's.

Dear God—

Elias continued, sliding the letter back into his robes. "When I came to retrieve the boy, I was told he'd disappeared, along with his mother. Her body was discovered a few weeks later, but the boy . . . he was never found. A shame."

Cam couldn't breathe. The ringing in his ears drowned out everything. Somewhere far away, Annie tugged on the front of his shirt, whispering his name.

The stranger had chuckled at him. "I'm sure he'd love to see you burn."

"Somewhere his father won't find him."

"Goodbye, Camden. Remember I love you."

His fire caressed his cheek, crooning sweetly. *Kill him.*

Cam closed his eyes. *I'd love to.*

Someone screamed as the world around them exploded into smoke and flame.

CHAPTER 39
ANNIE

Annie crumpled, the air rushing from her lungs, as the manor disappeared into a vortex of fire.

Charlotte screamed, the sound muffled as a shield snapped in place around her. Rock fell from the ceiling, burying her.

Annie managed to lift her head, opening her eyes, and was greeted by the morning sky outside. The manor roof was gone, along with the top two floors. Mr. Price was on his knees, holding a bubble of wind around him and Lady Duskin.

Frank and Elias Bennett were nowhere to be seen.

The wood flooring encircling Annie remained uncharred. Cam stood over her, staring blankly to where the far wall had been—where *Elias* had been a moment before.

The fire around him embraced him like a lover, holding him as tendrils of flame whispered in his ear.

He didn't look *human* anymore.

The fire inside him crawled through his veins, showing through his skin with a bright orange glow. His brands cracking, the fire spiderwebbing across his cheeks, meeting the flames in his eyes. Nothing remained of his boots or the shirt under his coat.

He noticed her watching then and smiled.

Cam knelt and helped her stand, leaning her against the wall. The heat of his breath burned her fever away. "Let's get out of here, Kitten. I'll get you to the boat in the tunnels, but then I need to take care of them."

"No." Annie met his stare, soaked in the unrelenting, violent rage. *If I could meet the man who killed my father, with that power?* "I'll go myself. Make him pay. For *her*." The nearness of death made her bold. She took his face between her hands, pressing her forehead to his. "Make him pay for *us*."

He brushed his glowing fingers down her cheek, down her neck, then grinned. "For *us*."

Outside, rock exploded with a loud crack, revealing Elias standing in the center of the rubble—robes torn and tattered—undulating lightning crackling around him. Moments later, Frank rose, spitting blood.

Cam whispered in her ear. "Hide. I'll find you soon." He turned and disappeared into the lingering smoke without a second look.

Annie clutched her chest as she broke into violent coughs, the taste of blood in her mouth.

Mr. Price let his shield fall, breathing heavily, and scrambled to his feet. "Miss Annie, we need to—" There was a loud crack, and his eyes glazed over. He fell, ash pillowing around him. Behind him, Lady Duskin held a broken glass bottle, grinning like a madwoman.

Shouts rang out from where the kitchen used to be, and as rubble shifted, a dozen or so men poured out of the tunnel entrance—running, guns drawn, for the lawn. A fresh rush of smoke and fire filled the sky, illuminated with random bolts of electricity.

Annie groaned as she steadied herself, the adrenaline alone forcing her legs to carry her weight. There was a shrill laugh, and when she turned, Lady Duskin curled her finger toward her, admiring the jagged glass in her hand. "We're not done, Annie, dear."

Elain formed beside Annie and gripped her arm. She mouthed, *Run*.

CHAPTER 40
CAMDEN

The fire . . . it enveloped everything. Every cell of his being. Every part of his soul.

And it was *his.*

Mine.

Cam waved his hand, and the smoke parted for him like a curtain, revealing Elias watching him from what remained of the Duskins' manor. Lightning cracked around Elias' fists as he let out a slow laugh. "Oh, *Mr. Barnes*, I remember you promising me you wouldn't use your powers."

"Oh, Elias." Cam stepped barefoot onto the lawn, and the grass burned where his skin touched. "But it's so fun, and I've gotten good at breaking my promises lately."

"So, I've heard." Elias glanced at Frank Boyle, shaking himself free of the rubble. "Sorry to hear about your captain. At least your navigator made it. What was his name . . . Nathan?"

Frank wiped the blood dripping from his nose onto his dusty sleeve. "Nathan. I'll remember that while I burn him to dust, just like I did you."

Shouts and rushed footsteps approached, and armed

guards appeared from the ruined manor. Cam watched them over his shoulder as they trained their weapons on him. He just sighed. "And here I thought you'd go easy on me."

Elias gave the signal to shoot, and chaos erupted.

Cam raised his arm, as if brandishing a shield, and a wall of flame sprang up between him and the Revenants. It held while he drew Thomas's revolver, taking out the first three guards with a bullet between the eyes. Shouting orders, they reloaded and continued their barrage. He switched his flame wall to the opposite side, the heat absorbing the bullets before they could reach him.

When Cam drew his saber and lunged, Frank was ready to meet him.

His own sword clashed with Cam's, spraying sparks. The gunshots continued, and Cam prayed his shield would hold.

Elias stood back, raising his arm to prepare for an attack, but was knocked back into the trees by a sharp gust of wind. Frank swung for Cam's side, but he parried, just as Julian landed beside him.

Blood streamed down Julian's face. "I'll keep my brother busy. Take care of Boyle." He leapt back into the air. Frank drew his pistol to take a shot at him, but Cam pushed forward.

Their swords collided again, and Frank let out a laugh. "If only you'd fought so well before, your crew might have lived."

A flash of metal shone over the edge of Frank's boot.

Cam smiled. *You idiot.* He slid his sword down Frank's blade until they were nose to nose and grinned. "And *you* should have learned your lesson the first time." With his opposite hand, Cam reached forward and jerked the knife out of Frank's boot, then plunged it into the base of his neck.

Frank's eyes grew wide before they dulled.

Cam's wall fell as Frank slumped to the ground. The remaining guards took aim and fired. Cam cursed as a bullet grazed his shoulder. He crouched in time for another bullet to fly over his head. He shot the last three bullets in his revolver, taking out two more guards, then ducked behind some rubble.

He pressed his back against the rock, breathing heavily as he reloaded. *I don't have enough ammo for this.* He needed to save some for Elias. He doubted he'd be able to get close enough to run him through with his sword.

The remaining guard shouted. The crack of thunder shook the air. Cam looked up. Storm clouds gathered on the north end of the grounds at the base of the volcano. A gust of wind yanked at Cam's clothes as it closed in on the storm, swirling the clouds into a tornado.

Julian. Cam gritted his teeth and peered over the rubble. A bullet pinged off the rock a few inches from his face. The guard dove behind a chunk of wall, too fast for Cam to get a shot off.

Blazes. Cam tried to settle the fire building in his throat, pulsing in his veins. *Wait—* He glanced down at his glowing hands. He could use this. *God, I'm the idiot.*

Another inhale. Smoke coated his tongue. *Here goes nothing.* Cam stood and waved. "Hey yo!"

The guard peeked over his cover, brows rising, grey uniform speckled in blood.

Cam's fire reacted as the man took aim and fired, sending out a wave of heat that swallowed the guard whole. The screaming only lasted for a moment before all that was left of him was a blackened lump.

A pang of guilt shot through Cam's gut, but he shook it away. *Later. I'll think about that later.*

Right now, Julian needed him.

He sprinted for the volcano, his fire bringing new life to his muscles, pushing him faster than he ever thought he could run. *I could get used to this.*

Elias' storm blocked out the sun, covering the lawn in

shadow. The grass faded into crunchy, black rock as he approached the mountain, tearing into Cam's bare feet. Old, burned tree trunks littered the base, remnants of its last eruption. Cam startled, nearly falling, as a blast of lightning flew out of the charred forest.

There they are. Cam continued forward in a crouch. If only he could get a shot off on Elias before he was noticed. His feet left a red trail on the rocks as he moved, and he peered down into a small ravine. *There.*

About a hundred yards below, Julian was on the ground, his expression pained as blood leaked from a wound in his thigh. Elias knelt over him, whispering something that had Julian spitting in his face. Elias sat back, wiping his brow on his sleeve, then waved his finger in the air. A ball of electricity formed on his fingertip. Julian struggled, but his body shuddered as more electricity coursed through him.

Hang it all. Cam drew his revolver. *He can't move.*

Cam put his knee to the ground, aiming down the barrel. A sharp breeze stung his eyes, and he cursed. *I don't know if I can hit him in this wind.* Back with Resh's crew, he'd made riskier shots in worse situations, but he couldn't risk hitting Julian by accident.

A deep thrumming rose from the earth, through his knee, and spread into his bones. His fire purred, absorbing the sensation, bonding to it. Cam clenched his chest, gasping, as a new warmth spread into his blood.

The volcano. Cam's eyes widened. The ravine—it was a lava channel.

Trust me. Slowly, Cam spread his hands on the ground. The thrumming spread up into his fingers, into his arms. His fire seeped into the earth, and he felt that beast again—the one that had poured from him during his first fight with Frank. *Trust me.*

I will.

The volcano . . . it remembered. It wanted to be alive again. Cam exhaled, releasing all the holds and barriers he'd raised in his soul to contain the power hiding there, and just . . . let it go.

Thank you, his fire whispered.

Cam gagged as flames poured from his throat, spilled from his pores. It poured from him into the rock, burning a hole straight into the mountain. Searching, searching, until it found what it so desperately wanted: magma.

Cam trembled, his hands cementing to the molten rock. The ravine began to shake.

Elias knelt over Julian, lowering his hand to push the ball of electricity into Julian's chest. He paused when the rumbling knocked him off balance. The interruption broke his focus, and Julian kicked him in the gut, sending Elias flying into a stump.

Julian scrambled back and made it to the edge of the ravine.

Elias stood from the mess of blackened wood, dusting off his robe. He turned then, his golden eyes locking onto Cam. His brands flared, electricity crackling in the air around him.

The ravine shook again, but this time it split in half—spewing and filling the channel with molten lava. That monster—almost humanoid—rose from the fiery river, laughing. It grabbed Elias by the ankles. He tried to fight, but it dragged him under.

Somewhere in the chaos, Elias screamed.

Cam gasped as the rock released its hold on him. *What the blazes.*

"Cam!" Julian clawed himself up the side of the channel, his pant legs peppered with holes where he'd been splattered with lava. Cam climbed down and reached for him. Julian gripped his elbow.

Once on the bank, Cam lay back, trying to catch his breath.

Whatever his fire had done, it sucked the energy out of him. Every part of him ached like he'd been beaten by a couple of drunken thugs.

Julian got to his knees, panting as he clutched the wound on his thigh. He watched—with wide eyes—as the ravine cracked and widened, releasing more magma. "W-what did you do?"

Cam managed a low laugh. "I have no idea."

"Whatever it was," Julian groaned, climbing to his feet. "Thank you."

"No problem."

He stepped to the edge of the ravine, the fire glowing off his pale skin. "Do you think he's gone?"

"Elias?" Cam sat up on his elbows. "Probably not."

"You'd be correct," a voice growled from their right.

They turned as Elias crawled out of the side of the river, his lower legs splitting and blistered.

A bolt of lightning shot into Cam's chest.

He dropped his gun, seizing as he fell. Cam's back arched off the ground as he cried out.

Julian tried to help him. But as he reached for Cam, his entire body went rigid.

Cam's vision cleared just in time to watch Frank Boyle run his dagger across Julian's throat. He slumped, falling face-first to the rock.

Frank wiped the blood off on his coat sleeve. He let out a dark laugh, pulling back his shirt collar to reveal the hole that Cam had left in his neck—now sealed and cauterized. "The funny thing is, Cammy, you're supposed to *pull out* the knife after you stab somebody. It lets all the blood leak out, you see."

Elias braced himself against Frank, then nudged his brother over with the tip of his boot, inspecting Julian's opened throat. "I wish it hadn't ended this way."

Cam rolled over onto his knees, reaching for the revolver, but another burst of electricity arched through him, freezing his muscles in place.

Frank chuckled as Elias knelt and lifted the gun, checking the chamber.

Cam's muscles screamed, struggling against the power that held them.

Elias aimed at his head. "That's for you as well as him. You had so much potential, Camden." He cocked back the hammer. "It's such a waste. Don't worry, I'll put the girl out of her misery before The Rot takes her."

CHAPTER 41
ANNIE

"You don't have to run, dear." Lady Duskin's sing-song voice echoed through the darkened tunnels.

Annie's breath came in ragged gasps as she stumbled down the hall, bracing herself against the damp black rock. Her lungs were filled with knives. Sweat poured from her pores as the fever returned. Her dress had torn, revealing the blue blisters forming on her shins. Elain tugged on her arm, barely audible as she begged for her to keep moving.

"Annie?" Lady Duskin cooed. "Are you listening? Don't be scared. Mommy's here."

Just a little further. A boat waited for her in the receiving chamber. She just had to keep going a little longer. *Why does it matter? You're going to die anyway.* Annie shook the thought away, forcing herself to continue down the hall despite the agony coursing through her limbs. *I refuse to die here.*

Anywhere . . . she could die anywhere but here.

"Annie?" Lady Duskin turned the corner, the remaining light reflecting off the broken bottle in her hand. She grinned. "Ah, there you are."

Just a little longer. Annie raised Cam's gun and fired, the bullet ricocheting off the lava rock walls. It didn't hit her target, but it slowed her down long enough for Annie to scramble forward, letting Elain guide her through the darkness.

Both the captains were there. The grey one held the dark one at bay as he tried to claw at her face. She and Elain rushed into the patient's quarters. Annie leaned on one of the cell doors, trying to get air past the inferno in her chest, but Elain forced them to keep going until they reached the cavern's outer chamber.

In the open area before the docks, the white crosses—all the men and women she'd buried—looked so stark against the darkness clouding her vision.

Annie slowed, bracing herself against her trembling knees. She couldn't keep running. She didn't have much left. Her hands shook as she checked Cam's gun. Three more bullets. She'd used too many.

Running footsteps entered the cavern.

Elain tried to keep her going, but Annie pushed her away. *I'll never make it to the boat.* It was only two hundred feet away —floating just off the dock—but it could have been two thousand at this rate. No . . . she had to find a way to keep Lady Duskin from following her—and there was only one way to do that.

Annie groaned as she straightened, limping into the graveyard. She ducked behind one of the crosses, wide enough to conceal her, and pressed her back against the white stone. Elain watched the cavern entrance with panicked eyes.

Annie covered her mouth, willing her rattling breaths to slow.

Lady Duskin's steps were so faint as they pressed into the soft earth. "Annie?" She clinked the jagged glass with her long, manicured nails. "Come on out. I've been dreaming of this moment for *so* long." Annie could almost hear her smile. "I'm sure Elain, Rose, and little Nathan miss you."

So much death. Annie grimaced, holding her bloated stomach. *So many lives I could have saved if I hadn't been such a coward.*

Lady Duskin crept forward, the toe of her boot visible from Annie's hiding place. She pressed Cam's gun to her chest, her hands barely strong enough to grip the pearl pommel.

Lady Duskin leaned over the top of the cross, her brown curls falling over her shoulder and into Annie's eyes. "There you are."

Annie closed her eyes and squeezed the trigger, the force of the gunshot enough to launch the revolver out of her hand. The bullet blew off Lady Duskin's ear. The gun landed a few feet away, in the muck.

Annie scrambled for it, but she couldn't think over Lady Duskin's screaming.

The grip on Annie's shoulder swung her onto her back, and Lady Duskin straddled her—wild-eyed with blood streaming down her neck. She plunged the broken glass toward Annie's neck, but she managed to jerk far enough to the side to avoid it. Annie reached up and grabbed the stump of her ear and twisted. She screamed again, crumpling long enough for Annie to pull Cam's dagger out of her belt.

Not here, not here. Anywhere but here. She plunged the knife upward, just as Lady Duskin lunged again with the glass. Their forearms collided, holding the knives at bay by only inches.

She grinned, pressing her weight against Annie's arm, their skin slippery from the wet blood coating them. Annie's limbs trembled from the pressure, from the tip of Lady Duskin's bottle brushing against her breast.

"You know," Lady Duskin huffed a strained laugh. "I

almost wish you could live to see me become who I was always meant to be. I wonder what kind of power I'll have?"

"Elias is lying to you," Annie panted. "You won't become a Revenant."

"How dare you," Lady Duskin hissed, but her eyes flashed with concern. With her wedding band gone, Annie noticed a small, black phoenix tattoo on the underside of her ring finger. *Just like Mr. Boyle's.* "Both of my brothers turned. Why wouldn't I?"

"Because you've been using." The glass cut through Annie's dress, brushing against her skin. "Mr. Bennett said Camden burned down a building when he was exposed. Mr. Boyle leaked smoke from his body until he died." Annie managed to laugh. Lady Duskin's eyes continued to widen. "The Pearl Dust has done nothing but turn you into an addict, Mother. Elias knew better. He used you. It doesn't make Revenants. Only helps predict them."

"*Liar!*" Lady Duskin reeled back, taking the bottle in both hands, and lunged again. Annie braced, but her arms gave out. She cried out as the broken glass sank deep into her chest— just as Cam's knife plunged into the base of Lady Duskin's throat.

Lady Duskin looked so confused and stunned as she pulled the knife from her neck. Her eyes glazed over as the blood poured from her throat. She tried to inhale, but only a gargle escaped her lips. As she folded, rolling onto her side, her breaths went silent.

Annie stared at the black ceiling, feeling the water drip from the rocks above onto her skin. A warm wetness pooled under her collarbone, dripping down her ribs. Elain knelt beside her, weeping, and laid her head on Annie's chest.

Oh, Elain. "Don't cry." Annie stroked her sister's back, little whisps of ether floating around them. She didn't know what else to do but sing, despite the fluid filling her lungs. Just as her father had sung to her. *"Hush, hush, now. Close your eyes and dream."*

When Elain's head rose, her skin was no longer grey, her skin no longer cracked. She'd become whole and beautiful again—like before. But her eyes . . . they were solid white.

Annie's chest shuddered. *"Hush, hush, now. You're home now. Close your eyes, so free."*

Elain held Annie's palm against her cheek. There was a loud grunting, and she glanced over her shoulder. Annie followed her gaze.

The two captains battled, one bathed in light, the other in darkness. Their swords clanged violently, teeth bared, until the angry captain disappeared in a wisp of black as the other slashed through him.

The light-filled captain looked like Edmund Resh again as he knelt over her, his expression saddened as he took in the blood pooling around Annie's body.

Something struck her then.

The ghosts . . . they'd never come to her until she'd arrived on New Havana. Until she'd started working every day in the presence of Pearl Dust. Touching it. Inhaling it.

Annie smiled, her mouth tasting of iron. She yanked the glass out of her chest, letting it fall to the dirt. *Better this way than The Rot, I guess.* "You're not ghosts at all, are you?"

They shook their heads. Elain held her hand and smiled, mouthing, *"Helpers."*

A tear leaked down Annie's cheek. She'd never been alone. Not really. They'd been waiting for her. "Will you stay with me?"

Elain nodded and snuggled up to her side, her head resting on Annie's shoulder.

I wish I could have seen him again. She hoped wherever she went—whether here or there—she'd remember Cam's face, the feel of his hair between her fingers, the way his smile made her heart sing.

Annie stared at the ceiling until it faded away.

The pain disappeared. Her breathing slowed until it stopped . . . as did her heart.

And she slept.

For how long, she didn't know.

She twitched as a burning sensation crawled up her limbs, neck, and chest before settling on her jaw.

Breathe. She opened her eyes. The world around her was nothing but mist and sky.

Breathe.

She inhaled. Annie's lungs expanded, crashing into her heart, sending it into violent spasms. Everything spiraled back into her body in a crushing wave of darkness, salt spray, blood, and gunpowder.

Elain stood over her, holding out her hand. Behind her, a void had been cut into the air itself. A moaning cry of pain filtered through the portal, echoing off the walls of the cavern.

Camden.

Annie reached for the wound on her chest but felt nothing but unblemished flesh.

Elain smiled as the captain stepped up beside her.

Annie took her hand and rose, snatching Cam's gun out of the mud before stepping through the void. They followed.

She was not afraid.

Not anymore. Never again.

CHAPTER 42

CAMDEN

Elias pressed the muzzle of the revolver between Cam's eyes. He couldn't move as the cold steel bit into his skin.

Julian lay bleeding out on the rocks beside him.

He'd been so close. He'd just wanted to get Annie somewhere safe. To keep her comfortable for whatever time she had left. He couldn't even give her that. Nathan would die. Pulley, too. *I failed them all.*

"You know." Elias gave him a thoughtful look, like he so often did back on Shar-Crue. "When your father told me about the incident in his study, I didn't believe him at first."

Cam couldn't speak. The lightning had wired his mouth shut. He just watched Elias, silently fighting against the electricity binding his body.

Elias continued, using his free hand to scratch his chin. "I mean, thousands of people who've died under the influence of Pearl Dust have become Revenant, with no indication prior."

Frank paced, honed in on Cam like a hungry animal.

"But then, I realized that itself must be the connection,"

Elias said. "What about you made the difference? Since I didn't have you to experiment with—thanks to your mother—I'd hoped I'd find my answers through Richard Duskin's research, but only Mr. Boyle turned . . . why did he show signs when so many others haven't? Why did you?" He glanced to Frank, who just smiled. Elias returned his gaze to Cam. "I could continue my research on you now, but I doubt you'd cooperate."

Cam poured every ounce of hate he had into his glare.

Elias just chuckled, pressing his finger to the trigger. "I thought so. Goodbye, Camden Callahan."

Cam scrunched his eyes shut, a tear escaping down his cheek. *I'm sorry, Kitten. I tried.*

A gunshot sounded, echoing through the ravine. Hot blood sprayed over Cam's face, the taste on his tongue, as his body hit the ground.

But it was Elias who screamed.

Cam's heart still beat.

He opened his eyes. The sound that escaped him was half a sob and half a laugh. *I'm not dead.*

Elias lay on the ground, writhing, in front of him, clutching at the split, meaty stump that used to be his hand.

Frank moved toward the ravine, his expression a mixture of fear and rage, but he wasn't moving toward Elias.

Cam sat back on his knees, following Frank's gaze.

Annie held his revolver—aimed at Elias—and smoke leaked from the barrel as she stepped out of a hole cut into the world. The swirling, grey void closed behind her. Blood stained the length of her moon-white hair red. Strips of her pale skin showed through the slashes in her bodice.

Thin, black, swirling patterns—like spider-webs—trailed from her limbs up to her jaw.

Brands. Cam forgot how to breathe. *She's Revenant.*

Her blue eyes found his then, and she smiled. Truly smiled. "Camden."

His tongue remembered how to form words. "Annie?"

"It figures you'd show up." Frank strode toward her, drawing his sword. "You always know how to ruin a man's fun."

Cam leapt to his feet, diving for Frank as he swung his blade, but Annie managed to catch his wrist.

Frank paused, staring down in confusion where their skin touched. A darkness spread into his body, snaking up his arms until it spread into his lips and eyes. A glow seemed to be *leached* through his blackened veins towards Annie's grip.

Frank screamed and dropped to one knee. His limbs went limp as he struggled to free himself.

Annie looked just as surprised as the glow transferred to her body, turning her black brands a pale iridescent.

Frank moaned as he became nothing more than a browning husk.

Annie jerked away, staring at her hands.

Elias let out a low laugh.

Cam moved to Annie's side, his every muscle aching from the electricity that had poured through him.

Elias wrapped his ruined hand in his clothes to staunch the bleeding, still on his knees. Between the blood loss of his hands, and the burns on his legs, his body was destroyed. Shock had stolen the color from his golden skin.

Elias looked Annie up and down, filled with awe. "And here's something I thought I'd never see again—a Death Brand."

Annie stared at him, expression blank, her brands now a pearly white. "Explain."

"They traced the rare occurrences of Death Revenancy to a

few families in the North." Elias winced but never took his eyes off her. "I imagine that's why they sent us to collect you."

Annie's expression darkened. "My family was murdered. I was sold to Lord Duskin by slavers." Her eyes widened. "Wait —what did you mean by *collect* me?"

"I remember you now." Elias shook his head. "My associate at the time sold you off before we made it to our arranged destination. There are those in the Order who tried to pay a pretty price to have you. The slavers offered more." His lips curled menacingly. "But my associate's greed got the better of him in more ways than one, didn't it?"

Annie's gaze was nothing short of cold, calculated murder.

"You're going to die, Elias." Cam turned to Annie. "Should I kill him now, Kitten, or would you prefer I beat some answers out of him first?"

"No." Annie handed him his revolver by the barrel, the pearl handle gleaming in the morning light. She gave him a grim look. "We'll find our own answers. I've had enough of him." She brushed his fingers, leaving a tingling sensation where she touched. "What was your mother's name?"

Cam's breath caught as he took his gun from her. "Cassandra."

Annie nodded, holding her pinkie finger out for him. "For Cassandra. For my family. For you." She spat on Elias' face. He squirmed. "For *me*."

He looped his free pinkie through hers and squeezed. They just watched each other. She was alive. *They* were alive.

Cam finally smiled. Annie mirrored it as he said, "For us."

Annie nodded.

Cam turned and fired.

Elias fell, a hole blown through his eye and out the back of his skull.

The sound of the gunshot echoed through the mountain.

A soft gurgling sound caught Annie's attention. Her face fell when she noticed Julian's mangled body. She knelt beside him, running her fingers over his open throat. Her eyes widened. "He's still alive."

"He can't be." Cam knelt beside her and pressed his fingers to Julian's wrist. Sure enough, despite his glazed-over eyes and the grey sheen his skin had taken, he had a weak pulse. Cam shook his head sadly. "There's nothing we can do for him. He's lost too much blood."

Annie stared at her hands for a moment, chewing her lip. "I can't believe I'm doing this." She grabbed Julian's wrist, her expression fixed in concentration. A bead of sweat budded on her brow as her brands flared to life. This time, instead of darkness, a pale light spread through Julian's veins, racing up his arm.

Cam sat back, his lips parting in shock as the wound on Julian's neck began to knit closed. His silver eyes shot open, and he sucked in a desperate breath, his gaze racing between them. It settled on Annie, and he sat up.

Julian finally exhaled. "I'm not sure if I should congratulate you or offer you condolences."

Annie's lips curled up at the corners. "Either is acceptable."

"And Charlotte?"

"She's dead," Annie whispered. "I'm sorry. She thought she'd come back."

Julian glanced over at his brother's corpse. "Elias had her fooled."

"She's not the only one." Cam offered Julian his hand and pulled him to his feet. He nodded to Elias. "Sorry about that."

Julian, to his surprise, laughed. "He had it coming." His brows furrowed when he noticed Frank face down on the rocks. Cautiously, he rolled him over. Frank's skin was webbed in black, his body withered—like a dried plant—but he still breathed.

Frank's eyes fluttered open, focusing on Julian's face. He attempted a smile. "Your pardon, *Jules*. Elias paid well. You can understand?"

Julian just nodded, then turned to Cam. "Do you have enough ammo for one more?"

"I do." Cam squeezed Annie's fingers again. "But I promised Kitten she could make the final shot." He loaded a bullet into his revolver and offered it to her. "Would you like to do the honors?"

She blinked at him, conflicted. After a pause, she glanced up at the sky. "It's getting hot out."

Cam's mouth slowly spread into a grin. "It is, isn't it?"

She bent over, brushing the back of her hand against the rock. "The sun will turn it into an oven out here soon. A man could die."

The lava had begun to bubble over the edge of the ravine, creeping towards them.

"I imagine it could. I'd hate to be *stuck* out here." Cam knelt until he could smell the old coffee stink of Frank's breath. "Hopefully, you can get up in time, Frankie. You might burn up out here, all alone."

Frank just smiled at him. Defiant to the end.

Cam patted his cheek, blistering him. "Enjoy your stay in hell."

Frank managed a laugh. "I'll do my best."

CHAPTER 43
ANNIE

She found him by the sea, watching Pulley and the crew load supplies onto their new warship.

It had been a week since Lord Duskin's death. The island had descended into mayhem.

Cam handled it beautifully, with Mr. Price never far from his side, advising him.

Now, the Carters were taking over ownership of the island. They would see that New Havana would continue. That the patients would have somewhere safe to heal and recover before sailing home.

Most of her time had been spent helping Nathan through his Pearl Dust withdrawals. He'd started to treat her more cordially now.

Mr. Price had pressed for details about what had happened to her in the bunker. How'd she'd died, how she'd come back. She thought he had mostly wanted to hear about the last moments of his sister's life.

Cam never pushed her, though. He just let her continue on with her day like nothing happened, and she was grateful for it. One day, when she was ready, she'd tell him—tell all of them—but not today.

One day, she'd think about what Elias Bennett had watched happen to her. That he'd *been* there and done nothing.

But not today.

Annie strode down the dock. As she grew closer, Cam's heat brushed against her arm—a greeting. Her brands flared in response, welcoming the gesture.

Her *brands*.

She was Revenant now.

Another thing she tried not to think about.

Cam turned and smiled at her, the salty ocean breeze brushing through his hair. He wore a simple fitted shirt and vest. Nothing like the over-the-top formal wear he wore for the Duskins.

She stepped to his side. He carried a thick letter in his hand. She nodded toward it. "What's that?"

"Read it." He passed it to her. "I found it with Elias' things. Along with this." He held out a large, silver ring emboldened with the symbol of a phoenix.

Annie examined it. "Charlotte and Frank had that same mark tattooed on the inside of their fingers."

"Curious." Cam shoved his hands in his pockets. "A cult, perhaps? Elias mentioned an order."

"Maybe." She took the letter and unfolded it. The creases were well-worn, the script small and elegant.

> *Master Bennett,*
> *I paid you to bring my son back to me alive, not ship him off to New Havana to flounce him around with such lowlifes as the Duskins. I had my reserva-tions about working with you again after our previous*

fallout, but my advisors assured me you were a changed man.

I assure you, they'll be searching for new jobs, and you'll be searching for a new head if you don't fulfill the terms of our contract.

And please, don't think I haven't heard what Camden has become. If I learn that you were behind the attack resulting in his turning, I promise your fate —in my hands—will be far worse than anything he could ever do to you.

I expect a prompt response,

Alexander H. Callahan

Annie handed the letter back to Cam, brows furrowed. "Interesting. It almost sounded like he cared."

"Agreed." Cam stared at the paper in his hand. "Which leaves me with more questions than answers. If you hadn't come when you did, Elias would have killed me. Why? Why not just return me, get paid, and avoid angering one of the most powerful people on the planet?" Cam shoved the letter in his coat pocket. "Why pay Elias to return me when my father was the one who sold me out in the first place? Why murder my mother, but leave me alive? None of it makes sense."

"Maybe she refused to let Elias experiment on you," Annie mused. She couldn't imagine many mothers would *willingly* submit their children to that fate. "And he was getting her out of the way?"

Cam blew out a frustrated breath. "Then why not have his assassins deliver me straight to Elias?"

"I don't know. Maybe Elias was working with someone

else." Annie tucked a loose strand of hair back into her braid. "Or *for* someone else."

"But who?"

"I have no idea," she admitted.

"That's what I plan to find out." Cam rubbed his face, brands blazing brightly. "I also intend on finding out what he meant about you being a Death Brand. Richard talked about the Northern moon-veins once. Maybe it's connected?" His jaw clenched. "And if Elias was behind what happened to you and your family, I want the names of every person involved. Every. Single. One. I'll deliver their heads to you on a silver platter."

Annie's lips curled as her brands flared, shimmering iridescent on her skin, making her palms warm. "And how do you plan to do that?"

Cam turned to her then, smiling that lovely smile of his. "I promised I'd take you West, didn't I? We'll go West. Commander Carter will hold New Havana." He nodded to the second, smaller frigate floating offshore. *The Apology.* "A fitting name, isn't it? I'm sending Thomas to Shar-Crue to return the Pearl Dust to Vernon Douglas. Hopefully, that will smooth things over."

"You trust him?" Annie asked.

He shrugged. "I don't trust anyone outside of us. But he could be useful in the future. I don't need more enemies."

Annie let her eyes roam over *The Armageddon*. Steam billowed from the funnels over the deck, filling the air with the gritty scent of coal. "How are you going to afford to keep that thing fueled all the way out West?"

"Haven't you heard?" Cam straightened his vest. "I'm a wealthy man now. Elias promised me triple when he sent me here, and I'm taking it. Everything on that ship, all his treasure . . . it's mine now. I refuse to face my father again as a beggar."

Annie's heart sank.

She didn't know why she expected them to stay together, but of course, he'd go find his father. He didn't need her for that. *He said we were friends, but maybe that means something different to him.* Instinctively, she stroked the jade pendant hanging around her neck, her collateral. Somehow, she and Jenny would find a way. They had no choice.

Cam shot her a nervous glance, running his hand through his hair. "I-I finally figured out a way to get you through Western customs without all the trouble or paperwork. It's kind of a foolproof plan, really."

"Oh?" Annie said dully, letting her mask fall back into place. She didn't want to talk about leaving anymore. "How's that?"

Cam drew his revolver out of his holster, twirling it around his fingers, before holding it out to her, pommel first.

Annie took it, raising a brow.

Cam chewed his lip. "There's a compartment on the bottom. Open it."

She turned over the gun. She flipped the small switch on the underside of the handle, and the hidden pocket opened. Inside sat a small, wrapped package. She shot him a skeptical look, and he gestured for her to continue.

As Annie unwrapped the cloth, her heart nearly stopped. A stunning woman's ring shone up at her. Its band was dainty and gold, holding a teardrop-cut fire opal. The sun reflected off the stone, setting it ablaze.

Cam chewed his lip until it bled. "If you marry me, you'd get immediate Western citizenship. Plus, we can pass Jenny through as your handmaiden. And as a Callahan, you could get a job at any hospital you wanted. They'd fire someone to make room for you."

You and me. He'd said that in the tunnels. Maybe he meant it.

Somehow, she kept her voice steady. "For how long?"

"For as long as it's beneficial to you. Friends?"

"Friends." Annie slid the ring onto her wedding finger. *His mother's.* It fit like a glove. She allowed herself to smile at him, her heart thundering. "And whatever else I want?"

His returning smile took her breath away. "Yes . . . and whatever else you want. Always."

"I accept." She looped her pinkie through his, watching the warship rise and fall in the waves.

Cam's throat bobbed as he followed her gaze. He squeezed her finger. "Our ship needs a new name, you know. Any ideas?"

Annie thought for a moment. "*The Elaina.*"

"*The Elaina* it is." His brands flared, his fire spreading into his veins. Whatever power hiding inside her stirred in response, vibrant and alive.

Alive.

They were alive.

They were free.

"Kitten," Cam purred. "I think it's time we set the West on fire."

ACKNOWLEDGMENTS

Wow.

This book has been an absolute journey.

Like, battling dragons and evil wizards kind of journey. I wrote the original draft of this story back in 2017. I fell in love with it, but I knew it could be better. *I* could be better.

I sought help and was told it was garbage.

After a lot of tears, I shelved this story. I was pretty salty about it, not going to lie.

Fast forward to 2023. I've written several books. My knowledge and craft have grown considerably. I never forgot about Cam and Annie. When I made the switch to being an independent author, I realized that nothing and no one was stopping them from being introduced to the world now. I rewrote their story from the ground up, and I'm so thrilled to present them to you—my heart babies.

This story would never be what it is without you, Samantha. You've been there for me since the start. Tricia, Jessica, Sara, Cait, Kimberly, Sarah, Brittany, and Ashley—thank you.

To my editor: Melanie, you're the best and sorry for my fat fingers!

To Michaela: I'm glad I can always come to you if I need new, morbid ideas!

To Mom: I'm so sad you never got to read this one. You would have liked it. There's nothing worse than picking up my phone, excited to call and tell you all about my new ideas, but then I remember you're not there.

But most of all, thank You Lord. Thank You for redeeming the irredeemable. For giving the broken and fallen feet to stand again. I'm nothing without You.

"But God chose the foolish things of the world to shame the wise; God chose the weak things of the world to shame the strong. God chose the lowly things of this world and the despised things—and the things that are not—to nullify the things that are, so that no one may boast before Him." – 1 Corinthians 1:27-29

Don't miss Cam and Annie's next
adventure in—

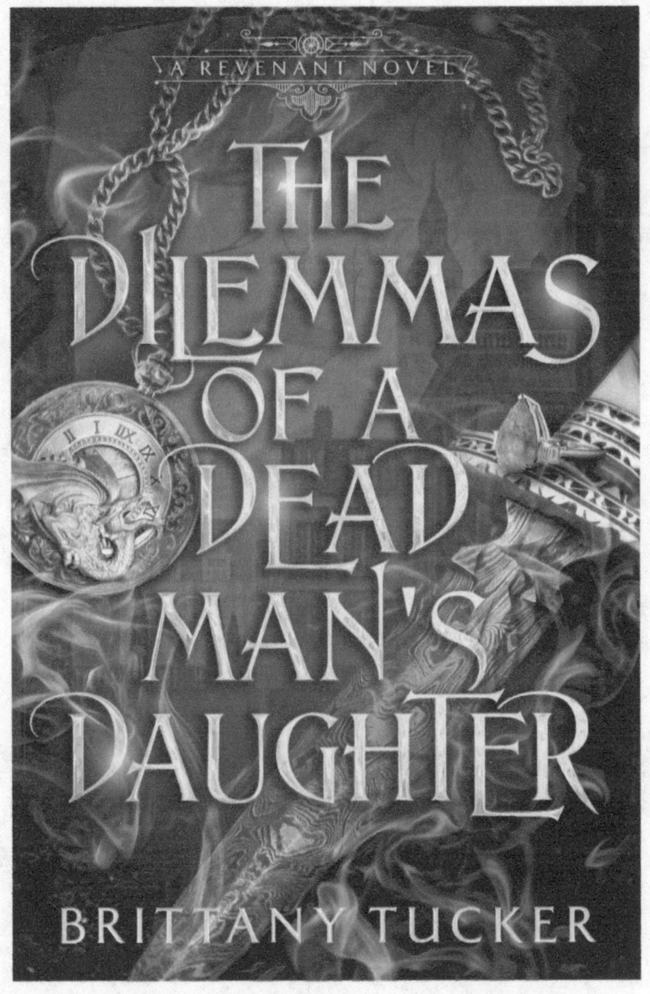

Available December 2025

ALSO BY BRITTANY TUCKER

The Revenant Series:

The Calamities of Camden Callahan

The Dilemmas of a Dead Man's Daughter

The Sunshine Series:

Sunshine's Syndicate

Others:

A Dowry of Snails and Mud

Noah's Not So Super Summer

ABOUT THE AUTHOR

Brittany Tucker lives on an island off the coast of Washington state with her husband, daughter, a menagerie of fur-children, and her imagination. She prefers generic cereal, collects tattoos and action figures, and was in the top 5% on the planet for ship's sunk in *Assassin's Creed III*.

Brittany also likes to write books from time to time.

(Just kidding. All the time.)